The Misfit Guild

R. Linn Curtis

First hardback edition 2026
First paperback edition 2026
First ebook edition 2026

Cover design by Emily N. Goff
Map by R. Linn Curis

ISBN 979-8-218-90279-7 (hardback)
ISBN 979-8-90-329098-7 (paperback)
ISBN 979-8-218-90280-3 (ebook)

The Misfit Guild

Map of Argodoth

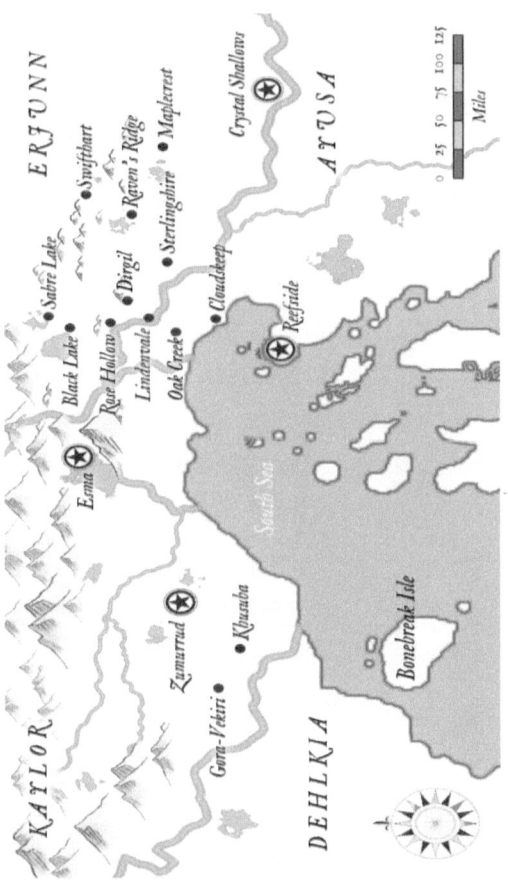

*

This novel includes some adult language and references to religious trauma and abuse, child abuse, racism, self-harm and suicide, sexual assault, violence, sexism, and implied sexual activity between consenting adults. A sexual assault takes place on-page.

Please take care when reading.

*

Part One

Prelude:

Of Wings and Worries

Three Months Ago

Given the choice, the Queen of the Faeries would have preferred to remain permanently aloof and sequestered, sipping nectar and warming her dusky purple skin atop a sun-drenched rock. But duty called, and another year without her partner meant that it was she and she alone who could administer discipline among the colonies.

Talu knew that her frustration was not only useless, but inappropriate. She had been given a remarkable position among the four Guardian races; only the faeries had chosen to pay fealty to a ruler, meaning that Talu's rule was absolute. Of course, near-eternal command of an entire species had its perks, but today, she was required to leave on the type of journey that she had come to dread and despise.

She was to be responsible for the execution of another wayward faerie.

Chapter One:

Of Baking and Book-Lending

Alvyx Autumnsong was rumored to be a druid, and not a very good one, according to his neighbors.

Alvyx, everyone agreed, was much better at baking.

The piping-hot blueberry pie on the table, with its golden, cinnamon-sprinkled crust, was delicious proof of that.

Rinah watched spirals of steam curl upward and dissipate into the air. "Papa, it's *perfect!*"

She breathed the word with such veneration that Alvyx had to laugh. "Although our bellies never know the difference, I've always believed that a pretty pie somehow tastes better than a plain one. Now, tea, my dear."

Rinah filled the kettle with spring water and hung it on the hook above the fire, then prepared two cups, dividing dried leaves between them. Alvyx pulled a small notebook from the shelving underneath the table. He tapped on his chin with his charcoal stick.

"Now, have we decided what type of fruit tarts young Miss Rallis would like for her birthday party this year?"

Rinah didn't hide her scowl. "Pear and pomegranate," she sighed. "*Of course,* she wants something out of season."

"That's her prerogative. Her parents are willing to pay for it," Alvyx mumbled as he scratched some numbers into the book. "We could go to the market just west of the Eliki Groves for the pomegranates; I imagine we'll get a decent price there, but they won't have pears…"

"Why does she make everything so difficult?"

Alvyx did not look up from his calculations but asked, "This isn't about the tarts, is it?"

"Of course, it's not. I don't like what she says about you."

He chuckled. "These days, I care very little in regard to what is said about me."

"I know, but my point is that she's allowed to say whatever she wants without any consequences. If *I* said something about *her* father—"

"What have you said about the provost?" Alvyx asked, his tone sharp.

"Nothing!"

"Keep it that way," he advised. "Pettiness is unbecoming for a young lady."

"Tell that to Xinny," Rinah muttered bitterly. "She's going on about you being a diviner."

"Oh, people have been saying *that* since before you were born. Idle talk always comes full circle." Seeing the concern on his child's face, Alvyx added, "If her father *really* thought it was true, he'd bring in the Zealots and lead the mob himself, pitchforks and torches blazing. Xinila just likes the attention the gossip brings her."

The kettle released a shrill whistle, and Rinah hopped up to remove it from the fire. The crisp scent of sage filled the little cottage. She dropped a dollop of honey into Alvyx's cup. He idly stirred it and mused, "So, we do not look with a favorable eye upon Xinila Rallis these days. What of her brother?"

"Everyone adores Galen. I wish Xinny had *two* brothers. One for Charis and another for me."

Alvyx laughed. "It's good that you and Charis are still close. She's always been on the fanciful side. And you're more serious. You balance each other out."

21

"Well, Galen has a serious side, too. I think they're going to be very happy together."

Alvyx blew on his tea, thinking on Rinah's concerns. Xinila's recent comments were hardly unique. He had been the subject of gossip before. He had to admit that he *did* possess the somewhat unbalanced air of a man whose secrets were slowly driving him insane. Perhaps he should consider brushing his hair more often.

Still, no matter how wild the rumors became, they never seemed to put anyone off his celebrated fruit pies.

It was over bowls of batter and baskets of berries that he first shared stories of his youth with his daughter. Then, as she grew older, he took her on hours-long walks in search of herbs and flowers to make poultices and tinctures. Providing food and supplying medicine, he used to tell her, were two ways that they could show kindness to others. As he nurtured her gentle, inquisitive spirit, she developed a veneration for the talents and experience of those around her. Even as a young girl, she loved to watch the town's tailor, Ms. Quadira, measure and snip fabric for new gowns, or help Mr. Adelfi, the innkeeper, make huge pots of stew for the guests. Alvyx liked to remark that his daughter was "an old soul," but he knew she simply preferred the company of storytellers. And older folks, Alvyx taught her early, were the best storytellers.

*

Most of the time, Rinah liked that her papa's cottage was on the outskirts of Lindenvale. Though the house was small (her bedroom was just a loft above the kitchen), their garden was as fine as that of any noble family. Rinah cared for the herbs, the flowers, and the shrubs as tenderly as though they were her own children. A weathered, shoulder-high stone wall had once encircled their home, but several of the blocks had disintegrated over time, erasing much of the barrier between cultivated land and the wilds beyond. A rippling stream snaked its way through the trees just outside the wall; it had been a source of wonder for young Rinah, who had spent long summer days splashing about in it with the graceless joy of a child, begging for Papa to join her, but often settling for a timid Charis instead.

The Autumnsong cottage was a cozy place to welcome friends and enjoy a cup of tea and a scone, a tiny paradise shielded from the noise and crowds of the town. But on days like this, blue-skied and sunny, full of promise and the scent of summer blooms, Rinah preferred to lose herself in the bustle of her lively village. Children chased each other around the fountain in the town square. Young boys dangled crudely wrought fishing rods from the stone bridges, yelping with pride every time they reeled something in, no matter how small. Wagons and the occasional horse-drawn cart rattled over the cobbled paths, and boisterous music streamed from Adelfi's Inn. Its newly minted proprietress, Ioanie, flung open the windows and filled the busy street with the sound of buskers, minstrels, and balladeers, all of whom stayed in her rooms for a reduced rate—as long as they sang for their supper. Traveling merchants frequently stopped in Lindenvale, as it was so near the borders of two neighboring nations. They brought a wonderful assortment of spices and goods, all of which contributed to the multicultural flavor of the little town. That flavor was something that Rinah had come to treasure. Elves, orcs, dwarves, and humans—and almost any combination thereof—called Lindenvale home and brought their respective traditions to the table. As small as it was, the town boasted temples dedicated to all four of the Gods Below (two, in fact, to the earth goddess).

Lindenvale's library, situated on the second floor of the town hall, was a far cry from what a big city dweller might call a public archive. Still, the building stood proudly across from the chandler's shop and one of the village's taverns as though inviting ale-addled brains to spend time among books instead of beer.

Rinah greeted Tzaki Naoum, the half-elf curator, who sat behind a scuffed desk. She set her books down. "I loved this one," she stated, pointing to the romance novel, "and this one was..." Rinah made a face at *The History of the Dwarven Mountain Wars.* "Honestly, I'm not even sure why you recommended that one to me."

With a cocked eyebrow, Tzaki asked, "Did you learn anything new?"

"I learned that dwarven history is very dry," Rinah admitted. "And I also learned about dwarven axeheads. I didn't know that the shape is based on tribal heritage."

"It's never a waste of time if you learned just *one* new thing. Besides, dwarven history is no more or less dry than anyone else's. It all depends on the author." Tzaki pulled a leather-bound tome from a drawer. "This one is more to your liking, I would wager. I bought this one a few days ago when I was in Maplecrest. I'd like you to be the first to borrow it!"

The cover was green with a delicate illustration of swirling ivy leaves. *"Traditional Herbal Remedies of the Lowland Forest Elves,"* she read. "Thank you, Mr. Naoum!" She immediately flipped through the pages, announcing the chapter titles. "Potions for Restful Sleep… Therapeutic Uses for the Purple Coneflower… Benefits and Dangers of White Snakeroot. Oh, this looks marvelous!"

"Will you, by chance, be passing by the forge sometime today?" he asked. "I have a book that one of the apprentices was asking for."

"I wasn't planning on it, but I'm happy to take it there." Mr. Naoum gave her a thin, paperbound book, little more than a pamphlet. When Rinah saw the title, she couldn't suppress a smile. "Mr. Naoum, is this *love* poetry?"

She was met with a disdainful huff. "The Northern Dwarves do *not* write love poetry," he asserted. "I'll have you know that *The Ardor of Bera Brannbarn* is over nine hundred years old! It's the oldest known dwarvish poem in recorded history, and it references warfare thrice as often as it does marital relations. It's a death hymn written by a widow on the occasion of her mate's assassination at the hands of an enemy tribe's spy. Whom she later married."

Rinah frowned.

"Wartime treaties and whatnot," clarified the librarian. "Thank the gods we live in more civilized times. Enjoy the rest of your day, Miss Autumnsong."

As soon as Rinah left the town hall, she heard a familiar, sing-songy voice. "Your papa told me you'd be here!" Charis Soter waved excitedly from across the square and bounded over to her friend.

Arm-in-arm, the girls strolled down the cobblestone path toward Adelfi's Inn. They could smell Ionie's peppery rabbit stew from blocks away. With eager grins, they decided it was time for lunch.

"Have you heard anything from Dargah yet?" Charis politely dipped her head as a male dwarf, leaving the inn, held the door open for the young ladies.

Rinah shrugged. "Nothing after that first letter from Fairbrooke, and that was—what, two weeks ago?"

"Are you worried about her?"

Dargah was a good head and a half taller than Rinah and worked as a blacksmith. There had never been, nor would there ever be, a reason to worry about her. "No. But as for her brother when she gets a hold of him…"

Inside, Ioanie greeted them cheerfully over the heads of her chatting patrons. She was their age but had been helping to manage the smaller of Lindenvale's two inns since she was just ten years old. Her parents still puttered around the place, her father making minor repairs and her mother mending curtains and brewing tea. However, at Adelfi's, now Ioanie's word was law.

The two friends slid onto stools at the bar counter, where Mrs. Adelfi was filling a tankard with golden suds. The inn was known for its sub-par ale, but that was because Mr. Adelfi was a rather talented vintner and put more care into his wine casks than into hops and malted barley. His small batches of blackberry wine were a treasured local specialty; only Alvyx's recipe rivaled his.

Ioanie presented Charis and Rinah with two large bowls of savory stew and a sizable chunk of the inn's signature sourdough bread to sop up the gravy. She seemed as though she wanted to chat, but hungry patrons continued to pour through the door, and she hurried back to the kitchen.

Talking around a mouthful of food, Rinah said, "Have you given any thought to the Adoration of Ayusa yet?" The celebration was six weeks away, but she knew Charis was already considering decorations. She was happiest when planning a celebration, or hosting a celebration, or attending a celebration. Charis was the flighty social butterfly Rinah was not, but they shared an eye for detail and a knack for problem-solving—gifts they put to good use in the town of Lindenvale. With Alvyx inevitably providing the sweets, the girls had helped plan and organize at least half a dozen of the village's celebrations in the past year, from weddings to festivals and birthday parties. But while Charis was the effervescent hostess, Rinah always preferred the role of the vigilant steward, refilling plates of treats, pouring beverages, and folding napkins to ensure no one would run out.

"Of course I have!" Charis exclaimed. "I found out that a brand-new orcish theatre troupe will be passing through next month, and I was hoping we could convince them to stay long enough to perform at the festival. No one does drama better than orcs, so it'll more than make up for last year's… um… challenges."

Charis's tender heart had gotten her in trouble the previous year when her trio of cousins had convinced her to let them present a dance in honor of the water goddess Ayusa. The only issue, they learned far too late, was that her cousins were terrible dancers.

"The orcs won't be performing the Dance of Dalliance, will they?" Rinah wondered. As children of the earth goddess Dehlkia, orcs were a passionate people. They enjoyed expressing their sensuality in any number of ways, most of which the easygoing humans of Ayusa tolerated. But Lindenvale's leadership had drawn the line at the female-only Dance of Dalliance, which was, in their words, "not merely suggestive, but just shy of a public orgy."

"Absolutely not! Besides, I think that's kind of a unique thing in Inbar, and this troupe is from Granaat."

Rinah had poked around in enough Dehlkian history texts to know that Inbar was a rough place to be a woman; it was the only one of the orcish kingdoms in which females did not enjoy the same basic rights as males. Granaat, however, the empire in which Dargah's family lived, was egalitarian in regards to gender. Queens could even rule without a consort or regent in Granaat! A dance troupe from there was more likely to land well in Lindenvale, so she agreed. "And they don't mind performing at *Ayusa's* festival? That seems rather open-minded."

Charis nodded. "They're not linked to any of Dehlkia's temples. They're a secular troupe. They don't care where they dance or who for, as long as they get paid. So, let's see. Their presentation can be the focus of the celebration, once the temple procession clears out. We'll have the merchant and artisan stalls lining the town square like we always do. Or do you think maybe we could change it up and—"

"Help! Please, someone—we need help over here!"

The girls turned as one at the sound of the gruff voice. At the door were two local men, worried eyes wide open, with a bloodied male body hanging between them.

*

The faint smattering of applause was more appreciation than Runo had ever received for his music. He bowed low, smiled, and skipped off the stage. As he made his way through the sweaty mass of patrons and back to his table, he realized that his seat had been taken.

By his sister.

Older than Runo by a decade, Dargah was an imposing figure. Unlike him, she had inherited the sleek, solid musculature of an orc, was considerably stronger than he was in at least a dozen ways, and his lifelong protector.

34

Of his four siblings, Dargah had always been the one Runo loved most. But, as he met his sister's unreadable, inky gaze, his guts began to flop around like a fish on a hook.

"Ruh Noor," she said. "Come. Walk with me."

He nodded weakly and cast a final glance behind him at the shoddy stage. He tried to savor the moment, even as anxiety dampened his palms.

Outside, the night air was hot and humid, but Runo shuddered. He hugged his drum close to his chest and forced a cheerful, "Dargah! I had no idea you were in town!"

Without a word, she continued to stalk away from the tavern. Runo quickened his pace to keep up, wiping clammy hands on his tunic. His sister was not much of a strong-and-silent type. She never had been. No, Dargah was a strong-and-tell-it-like-it-is-even-if-nobody's-listening type. This was going to be bad.

"Are Appa and Umma doing well?" he tried, noticing that tension had shot his voice up nearly an octave. "And what of—"

"Do not mock me, brother," Dargah said, her voice sharp. "No one's heard from you in a month, and Umma assumed you dropped dead somewhere. Fortunately for me, you are about as subtle as a sandcat in heat, so tracking you down was not a challenge."

The comparison made Runo wince.

"What I want to know is," she continued, ignoring his petulant frown, "why aren't you with Savta and Yalniz right now? And how long have you been on your own? And how did you manage to survive with nothing but the shirt on your back? And why couldn't you be bothered to write to *me* about any of this? You know I would have helped you."

"I'm fine. I've been singing for my supper," he replied. "I haven't starved, clearly."

She stared at him, unblinking, until a drop of sweat skidded down his face.

"I've been sleeping outside and stealing food," he admitted, and she rolled her eyes. "Look, I couldn't stay with Savta. She's a spy for Umma! I couldn't even sneeze without her writing to Umma that I was dying of the Khusubian *catarrh*. And Yalniz is a jerk. He's always been a bully, so I figured I'd be better on my own. And I was right! I did get a gig tonight! You saw! And I have another one lined up near Sabre Lake next week!"

She snorted. "I cannot *believe* Umma and Appa let you do this! Just up and leave!"

His face fell. "So, it's all right for you but not for me?"

"That isn't what I meant. For you to leave home without a—"

"I didn't *leave*. Not permanently. They wouldn't let me. Not after what happened to you," he said, his voice softening. "We agreed it was only for a few months."

"You might as well have left for good! Look at you. After you *promised* to stay with family, you're out here completely on your own, in taverns, looking to impress people who would just as likely rob you as they'd enjoy your music!" Her piece finished, Dargah crossed her arms and challenged her brother to reply.

He gave her a moody but knowing pout. "So, what are you *actually* mad about?"

"Nothing. You. Waiting to hear from you, not knowing if you were alive or dead."

Runo took in her defensive stance and decided he'd risk further irritating her. "That's only fair after what happened with Parviz. *Three months*, Dar!"

At the name of her former trainer, the corners of Dargah's mouth turned down. "That is different," she insisted. "I was twenty-two, and my situation was nothing like—"

"It's the same. It's *exactly* the same. No one knew where you were! I kept having dreams that you were dead somewhere."

Her expression went blank. "Well, I wasn't."

"But we didn't know that!" Runo argued. "Appa was on the verge of defending our family's reputation in the ring!"

Dargah rolled her eyes. Though more ceremonial than anything else, orcs could still defend the honor of their loved ones by publicly insulting the offender and drumming up support in their favor. It was little more than posturing nowadays, but it did count for something. She knew her father would have gone down swinging on behalf of his own bruised pride if not his daughter's, but no good would have come of it. "And he'd have wound up dead," she concluded. "Besides, what future was he talking about? My time at the Games was essentially over, and Parviz was my last chance to… oh, for gods' sakes, it doesn't matter."

"It does!"

"This isn't about me," Dargah said, her tone firm. "This is about you *lying* to our parents. At least I had the decency to be upfront about what I was doing with my life before I left home."

Runo realized that his opportunity to make his point had passed, and further talk would be met with silence. "I'm sorry," he said with genuine contrition. "But I kind of liked having a little bit of freedom. And it's been an adventure!"

"Yes, starvation is such a thrill."

"I wasn't *starving*."

"You've lost weight." Dargah cast a mildly disdainful glance toward her brother's wiry frame.

"I'll fill out," he insisted. "Umma says the males in our family just take a little longer."

"Umma says a lot of things." Dargah uncrossed her arms, an unspoken sign that their squabble had ended. "Now, I assume you don't have a place to stay for the night. I have a room at the inn. Come on."

Knowing that protest of any kind would be useless, Runo nodded and followed her like an obedient puppy. At least he'd sleep in a warm bed tonight.

Chapter Two:

Of Family and Flirtation

"Help! He's bleeding everywhere!"

While a few patrons staggered out of their path, Rinah moved forward to help the men. She shot a questioning glance toward Ioanie, who asked calmly, "And you brought him *here* instead of to the infirmary?"

"He said he don't trust no physicians." The younger of the two men glanced back at the victim's bruises, listened to his muffled groans, and realized the absurdity of his statement. "Yeah, maybe best not to take his advice now, huh? But that's all we got outta him - his name, an' that he hates doctor-types."

Ioanie gestured. "Room three is open."

Charis leapt to her feet. "I'll get Doctor Jayce anyway. Just in case."

As the men eased the unlucky traveler into the room, Rinah took in the victim's injuries. She had already cleaned her hands in the wash basin on the nightstand.

"Hullo, Miss Rinah," one of the men said shyly. She recognized him as Ida Drepani, the teenaged son of a nearby tailor. And the shorter man was his step-brother Solan. "We think it was them bandits that the provost was warnin' people about."

"Can you help him, you think?" Solan asked Rinah. "His name's Bram."

"I think his injuries are largely superficial," she said. At Ida's confused frown, she added, "I don't think he's going to die." Then, to the groaning man on the bed, she announced, "Bandits must be getting bolder, picking on a big, strong man like you, in broad daylight no less!" Her bedside manner, Alvyx always reminded her, was as important as the treatment she gave her patients. That was the reason apothecaries were still preferred over physicians in so much of Ayusa, at least for treating minor issues. Rinah drew near to the injured man. Indeed, one of his eyes had swollen shut, and there were scratches and cuts all over his face and neck. At any rate, he appeared to be handsome under the bruises—and quite likely to survive.

"Four on one," wheezed Bram. "Not fair."

While she dabbed at his wounds, Rinah answered, "Four were too many for *you* to handle? That's hard to believe!"

Bram's cracked and bloody lips curved into a smile. "You lads brought me to a *lady* doctor?" She thought he attempted a wink, too, but it was hard to tell with that swollen eye.

"The physician is on his way, but I can help a little until he arrives." She pulled a small jar of salve from her bag. After she had carefully cleaned the deepest scrapes, she smoothed the ointment onto them.

"I don't like doctors," mumbled Bram. "They always get me in trouble."

"I don't care," Rinah replied pertly. "You need a proper examination."

Solon announced, "Me and Ida were headin' to the far side of the creek to do some fishin', and when we got

45

there, we heard this moanin' and groanin', and I said to Ides, 'That ain't no fish makin' that noise,' so we looked around, and sure 'nuff, couple yards away was this fellah, all busted up. So we threw him in our wagon, and here we are!"

"You're both proper heroes, then," Rinah said. Ida blushed, and Solon ducked his head.

The village's physician, Farzaan Jayce, bustled into the room. "I ran into Miss Soter just across the street, and—oh, thank you, Rinah," he said, eyeing her handiwork. "I've got it from here."

"Hey," mumbled Bram, jerking his chin at the well-dressed half-orc leaning over him. "What can you do that *she* can't?"

"Well, she can't set broken bones, for one," Farzaan replied.

"Yes, I can!" protested Rinah, though quietly.

"No broken bones here." Bram wiggled his fingers and then flexed his arms and legs.

"I will be the judge of that." Farzaan began to prod, perhaps a bit too aggressively, at Bram's bruises. As his patient stifled a yell, he said to Rinah, "Thank you for your assistance, Miss Autumnsong. I'm sure I have the situation under control!"

It was as polite a dismissal as Rinah could have expected, so she smiled at all four men, then made her way back downstairs to Charis. "Bandits, and he'll live," Rinah answered the questions on her friend's face.

After finishing their meal without further interruption, they meandered back into the sunshine. Charis effused about some new fashions coming out of Raven's Ridge. Though no longer little girls, the two sometimes fantasized about what they would wear if they were Ladies of Great Means. And today, as Charis's relationship barrelled toward marriage, she dreamed of a long, pale-purple dressing gown trimmed with handmade lace. It would billow dramatically behind her, she explained, while she stood alone on a windswept moor at dusk, waiting for her lover to whisk her into his arms. Rinah was about to tease Charis about her highly specific daydream, but heavy, lumbering footsteps interrupted her.

"Miss! Ladies! Wait!"

The girls turned as one. Out of the inn, unaided by his rescuers, walked Bram. The physician fussed after him, noting that he should get some more rest, but Bram declined. "Thanks for your help," he said, pulling a single gold coin from under the cuff of his boot. He grinned. "Ha! Bastards didn't bleed me dry."

"Nonsense," Farzaan responded, returning Bram's dismissive wave. "I did very little, and certainly nothing worthy of *that*. If you're staying in town over the next day or so, buy me a drink here or at the Screaming Siren down the road, and we'll call it even."

Having recovered well enough to flash a disarming grin at Rinah, Bram agreed, "Fair enough. I'm looking to stay here a good while, actually. Working for my Aunt Vigga. Know her?"

Vigga Ilsted was a ruddy-faced, old but somehow ageless half-dwarf. She was sharp-tongued, steel-jawed, almost deaf in one ear, and as grumpy as an underfed billy goat. As long as most residents could remember, Vigga had managed her own forge and taken on dozens of apprentice blacksmiths over the years.

Everyone knew Vigga, whether they wanted to or not. She made sure of it.

Rinah noted, "Bram, you'll be working with my friend Dargah, too! I'm sure she'll help you settle in."

"Well, then, how about a formal introduction, ladies?" Bram's easy charm shone through the bruises on his face as he dipped his head in respect.

"I'm Rinah Autumnsong, and this is my friend Charis Soter. We're sorry to have met you under these circumstances, but welcome to Lindenvale nonetheless." She and Charis offered quick curtseys.

"We wish you a fast recovery. I'm sure we'll see you around!" Charis added before the two girls left for the shops on nearby Halcyon Street. At once, she was in Rinah's ear. "He was *flirting* with you!" she hissed.

Rinah chuckled. "I know you want everyone to be as happy as you are with Galen, Charis, but I think you're imagining things."

"I'm not! He didn't even *glance* at me."

Charis was well-meaning, but Rinah was growing impatient with her friend's attempts at matchmaking. Two months ago, the girl had roped her into an evening at the theater with one of the men from Galen's garrison. Although Charis has insisted that he was "darling," he'd embarrassed both himself and Rinah by yelling drunkenly at the actors during an intense, intimate scene, demanding that the female lead "take it off, already." And only last week, Charis had begun dropping hints about a neighbor who might "have a friend" for Rinah.

"I think we need to make some decisions about the festival." Rinah abruptly changed the subject, suggesting, "We should talk to Xinny and see if she might like to play. You know she'll be offended if we don't ask her."

Charis wrinkled her nose. "The only thing I like about that stupid flute of hers is that she can't play it and talk at the same time! She never used to be like this, but since Galen and I have gotten closer, she's always there, pulling him away with some excuse or another. Or she's interrogating me like I'm a common criminal! It's obvious that she doesn't want Galen to marry me, but I still don't know why." Her anger slipped into confusion. "Is there something the matter with me?"

"Of course not. Oh, I have an idea! Ask Xinila to play her flute at the wedding. That way, she won't have the opportunity to bother you on your special day."

"And have her showing off the whole time, while people should be focused on *me* instead? Charis's eyes went wide with horror.

"Oh, fine. But do ask her about the festival. You'll be on her good side if you make a big deal about having her play. You should go now," Rinah insisted with a little shove on her friend's shoulder. "I wanted to talk to Mrs. Harek about a new pair of shoes for Papa." With that, she ambled away, leaving Charis flustered and alone with her own pleasant, purple-gowned thoughts.

*

Blazing shafts of sunlight assaulted Runo's eyes, forcing him back under the covers with a grumbled protest.

"Wake up," came his sister's bark, and the blanket was torn from his body. A bundle of clothing hit him in the face. "You smell like a dung heap," she announced. "Get cleaned up, and then we're leaving. I'll be waiting downstairs."

His eyes were still squeezed shut when he heard the door slam. He stole one more delicious moment, hugging his pillow, then slid out of bed. He shucked off his old clothing, splashed water on his face, and gave himself a sniff. Nothing out of the ordinary, but orc females were inclined to have a sharper sense of smell than the male, making them excellent hunters.

Hmm. Dargah might have a point.

Runo took a minute to tidy himself up, then unfurled the clean tunic his sister had given him. He slid it over his head, realizing that the color and cut made him look older. Maybe even more refined. He tilted his chin just so and thrust his jaw forward a bit. If he pushed hard enough, his tusks looked almost as big as a full-blooded orc's, right? They totally did. He tied the drawstring on his leather pants and slipped back into his well-loved boots. A good night's sleep and a fresh change of clothes made him feel like a new man.

Dargah was glaring at her porridge when he found her. A steaming bowl awaited him, generously sprinkled with pistachios—his favorite snack.

"How far is Sabre Lake?" she asked by way of greeting.

"About twelve miles."

"Well, then, we won't have trouble making it there before supper," came the reply. "We can eat a decent meal, something with meat"—she gestured to her bowl—"and we'll have time to load up on supplies before your performance."

Runo blinked. "We? I... I thought you came after me to drag me back home. Or at least back to Savta's."

"Gods, no. You're coming home with me."

"To Lindenvale? You mean it?"

"Your food is getting cold," Dargah announced.

Runo squelched the desire to jump up and squeal with glee. Instead, he nodded soberly, as though considering her offer. "This could work. When I become famous across the land, I will need a bodyguard to protect me from all the crowds of wild, adoring admirers. Think you're up to the task?"

"You are an arrogant little turd."

"I missed you, too." Runo's smile was crooked but genuine. "The past couple weeks were really scary, but whenever I thought about quitting, I thought of how you would kick my ass if I did. And that scared me way worse than anything else. So I kept going."

Dargah—too human of face—was not considered beautiful by orcish standards. But in that moment, the pride and motherly love radiating from her face made her look as majestic as a queen. And Runo couldn't be happier that his only sister, his most trusted, best friend ever, was back in his life for good.

*

Rinah plucked a final blueberry from the bush and stashed it in her already overfilled basket. She moved to return to the cottage but paused as she saw a vaguely familiar figure striding along the path near her home.

"Oh! Bram! Hello. It looks as though you've recovered."

The half-dwarf pushed fluffy blond hair out of his eyes with one hand and tipped his hat with the other. "That I have, Miss Autumnsong! Thanks to the good people in this town. It was a humbling experience, being ambushed by bandits. If those two boys hadn't happened upon me, I'm not sure I would have made it here at all."

"Is your aunt well? She must be so pleased to have you here to help her."

Bram laughed, a cheerful, booming sound. "Well, even if she isn't, *I'm* glad to be here. Folks have been nothing but welcoming all week."

"So, just out enjoying the sunshine, or is this a social call?"

"A bit of both, Miss Autumnsong." He presented her with a single daisy he'd plucked on the way there. She smiled and tucked it behind her ear. Its petals were almost swallowed up entirely by her voluminous curls.

"Thank you. Just Rinah is fine."

"Absolutely not. If my mother heard I was addressing a young lady by her first name, she'd have plenty to say about it," he warned. "But I heard that you do some potion-mixing, and I need a little relief for my shoulder." He rotated it, then winced. "It's the only thing still bothering me."

Mild indignation flushed her cheeks. "A *potion-mixer*? I'm learning the apothecary arts, if that's what you mean. But yes—of course, I can help you." Rinah realized that she should have invited him into the cottage by now for the sake of hospitality, but Alvyx wasn't home. "Have a seat," she offered instead, gesturing to the wooden benches in her garden. As he eased his solid frame onto the bench closest to her, Rinah slipped into the house, placing the berries on the kitchen table. From the shelf that hung over her worktable, she grabbed a small pot of peppermint-scented muscle balm.

When Rinah handed it to Bram, he asked, "How much?"

"Oh," Rinah shrugged. "That salve is so easy to make; I couldn't charge you for it. I hope it works quickly for you."

"You won't take any coin for it at all?" She shook her head. "Huh. The healers in this town! Then I will owe you an ale at the tavern, too," he promised. "Or wine, if you prefer. I heard something about blackberry wine being a big deal around here."

"It is, very much so. And your offer is sweet but not necessary. I'm happy to help."

"I insist. Thank you, Miss Autumnsong. I am certain I will see you sooner rather than later." With a nod and a tip of his cap, he was on his way back toward the town. Then he paused. "Wait! I was wondering, do you all celebrate the Adoration of Ayusa?"

"We celebrate all the Adorations," she answered.

"I don't know how it's done here, but my hometown is mostly dwarves and humans, so Ayusa's festivals get pretty wild. Lots of dancing and amazing food. Maybe if I'm a lucky man, I'll have the chance to dance with you. Have a pleasant day, Miss Autumnsong." Again, he touched his hat and made his way up the path.

Rinah smiled to herself. She relished seeing someone benefit from her remedies. And it certainly didn't hurt when that person happened to be a handsome blonde gent with two perfect dimples.

Chapter Three:

Of Singers and Sisters

"Can you *please* sing something else?"

Huddled over a small desk, Dargah was attempting to scratch out a letter to her parents, explaining that her brother was safe with her and would not be returning to Savta's house. Runo had been singing "The Ballad of the Orcish Fishwife" since breakfast, and now it was well past noon.

"Why not 'Dehlkia's Golden Fruits'? Or 'Daughter of Earth and Sky'? You know those," she suggested.

Runo gasped. "There might be *children* listening!"

Dargah considered the lyrics for a moment, then shrugged. "They're gonna learn about sex one way or another." Trying another approach, she asked, "If I give you money, will you go away?"

Earning his keep was going to be easier than he thought, Runo realized with delight. "Absolutely, I will, yes, ma'am—"

She closed her fist around the coins she was about to offer. "Not for *you*. To go run an errand for me."

"All right, yeah. What do you need?"

"I need you to find something to do as far away from this inn as possible." Dargah dropped three small coins into her brother's hand. She loved the kid to death and beyond, but she'd almost forgotten how nonstop his chatter could be. "Don't come back 'til supper, and promise you won't do anything stupid." .

"I promise nothing!" Runo placed his drum on the bed with gentle reverence, then gave Dargah a theatrical bow and left the room.

She signed the letter and wrapped it up in a parcel—her portion of the household expenses. Leaving home without a mate was strange enough for an orc, so Dargah had decided years ago that she would soften the blow by reimbursing her family for every damn coin they spent on her training. She still had a substantial cache of gold saved up from her winnings at the Games, and Vigga paid well. Not to mention, Rinah kept her supplied with sweets that she and Alvyx baked, and Ioanie snuck a bowl of stew up to her room every so often at no charge. Funds were good, and friends were good.

Dargah's life was not exciting in Lindenvale, but it was peaceful. And right now, that was enough.

*

The resounding clangs from the blacksmith's shop were so familiar to Rinah that she didn't even notice them anymore. But today, refreshed by a quiet stroll in the woods, she heard a wholly unnatural sound from inside the forge.

Vigga was *laughing*.

Rinah popped her head inside the shop to find the source of the smith's delight. There, seated on wooden stools, were Vigga and Dargah. "What is this sorcery?" Rinah asked with mock horror, entering the shop. She dramatically placed a hand over her heart and added, "For, to be certain, only *dark magic* can bring a smile to milady Ilsted's face!"

"Quiet, you." Vigga snapped a damp towel toward Rinah, who skittered out of reach, giggling. Then the smith wiped her sweat-soaked face, stretched, and mumbled something crude and dwarven under her breath.

"You didn't let me know you were back!" Rinah chided Dargah, reaching over to give her a hug. "Do you have news of your brother?"

"Runo's sleeping on my floor right now. He's fine."

"He's *with* you? Is he all right? Why didn't you hear from him?"

Dargah gave her a half smile and slid off the stool. "Patience, little lady. I figured you wouldn't mind crashing our family reunion, so meet us at the inn this evening for dinner, and I am sure he'll tell you all about his adventures. You come, too, Vigga. If you can put your mallet down for more than two seconds."

"I'm just relieved he's all right!" Rinah announced. Though she'd never met Runo, she knew that there was no one in the world more precious to Dargah than her baby brother.

"You're monopolizing the time of my best employee," grumbled Vigga. But she was smiling now. "If you're here to see Bram, girl, he's not awake yet. But I bet if he knew you'd be here this early, he'd have been out of bed hours ago. Done up his hair or something."

Rinah was rescued from embarrassment by the arrival of a customer in fine attire and proud bearing. A sneer spread across Vigga's face when he entered.

"Greetings, Madame Ilsted," he said in a too-smooth voice.

"Unless you're bringing me payment for services rendered, you turn that smug little face of yours around and march yourself all the way back to Black Lake."

The man frowned a bit at her words but did pull a small pouch from his satchel. "From my mistress. This is to pay for the attire Mr. Jernhorn will require while living here."

Vigga snorted. "He came with three trunks of clothing, which is two and a half trunks more than *I* have. What else does he need?"

"His mother is concerned that the environment here will cause irreparable damage to several of his garments. He will need to have more... *rustic* clothing fashioned in order to preserve the finer pieces of his wardrobe."

"Damn his mother. Is his personal cook being sent out here as well?" Vigga replied. When the messenger reached into his bag again and pulled out a sealed parchment, she shook her head. "Just throw it in the fire."

Dargah's hand darted out faster than the messenger could withdraw his and she snatched the letter from him. "My thanks, good sir. If you don't have anything further," she said imperiously, "you're free to go."

Rinah looked in astonishment at her friend. She knew Dargah was gutsy, but defying Vigga took a level of recklessness that few in Lindenvale ever reached. After the man offered a brief bow and took his leave, Vigga tried to grab the letter from Dargah.

"It looks fancy," the half-orc noted, holding the paper out of Vigga's reach.

"I swear," the older woman grumbled, "if you don't give me that damned letter, I'll chop off your legs at the knee, and *then* we'll see eye-to-eye."

"You wouldn't," Dargah replied mildly, "because you can't reach the top shelves in here without me."

"I did just fine before I hired you!" returned Vigga.

By now, Dargah had already split the wax seal and begun to read the letter. "*Oh*. I can see why you and your sister aren't close."

Vigga swatted at Dargah, but her heart wasn't in it. "She can go to the crows, for all I care."

"That's a bit harsh," Rinah noted, reminding the two that she was still present.

"It's the truth," was the reply. "She's always been selfish. And now, she's paying for a brand new wardrobe for her son but still hasn't paid *me* what she promised to house the boy until... until she's ready for him to return. Something about getting housing sorted out." She hefted the purse and sighed. "At least it's a boon for Qadira. I'll send him to her shop later to have his measurements taken. And you"—she pointed up at Dargah and swiped the letter—"I should dock your pay for all this... this... *disrespect!*"

"But you won't."

"Get back to work."

Dargah thumped her fist against her chest in acknowledgment and returned to polishing a decorative door knocker, her eyes still on Rinah.

Rinah searched Vigga's drawn face. "Is there something I should be worried about?" she asked. "I mean, Bram hasn't been anything but kind to me."

"Ah, girl," she replied. "I know he's a charmer, but he's so much more trouble than he's worth. Too much of his mother in him."

"But why don't you and your sister get along? Surely, it's not just that you have different personalities, is it? Is she all that terrible?"

"Making me miserable was Fritjof's full-time job. For as long as I can remember, she was the one picking fights, blaming me for her own mistakes, then trying to sweet-talk her way back into my good graces. Just like she is now." She crumpled the letter into a ball. "Just be glad you're an only child, Rinah. Sisters are hell."

Chapter Four:

Of Boasting and Balladeering

Charis was at Adelfi's Inn because Rinah had invited her; Galen was there because Charis had invited him, and Xinila was there because Galen had invited her. And Bram, dragging a reluctant Vigga with him, approached their table and wondered if two more could join the party and meet Dargah's little brother.

Dargah didn't mind the extra company, but she wasn't shelling out coin to feed half of Lindenvale. "You're gonna need to sing for your supper," she muttered to her brother. "Literally. I told Ioanie you're broke, and she said that you'd better haul your green ass onto that floor and serenade us."

Runo glanced over his shoulder, took in the sight of Ioanie's well-formed figure and pretty face, then grinned. "That's her? And she actually mentioned my ass?" he asked, raising an eyebrow. "Did she say anything else about it?

She smacked his shoulder. "She's spoken for. Now get up there. *Someone's* got to pay for this roast."

Runo wiped his hands on his tunic, then took his goblet drum up toward a small open area near the bar counter.

"Your brother seems like a great kid," Galen remarked.

Dargah swirled the heavily-watered wine in her cup. "He is."

"You teach him to swing a hammer like you do, and he'll be even greater," observed Vigga. Dargah watched as the older woman hovered at the table as far away from her nephew as possible.

Xinila was expressing her disappointment in the birthday tarts Rinah had provided last year when Bram's broad form squeezed between them. He introduced himself to Xinny, who nodded coolly but allowed him to kiss her hand in greeting. Galen welcomed the half-dwarf to the table by drawing him into a conversation about—of all things—local fishing spots. Galen didn't even fish.

Just then, Runo's rough tenor soared over the clattering and clamor of the dining hall.

Dargah nodded proudly. He *had* improved over the past few months, and Ioanie's patrons shouted their approval. He was persuaded to sing several more songs (including that damned fishwife ditty) before he returned to their table, eyes bright and tunic streaked with sweat.

"Did you write that yourself?" Rinah asked him, clapping.

Runo dipped his head modestly. "The second song, yeah."

"Hey, that was great," Galen said, slapping Runo on the back. "Xinny, maybe you two could play something together sometime! She plays the flute."

"I play an *aulos*," she corrected, tidily slicing her roast beef.

"Do you prefer the Ayusan style or the Erjunnian style?" Runo asked.

Xinny allowed herself a brief glance in Runo's direction. "I learned on an Ayusan flute, but I play an Erjunnian one now. The fingering is more difficult, but the clarity of tone is worth it."

Ah, a fellow musician, and a pretty one! Runo grinned at Galen, eyebrows raised. Galen shook his head. "Don't even bother," he mouthed.

"See, I can't even think words like that in my head, and you go and turn them into music," marveled Bram. "That's amazing."

The rest of the evening passed pleasantly, with Runo sharing stories of his childhood in Dehlkia and the challenges of living with four much older siblings. Dargah chimed in with her own memories, mostly of Runo's early years. When he turned to stories of her athletic prowess, however, she announced, "I'm going to call it a night."

Runo leaped up to hug her, then turned his attention back to his new friends. "Now, someone pass me those raisin cakes, and I'll tell you about the time my oldest brother got trapped in a pigpen overnight. Twice."

*

Even after Rinah, Vigga, and Bram bid him a pleasant evening, Runo continued to regale the table with

75

stories of life in the desert-towns of Granaat. And most of them were even true!

Charis, in particular, was open-mouthed and rapt as Runo waxed poetic. He caught her eye a number of times, winking at her more than once. Galen just seemed happy to have additional male companions in the group; between Xinny, Rinah, and Charis, he joked to Runo, he felt like a thorn among roses.

Charis wanted to know more about Runo's family, asking why he and Dargah were the only ones who had left home. "Orcs usually stay at home until they find a mate. Hashem's too clueless to find a wife, Omir is married to his work, and Talor-Vahan is probably still pining away for a girl who got married last year. And Dargah... well, uh, she's her own woman, you know?"

Xinny spent most of the evening picking at her food, with her chin resting on her folded hand. Her glance bounced between Charis and Runo as though she was trying to determine Charis's level of interest in him. Or maybe she was jealous? Runo flushed a bit at the idea of two pretty young ladies equally enraptured with him at first glance. That would make a great song.

"Do they bite?" Charis was asking.

"Huh?"

"Do sandcats bite? Or scratch?"

Oh, that was right, he'd been telling them about the wildlife in the slum where he and Dargah had grown up. "Nah. They're pretty docile, generally. Except mothers protecting their babies. Or males fighting over females. They make awful pets, though, since they're most active at night. We tried to keep one once, but it was up 'til morning, knocking things over and screaming. And it slept all day, so we couldn't even play with it."

"So, pretty much exactly like a regular, non-Dehlkian cat," Xinny remarked.

"But they're smaller, so that makes them cuter," Charis noted.

"*Much* cuter," Runo confirmed.

"I've always wanted a cat. I do have a goose, though," she said.

"A *goose*-goose? Like for a pet?"

"His name is Linus, and he is the sweetest thing ever," Charis said, dipping a spoon into her custard.

"I still don't know why your family won't just eat him," Xinila said to Charis.

"Linus is not food! He's my friend." To Runo, she explained, "He was left behind by his mother because his wing got broken. He would never have survived on his own!"

"That goose is a terror," Xinila persisted. "It guards the Soters' house like a dog. It bit me once!"

Charis frowned. "You were bothering him."

"I wasn't even in the room with him, and he just came after me!"

"Maybe you spooked him." She narrowed her eyes. "Sudden movements and *shrill sounds* scare him."

"And that's not the worst of it," seethed Xinila. "There's a raccoon that comes around their house. And Charis stays up late to *hand-feed* it!"

"If I feed her, she doesn't try to sneak into the pantry! Have you ever been woken up in the middle of the night by crashing pots and jars, only to find a raccoon in your kitchen? I swear, she scared me half to death. But she'd never tried it again since I started giving her my leftover dinner!" Charis exclaimed.

"She's obese."

"She's *pregnant!*"

"So she'll teach all her filthy little babies to beg for food, too." Xinila shook her head scornfully. "There goes the neighborhood."

Then Charis, simple, sweet-faced Charis, stood up and threw her soiled napkin at Xinila. "I'd prefer having a hundred filthy, dirty raccoons begging at my door over having just one of *you* in my neighborhood any day!" She turned on her heel and marched out of the inn, pushing aside a dwarf who'd gotten in her way.

Galen, his mouth hanging open, glanced between his shocked sister and a bemused Runo, then took off after Charis, apologizing on her behalf to the disgruntled dwarf.

Runo finished the last of his ale and tilted his head at Xinila."So, you're not an animal person, then?"

*

In her dreams, the little makeshift campsite is distorted. Unreal. Instead of the single, humble tent Rinah remembered, it's a vast maze of animal-skin dwellings and cooking fires scattered across a huge, wide field. It's raining, and all the fires are sputtering. Her parents are in one of those battered tents, she's sure of it, but she can't find the right one. Each half-open flap holds a fresh horror for her young eyes—a deer carcass, a bloody nightgown, a dead child. And in every dream, it's always the last one she approaches that holds her parents.

She sees the bulk of her father's brawny frame, half-hidden beneath a blanket, his pale, outstretched hand caked with dried blood. The air suddenly smells foul. Sour. She hears the soft voice of a three-year-old child. Her own voice, a whispered plea. "Dada? Dada!"

Her fingers stretch out toward him, but they are not the calloused fingers of an adult. They are the chubby, curious fingers of a little girl. She tries in vain to stop the child from looking, to pull her away and to hold her tightly, to keep her from—

"Rinah!"

Soft blue eyes stared into her face, and Alvyx gently wiped the sweat from his adopted daughter's forehead.

"You haven't had that nightmare for a few years now. I was hoping that those dreams were gone for good. Are you all right?"

Rinah sat up, blinking in the glow of Alvyx's candle. "How did you know it was *that* dream?"

"You were calling for your daddy, my girl."

Rinah nodded and took the cup of water Alvyx pushed into her hand, drained it, then gave it back to him. He had never told her to call him "father," and she'd never tried to. Asking a toddler to wrap her mouth around the name "Alvyx" was a losing battle, so he'd given himself the same name he'd used for his own grandfather. And every time he heard "Papa" in her little sing-songy voice, his heart filled with more love for her.

Tonight, as he watched color return to her face, it was no different.

"Thank you." She pushed open the small window next to her bed, and the cool night air flooded in, kissing the sweat on her skin and calming her. "I'm sorry I woke you."

"No, no, dear, I was just saying goodbye to Nell. I was up."

Rinah gave him a little nudge. "She is keeping you out all hours of the night lately. And I *still* haven't met her!" When Alvyx didn't explain, she kissed his cheek. "I'm fine. I love you. Go to bed."

Rinah lay awake for some time. Papa was right; the last time she could remember having the nightmare was when she'd had a fever last autumn. When she was a child, though, she woke nightly, crying and screaming for her parents, then finding comfort in Alvyx's fatherly embrace. She had always resented the fact that her only memories of her biological family were tangled up in their deaths. She had sweet recollections of Elpida Soter singing her lullabies and of playing tag with Ioanie, Galen, and the other neighborhood children. She even remembered her first birthday in Lindenvale and being celebrated by all her new friends. But nowhere among her memories were clear, precious images of her parents. She could only recall that her mother rarely smiled, and her father used to hug her like he'd never let her go. Like he'd have to die before he'd release her. Perhaps that was exactly what had happened twenty years ago. She tried to put the dream out of her head until she realized something was wrong this time.

Her mother wasn't there.

Every time the memory invaded her dreams, she saw her father's arm thrown over her mother's body, as if to protect her from their attacker. Her mother was always curled up, scratched hands covering her face like she died ashamed or afraid.

But not tonight. There was an empty space where her mother should have been.

Tonight, her father died alone.

Chapter Five:

Of Betrothals and Betrayals

Orlaeth Silverwillow sat on a stiff-backed chair, facing her intended husband.

Neryn Sunstorm was taller than her, as he'd always been, and had a sharp jawline. As with all pure-blooded elves, his skin, eyes, and hair were of a similar tone; in his case, they were a warm, dusky bronze. His hair was carefully braided, his expression pleasant and mild. Beneath his tunic, his chest was broad, his waist trim. His left cheek dimpled when his smile was genuine, which, Orlaeth noticed, was not often. He was poised and well-spoken, inadvertently attracting attention wherever he went. Frankly, he was perfect.

Orlaeth wanted to vomit.

Instead, she nodded, acknowledging his gaze, and turned her attention to the bowl of chestnut soup in front of her.

With an admiring smile, Neryn said, "The Disciple has remarked on more than one occasion that he is consistently pleased with your copywork. Surely, your father is grateful to have had you assisting him in the Archives on his travels."

Orlaeth responded, "Yes, I find them to be a place of peace. The Archives provide calm, quiet surroundings that I enjoy. I wish I could spend all my time there." It was the most she had said to her betrothed in the week since their engagement had been made public. Though they had been quite close as children, their respective duties had forced them apart in recent years, and she couldn't remember the last time she'd had a real conversation with him.

Neryn thought on her response for a moment, then, leaning a bit closer to Orlaeth, he suggested, a bit wryly, "I wonder, does that quiet elude you here?"

His playfulness lost on her, Oraleth blurted, "Always."

Aine Silverwillow had borne six healthy children. Early during the course of his leadership, the Disciple began to encourage his followers to consider bearing more than the one—rarely, two—children customary for elvish couples. Yes, he told them, he understood that the biology of elvish females made multiple pregnancies a bit of a challenge. Still, it was the duty of those faithful to the god Erjunn to bring as many of his future followers into the world as possible. Orlaeth's parents had been dutiful in carrying out this command. Although their daughter was ten years old at the time of the Disciple's suggestion, they went on to have an additional five children, and Aine was pregnant yet again. She glowed with maternal warmth tonight, but Orlaeth knew the luminous smile was artificial. Only hours before, while she'd been preparing the evening's meal, her mother had to stop at least three times to flee outside and vomit into the bushes, nausea lasting well into her tenth month. Orlaeth didn't mind taking over the preparations, but she did feel some anxiety for her mother's health. The next three months might prove very difficult for her, in spite of her serene attitude.

Now, though, before her special guest, Aine Silverwillow was a vision. Her hair and skin were almost as fair as Orlaeth's, but where Orlaeth's appearance was ethereal and sylphlike, Aine glowed golden, a star shimmering brightly next to the wan crescent moon. She carried herself with a benevolent grace, correcting her younger children's improper posture and reminding them to eat without spilling their food. Even with the celestial aura of their mother hovering over them, the boys, Hallor and Kyrell, were fidgeting and beginning to fight with each other. It was only a matter of moments before their food ended up on the floor, in their hair, or anywhere but their mouths. The middle child, Eorna, was in a foul mood, muttering under her breath and barely remaining civil toward the siblings between whom she was seated.

Orlaeth tried hard to ignore the tension brewing at the other end of the table. She appreciated Neryn's attempts at conversation, but even his courteousness and her favorite meal weren't helping to ease her sadness. She stirred the soup idly, poking at the herbs sprinkled on top.

"How many children will we have, do you think? Three? Five, perhaps," he went on. "I imagine your mother already has names chosen—for her own child as well as ours."

Tradition held that a firstborn infant's maternal grandmother received the honor of naming the newborn, and Neryn's guess was correct. Aine had already written out a list of names that she was considering bestowing upon her first grandchild. Orlaeth's stomach turned again. "Please excuse me," she whispered, placing her spoon next to her bowl. Shaking, she rose and swept out of the room, quieter than a ghost.

Orlaeth hurried past her parents as she left, murmuring something about fresh air, and she didn't stop walking until she was outside of the large wooden lodge that served as the community's public meeting house. The cramped quarters of their own home were hardly the place for a friendly engagement dinner. A more formal affair was planned for the following week, and that celebration would include the entire village. The sacred ceremony binding them as mates would take place in less than a month.

She took several deep breaths of the evening air, enough to help calm the trembling of her hands and the twisting inside her gut. The setting sun tossed streaks of pink and purple into the dusk sky. It was almost beautiful enough to distract her from her concerns.

Orlaeth understood her duty. She understood the duty of all elves of child-bearing age. She understood the need to protect the purity of magic at all costs. She understood the need to bring new followers to the earth for Erjunn and raise children with the knowledge of his goodness and his kindness. How else could the world come to love him as she did?

But she didn't understand why the cost *she* had to pay was so great.

The memory of her mother clutching her swollen stomach and heaving its contents into the bushes for days on end made Orlaeth light-headed. The muffled groans from the birthing house rang in her ears for hours after her monthly midwifery duties were complete. When her fears overwhelmed her imagination, it was Orlaeth and not her mother, whose heavy belly jutted perpetually before her like the prow of a ship, making her struggle to breathe, and walk, and speak. And in those awful daydreams, her mate—he never had a face or a form in her mind—took from her the quill and ink and parchments that brought her so much clarity and structure and instead filled her arms with a squalling, starving infant she could not bring herself to hold to her breast.

Orlaeth chewed her lip. She bit her lips so often that the corners had become cracked and dry, and she found herself picking at the flaking skin around them. Almost daily, her mother chided her to keep her hands away from her mouth, but the habit had become soothing for Orlaeth. So now, she rubbed at her lips with a fervor that helped to ease her troubled thoughts enough for her to try to think rationally.

Neryn was a respectable man with a good reputation and unquestioned devotion to the Disciple. Orlaeth was fortunate to be matched with him; even she had to admit, she could not have chosen a more dignified mate from among her peers. She knew that life with him would be orderly, simple, and peaceful, especially since he knew that she thrived on such structure. He would be a good and loyal husband and, she surmised, a patient and caring father, too.

The bile rose again in Orlaeth's throat. The thought of Neryn inviting her into the marital bed, of consummating their union, of her slim, boyish body stretching and growing heavy with child, overwhelmed her. Orlaeth turned and retched into a nearby bush.

As she wiped acid from her mouth, she was grateful that the rest of the community was indoors, enjoying their own evening meals so that no one could witness her fit of self-loathing. After all, Orlaeth Silverwillow, the eldest daughter of Aine and Maolyr Silverwillow, the quiet, soft-spoken Orlaeth, with her milk-white hair and moon-pale skin, was the picture of obedience. Of grace. Of daughterly love and sisterly charity. Orlaeth was the studious, penitent young woman who spent hours alone among the sacred texts, copying rites and incantations and genealogies for the Disciple. It was Orlaeth, who, when mated to Neryn, would be an ideal bride, perfect and discreet. She would continue to keep her eyes demurely downcast throughout three, five, nine pregnancies until she had provided the commune with a sufficient number of babes for the next generation of magic-wielders. If she survived childbirth, her fragile, healthy, and haunting beauty would eventually fade, just as stars do when the sun rises, and her children would rise up, as beautiful as she, to continue the cycle until the end of time.

Orlaeth knew she needed to return to the meal, and it was important for no one to see any change in her disposition. Even after years of perfecting a smooth, pleasantly vacant expression, it was still a challenge to keep fear and worry from her face tonight. She closed her eyes and swept her hands over her brow, her mouth, her nose, as though blending away the lines of worry that knit them all together. Satisfied that her mask was again in place, Orlaeth returned to the buzzing hive that was her betrothal supper.

During her brief escape, her sister Fyoled had deposited herself in Orlaeth's chair and was now smiling at Neryn but saying nothing as he ate. He appeared grateful for Orlaeth's return. "I have never before," he whispered, once Fyoled had returned to her seat near her father, "had such an attentive audience while I ate."

Orlaeth turned up the corners of her mouth and gestured to his plate, which had been filled in her absence. "It was she who prepared the lentils. I am certain she was here to ensure they met with your approval." Then, she added, "As she may be the next of us to receive a mate, I believe she would like to know she can provide for him the most wholesome food possible."

"How prudent of her," Neryn noted. "They are... well-cooked." Then they lapsed again into silence.

Orlaeth busied herself with counting the number of peas she could spear on a single tine of her fork until she heard her father's mellow voice, just loud enough to carry over the clatter of plates and childish prattling at the table.

"It would be a great pleasure for us all, I believe, if, as we are finishing our meal, our esteemed guest would close our time together with a prayer of gratitude to Erjunn, may his name forever be cherished."

Neryn lowered his head in a respectful nod. The whole company, all but baby Betrys, assumed the traditional posture for a time of reverence: eyes closed, face upraised, both hands on the chest, one placed over each lung—gratitude for the breath they received from Erjunn.

Neryn could easily have slid into a melodious, hour-long litany, intertwining the prayer with snatches of holy songs and even a short homily on domestic bliss, but he saw that the skies were darkening, and some of the younger children looked more than ready to be tucked into bed. He kept his invocation brief.

"Gracious Erjunn, who has given us life, we turn to you our faces and our hope. Beautiful Erjunn, who has given us breath, we release to you our words and our actions. Mighty Erjunn, who has given us protection, we thank you for our families and our homes."

As was customary, the host released the family from the table only after the guest of honor stood up. As soon as Neryn did so, Orlaeth blurted out her required niceties, then hurried to her mother, asking if she could have the honor of cleaning up after the meal. When Aine shooed her, Orlaeth reminded her of how ill she had been earlier and how important it was for her to rest and remain strong and healthy for her unborn baby.

"Then you need not worry about the cleaning here or about me," she insisted. "And fear not if I am home a bit after moonrise, Mother. The night is so beautiful that I may, if you please, enjoy an evening walk before I return home."

"It will be as you ask," Aine said, gratitude in her eyes. "Our house *is* sometimes a bit crowded for you, I imagine, daughter. You have such a tender nature that it makes sense for you to need time alone to soothe your spirit."

"Yes," Orlaeth agreed. "Rest well, Mother."

"And I ask you, Mother Silverwillow, to allow me to assist my future mate as she clears the table," Neryn added. As he approached, his posture and tone were respectful, but his mouth was twisted in an almost roguish grin, reserved for Orlaeth alone. "Practice for a blissful marriage, to be certain."

"You will do no such thing," Aine scolded. "Her sisters are capable of helping her. There is no reason to have the Disciple's Counselor tidying up my family's dirty dishes!"

Neryn straightened a bit. "I have two hands and two feet, Mother, same as you, and I will use them to assist others in whatever way I can. Now," he said with finality, "You owe your child a healthy mother, and you must rest. With my help, your daughters can return to you that much sooner."

Aine's husband placed a gentle hand on her shoulder, commanding his wife without words. He steered her towards the door, casting a grateful glance towards the young man he already considered a son. Their smallest children followed, leaving behind Fyoled and Eorna.

Quick as a wink, Neryn slipped his hand into Orlaeth's, leaving behind a small velvet pouch. Her eyes widened. The exchange of gifts between unmarried elves was strongly discouraged within the Remnant, and it was unlike Neryn to flout tradition. She hurriedly hid it in her apron, turning away to help her sisters.

True to his word, he made quick work of the dishes, then offered to escort the Silverwillow ladies home. Eorna, tired and yearning for her bed, set the pace. Fyoled tried to engage her in a conversation about marriage, likely to impress Neryn, who hung back with Orlaeth.

She said nothing as they walked, her eyes focused on the lantern she carried. When her sisters were out of earshot, Neryn murmured, "You are not going to open your gift?"

She shook her head. "Counselor, a token of any kind from you is not proper right now."

"No, indeed. But it is not from me."

Orlaeth's gaze darted towards her sisters, who had lost interest in the couple and were now bickering over a stolen hair ribbon. Her curiosity awakened, she examined the bag. Inside it was a smooth, ivory-colored pendant—an unexpected reminder of a reckless childhood adventure. *The noisy market. The colorful tent. The she-orc with her strange words. The books and bottles.* A smile of genuine affection crossed Orlaeth's lips and she whispered, "Erjunn forgive me, but I had forgotten about this!"

"I have carried them with me, your charm and its twin, all these years," he said, tapping his baldric. Where most men would stow their weapons, Neryn carried instruments of peace—a collection of healing herbs and a miniature book of prayers.

"You took all the blame that day," she recalled, "and I never breathed a word of what happened."

"You have proven yourself mature and trustworthy with secrets," Neryn said, his eyes twinkling, "And so what was once yours is now yours again." After a moment, his expression grew serious. "There are things I would discuss with you, Orlaeth."

"Things regarding our marriage?" she asked, her voice catching.

"Things of much more significance than the two of us," he replied solemnly. "Things regarding *all* our people."

She turned a worried face towards him. "Perhaps such a discussion is best had with the other Counselors," she suggested, "or the Disciple?"

He shook his head with a sad smile. "Only the Lady of the Quills can help me," he noted, using the affectionate title her father had given her. "But I see that my words trouble you. Tonight is not for troubles, but for family and for peace. Talk can wait."

The soft sounds of nightbirds and insects enveloped them as they walked. Orlaeth's fingers made their way to her lips, picking at them. She stole a glance at his profile, took in his straight nose and full lips—slightly pursed in a contemplative pout, as always—and his jawline. For once, it was not set in a determined clench, but relaxed, at peace. Orlaeth wished with her whole heart that she could feel that kind of peace, but she hadn't known real peace in seventeen years.

Not since Liadayn Sunstorm died.

And, if she married Neryn, Orlaeth knew she would never feel peace again.

*

"Papa, go to bed." Rinah's voice drifted down from her cozy loft.

"I'm just about to," Alvyx called back.

"Is everything all right?"

"If you must know, the truth is, I've just been a little worried about you."

She leaned over the edge of the loft. "Why?"

Alvyx looked up at her, the candlelight casting eerie shadows across his face. "Oh, I guess I just thought you would be my little girl forever."

"Of course I will!" She threw off her blanket and clambered down the ladder, then gave her papa a hug.

"Ah, I'm not blind, daughter. I've seen the young man—the blond—hovering around here. He hasn't been here two weeks, and he's already got eyes for you. He's handsome enough and well-dressed, and if he's Vigga's nephew, he comes from good stock…"

"Papa, we've seen each other perhaps three times and had hardly more than polite conversation so far. I think you're jumping to conclusions. You and Charis both!"

"But I can see you blush, even in the dark," he noted.

She swatted his shoulder. "I'm enjoying getting to know him," she admitted. "But that's all."

"Then you'll be my little girl a bit longer?"

"Forever."

He kissed her forehead, patted her cheek, and shuffled off to his bedroom. Rinah returned to her bed. Tonight, she would not think of troubling things. Long after Papa's candle had been blown out, long after the moon was high in the sky, she lay still, her heart filled with gratitude and love. Papa was so good to her. Charis and Galen were smitten with each other. Dargah was back in town with her baby brother, and both were safe and well. Rinah decided those were reasons enough to enjoy a little self-indulgence. She climbed down from the loft, grabbed a lantern, and slipped outside wearing only her thin shift.

Her garden always seemed different at night. The aromas were different, of course, with certain flowers shying away from moonlight and others thriving in it. And the sounds were different, too. But there was something else out here this evening, something Rinah couldn't quite identify. Whenever she thought she had a name for what she sensed, the feeling disappeared like butter melting into warm bread. It was a good feeling, though, like the warmth of a rabbit's fur or the aroma of a favorite meal. She took it in tonight, then allowed it to escape without trying to chase it.

It would come back to her someday.

*

Makoa listened to the familiar sounds of twilight. The thrumming symphony of the cicadas. The haunting hoot of a nearby owl. A warm breeze nudged the scent of lavender and sweet basil toward him. He felt himself relax; the tightness in his muscles released. He flicked his wings outward one final time before letting them drape like a cloak down his back.

The muffled tread of footsteps roused him from his blissful stupor. A form carrying a lantern was moving through the garden. Makoa leaned forward on his branch with a mischievous grin. He'd been chided as a young faerie for expressing too great an interest in the daily lives of the Created races. He needed to know about their potential dangers, he was told, not about such trivialities as how they take their tea (dwarves tend to dislike it altogether, he had still managed to learn). But Makoa thrived on discovering such details. After all, wasn't attention to detail one of the traits that made him such a successful scout? He narrowed his eyes and assessed his visitor.

Smallish. Definitely female. A dwarf? Not quite as stocky as most he'd seen. Her gait was relaxed, and over the sound of her feet shuffling on the grass, he thought he heard her release a long, contented sigh.

She made her way around the crumbling stone wall and placed her lantern on the ground. Then she rose and, in one fluid movement, stripped off her gown. She slipped silently into the stream, wading until the water reached her waist. She disappeared for a second, then resurfaced, flinging a wet mane of ringlets over her shoulders. Water dripped from her body like diamonds in the moonlight.

Now, Makoa reflected, female faeries were beautiful. Of that, he felt there was no doubt. Like nature itself, they blossomed in every color, all with lithe, limber bodies and vibrant wings, eternally young, fresh-faced, and always flushed with what looked suspiciously like an orgasmic glow.

But this female possessed a different kind of appeal. The moon was only a sliver in the sky, and the flickering light of her lantern was only bright enough to illuminate her silhouette, but it was... remarkable. She was all curves, swooping and dipping, a far cry from the lean, willowy shape of his own kind. Her breasts were heavy and full, and her hips wide. The curve of her belly was soft, round. Everything about her form spoke of warmth. An earth spirit—rich and lush and heavy, her body radiant with promise. Blades of grass burdened with morning dew, the blanket of vapor hanging in the air before a hot summer rain. Heavy, ripe grapes weighing down their vines, dangling temptingly close, ready for harvest.

His mind may have been locked in the ivory-tower haze of a half-drunk poet, perhaps, but Makoa forced his eyes shut as a wave of embarrassment washed over him. This wasn't who he was. Watching an oblivious woman bathing by the light of the moon? It wasn't right. Not when he had orders from the Queen. Not when he had standing invitations into the arms of a dozen females in his home colony. The essence of his very role as a Guardian was loyalty without question. Honor above reproach.

He denied himself a final glance at the curvy figure in the darkness as he stretched his wings and took off to complete his rounds.

Chapter Six:

Of Secrets and Stealth

With a whispered "Good night," Orlaeth closed the door behind her. Neryn's affectionate kindness was too great a burden to bear, and she pressed her forehead against the warped wood of the door.

Only one option remained for her.

Moving with noiseless grace, Orlaeth stepped into the room she shared with her sisters. She listened to their soft snores and the grinding of Fyoled's teeth in her sleep. Orlaeth's cot was closest to the door, so she knelt down and pulled a small satchel from underneath it. She threw every possession she could call her own into the bag: a sealed pot of ink, a handful of decent quills, scraps of unused parchment, a handwritten copy of both holy books, a few pages of research, a clean chemise, and a thin cloak. Three raisin cakes and some dried fruit, leftover from supper, filled the bag to the top. She stood again, committing to memory the sound of her sisters sleeping.

A shaft of moonlight crept into the room as the curtains shifted, and a dull shimmer caught Orlaeth's attention. She turned toward the pendant strung up above her cot. Each daughter of the Remnant, upon her tenth birthday, was given such a necklace. The swirling sigil of Erjunn, hammered into a bronze disk, represented her promise to meet her family's expectations. It would someday be presented to the mate the Disciple chose for her.

But Orlaeth's pendant would never find itself around the neck of another. She plucked the pendant from its hook and swung it around her own neck. It was the only thing of value that she would allow herself to take with her. After all, if she completed her plan, she would never have the right to claim anything of the Silverwillow bloodline again. Not even the name, she mused, which meant that she would have to come up with something else to call herself.

As she moved back through the house, she let a few currents of air have their way in the common room. Perhaps, if she left behind a mess, her family would think she'd been abducted.

Not that she defied the laws of the Disciple for her own selfish gain.

Not that she'd chosen to run away from her beautiful betrothed.

Not that she fled in the night like a coward.

*

"It's… it's a mop closet."

Having been dragged back out of her own bed, Dargah eyed the space her brother was given for the night. Pails, brooms, mops, bottles of solvents, and shelves piled high with washcloths lined one wall, and a cot was pushed up against the other. "So it is. You get what you pay for. Sleep tight, kiddo."

Runo squeezed into the room. "It's cozy," he said with a grimace.

"It's better than sharing a bed with cousin Yalniz."

"Sleeping in a pile of manure is better than sharing a bed with cousin Yalniz."

Dargah snickered. "If that's what you want, I can have Ioanie make some room in the stables for you."

"Nope. This place is a palace." Runo collapsed onto the cot. "Thanks, though. For finding me and stuff."

Dargah hung the lantern on its hook next to the door. "Bathhouse is outside and to the left if you need it. Privy's there, too. It's for Adelfi's patrons only. G'night, Ruh." She started to close the door, but her brother spoke again.

"I really don't have to go home?"

He looked small, like the child who'd broken his wooden toy horse and was trying not to cry. Ten years later, Runo still had those big brown eyes that betrayed his every feeling, no matter how fleeting. And just as she'd comforted the sad-faced boy, Dargah eased into the room and pulled Runo into her arms. "Nope. I'll tell Umma and Appa you're staying with me forever."

Runo choked back a sob.

"We'll figure something out," she went on. "I'm sure Ioanie could use help here. Maybe as a groom in the stables or working in the kitchens. We'll make you earn your keep."

"I missed you."

"I know. I missed you too."

"We're different, Dar," Runo whispered. "We're not like Umma or Appa or Hashem or any of them, are we? Not really."

She ruffled his raven-black topknot. "Maybe looking at us reminds them they've got human blood, too."

He pushed her hands away and smoothed his hair back into place. "I don't think they like that."

"Probably not."

"But I don't mind. After all, it could be so much worse."

Worse than their mother's disregard for her, still relentless after all these years? "How so?"

"We could be orc-dwarf hybrids instead, and *gods*, would we be ugly."

*

With only the most pitiful lantern for light, Orlaeth slipped through the forest like a phantom. She'd only stopped once since leaving Dirgil, and that was to dig a pebble out of her shoe. The adrenaline coursing through her veins would overwhelm her, if she allowed herself time to consider her own actions. So she didn't consider them.

When the faintest glow of a sunrise warmed the night sky, she quickened her pace. Where she was going, she did not know, but she was in a hurry to get there. To disappear into one of the half-dozen bustling towns south of Dirgil. Better still, a big city! Maplecrest and Raven's Ridge were to the east, she knew. Her father had taken her to both cities before, years ago, when they were in search of manuscripts for the Disciple, and she remembered the way. But no. There was a chance, even a small one, of being recognized, and Orlaeth wouldn't risk it. To the south it was, then.

Reinventing herself was turning out to be far more difficult than she had imagined. She was not a very creative woman; her highly specialized strengths lay elsewhere. Who to become? What kind of person? No one would believe that she was a traveling minstrel or bard. She had no musical talent to speak of. In fact, her father had once asked her to refrain from singing during the midday adoration of Erjunn because she'd thrown the rest of the family off-pitch. But, worse still! What if people assumed she was a fallen woman, trading her own body for coin? Orlaeth buried her face in her hands. Being eaten up by sex-hungry males—that was the one fate she could *not* survive, she decided. But why would a woman be traveling alone? How could she explain her predicament? Perhaps a grieving widow. Yes! People seemed uncomfortable around those in mourning, so that might keep people from asking her too many questions. Brilliant! Yes, a childless young widow who had just lost her husband and left her home because the memories there were too painful. Perhaps she might gain sympathy from an innkeeper or gentle soul who would take her in for a few days, just until she could figure out how to make a living and return their kindness.

That part was the most daunting to Orlaeth. She was certainly no stranger to hard work; like every other female on the Remnant's property, she farmed, cooked, cleaned, mended clothing, delivered babies, tended to children, and cared for the sick. She could find work doing any of these, but would any of them allow her time to fulfill her true dream?

She had known her purpose since she was a girl of thirteen. For many years, she nurtured hope that the Disciple might hear the voice of Erjunn as clearly as she did. While she waited, she gave herself over to her duties, to obedience, to her self-appointed role as the handmaid of her perpetually pregnant mother. She followed her father on his assignments, cherishing the time with him. Rare was the daughter who was allowed to serve alongside her father, and Orlaeth knew that only her impeccable handwriting and silent tongue allowed her that privilege.

But, the closer she came to the age she could expect to be married, the further into herself Orlaeth withdrew. Her prayers that Erjunn would move the Disciple's heart had been heard, she knew, but not answered in the way she wanted.

Instead, just days after she turned thirty, her parents welcomed the Disciple into their home, their excitement palpable. He was coming, they whispered to their children, to reveal the identity of the male Orlaeth would marry.

After the evening meal he had partaken with them, the Disciple dismissed all Silverwillow children except the eldest. He said, "I have prayed that each man in our community would receive a wife fit for him, a wife as dedicated to him as he himself is to our great and magnificent god. It seems that, in his goodness, Erjunn has heard the cry of my heart yet again." His austere face broke into a warm, fatherly smile and he reached out to take

Orlaeth's icy hand. "Yesterday, immediately after the daybreak vigil, he confirmed to me that Neryn Sunstorm was to take Orlaeth Silverwillow as his mate."

While her mother wept tears of joy and her father bowed in humility, Orlaeth protested as vehemently as she was permitted. "But I have done nothing to be so greatly favored, Revered One. Such an honor I do not deserve."

"Perhaps not. And yet Erjunn has picked you, as one may pick a beautiful, fragrant flower, to bring happiness and children into Neryn's life. In his wisdom, he has allied two gentle and faithful souls with each other. It makes my heart sing to think of the joy you will bring to him. I will make the announcement after tomorrow's midday vigil."

Aine had taken his hand then and kissed it. Everyone knew that the Disciple treated all the young men in Dirgil with equal benevolence. Still, some assumed that Neryn would one day lead the Remnant; the Silverwillows were among this group. And if so, their beloved daughter would be by his side. Could they imagine a more beautiful future?

Orlaeth could, and it did not include a steady procession of newborn babes suckling at her breast.

Interlude I:

Of Fountains and Foundlings

Nineteen Years Ago

No one knew the exact moment when the little girl wandered into Lindenvale. She was toddling around the town's modest fountain, peering into its depths and hoping to see—what? Fish? Coins?

Elpida Soter was the first one to see her, her own infant daughter in a sling across her chest. She had been out quite early. Waking before the sun and taking her baby on a leisurely walk around Lindenvale at its quietest was a pleasant little ritual she'd adopted as soon as she was able. Before the busyness of the day, she could enjoy precious time with her child.

Elpida approached, humming to herself. The girl turned and stared up at her with a tear-streaked face. Offering a motherly smile, Elpida took her hand and walked her away from the edge of the fountain so she could not fall in. Then, she knelt and looked into the girl's pretty eyes.

"Hello, love," she said. "What's your name?"

The girl looked at the hand holding her own, then at the fuzzy-headed babe snuggled up against Elpida's bosom. "Baby," the girl announced, pointing.

"Yes! This is my baby. Her name is Charis. What is your name?" The girl seemed to hesitate, so Elpida continued in a gentle tone, "Where are your parents, dearheart? Your mother? Mama? Shall I take you home?"

"Mama," she repeated.

"Where is Mama?" Elpida rose to follow the girl, who was now toddling toward the woods beyond the village. "Be careful, love!"

The forest thinned into a clearing. There stood a lopsided tent, stitched together from animal hides. The remains of a campfire smoldered, and a half-roasted quail was still suspended above the ashes, a pitiful meal left uneaten. Next to the campfire was an elegant dagger, one that bore little resemblance to the simple, functional ones created by the town blacksmith.

On its slender blade had dried a line of deep red blood.

Chapter Seven:

Of Widows and Webs

Though foraging was not her preferred pastime, Orlaeth had learned enough about the land to know what to avoid, what to ignore, and what to fear. She even managed to build a small fire when darkness and fog finally forced her to rest on the second night of her escape. She slept only a few hours and was on the move again before daybreak. If nothing else could be said about her, Orlaeth was single-minded and had the determination of a bull. Even the wild animals seemed to sense it and watched her from a respectful distance, never daring to meet their own reflections in her moon-white eyes.

Less than two full days after fleeing Dirgil, Orlaeth found herself outside of a small town. A middle-aged human male drove a mule past her, and a wagon full of crates and jars clattered behind them. He waved a cheerful greeting. She offered what she hoped was a pleasant smile. Then, she turned her full attention to the village in front of her. How many miles had she traveled? And how long had she held back her fear? For how long had she kept it pressed back beneath its iron gate, refusing to acknowledge its growls and then its roars? Something was terribly wrong with Orlaeth if she trembled with dread upon seeing a mother suckle her babe, but threw herself headlong into an unplanned flight into the forest without hesitation.

But she was here now, and what was done could not be altered.

This was a pretty enough place, Orlaeth mused. In their early childhood, she and Neryn enjoyed visiting small towns with their mothers, setting up little pavilions to sell their homemade wares. They rarely ventured to any large cities, but even the villages—so bright, and crowded, and loud!—had been enough of a challenge for Orlaeth to navigate, and she had always turned to Neryn to distract and shield her from the commotion.

Now, she stood in the middle of a well-worn dirt path, listening to the shouts of children, the clanging of bells, the rhythmic slam of hammer on steel, and the laughter of men from the tavern. She smelled the earthy stink of animal dung at her feet, the sharp green spice of the pine trees, the savory scent of garlic and onions roasting in a nearby home, and the collective tang of unwashed bodies and unbrushed teeth, mixed with fine perfume and lilac bushes.

For the first time since she'd left the compound, Orlaeth felt a swell of anxiety so intense that she had to leave the path and sink down onto the soft earth. Her chest tightened until it felt like a strong fist was squeezing her heart. She let out a soft whine, took as deep a breath as she could, and began to murmur to herself, a prayer in the Old Tongue, one that only Erjunn would understand.

"Excuse me, friend, do you need help?"

Orlaeth forced herself to look upward. She met the concerned face of a plump young woman, standing several feet away from her. The elf tensed, like a rabbit that had just spotted a prowling fox. She shook her head, then looked away, rubbed her hands together, and continued to mutter under her breath.

The girl knelt down in the dirt, setting aside the basket she'd been holding. Offering a soft, pretty smile, she maintained her distance and placed her hands in her lap. "Are you hurt?"

Orlaeth shook her head again.

"Are you in danger?"

Orlaeth shook her head so furiously that her milk-white braid swung between her shoulder blades.

"Are you afraid?"

With a flash of watery eyes at the girl, she nodded.

"Why are you afraid?" When Orlaeth didn't reply, the girl said, "Is it all right if I stay here with you for a bit?"

Orlaeth dipped her head twice. The two young women sat facing each other, not making eye contact but listening to each other's breathing. The cacophony of sounds pelting Orlaeth had already been drowned out by the rush of blood pounding in her ears. The thick swirl of various odors was still overwhelming, but if she honed in on the one scent she found least offensive, her keen elvish senses allowed the others to fade somewhat. So she closed her eyes and breathed in deeply the aroma of the pine trees. And she focused on that. Green. Crisp. Fresh. Heavy. Earthy. Sharp. She imagined the scent like a bright emerald woolen cloak, prickly but comforting, and reached her hands up to her shoulders to draw it tighter. Several moments passed. Then, she opened her eyes and dared a glance at the girl.

She was calm and still motionless. Her eyes were gentle, bright, and doelike, fringed with thick lashes. They were an unusual shade of reddish-brown that seemed both warm and intelligent.

Orlaeth took a final deep breath. She did not smile, but she said, "Thank you."

"You're welcome." The girl began to extend her hand in greeting, but let it fall back into her lap. "I'm Rinah. Can I ask who you are?"

Orlaeth had been unreasonably indecisive about a new name, imagining herself as an Enfys or Menyn, before she settled on Ysella. She liked the way the words felt in her mouth, how her lips and tongue curled around the sound. "Please call me Ysella Evenstar."

"It's nice to meet you, Ysella," the girl called Rinah said. "Are you feeling better?"

"A little. Thank you."

Rinah stood up, brushed the soil off her skirts, and picked up the basket, filled to the top with fat, glossy, dark red berries. "I was just about to take these strawberries home and make tarts. Are you hungry?"

Orlaeth realized that she was. Very. She nodded and stood up, picking at her lip.

"Would you like to come with me?"

Orlaeth hesitated. Worry gnawed at her insides again, but she muttered to herself the same strangely musical phrase she had repeated earlier, then nodded again. "Yes, please. I can help you."

Rinah beamed and began down the path, encouraging Orlaeth to follow her.

"Then let's go. Welcome to Lindenvale, Ysella."

*

Though small by most standards, the cozy Autumnsong cottage seemed huge to Orlaeth after two decades of sharing a cramped bedroom with her sisters. Rinah spoke as she moved around the kitchen, pulling bowls and knives out of drawers. "My papa lives here, too, but right now, he's out gathering wild rosemary to make a batch of ointment. He has to deliver it to Sterlingshire tomorrow. He said he'll be back in a few days, but he always ends up running into an old friend or something and staying longer, so I have no idea when to expect him back," she laughed.

"Ointment?" Orlaeth repeated, sensing it was her turn to contribute to the conversation. "Do you make it?"

"We certainly do!" Rinah took a strawberry for herself and offered one to Orlaeth. "Look!" She pointed out a long table pushed up against the far wall of the cottage. A window just above it overlooked a lush garden. On the table were various mortars and pestles, jars, tubes, bottles, and flowers, plus a ball of twine and a pair of scissors. Hanging above the table were dozens of bouquets of herbs and plants in varying states of the drying process. Orlaeth's appreciative nose picked out notes of sage, mint, rose, and yarrow, but there was something swirling beneath the fragrance of flowers. Something delicate, but vibrant and primal. Something that Orlaeth couldn't quite place, but something she had once felt, rather than smelled.

"Are you an apothecary?" queried Orlaeth.

"Sort of. Someday, I'd like to have a whole shop and maybe even an apprentice of my own! But for now, I just work out of the kitchen. I still have plenty to learn."

"It is a good choice in life," Orlaeth said simply, "to want to ease another's pain."

"Here. This might help with your chapped lips," Rinah said, offering her a small jar of sweet-smelling balm. Then, she set to slicing the berries. "Where are you from?"

Orlaeth had practiced her speech several times during the final hours on her trek through the forest. Not only did it help get the story stuck in her head, but it staved off fear and panic. "I lived with my husband in Swifthart," she answered, using the name of one of the towns where her mother used to sell jewelry and ceramics. It was far enough away that, she hoped, the residents of Lindenvale would not be too familiar with it. When Rinah nodded but didn't exclaim that she had friends or family there, Orlaeth continued, relieved, punctuating her words with what she hoped was a crestfallen sigh. "He drowned in an accident at the lake out there."

Rinah's hand flew to her mouth. "No wonder you're so upset! I'm so sorry!" she gasped. "That is *terrible!*"

Her reaction made Orlaeth uncomfortable, and she found herself searching for a way to quash Rinah's distress. "He was not a good man!" Orlaeth added, blurting, "He gambled away all our money, and he fraternized with women of ill repute." Rinah's face hardened, and Orlaeth breathed a sigh of relief.

"*That* is terrible," she repeated. "How could he do that to you?"

Orlaeth had no story prepared to explain his vices, so she deflected. "I did not have enough money to pay the rent, and I had no relations in Swifthart, so... so I left."

"What about *your* family?" Rinah had already made quick work of the strawberries, and she was dusting the tabletop with flour. Orlaeth attempted to help by gathering the berries into a bowl. Rinah topped them with a few spoonfuls of honey, then asked, "Can you mash that up for me, please?"

Orlaeth obeyed and answered with the one tale she didn't have to invent. "To be certain, my family is deeply disappointed in me, and I cannot go back home."

Rinah's face fell. "You have nowhere to go? *No people* to take you in?"

Orlaeth's face was drawn as she stared into the bowl of broken berries, red as blood. "I do not."

"In that case, you will have to stay here."

"Here in this house?" Could Erjunn have answered Orlaeth's desperate plea so quickly, in spite of the lie she'd just told? Her breast filled with hope.

Rinah glanced up towards her loft bed. "Well, if it comes to that, yes, of course, but I'm sure we can find decent lodgings for you in town."

"I have no money," repeated Orlaeth. "I will need to find work to pay for lodgings first."

A sharp knock at the door interrupted them. Orlaeth instinctively moved toward a corner, eyeing the room for a place to hide. *They found her. They found her, and now they were going to punish her and keep her there forever, back where she couldn't breathe and couldn't think, and her home was so crowded, but wait, no, she would be living with Neryn soon, and sharing a bed with him—*

"Well, hello! Good afternoon, Bram," Rinah enthused.

From her position, pressed up against the worktable, Orlaeth dared to draw a shallow breath. A male voice answered, "Hey, sweetheart! So, I was thinking, maybe we could have a picnic lunch today?"

"That's a wonderful idea," she replied, "and I'd love to. But I… I have to build up my stock for the festival."

Disappointment hung in the air. "Really?"

Rinah laughed a bit while she moved her body to block the doorway. "Some of us have to work for a living," she joked.

"I'm pulling my weight at the forge," the man protested. "Maybe I can help you?"

"Oh, no, I couldn't ask that of you, not after you swung a hammer all morning." Rinah leaned forward, and it appeared to Orlaeth that she might have given him a quick kiss. "Maybe another time?"

There was a pause. "Isn't your papa leaving town tomorrow?"

"He's going to Sterlingshire, yes. I usually go with him, but I'm so behind on my work this time. I'm staying here."

A soft chuckle. "I think you made the right decision. Well, if you've really got things to do, don't let me bother you. At least take a snack?"

"You know you're not a bother..." In an undertone, Rinah said a few more things to her visitor, then closed the door, a green apple in her hand.

Orlaeth pointed. "That man is your lover?"

Her new friend laughed, shaking her head. "That man is *not* my lover. But who knows, maybe that will change. We *have* gotten close. His name is Bram. He arrived here not too long ago. I should probably introduce you so you can both get to know Lindenvale better."

"That is not necessary. I am certain that you will be an adequate guide," Orlaeth announced. "Do you truly have tasks to complete, or did you send him away on my account?"

Another laugh, this one more subdued. "Both. Bram's got a big personality, and I think he might overwhelm you a little right now."

"That is considerate of you." Orlaeth cautiously returned to her seat at the table, her gaze lingering on the door.

Rinah sat, too, then sliced the apple in half. She offered some to Orlaeth, who accepted it with silent gratitude. She then went back to preparing the tart. "What were we talking about?"

"I need to find work."

"That's right. Well, with the festival in a few weeks, there's always vendors and traders who need help getting ready, and they aren't picky about who they hire." Rinah paused in her prodding of the dough. "Did you work at all in Swifthart? I know some elvish men don't allow their wives to carry on outside the home, so I don't want to assume anything."

"I am an excellent scribe and copyist," Orlaeth announced proudly.

Rinah clasped her hands under her chin. "That's marvelous! I'm sure you will find work right away!"

"Yes. That is my hope. I want only to be useful."

*

"Indeed, my sons, we serve a peaceful god, but is not Erjunn also a god of purity? And does not even the mercy of a god have its limits? Does not our god long to set wrongs right and to restore balance in this battered and broken world? Does he not call his followers to lives of integrity and truth? Yes, he does, and it pains me beyond words to confess that only as of late have I realized how gravely we have failed in our mission to honor him."

What did the Disciples's words have to do with Orlaeth's disappearance? Neryn was still rattled from the news, and he had hoped that his leader would address it as soon as his counselors had gathered around the table. Perhaps there was a connection between this ominous announcement and his own lost bride? It was rare for him to speak out of turn, but today, Neryn's concern for Orlaeth's safety outweighed his respect for formalities.

"Forgive me, Disciple. Many of us are deeply troubled about Sister Silverwillow. She has not been located yet, and we seek your wisdom and guidance. What could possibly have happened to her?"

Standing at the head of the table, the Disciple of Erjunn bowed his head. "Your concern is noted and appreciated, Counselor. Believe me when I say that her disappearance cannot be separated from what I am about to discuss." He unrolled the parchment in front of him. Neryn eyed the unmistakably tidy lettering of Orlaeth's copywork. The Disciple addressed the twelve men seated before him. "We have long known that Erjunn's desire has been to see his people embrace wholeness—oneness with him and each other."

"And so we do, my lord Disciple," Tiarnán said with caution. "We seek unity with our mates, within our families, and in our entire community."

The Disciple pursed his lips. "And yet, we have done nothing but make concessions! My brothers, look at us. Even our names are a compromise! Our great families have taken on the clumsy Common Tongue, and our children do not even know their true names. Their true *identities*! Tiarnán, you are of the Dwyer-Melys people, and yet your forebears adopted the base translation of *Sweetwater* as your family name?" He shook his head. "We are blessed to be males of magnificent lineage. Yet we allow such indignities to flourish, affronts to the craftsmanship of a most spectacular god. Hear me, sons of Erjunn. I possess the fresh revelations of our god, whispered to me in dreams and visions these past seven days." He looked directly at Neryn, his eyes welled with sorrow and... guilt? "Yes, in these seven days since I pledged Orlaeth Silverwillow to you and you to her, the Highest One has spoken to me almost unceasingly."

"Do we dare ask you to share his mind, Disciple?" Maolyr's tone was mild, but he tensed at the mention of his daughter's name.

The Disciple dragged a finger down the neat rows of letters and read, "'And that which is half itself, a thing half done or half begun, is to Erjunn as a sickness, a foul taste in his mouth. For Erjunn is a patron of wholeness and purity. Never must his people be of half a mind or half a heart, but instead, they must place all of themselves wholly into his care."

The weight of those sacred words, unheard by elven ears until that very moment, plunged the room into a thick stillness. Neryn shuddered. If only Orlaeth hadn't seemed so overwhelmed the night before, he could have learned ahead of time about these verses; surely she would know if—

"Our god speaks anew." It was Felan Windrider who dared to break the silence, his words a reverent whisper. Seated next to him, his father Arweyd nodded solemnly.

What did any of this have to do with Orlaeth? "But have we not lived as he has commanded?" Neryn asked, looking at each man in turn. "In what area have we failed him? Failed ourselves?"

The Disciple responded, "I find this newly unearthed command perfectly clear, Counselor. Surely you must understand it as well! His holy mission for us is so much simpler than we have made it out to be. His love for us is less about what we are and more about what we are *not*. Why is it, my sons, that Erjunn continues to bless this community—Dirgil, specifically—while so many other centers of his worship have broken down, have become corrupt, have suffered famine and pestilence, have given themselves over to lust? We have never, for a single season, gone hungry. We have seen neither flood nor fire tear apart our homes and sweep our loved ones into the Other Realm. We are so greatly blessed because we have remained pure. Our lives, yes, our bodies. But also our blood. Our blood is untainted, blood from the veins of Erjunn himself.

"What father would not take pride in children who follow after him with such passion? Children who compromise nothing and who live as reflections of himself? Children who would take up arms against no one and nothing but in defense of their god alone? I have long known that the Remnant was to bear a great burden for the sake of Erjunn. And I have hoped against hope that it was not to be a declaration of war. But war is what we face, my friends." Seeing his advisors' troubled faces, he continued, "Not war against a nation. Nor even against another fold of our less enlightened kinsmen. We war against the *compromise* that has led Argodoth to this—its moment of gasping, dying desperation."

"Who must we battle, Good Father?" Even his distress over his daughter's disappearance had not kept him from maintaining decorum at the morning's meeting, but Maolyr hesitated before asking. "When do we go to war? What training must we complete in order to prepare?"

"We do not battle a *people*, Counselor. We battle a *plague*. We grapple with the very lust and carelessness that endanger our purity. We confront the selfishness that brings each generation closer to a world without magic. And it is no coincidence that this revelation was provided to us by the hand of your own beloved child, whom we learn, to our great anguish, is missing. The Restless Dead have become angered with the awakening of this secret knowledge, and Orlaeth's disappearance is proof of how swiftly their wrath can strike! I can only conclude that the enemies of our god have stolen her away from us in retaliation for our obedience and earnest love for Erjunn." He quieted, eyes focused on something just out of sight. His voice cracked. "By the sweet breath of the god, *I* am to blame. I truly fear that in allowing her to serve alongside her father, I myself have been the cause of Orlaeth's disappearance. If I had not betrayed my own convictions, if I had denied her permission to tend to the archives, then she would have escaped the notice of prowling spirits and would never have fallen victim to them. Her disappearance is to *my* deep shame, and I hold myself accountable for our terrible loss. But, my brothers, my sons, even as we mourn, we must ready ourselves for battle. Go in peace, and prepare your hearts for war."

As the Disciple, shaken by his own confession, dismissed his advisors, Neryn reflected on his words. Since childhood, he and his peers had been warned about their invisible enemies, the Restless Dead—the souls of elves who had not served Erjunn in life and, accordingly, were denied entry into the Other Realm. They appeared to the living as shadows or as mist, his mother had told him, dark and cold figures hunched over and bearing the invisible weight of their evil actions. She reminded him regularly that they were never more than a heartbeat away from the living, always watching for the opportunity to whisper lies into the ears of Erjunn's children, eternally seeking to increase their ranks.

He had never been told that the eerie apparitions could steal away a full-grown woman in the middle of the night, and, for the first time in his thirty-two years, he wondered, for the briefest of moments, if the Disciple might be wrong.

Chapter Eight:

Of Hospitality and Heroism

After scooping some warm, savory tart onto Orlaeth's plate, Rinah served herself. The elf peered at the muddled mash of berries and the swirls of lemon zest atop it. The food was vibrant, almost jewel-like, not the humble, beige foods she was used to. She took a small, hesitant bite.

Unfortunately for Orlaeth, the presentation far outweighed the flavor.

It wasn't *bad*, really. No, she could tell that there was no error in the recipe. And it was evident that Rinah was confident as a baker. But the combination of sweet strawberry with minty, peppery thyme was off-putting to Orlaeth. In Dirgil, food was as simple as possible: vegetable stew, brown bread, and fruit. Never any meat or fish. No cheese or cream. No honey, not even in raisin cakes.

Orlaeth could tell Rinah was trying to gauge her reaction to the food, so she crafted a smile around the mouthful of tart. "I have never eaten anything like this before," she said truthfully.

Rinah grinned. "Enjoy. I have some errands to run today, so let me get my bag, and we will go find you some work when you're finished eating!" She pulled a large, threadbare bag from the wardrobe near the door, then puttered around on her worktable, filling the bag with jars of cream and ointments.

Orlaeth looked at her plate, then dumped her portion back into the communal dish. Perhaps her new friend would not notice.

Rinah removed her apron and hung it by her tools. Orlaeth gazed longingly at Rinah's soft, lightweight chemise and loose, flowing skirts. Her stiff bodice was laced quite tightly to support her heavy bust, but Orlaeth, with her slender, almost boyish build, needed no such undergirding. She longed to find a dress and shoes more comfortable than the ones she was wearing, but that would have to wait until she had enough coin. *Imagine that! Earning her own pay and buying her own fabric for a dress! Soft, flowing fabric that didn't scratch her skin—fabric as bright as a buttercup or as deep as the midnight sky!* She followed Rinah outside into the sunlight, spirits buoyed.

Rinah wound her way through the village, waving at neighbors and friends and pointing out to Orlaeth every building along the cobbled path. "That's one of the taverns, and over there is the tailor's shop. I don't think any of my things will fit you properly, so we can talk to Ms. Qadira next week about clothing for you. And my friend Charis Soter lives there. And down that way is the blacksmith's forge. Vigga Ilsted runs it. That's why Bram's in town. He's her nephew, and he's going to help her out. My friend Dargah works there, too. A few blocks that way is Adelfi's Inn. If we can't find anything else for you, I'm sure Ioanie can use help with cleaning or cooking. She just hired Dargah's brother, but they're always busy there, so it's still an option. Up the hill way over that way is the temple of Erjunn. There are a lot of half-elves here who worship daily. And there's a library on the second floor of the town hall, so let's go in and see if Mr. Naoum needs help..."

Orlaeth tried to note each location on a mental map, but, as they did earlier, the sights and sounds battered her senses. She took a few deep breaths and whispered a prayer to comfort herself. Her panic subsided just enough for her to look reasonably interested when Rinah stopped before a tall, tidy-looking building. The brilliant blue-and-white banner of Ayusa flapped atop the building's steeple.

"This is the town hall," she announced, hopping up the three steps to the landing. She led Orlaeth beneath a low archway, through a simple, open atrium, greeted a handful of officials and administrators milling about, then bounded up one flight of stairs.

Orlaeth was immediately soothed by the scent of parchment, ink, and old books. Her sigh of relief bordered on a sob as she placed an appreciative hand against one of the tidy, organized shelves flanking the doorway.

"Miss Autumnsong! Two visits this week? I am a blessed man, indeed," Tzaki removed his spectacles and polished them with a soft cloth. He put them back on and looked at Orlaeth with owlish eyes. "A new friend?"

"Mr. Naoum, this is Ysella Evenstar. She is new to Lindenvale and seeking work." Rinah nudged Orlaeth a bit, encouraging her to introduce herself.

"Hello, and greetings to you, sir," she said, making the effort to look into his face. "I am a skilled copyist. Have you a need for a worker with my talents?"

Tzaki chewed on his finger. "Well, I haven't ever needed help here. It's something of a one-man show…"

Orlaeth didn't think she was supposed to notice the pleading expression Rinah gave him.

"But," he amended, "I'd like to expand the business somewhat. I've been thinking about selling books and not just lending them out. I could save a great deal of coin if I could copy them in-house. Why, perhaps this is fate nudging me in the direction of my dreams! Do you have any samples of your work, Miss Evenstar?"

Orlaeth shook her head, so Tzaki offered her a scrap of parchment and an ink-filled stylus. It was heavier than her quills, but Orlaeth was delighted to learn she did not have to dip it into an inkwell. After a blotchy start, she recovered and wrote out several lines from *The Path of the Wind*, each letter perfectly formed. She slid it across Tzaki's desk and waited for him to review it.

"How soon can you start?' he asked.

*

"You'll love working with Mr. Naoum," Rinah gushed as they left the municipal building. "He's a lovely person. Very intelligent. And patient."

Orlaeth flushed. She neither expected nor deserved such open-handed kindness. As Rinah continued to show her important locations within the little town, she asked Erjunn to bless her new friend. Bless her with something she had always wished for but never thought possible. Orlaeth liked praying that prayer because the idea of unexpected surprises, while paralyzing to *her*, seemed to bring joy to many other people. And she could tell that Rinah deserved joy.

*

Though an amicable man by nature, Alvyx was not pleased to learn that Rinah had adopted a stray elf and offered to house her in their cottage. He didn't take issue with the fact that his guest was an *elf*, of course. He just didn't have anywhere to put her, and just before dinner, he pulled his daughter aside to say exactly that.

"She can sleep in the loft, and I'll take the sofa. Or—or I'll even sleep outside! It's certainly warm enough," Rinah begged. "I don't mind! Papa, please! I can't bear the idea of a brand-new widow in a strange place, not knowing a single person and having to start her whole life over! She must be terribly lonely."

"And you're the one to take her under your wing?" Alvyx asked with a gruff expression.

"I learned that from you," she pointed out.

As usual, her enthusiasm and compassion won him over, and he returned to Orlaeth with a pleasant smile. "It seems that my daughter refuses to allow you to suffer even a single night of solitude, Miss Evenstar. I'm happy to offer you a place here until you feel comfortable finding a home of your own."

Orlaeth, almost melting with relief, took his hands but, unsure what to do with them, simply bowed and pressed them to her forehead. "I am very grateful. My god has blessed me in bringing me here, of that I have no doubt."

Alvyx shooed her away. "I suppose it's rather convenient that I'll be out of town for a few days. You girls will have to fight over the bed."

"Did you need me to make another batch of ointment for Sterlingshire, Papa? Does the temple there need more candles? Or the oils the priestesses use? I can whip up—"

"Rinah. Stop. It's not an exchange. Ysella is allowed to stay here, regardless of the amount of potions you brew." He cast a helpless glance Orlaeth's way. "She's always been like this."

The elf cocked her head, her sky-pale eyes resting on Rinah's. They looked even lighter than they had that morning, giving her the appearance of a marble statue. "If I perceive correctly, Mr. Autumnsong, Rinah is among those people who feel as though they need to justify their own existence, often through servitude, thoughtful gestures, and accommodations, even those that may interfere with her own desires, in spite of such expectations never being expressed."

"Indeed." Alvyx pressed his lips together. "And she just met you this morning," he chided his daughter.

"I know many people who bear the same burden," the elf volunteered.

"What's a burden about being a decent person?" Rinah asked.

"We can discuss this later," Alvyx said, ending the conversation. "I need to pack and get over to the Soters' place. They've graciously agreed to lend me their horse and cart." And thank the gods for that! The last time he'd used his own animal to visit Sterlingshire was over a decade ago, and had been a miserable experience. That damned donkey had three hooves in the grave, to begin with, and he was half-blind, with a temper to boot. The journey had taken nearly twice as long as it needed to because that mule was so stubborn. It was no surprise that he gave up the ghost not long after their return. Despite the old donkey's sour disposition, twelve-year-old Rinah had wept for days, insisting they have a proper burial for Mr. Shivers. She had even made a wreath of wildflowers for his grave.

"Who *buries* a donkey?" Alvyx had spluttered. "We can just tan his—"

"No! Mr. Shivers carried me on my first visit to the 'Shire!" Rinah had protested.

Years earlier, she'd been permitted to accompany Alvyx on his quarterly visit to the town to restock the supplies used in the small Ayusan temple there and provide wares for a few shops. Although Sterlingshire had its own well-respected apothecary, the high priestess had once lived in Lindenvale and refused to use any products but those made by Alvyx Autumnsong. So he'd plopped Rinah atop a much younger Mr. Shivers and they'd made the journey, with Rinah both terrified and overjoyed to be *riding an actual animal.* She'd come to spoil that animal rotten, brushing his mane and offering him the shiny red apples that Alvyx had bought especially for her.

Of course, he had caved and arranged to pay a ridiculous fee to bury his donkey just outside the necropolis (the authorities would not allow livestock to be buried within its borders, of course, despite the urgent pleading of a distraught young lady). And every season, around the time of his pilgrimage to the 'Shire, Rinah made another wreath to honor that beast.

This year, he supposed, she would coerce her new friend into making one as well, and the grave would be graced with twice as many flowers.

"Please allow us to assist you in additional preparations," requested Orlaeth.

Alvyx accepted her offer, and the three of them got to work.

*

Neryn composed his face into solemn lines before he approached the Disciple. When he was granted entry into his leader's private chamber, he knelt at once.

"Most Merciful One," he began, "I come to humbly request your favor."

The Disciple smiled. "Of course, Counselor. What is your desire?"

"I ask your permission to learn what has happened to my intended bride."

For a moment, Neryn was not speaking with his spiritual leader. He was just a grieving man facing another who had buried his own wife years before. When he had been known only as Kaedryn, the Disciple was a softer man. For the length of a heartbeat, Neryn again saw that man. "Perhaps you feel," the Disciple said, almost to himself, "that I have erred in assigning Orlaeth Silverwillow as your mate. Indeed, you *must* feel this way. You may even resent me for putting her in harm's way, even inadvertently."

"In no way, Gracious Minister," Neryn asserted. "In fact, I feel so strongly that you have chosen well that I must find her, wherever she has been taken."

Something sorrowful glistened in the older man's eyes. "Do you feel that she left our family of her own volition, Neryn?"

"Certainly not! You said that her disappearance is the result of wicked spirits. As I have never known Orlaeth to be a disobedient daughter, I fear that she must have been spirited away in the night by some cruel and unseen forces. We know that highwaymen and thieves, while not common, have appeared more than once at our doors. Could one have entered into our sanctuary, cloaked by a malevolent power, and stolen her in her sleep? One cannot say. And so I invoke my right as her betrothed to recover her and bring her back to the safety of the Remnant, if such a thing is possible."

The Disciple steepled his fingers and said, "Your bravery and commitment fill me with admiration. Yet, should you find that she *has*, in fact, chosen to dishonor her betrothal vows, Counselor, what then? After she receives the proper chastisement, will you take her to mate in spite of her disobedience? Will you allow her such grace, and the mercy of your love and protection?"

The shift in tone was jarring, but Neryn did not falter. "After she is disciplined in whatever way you determine to be most glorifying to great Erjunn, my lord, I will indeed receive her as my own. *You* have chosen her for me. It is for this reason that I feel so strongly the resolve to find her, wherever she may be."

"I fear that you will find no trace of the Silverwillow girl alive in this world, Neryn, and my heart already grieves with yours." The Disciple's ever-present, serene smile faded. "Still, let it never be said that I dishonor her or her family. It may be that she yet lives, awaiting your rescue. I release you to search for your intended. Go and find peace for your soul if you can. Take with you Tiarnán, for I trust him to protect and assist you. I will confer your daily duties upon another for the time being. Return swiftly, Counselor, for I will feel your absence every moment you are away. May Erjunn guide your path."

Neryn dipped his head low and hoped that his eyes shone with gratitude when he looked back up at the Disciple. "Your kindness overwhelms me. Thank you."

Chapter Nine:

Of Reunions and Regret

Neryn and Tiarnán were provided with rations, supplies, tools, and enough coin for a weeklong rescue attempt. The Disciple's reasoning was that, since Erjunn had been speaking directly to him for seven days, that in another seven days, the truth of Orlaeth's whereabouts would be revealed, for better or worse.

The men received a public blessing from the Disciple, and Neryn, uncomfortable with the lavish praise, stared stoically at the horizon instead of meeting anyone's eyes. Much depended on his success; a grieving family needed it, a shocked community needed it, and Neryn yearned to know what had truly happened to his bride. Did he have even the slightest chance of recovering her alive?

As they exited Dirgil to the sound of chanted prayers and well-wishes, Tiarnán turned to Neryn and said, "If the Disciple believes that some terrible evil has lashed out against Sister Silverwillow, you must be careful. I fear that this evil seeks to punish you as well."

"And how does one avoid an enemy one cannot see?" Neryn returned, half-serious.

"With prayer and vigilance!"

"Then I am well-prepared to face anything."

*

The first town Neryn and Tiarnán encountered could hardly be called such. A shabby lodge, a cobbled altar to the humans' goddess Ayusa, and a handful of roughly-built houses were clumped around a small community well. Most of the males in the town were either children or old men. The idea of one of *them* spiriting Orlaeth away, or of her being there at all, seemed almost laughable. Neryn urged his companion to press onward. He was growing tired of the dusty, pebbled path. Though the complaint would never cross his lips, he felt rather put out that the Disciple had not considered the mission important enough to loan out his pair of well-fed horses, forcing Neryn and Tiarnán to travel on foot. They were already at a disadvantage, leaving Dirgil at least half a day after Orlaeth disappeared, but the horses were needed for a crucial diplomatic mission, apparently. Neryn grimaced as he yet again wiped mud from his boots, but there was nothing to be done for it now.

They passed two more small towns, with their increasingly desperate search bearing no fruit. One chatty woman kept them in conversation for a good half-hour, buoying their hope, until the elves realized that the woman she was describing was actually the main character of the novel she'd been reading, and not a real-life missing bride. Neryn forced himself to be civil as he thanked her for her time, even as Tiarnán muttered about "daft half-breeds" under his breath.

Well into late afternoon, they came upon a much larger village. An artfully scrawled wooden sign proclaimed the town's name as Lindenvale.

"Ah, look, something resembling civilization," noted Tiarnán as the two men took in the sight.

"Though I doubt we will fare better here than anywhere else," Neryn heard himself announce, "we can save time if we go our separate ways for a while."

"My lord Suppliant," Tiarnán objected, "the Disciple would be grievously troubled if he knew that I left your side at any time while in the presence of this rabble!"

He gestured, with no attempt at subtlety, to the people milling about around them.

"Your devotion does you credit, Counselor," Neryn replied. "But I am in no danger. I carry little of value. And I will pose no threat. I will simply go to the tavern and then the temples. Perhaps you may seek out the local authorities. They might be of assistance to us."

Tiarnán did not repress a shudder. Still, he inclined his head. "I fear that we must spend the night here. If you like, I will obtain lodging and begin a prayer of purification before you enter. Would that be acceptable to you?"

"In surrounding ourselves with this kind of... people... I do not know how easily we will sleep, regardless of prayer, my friend. But yes, I agree to your plan." Neryn gripped Tiarnán's forearm as a sign of respect, and then the younger man was gone, swallowed up in the crowd of bodies so very unlike his own.

Neryn turned his attention to the inn ahead of him. With a wrinkled nose, he realized it was the most reasonable place to begin his search. With his god giving him strength, he plunged into the sordid comings and goings of the unwashed.

*

"You weren't fired, were you? You're never here on Friday afternoons."

Dargah grinned at Rinah's alarm and took a gulp of watered wine. "Vigga would never fire me. But she had me working extra hours to train Bram, so she gave me the day off to make up for it. I get to enjoy myself here for a change." She watched her brother cross the room to offer a mug of tea to the foundling elf Rinah had adopted. The woman seemed touched by his thoughtfulness and accepted it with a shadow of a smile, then returned to the book she was reading.

"Got a letter from my parents yesterday. They're not happy Runo decided to stay with me. They're telling me to send him back their way."

"Oh. He's the baby, right? Maybe they don't like having an empty nest?"

Dargah snorted with laughter. "They'll *never* have an empty nest. None of our brothers will ever find mates."

"Well, what about you?" Rinah asked. "I'm guessing there was no spark with you and—oh, what's his name? The thin man, the one you saw before you left to find Runo?"

"Tufann? He made it a whole ten minutes into our conversation before admitting he had always wanted to be 'dominated by a voluptuous, leather-clad, whip-wielding orc maiden'—his words, not mine. I just got up and left."

Rinah lifted her shoulders, glancing at her friend's dramatic curves. "Well, you *are* voluptuous."

"A *maiden*, though?"

172

"What about the merchant—the one I met this past spring? Baros? I liked him."

"Baros is attractive, successful, and popular. He's got to be hiding some awful secret." A curious frown pulled at her lips, then she asked, "Hey, who's with your new friend over there?"

Rinah turned to see Orlaeth sitting with a man unfamiliar to them. Her hands covered her face, and her body shook with sobs. Rinah blazed with indignation as she crossed the room. Dargah leaned forward to watch with admiration.

No one made Rinah's friends cry.

*

When Neryn caught the flick of a silver-white braid, he knew that he had found his runaway bride. Her back was turned, but the posture, the waifish build, the long, cream-white fingers turning the pages of a book—it was her. He almost sank to his knees in relief. Erjunn be praised! He swallowed the joyful cry that leaped to his throat and, instead, made his way swiftly through the almost empty room. Once at her side, he slid into the chair opposite her and whispered her name.

She started and looked up at him with genuine fear in her eyes. "No," she said to herself. Then, louder, "No, no, no, no, no. This must not happen!" She tried to stand up and caught her skirts on the edge of the table. She sat back down, dropped her book, and began to tremble, shaking her head and covering her face. Despite the warmth of the day, a chill breeze swirled through the room, ruffling the too-quaint curtains behind Neryn.

He reached a gentle hand toward Orlaeth, ready to offer words of comfort, but before he could do so, a woman's voice interrupted him.

"Don't you touch her!"

The owner of the voice was a short—what was she? She looked human in appearance, with two thick braids framing her round face, but her ears had just the slightest point to them, hinting at dwarven or elvish heritage. Neryn guessed that she was one of the *anathema* the Disciple often mentioned—unfortunate creatures whose ancestry was so tangled up that even humans sometimes called them "patchworks." However, it didn't look like what he called her mattered much, because she was already upset.

"Excuse me, sir, but I said *don't touch my friend,*" she repeated, leaning forward to smack his hand away from the shivering Orlaeth.

Her insolence stunned a wide-eyed Neryn into silence.

"She doesn't look happy to see you, whoever you are," she added. Then she leaned down, bringing herself into Orlaeth's line of sight. "Ysella? Are you all right?"

He found his voice. "What did you call her?"

"Her name," the girl snapped over her shoulder. "Allow me to have yours as well so that I can ask you to leave."

"Rinah?" Now, a gangly man-child of orcish origin was leaning over the bar. His curious expression melted into one of suspicion. "Hey, is there something I can help you ladies with?"

At the sudden authority in his voice, a few nosy patrons glanced towards Orlaeth, her shoulders still shaking. Neryn swallowed a groan. He was failing spectacularly in his attempt to be subtle. This wasn't good. He put his hands up and pushed away from the table. He'd already attracted too much attention. He pitched his voice low and spoke calmly. "I am not here to cause any trouble."

"Could've fooled me."

Oh, gods, another one. This interloper was a tall, powerfully built female, some kind of orcish hybrid. She appeared human but for her skin, a muddy shade of olive green, and her ears, almost as sharply tapered as his own. A razor-thin scar ran beneath her right eye, across the bridge of her nose, and across her high cheekbone. She was unquestionably some type of thief or brawler. With her cool gaze still trained on him, she positioned herself between the table and the door, then asked the shorter woman, "What's going on here?"

"I'm not sure yet. Ysella?"

Orlaeth stared at the white hands twisted in her lap, her heart thundering. She began to mutter under her breath, words in the Old Tongue that Neryn couldn't quite decipher.

Two patrons were murmuring about the situation, loud enough for Neryn to hear. Low-minded fools! He was not here to be a source of idle gossip; he was here to fulfill a divine mission! Reclaiming his dignity and poise, he said, "I am Neryn Sunstorm, Seventh Counselor and Suppliant Prime to the Disciple of the Remnant. I seek Orlaeth Silverwillow, eldest daughter of Maolyr Silverwillow, Keeper of the Sacred Texts of Erjunn, and his mate Aine, lately absent from Dirgil, and my intended bride. And which of you is her keeper? The imp or the barbarian?"

The short, curly-headed woman, Rinah, straightened to her full height and still had to crane her neck to glare at Neryn. "None of us have any idea what you're talking about," she insisted. "And did you just call me an *imp*?"

The barbarian cocked her head, one hand on her hip. "Watch your mouth, counselor, or I'll sic her on you. She's meaner than she looks." With a brash smile that irked Neryn, she took a seat at the table, then gestured to his chair. "Let's have a talk like the civilized people you clearly think we're not." Biting back insults, he sat. After a few stubborn seconds, Rinah followed suit. The orc signaled to the boy at the counter, then continued. "Now, my record isn't spotless, Counselor, but I dislike being accused of crimes I didn't commit. Neither of us has kidnapped anyone recently. To my knowledge." A raised eyebrow at the imp.

"Ysella came into town a few days ago. She told me she's a widow from Swifthart."

"Orlaeth," Neryn pleaded. The woman would not—perhaps *could* not—look at him.

"Are we completely sure your lady-friend was abducted, Counselor? No chance of her running off to avoid spending the rest of her life with you?" Another insufferable grin.

"Such an action would be heresy," Neryn returned.

Orlaeth made a noise somewhere between a gasp and a cough.

At that moment, the orc-boy appeared at the table with two tankards and two clay mugs. He placed the mugs in front of the elves and said, "Dargah, let me know if you need Ikraam." He flicked an eyebrow towards a hulking figure seated at the far end of the room, his face half-hidden in shadow. From what Neryn could tell, the orc's biceps were twice as substantial as his own thighs, which were rather sturdy, if he did say so himself. The immense Ikraam nodded once, an acknowledgement and a warning.

"Oh, I think we'll be fine, if we can coax the truth out of these two, Runo."

The boy retreated, his narrowed eyes not leaving Neryn's.

Orlaeth turned to Rinah, her voice tired and cracking, her pale eyes still clouded with tears, admitting. "I am treacherous, and my shame is revealed. It is doubly shameful to have lied to you and to my people."

Rinah's confused expression bounced between the elves. "What exactly is happening here?"

"I would also like an answer to that question," Neryn agreed, his shoulders tensing.

Orlaeth's frame drooped; the weight of their stares was nearly as heavy a burden as her decision to flee Dirgil. "I cannot marry," she said after a moment.

"Oh, *she* did run away?" Dargah asked, surprised by her own assessment of the situation. Rinah put a hand on her arm, stunned by the gravity of Orlaeth's confession.

Neryn wet his lips and leaned forward. "You cannot marry… me?"

"I know I have hurt you, and I am sorry." Orlaeth swallowed hard. "I have treated you so cruelly in spite of your kindness to me. I do not deserve forgiveness or freedom, Neryn, but please understand that I left in service to Erjunn—not in defiance of him."

"How can that be? I do not understand. The Disciple is the voice of Erjunn, yet you choose not to honor his choice of a mate for you? Have I somehow offended you? What have I done to upset you so thoroughly?"

Dargah took a heavy swig from her tankard; she noticed that Runo had supplied her with full-strength wine this time, assuming she'd need it.

"Nothing! You have done nothing wrong! Which is why my departure was so difficult—"

"Your departure was difficult because you chose to depart. What in the name of all the gods made you even consider leaving Dirgil, much less actually doing so? Do you know how deeply your parents grieve?"

"There are no words, I fear, that could make you comprehend my reasoning," Orlaeth replied. Though her body trembled, her voice did not. "You are a good man, Neryn, but you can never understand a woman's burden. Not fully."

He nodded then, his face softening. "You will not bear the same burden as your mother. That would put you in danger, and I would not allow it. A single heir is enough."

"This is awkward," Rinah whispered to Dargah.

"You adopted her," Dargah reminded her.

Orlaeth lifted her chin a bit. "My concerns go far beyond childbearing. If I told you—"

Neryn caught a glimpse of a familiar figure out of the corner of his eye, and he rose abruptly. "Tiarnán came with me. If he sees you, he will not tolerate *any* of your concerns, reasonable or not." A sharp breath. "Against my better judgment, I am willing to hear what you have to say, but it cannot be here and now."

"There is not a tree in Dirgil without ears," Orlaeth protested, her voice strangled. "I cannot speak freely—"

"Where can we meet? This evening?" Neryn barked at Dargah.

To her credit, the orc maintained her composure. "Two blocks east of here is a forge. Meet the three of us there at midnight."

"Three?" repeated the elf.

Dargah rose. "You walked into *my* town making claims on a terrified woman who doesn't seem very happy to see you. I'm sure as hell not giving you the chance to be alone with her."

Rinah looked up at her, eyes shining with adoration. Orlaeth's attention returned to her hands. Neryn hesitated, then hissed, "Agreed." He swept out of the inn, meeting his traveling companion in the street and guiding him towards

the river—away from the inn.

"Now. Orlaeth, is it?" Dargah asked, turning to the

despondent elf. "Let's have a little talk."

Chapter Ten:

Of Bargains and Beginnings

Escorted back to the cottage by Rinah, Orlaeth apologized for her deception a dozen times and was forgiven just as many. And although Rinah yearned to know more about this mysterious stranger she'd taken in, she could tell that Orlaeth was thoroughly exhausted. Whatever happened over the past few days must have taken a terrible toll on her body, so Rinah put her to bed, promising to wake her before midnight. Without a peep of protest, Orlaeth curled up like a cat and, within minutes, was sleeping so heavily that Rinah checked twice to make certain she was still breathing.

Taking care to be quiet, Rinah puttered around her worktable. It would not do to spend the rest of the day in fruitless anticipation. She poured a few candles and mixed a new batch of facial cream, but could not keep her thoughts from replaying the tense scene at the inn. Orlaeth was so fragile, and Neryn so resolute, that she didn't dare imagine what might have happened if she and her friends hadn't intervened. Rinah smiled to herself. Neryn was a big man, but Ikraam of Bayan-Taym was bigger, with a protective streak as wide as the sea. And if Ikraam didn't scare Neryn off, Dargah surely would.

Orlaeth would be kept safe at any cost.

*

186

Slinking to the forge long before the agreed-upon time, Dargah, Rinah, and Runo formed a protective triangle around their charge. Neryn, carrying only a lantern, approached just before midnight, his hands raised in a peaceful gesture. Ignoring all but Orlaeth, he began with, "You are fortunate that Tiarnán did not find evidence of your presence here—"

"You came to listen, not to talk," asserted Dargah. She stood nearly eye-to-eye with Neryn, and she was *not* unarmed.

"Must we have a discussion in front of these people?" Neryn asked Orlaeth.

"What's wrong with *these people*?" Rinah was starting to bristle like the half-orcs.

"Half-breeds and hybrids are inferior to the pure-blooded members of the races," Neryn returned. "Mixed blood is an outward sign of depravity and shame; therefore, I am not comfortable speaking of private matters in front of those who are not part of our community."

Rinah gasped, "*Depravity?*"

At the same time, Runo snapped, "What the hell?"

"Your reactions support my point," Neryn said serenely.

In a heartbeat, Dargah's dagger was at his throat. "How's *this* point, Zealot?"

Though he did not flinch, Neryn's eyes flicked to hers as he spat, "Reckless *ifrunn.*"

Orlaeth was the one to step in. "Please, stop. The threat of violence will not be conducive to reaching our goal."

"What *is* our goal anyway, Orlaeth?" Rinah's frown had grown impatient.

Ignoring her friend, the elf said, "Neryn, I trust these people. And I know that you trust me. They already know some of my story."

"Our story," he corrected softly.

"I have written myself out of your story, Neryn. I cannot expect you to understand, but…" She looked at him with a tenderness that bordered on pity. "I know that you are aware of the responsibility I have been given. That alone should have made you hesitant to accept me as a mate. If somehow, it was revealed that the wife of Neryn Sunstorm was able to—"

"This alone cannot be that this is the reason you fled," he interrupted, his mouth set in a grim line. "If it were, you would have left us years ago, after your fits first began."

"Yes. You are correct. I also left because I cannot serve you as a wife, as I will never be able to engage in any kind of intimate relations with you."

Hoping that the night hid the blush creeping up his neck. Neryn hissed, "Orlaeth! This is not an appropriate conversation to have in front of outsiders!"

The outsiders shifted uncomfortably.

As if not hearing him, Orlaeth went on. "You need not be offended. I made my decision based in part on my certainty that, for you, having no mate at all would be a preferable fate to having a childless one."

"How kind of you to consider my feelings before abandoning me," he uttered, incredulous.

"Of course I did. I care very much for you. I always have. And, as I know I cannot provide the future you desire—and deserve—so I removed myself from the situation entirely. It was the only option."

"But why? *Why* can you not provide that future? Is something... amiss?" He gestured vaguely to her abdomen, growing flustered.

He didn't possess the words to have this kind of discussion, and it did not appear that Orlaeth did either. And, Gods Above and Below, why were they even having it at all? Rinah groaned inwardly.

"Not with my physical body, no. Not that I am aware." Orlaeth offered no further explanation.

The silence stretched on, increasingly awkward, until Dargah spoke. "So. Counselor Sunstorm. Do you plan to club her over the head and drag her back to your cave now, or wait until morning?"

Eyes glinting like polished brass, Neryn announced, "I will not bring Orlaeth to Dirgil at all." Jaw tensing, he met the stares of Runo, Rinah, and Dargah in turn. "Though I cannot comprehend any of this, I will not take to wife a woman, even one promised to me, who is unwilling to wed."

"Unable," corrected Orlaeth, her hands clasped in submission or hope.

Refusing to let his shoulders slump in defeat, Neryn looked at her and said, "You are my oldest friend. You were the only person who mourned with me when my mother passed into the Other Realm. You have been nothing but good, and gentle, and faithful, not only to me, but to all of our people. Orlaeth, I will never understand this decision. But I will honor it." His breath hitching almost imperceptibly, he told Rinah, "She will remain in this community and do as she pleases for as long as she likes. However, this decision means that she can never return to Dirgil." Here, he turned to his former betrothed and added softly, "If you did, I could not spare you the consequences of your actions. Even my influence would not be enough to temper the discipline that a prodigal daughter would endure. And you know that I do not have the authority to break our betrothal. The only thing that can do that is death—yours or my own. You have no place in Dirgil now. You have carved your fate in stone, Orlaeth."

"I understand completely," she replied.

"And I never will." After another deep breath, he said, "Tiarnán and I will leave at first light. I will make every effort to keep him from speaking with anyone who is aware of your presence here." He nodded once, to himself, then stared at Orlaeth. "I wish you well." He turned to leave, but she stopped him with a hand on his arm.

"Take this," she breathed, tugging at the medallion around her neck, "as proof of my death."

"Orlaeth!" cried Dargah.

"My *symbolic* death," she corrected. "I know that my family will not rest until they learn of my fate. And so I think, if you give them this as proof you found my body…"

"That seems cruel," murmured Rinah.

"It does. But it is a practical solution," came the answer.

"To an unnecessary problem that you created in the first place," grumbled Neryn. "You request so much of me, Orlaeth. You are asking me to reject our marriage agreement, asking me to return home with a necklace and a lie."

"I know."

Neryn was quiet for a long time, examining the pendant in his palm, his expression unchanging in the flickering lantern light. When he finally looked into Orlaeth's face, he said, "There is no one but you for whom I would take this kind of unthinkable risk. You need not fear retribution. Yet I ask something in return."

Four pairs of eyes focused on his face.

"And what is that?" Runo wanted to know.

The barest hint of emotion that had glistened in Neryn's eyes turned hard and businesslike. "Before you left, I told you that there was a discussion I needed to have with you."

"I remember."

"I wanted to talk to you about some of the research you have provided for the Disciple's review."

"Ah. That is a conversation you are able to have with my father. He has been just as involved—"

"No, Orlaeth." For the first time, Neryn's voice took on a hard, desperate edge. "To your ears, my concerns are scholarly conversation. To Maolyr's, they are an incitement to sedition."

Rinah and Dargah exchanged a glance as Orlaeth waited for Neryn to continue.

"In spite of my relationship with the Disciple, I do not have unfettered access to his private study. You know that none of the Counselors do. Yet I must learn about the ones you most recently transcribed for him. Only you can provide that knowledge for me."

Without hesitation, Orlaeth vowed, "I will write down for you all I can remember, and it will be delivered to you before sunrise, if that is acceptable. But why is it of such great import to you?"

"With respect, Sister Silverwillow, at this point, you have your secrets, and I have my own. Thank you for your help. May you live long, and live well, with Erjunn's blessing." Without another word or glance back at any of them, he turned and walked away, his footsteps silent on the gravel path toward the inn.

*

Lindenvale's river was nothing like the lazy stream that wound its way around Dirgil, shallow enough, in places, to cross by foot. No meandering for this river; it was majestic in the moonlight, flowing toward the sea with assurance, finality. Tidy rowhouses and shops, illuminated by finely-wrought streetside lantern stands, told Neryn that the far side of the river was populated by the more privileged people in the town.

He had sat on a bench overlooking the shimmering water since his talk with Orlaeth. He counted the windows in each house he saw, watched fireflies wink at their reflections in the water, composed a new hymn in his head... anything to keep from thinking about the events of the past few days.

He reminded himself of holy verses demanding obedience and trustworthiness and duty, tried to ignite a fire of righteous indignation in his heart, but all he could feel was a dull, thudding ache in his head. He had failed. Neither his proud lineage nor his sterling reputation could ever soothe the wound that his bride—his *friend*—had dealt him. She had not only rejected him, but she had allied with the very people they had been taught to avoid.

And she'd destroyed his future along with her own.

Chapter Eleven:

Of Spies and Stories

Dargah had not expected to find herself trailing two pointy-eared Zealots through the forest on a gloomy Saturday morning, but it's not like she had other plans anyway.

When Rinah fretted about Neryn keeping his promise to Orlaeth, Dargah echoed her concerns. As she saw it, though, they had only two options; they could spend the foreseeable future fearing his betrayal and coming retribution, or they could ensure his compliance.

"How do you mean?" Rinah wanted to know.

"I'll just follow them back to whatever hole they crawled out of," Dargah answered, "and hear what he says for myself."

"You'd do that?"

After a peek at Orlaeth, who had been led to Alvyx's bedroom for the use of his writing desk, Dargah answered in a quieter tone, "You saw how terrified she was. No one should have to be haunted by their past like that."

"But what are you going to do if he tells his people she's alive?"

"You don't need to worry about that," came the curt reply.

Rinah wasted no time in loading a knapsack with supplies and pressed a sisterly kiss to her friend's cheek. "I really hope we're overreacting, but thank you."

"Make my excuses to Vigga," Dargah reminded her. "And to Bram. He's actually going to have to work tomorrow."

*

Dargah was relieved to learn that the elves had not been on horseback while traveling. She trusted her own two sturdy feet over four skittish, unpredictable hooves any day. Like a cat stalking a mouse, she sliced gracefully through the gloomy morning fog. The haze aided her efforts, even as it hindered the elves' progress. Though only half orcish, her sense of smell was keen, and the combination of floral herbs that they'd likely used to "purify" themselves was distinctive. Losing sight of them was of no concern.

What *did* concern Dargah was what she overheard the elves saying to each other.

"... your search has come to a sorrowful end, my friend," the one called Tiarnán was saying. "Exactly what did you learn?"

200

"Apparently, only yesterday morning, some traveling merchants discovered an elf matching Orlaeth's description drowned a quarter of a mile upriver from here. Once it was learned that she was not part of this community, the attendants at Erjunn's temple took responsibility for the body and provided a respectful funerary pyre. When I told them who I was, they offered me their condolences and something of far greater value."

Tiarnán took the pendant from Neryn's hand and examined it. "Yes, this appears to be Maolyr's craftsmanship. What a terrible blow for the man—to lose his eldest daughter just before his mate brings his youngest child into the world."

Dargah felt a prick of pity for the Silverwillow family. She understood Orlaeth's deep need for independence, but it came at the cost of wounding those closest to her. Then she thought of her own mother, who had hurled insults at Dargah when she left home. Before she could sink into a pit of self-reflection, she strained to hear Neryn's contemplative response.

"I wish that there was something I could have done to prevent all this. Had I been given any type of forewarning whatsoever, I would have done everything to keep her safe. I will forever remember this tragedy as my greatest failure." His voice was raw with sincerity, and Dargah realized that this part of his yarn, at least, was true.

After several quiet moments, Tiarnán spoke again. "I think we can agree that Orlaeth would have been a faithful and honorable mate for you, but, in the end, she was a smallish, frail sort of woman. Now that her fate is known, the Disciple can find for you a healthier female, one likely to bear many children. One of my sisters, perhaps. Una will be of mating age within the year."

Neryn simply replied, "Una is an agreeable female."

Rage darkening her face in the shadows, Dargah thanked the Gods Above and Below that it wasn't within her own capabilities to be *agreeable*.

*

Dargah wasn't thrilled about sleeping in the mud that night, but at least the clouds had cleared, and the night sky was bright with glittering constellations. While the elves dozed, she entertained herself by picking out the ones she remembered from her childhood. There, just over the horizon, was the rounded figure of the Royal Midwife. Above her was the jeweled crown given to the earth goddess by her consort Erjunn. The brightest star in the night sky, tinted a brilliant blue, was a perfect sapphire encircled by diamonds. The oldest orcish stories say that Dehlkia treasured the gift, but never wore it. For the lush goddess of the earth, only a circlet of wildflowers would suffice. She loved the pink-tipped desert rose best; Dargah recalled how brilliantly the petals glowed against that dense cloud of cocoa-brown coils...

But now, in the dreamy haze of the elves' fading campfire, with the low buzz of cicadas in her ear, her eyelids began to droop. She tried to make herself comfortable on the mossy side of a felled tree trunk. Two round yellow eyes, reflecting the moon, peered down from a tree, and Dargah recognized the gaze of a fellow predator. The owl murmured a wary greeting, then disappeared back into the leafy shadows. Strangely comforted by the bird of prey nestled above her, Dargah settled against the trunk and waited for the sun to rise.

*

The following day, clouds again crowded out the sunlight. Rain dampened and slowed the remainder of their travels. Having spent most of her life in the sun-drenched salt flats of eastern Dehlkia, Dargah loathed the muddy trails and spongy ground of Ayusan woodlands, made so much worse during the rainy season. There was no real winter here, as there was up north, no snow or icy roads.

But it got cold and wet, and there were puddles *everywhere*. All the time. She was focused primarily on keeping her footfalls as squelchless as possible when she heard, "Brother, forgive me, but might I ask you a question somewhat personal in nature?"

It was Tiarnán who had spoken. Dargah's ears perked like a dog's.

"Of course, you may," Neryn replied.

Dargah sensed Tiarnán's hesitation before he said, "Is it... inappropriate for me to experience the desire to lie with my wife?"

The response was succinct. "To lie with her is your duty, that she may conceive."

"But... there have been occasions when I have desired her, even when she was *unlikely* to conceive."

"I see."

"There have also been occasions during which... ah... *she* wished to initiate intimacy. Of course, I did not permit it, but it was more difficult to deny her than I

205

expected it to be. I fear that I am a disappointment in the eyes of Erjunn."

Dargah could not see Neryn's face, but his words were blunt. "Sexual congress is necessary for the raising of another generation. Otherwise, it serves only to distract us from our adoration and service to our god. Consider, brother, that the time you and your wife might spend engaged in fruitless exploration of each other's bodies is time that might also be spent in meditation or in acts of service to the community."

"Yes! These are things I consider endlessly. Yet the desires continue to return."

"And you will continue to resist them because you are a good man, a servant of Erjunn, and you will not lead your wife into frivolity and immoderation."

The younger elf let out a little chuckle. "I certainly will not. I suppose we are not orcs, after all."

Though she rolled her eyes, Dargah wasn't offended. She knew her people were passionate, vibrant, lusty, and full of life. It was what made them who they were. By contrast, these men of the Remnant, she decided, were less interesting than a pile of potatoes. At least the potatoes had potential. To thicken a hearty venison stew, for example.

Now Dargah was hungry.

Tiarnán spoke again. "It would be a proud and joyful service to minister to a wife as her body creates new life. I eagerly anticipate this blessing. Am I improper in expressing *that* desire?"

Neryn's response was thoughtful and quiet. "I do not think so. I firmly believe that nurturing a female in so delicate a condition is one of the most honorable things a husband can do in worship of his god."

Perhaps Orlaeth wouldn't have been treated like a broodmare after all? Still, Dargah almost laughed aloud. Only elves could be *delicately* pregnant. Orcish women, on the other hand, were so sturdy that they worked right up until labor began—and sometimes longer. She'd heard of orcs who delivered twins in the middle of a work day and had to be *forced* to go home to rest, though she'd never seen that happen herself. Still, it would not be impossible among a people for whom the pregnant female form is the height of beauty.

As she reflected, Dargah felt a sudden, uneasy hush fall over the woods. The elves noticed it, too. "A she-wolf?" Tiarnán guessed. He inched his staff into a defensive position. The fading light cast serpentine shadows, and a predator could be lurking within any one of them. Dargah was there, after all, unseen and unheard by the elves, as threatening as any wild animal.

Neryn sniffed at the air, then shook his head almost imperceptibly. "Cougar," he corrected. "With her cubs."

Dargah realized with alarm that the elves carried no real weapons. Many avoided bloodshed, so she'd been told.

Neither carried a bow or arrows, and the only blade between them was Neryn's pitiful dirk, hardly fit to cut bread. How would they protect themselves from a threatened mother cougar? At least Dargah was armed. She silently unsheathed the dagger strapped to her thigh and listened.

And waited.

The low growl finally came, and two pale green eyes peered down from the ridge above them.

"Careful," Neryn mouthed to Tiarnán. "Steady."

All at once and with as much grace as fury, the cougar sprung down from the ridge.

Or rather, she tried to.

Instead of planting all four clawed paws in the dirt, the mountain lion hovered midair. She seemed just as stunned as Dargah was, and she vainly stretched her paws toward the earth, claws fully extended. She lashed her tail and screamed in frustration. Underneath her, leaves and pine needles rustled in a noisy swirl of air. The half-orc had seen many unusual things in her life, but a floating cougar was a new one. She slowly turned her attention back toward the elves and swallowed a gasp of shock.

It was their magic. Real, elemental magic.

Neryn watched Tiarnán calmly as the younger elf concentrated on the whirlwind beneath the fumbling cat. "Now," he whispered, "do you think you can put her back on the ridge, or do you need my assistance?"

Tiarnán grimaced, but nodded. "I can do it." He made a slow, dismissive motion with his hands, and the cougar, still shrieking, rose several feet into the air. As soon as her paws touched the rocky slab above them, she disappeared, deciding that she and her cubs were better off fleeing than fighting. Neryn clapped Tiarnán firmly on the back.

"Yes, you have greatly improved these past few weeks!" he exclaimed.

"With your help," Tiarnán added with a hint of humility. "Thank you for your patience in working with me. I am eager to show the Disciple my improvements."

"Let not your progress open the door to pride, my brother," warned Neryn, not unkindly.

Dargah had seen pure-blooded orcs use magic, but somehow, moving great mounds of dirt to make way for paved roads wasn't quite as intense as what she had just witnessed.

Leave it to the elves to make everything more dramatic.

Chapter Twelve:

Of Falsehoods and Fairytales

"Oh. You've got a friend visiting."

Rinah glanced up from the stubborn weed she'd been battling and offered Bram a smile. "Hi. Yes, this is—" She shot a glance toward her companion, who was watching a bumblebee as it hovered over a peony.

"I am Orlaeth," the elf said without taking her eyes off the bee. She had been sitting in the grass for hours, moving seamlessly between times of prayer, short conversations with Rinah, and silent admiration of her surroundings.

"Well, hello there, Orlaeth," Bram said with a friendly smile, extending his hand. "My name's—"

"Your name is Bram, and you have a big personality," Oraleth announced to the bee.

"Yeah, you could say that," he laughed, stuffing his hand back into his pocket. Then, lowering his voice, he said to Rinah, "You forgot I was coming over?"

Another tug on the weed. "I didn't realize we'd finalized our plans."

"You did ask me to visit, though. When I stopped over yesterday."

"Oh. I'm sorry, I don't remember," she said with a grunt, having finally defeated the weed. "Well, at any rate, Orlaeth and I are almost done here. How about we clean up and join you for supper? I know! Over by the temple of Kaylor, there's a place with the most wonderful—"

"Nah, I don't think that's going to work," Bram said.

"What would you like to do, then?"

"I just wanted to spend some time with *you*, beautiful," he sighed.

She smiled, preening a bit at the flattery, but said, "I don't feel right leaving Orlaeth by herself. I'm happy to pay for her food. She can come with, right?"

"I guess." He looked away.

Unsure of how to respond, Rinah turned back to her friend, who was now entranced by a mantis she'd discovered hidden within a cluster of button-shaped, yellow flowers. "Orlaeth, be careful. I need to get rid of that plant!"

"It is a tansy."

"Yes. And I don't want it there. It shows up every year, no matter what I do. If I let it, it would take over the whole garden. And Papa gets a rash if he touches it. Lots of people do."

"Can't he just *not* touch it?" Bram interjected, trying to catch Rinah's attention again.

"May I take responsibility for the plant?" Orlaeth wondered, allowing the mantis to take a cautious step into her palm. "I dislike the idea of it being destroyed simply because it is not as appealing as other flowers."

"Well… do you want to put it in a pot?" Rinah removed her gardening gloves and tossed them Orlaeth's way. "We can stop at the stoneware shop across the river and get one that's large enough."

"Then we will not have to kill it?"

"No. If we transplant it and maybe move it out front, it won't be a problem."

"*Rinah!*" Bram barked.

Both women looked at him in alarm.

"I didn't mean to shout," he said quickly. He glanced between the two. "Look... never mind. I'll just spend the rest of the day with my aunt. Maybe I'll see you later this week, but I don't know. I'm working twice as hard now because I'm handling that orc girl's load today. What's her name again?"

"Dargah," they responded in unison.

"Yeah, she just never showed up this morning. Surprised me. I thought Aunt Vigga had a reputation for hiring reliable workers," he said.

Rinah wet her lips. "But… I stopped in to tell your aunt that Dargah was ill today. You hadn't woken yet when I got there. She… should be better in a few days, I hope."

"Huh. Guess no one ever told me. I think I'll eat with Vigga." He tossed a dimpled smile Orlaeth's way. "Nice meeting you, miss."

She merely blinked.

"All right, then." Rinah wiped her palms on her skirt as she watched him leave.

Orlaeth came to her, the mantis delicately balanced in her palm. "I was made aware a few years ago that, in certain species of insect, the female will sometimes devour the male during the mating process."

Rinah wrinkled her nose. She was already upset that she'd let Bram down, and now, her strange new friend was talking about cannibalistic bug sex. "Orlaeth, that's disgusting."

"Nature does not follow the same rules that we do."

"Why are you telling me this?"

Orlaeth gently nudged the mantis, who twitched and turned her huge, luminous eyes toward Rinah. "I think she is happier alone than with an unsuitable mate."

*

Based on her observations of the elves, Dargah had expected the community of Dirgil to encircle some kind of massive temple rising eerily up out of the forest, holy chants echoing while silver chimes carried prayer on the breeze straight to the ears of the wind god.

Instead, the elves' sanctuary was nothing more remarkable than a large campsite. Several cabins - all identical and unadorned, connected via crude dirt paths - were plotted around a central building, which she assumed was some kind of town hall or meeting place. Built slightly higher up on the hill, a smaller cabin seemed to watch over the rest. And higher still was something that appeared to be a pavilion or an altar. Lush household gardens dotted the land. A small wheat field and several vegetable patches lay beyond the cabins. Surrounding it all was a modest fence, likely more a deterrent for animals than anything else.

Dargah was not impressed.

Shouts of greeting drew her attention to a small welcoming party spilling out of the central building and heading for Neryn and Tiarnán, who approached the gate. Other elves heard their cries and emerged from their homes. Dargah scrambled up a tree, watching the reunion like a hungry hawk.

"My Counselors! Welcome home," said the slender, older man who led the pack. From her vantage point, Dargah could tell that he was advanced in years, but carried himself with the vigor and gait of a younger man. After both elves bowed low before him, he moved to embrace Neryn, then jerked back, his nose wrinkled in disgust. "By the breath of Erjunn, Counselor, you reek of... of..." He seemed to taste the air, then cringed. "A great many foul things. The gods only know what deviant creatures you must have encountered on this quest. You must both bathe in the sacred spring to purify yourselves before entering the compound." Then, the older man's tone softened. "But...you do not come triumphantly, Neryn Sunstorm. Tell me of your travels. Have you news of your intended bride?"

Dargah leaned forward as far as she dared. This was the moment. If Neryn told this man—obviously the Disciple—that he had found Orlaeth alive, she would leap out of the trees and claw off his face, consequences be damned.

Neryn drew a deep breath. His voice trembled as he spoke. "Yes, Holy One, I do indeed bear news of Sister Orlaeth Silverwillow."

A woman behind the Disciple let out a heart-rending cry and stumbled toward Neryn. Dargah could see her belly, heavy with new life—Orlaeth's mother. "I beg you, Counselor, please tell me that she is safe, somehow." Upon seeing his grim expression, she gasped. She could not speak further, dissolving into muffled sobs, as a man, probably her husband, pulled her into his arms.

Dargah felt a wave of pity for the woman. The poor thing was clearly not in a condition to receive bad—albeit false—news of her daughter's untimely demise.

Neryn bowed slightly to his would-have-been mother-in-law. "Tiarnán and I visited one of the small towns to the south, and, upon questioning the residents, we learned that..." He paused to arrange his features into a pained frown and allowed his voice to catch on his next words. "It appears that a woman matching Orlaeth's

221

description was found…" He stopped again, glancing at Tiarnán, as if for support. "Her body was found in the town's river. Her soul had passed into the Other Realm long before the local fishermen found her." At her mother's keening wail, Neryn closed his eyes, pressing on to repeat the tale he had told Tiarnán. He placed the medallion in her father's palm. "Did this belong to Orlaeth?"

The man nodded, supporting his trembling wife.

Here, the Disciple stepped in. "My dearest friends, the unexpected loss of your precious daughter is a loss for all of us," he said soothingly. "Orlaeth was a beautiful woman, a virtuous woman. We mourn with you. Allow me to assist you in the preparation of a memorial pyre." With his subtle encouragement, the small crowd began to disperse, muttering condolences. Some of them were crying, others shaking their heads. The Disciple turned back toward Neryn and Tiarnán. "Once you have purified yourself, Neryn, I will have you choose one of Orlaeth's favorite hymns to sing at the ceremony. Come to me, and we will discuss it." Tiarnán bowed and left after a final sympathetic nod.

"Disciple," Neryn said quickly, keeping his distance. "I… I know that Orlaeth had not yet become my mate, but I ask, if you see fit, to spend some time in private meditation. I would never think of taking a full week of solitude, but perhaps—"

The older man gave him a sad smile. "Of course," he said. "It is only appropriate that you have the opportunity to grieve in privacy. After your purification, instead of the customary trek into the wilderness for those in mourning," he suggested, "you may stay at the lodge by the healing spring this evening. It is not quite the same as being alone in the untamed wilderness with Erjunn's sweet presence, but it will allow you some quiet time to reflect. I will personally see to it that your belongings are sent to you and that no one disturbs you there. We will hold the ceremony tomorrow at dusk when you return." He seemed satisfied with his own response, then added, "Counselor, please know that I am saddened by this tragedy, and for your loss. For *our* loss."

Neryn bowed, his face crumpling with barely concealed emotion. "I am thankful for your great kindness, Holy One," he whispered.

The Disciple turned away, ushering the few remaining elves back toward their homes. Neryn was left alone and joyless, just outside Dirgil's roughly-hewn gates.

*

It was rare for Makoa to awaken during the day. He had discovered an abandoned, west-facing hollow inside a black locust tree deep enough for him to avoid the sun's brightest rays, and it had been his favored hidey-hole for some time now. The warm, sweet scent of the tree's flowers always helped lull him into a peaceful sleep before the intrusive blaze of sunset called him to task.

But today was different. The male cardinal who liked to preen on the branch above the hollow was chittering furiously with his mate. Something about nest-building, Makoa guessed, but his faerie heritage didn't magically translate animal-speak. It took decades—*centuries* to develop that kind of ability, and he hadn't even begun to scratch the surface of the forest's languages. Even after the bird had left in a huff, and the tree was again quiet, Makoa shifted on his soft bed of moss, still unable to relax. He watched the forest from inside the tree, hoping the swaying leaves and gentle wind might relax him.

Something bright and blue blurred past, trailing laughter like bells and the fragrance of violets. "Tahiri!" he called out, scrambling out from beneath his leafy covers. He sat on the edge of the hollow, legs dangling, and waited for the inevitable.

In a blink, his fellow faerie dropped out of the sky and hovered in front of Makoa, her iridescent wings buzzing as fast as a dragonfly's. "You're shorter than I remember," she announced pertly, fists on her lean hips.

"I miss you, too, Hiri," he laughed, making room for her in the nook.

She squeezed in next to him. "How long has it been since you started getting friendly with the owls? Feels like ages."

"Almost three new moons," he said, "and owls are the least of my problems. Night patrol is tough."

"I bet it's lonely."

Makoa knew what Tahiri's tone intimated; they'd restored each other in the past. His *lorica* reserve wasn't lacking, and he didn't have the physical energy to engage, so he pretended that her concern was consideration instead of proposition. "It's quiet, for sure. Took a while to get used to. But the night has its own rhythm, and I think I'm finding it."

"At any rate, it's an honor to be given the midnight guard." Tahiri's wide smile assured him that she was proud of him, but in no way envious of his new role. "It means the *tanaiste* trusts you."

Before he could reply, Tahiri heard her name drifting on the breeze. She let out a quiet, frustrated groan. "Kalama goes into a panic if she loses sight of me, even for a second. I wish she didn't worry so much." She gave his naked thigh a friendly pat before taking off. "Maybe I'll see you again sometime this year."

"Maybe," Makoa echoed as she leapt into the air. He waved her off with a smile. "But I wouldn't get my hopes up."

Chapter Thirteen:

Of Pride and Prejudice

Having retreated into the depths of the forest as soon as she heard Neryn's story, Dargah paused to weigh her options. She could simply turn around and make her way back to Lindenvale, but she doubted even her own sense of direction in the middle of a storm, and the gloomy dusk sky was threatening just that. They'd passed within a quarter-mile of a shabby village a few hours ago, and though it would be an unpleasant hike, she guessed she could make it to the inn there before night fell. Or, perhaps she could—

"Are you waiting for a formal invitation to approach me, *ifrunn?*"

Dargah didn't hide her surprise—and irritation—at the sound of Neryn's languid drawl. She realized then that she was within sight of the lodge the Disciple had mentioned and that Neryn was alone, his companion having quickly bathed to hurry back to the village and, presumably, a sense of normalcy. He hummed to himself, taking a towel to his wet hair. He wore a simple, pure white tunic that hung to his calves, contrasting sharply with his bronze skin. "Or should I assume that spying on unwitting males as they bathe is typical behavior for a she-orc?"

She stepped out of the brush, face defiant. "Don't flatter yourself. You aren't unwitting, and I wasn't watching you bathe."

"But you *were* spying."

"Only to ensure you kept your promise to Orlaeth."

"Come," he said, gesturing to the lodge. "I believe that we have things to discuss."

"You're joking," she huffed, crossing her arms.

"Joking is frivolous. Now, this may be a challenge for you, but think rationally, *ifrunn*. It was a long journey for both of us. You need rest and food as much as I."

Dargah's gaze darted from the cabin's dark interior to Neryn, then back again. "I don't trust you."

His expression was serene. Peacefully smug. "Nor I you. But all created races have basic needs that even *you* cannot ignore. I have food and drink enough for us both. Rest, and then be on your way." He went inside, then called out to her, "You are welcome to remain outside, although it appears that the sky again threatens rain."

Other than an involuntary shiver, she didn't move. "How long did you know I was following you?"

"To your credit," he answered, poking his head back out, "only the last few miles or so. You got a bit too close, and"—he smirked—"I caught the distinct 'reek of orc'. Tiarnán noticed something as well but could not identify it as your scent. I told him that he likely smelled a rotting deer carcass." When she remained stubbornly outside, he said, "If for no reason other than you and your friends welcoming Orlaeth into your community, I feel bound to offer a safe place to rest. You have done me a kindness in protecting her. I owe you a kindness in return. Is that not just and fair?"

A transaction. An exchange. Dargah could accept that more easily than she could open-handed pity or sympathy, especially from a Zealot. Still, she sneered as she brushed past Neryn into the cabin. He grimaced and flicked invisible filth from his damp tunic. "Are you going to need to perform some kind of sanctification ritual in this place after I leave?"

He grimaced and flicked invisible filth from his damp tunic. As he closed the door, he murmured, "Burning it to the ground is not an option, so yes."

While Dargah took in the complete lack of ambience, Neryn lit several lanterns and placed them around the room. Though the coming night was gray and cloudy, the cabin would have been as gloomy on a bright spring morning. A single window allowed in natural light, and even that, Neryn hurried to shutter and latch.

A long table, outfitted with several uncomfortable-looking chairs, was the largest piece of furniture in the room. Several papers piled neatly on it, as were quills, bottles of ink, and a few books. Two walls had floor-to-ceiling bookshelves, tidily organized and teeming with parchments, booklets, pamphlets, and loose pages in languages Dargah had never encountered. Next to the hearth was a small desk, on which rested a lyre, a set of reed pipes, a flute, and pages marked with musical notations. A low-backed wooden bench was in front of the hearth, its plump pillows the only scrap of hospitality in the room. A half-wall separated the main room from a row of cots. Beyond that was a closed door. Perhaps a necessary room. Neryn's people didn't seem the type to have old-fashioned pisspots under their beds. His people didn't seem the type to admit they had bodily functions at all, actually.

Her reluctant host had already gotten a few sparks to catch in the fireplace. Dargah was grateful, hoping to dry her hair and clothing from the day's multiple downpours and mud puddles. She eyed Neryn with envy as spring water dripped from his hair.

After a few minutes, he unpacked his satchel and brought forth the remainder of a dark, dense loaf of bread, several large mushrooms, a bundle of berries, a sack of oats, a jar of oil, and a canteen. Then he disappeared for a moment. When he returned, he was carrying blankets and two small wooden cups. He deposited one of each near

Dargah, then sat. Her pride instructed her to ignore the warm woolen blanket, but her body told her that it was clammy and damp and that she was doing herself no good by refusing it.

She wrapped it around her shoulders, then took the cup of water he had offered.

"Why did you fear I would not keep my promise?" Neryn asked. There was no anger in his voice, no suspicion, so she answered with equal frankness.

"Rinah and I know nothing about you, other than what you told us yourself. "

"Then it appears Orlaeth has surrounded herself with an apprehensive lot." His knife, clean but blunt, bit into the flesh of the mushroom, sawing it into jagged chunks. Then he sliced the bread.

"Not apprehensive. Diligent. I'm not ready to trust her future to a male I've never met."

"And you have known her for a mere two days. Surely then you can imagine my concern for her. I have called her friend for over twenty years."

Dargah snapped, "She's afraid of you."

Nonplussed, he placed the sliced mushrooms and a bit of oil in the pot hanging over the fire. "She is afraid of *marriage*, which is understandable. Many females are. You do not appear to have a mate. Perhaps you are afraid as well?"

This man hadn't done a thing to earn a telling of her story. Rage tightened her chest, but Dargah's words were measured. "You know nothing of my life."

"And you know nothing of Orlaeth's. Or mine." He turned back to her, adding, "None of that matters, now, of course. Her path and mine are now as divergent as east is from west. I do, however, acknowledge your boldness in following me here. It is an unattractive trait in a woman, but I appreciate that you have used it in your perceived protection of Orlaeth. Still, your actions were foolish."

"Why foolish?"

"The presence of a half-orc here is both unwelcome and unprecedented." Then, he added, with the slightest hint of a smile, "What is it, Dargah of Lindenvale, that you would have done had I told the Disciple the truth about her?"

Without missing a beat, she replied, "I would have killed you."

The gleam in Neryn's eyes winked out. He leaned back in his chair and crossed his arms. "And what makes you think you could have killed me?"

Dargah mirrored his pose and sputtered a laugh. "Over a decade of unarmed combat training and a three-year winning streak at the Dehlkian Games. I reached Champion. And I didn't need magic for any of it."

"Despite the Remnant's preference for peace, I, too, have been prepared for warfare," Neryn replied. "I am a highly accomplished mage and trainer."

"Magic's useless if you're dead before you know you're a target, elf."

Neryn clenched his jaw and stood abruptly. The soft golden-brown of his irises disappeared, and his eyes went as white as a full moon. Without speaking a charm or moving a single finger, without any spectacle, he released his power.

A gust of wind howled from one end of the cabin to the other, extinguishing every lantern and even the fire, which had grown to fill the hearth as they'd talked. Dargah's long braid flailed and tore at her face like a leather whip. The books on the table slammed into the wall and the paper streaked through the air like a thousand white flags of surrender. Even the wooden cabin creaked around them, strained by the pressure within.

The torrent eventually slowed to a gentle breeze, then faded altogether as Neryn returned to his seat. In the dimness of the cabin, his eyes, again the color of the dunes, fixed on her, awaiting a reaction.

She only offered a dismissive snort as she moved toward the fading embers in the hearth. The lyre drew her attention, and she reached out to caress its elegant curves.

"No," he said, the word sharp as an arrow. "I have offered to give you food and shelter. Touch nothing else."

Withdrawing her hand, Dargah asked, "These are yours?"

"I play the lyre, the harp, and the lute," he said without a hint of modesty. He pulled the pot from the hearth, and persuaded the embers to again ignite.

"My brother is a musician, too."

His laugh was an ugly sound. "I am sure his style is quite different from mine."

"No doubt it is." Shadows, thrown by the firelight, danced across her face. "Erjunn is the god of truth; yet you defied a command to bring Orlaeth back here, and then you lied on her behalf."

He regarded her with undisguised suspicion as he divided the mushrooms between two slices of bread. "Is that not what she requested of me?"

She picked a book from the floor—hurled there by Neryn's grandiose show of power—and began to leaf through it. "Yes, but how do you reconcile *your* deception with the commandments of your faith?"

Raising an eyebrow, Neryn steepled his fingers and replied as though lecturing a room full of fresh-faced students. "Laws are important. Rules and regulations are meant to keep us safe. They ensure that everyone consistently understands expectations. And they make it simpler to call out improper behavior without bias. I have spent my life memorizing rules. Reciting them. Enforcing them. Living them. It had never occurred to me, not once, before yesterday, that I would ever even speak the *hint* of a lie to the face of the Disciple." His eyes, like the shifting sands of her homeland, looked past her. "But when I saw the abject terror on Orlaeth's face—terror at merely *seeing* me—and when I realized that *I* possessed the power and opportunity to dispel her fears, there was nothing else to consider. Erjunn's primary command is to live a gentle life, easing suffering and promoting peace at every opportunity. Yes, honesty is a crucial part of obeying his commands as well, but... the thought of dragging her home—to *my* home, no longer hers—turned my stomach. If I did that, even though it was expected of me, I would be causing harm to Orlaeth.

"And yes, I know that, in lying about her death, I have spared her from harm while simultaneously causing harm to her family. Understand that I took no pleasure in watching the light fade from her mother's eyes. I do not think there was a solution in which I could satisfy everyone. And so I chose to honor Orlaeth. I have always respected her and her genuine love for Erjunn. It seems to me that, although I do not understand it, perhaps that very devotion to him led her away from the Remnant. She is a woman of deep and unshakable faith, and there have been times when it seemed as though she possessed more insight than us all." His voice carried a note of regret, and his expression was as solemn as Dargah had yet seen him.

She brushed away the pang of sympathy that caressed her heart. "If she had returned, would you have forced her to marry you?"

"You seem to think that would be *my* decision." Neryn seemed to brighten a bit at the confusion on Dargah's face.

"This Disciple," she murmured. "Tell me about this man. What does he do for your people, other than pairing them up like sires and brood mares?"

Irritated, he ignored the metaphor. "He is our spiritual leader, which is something you seem to lack." When she let out a sniff of derision, he continued, "He

241

seeks the wisdom of Erjunn and unveils it to us, and yes, that includes making matches among our people."

"How? By drawing lots? Through visionary dreams? I'm guessing affection and attraction don't factor into his decisions."

"Affection and attraction are fleeting at best," he scoffed. "Now, the heartbreak that so often follows emotional entanglements, well, that lasts far longer. The Disciple actively helps us avoid the pitfalls of ill-fated relationships, something to which I assume *you* are accustomed."

Refusing to rise to the bait, Dargah answered around a huge mouthful of food, aiming to be as unladylike as possible. "Because I'm a half-breed or because I don't have a mate?"

He offered her a patronizing smirk. "By virtue of your heritage and the appearance of your disheveled attire alone…" he began, gesturing to her partially-buttoned vest and mud-caked trousers.

"It's summer, and I just trailed you through what amounts to a swamp!" Dargah protested. "Looking *feminine* was not high on my priority list!"

He continued as though she hadn't spoken. "…I can assume that you are a woman who chases carnal pleasure while fleeing the emotional and spiritual investment of a stable marriage. While a reflection of your orcish ancestry, lustfulness is *not* a suitable excuse for embracing wanton promiscuity."

A decade ago, a spitting and hissing Dargah, hearing such a slur, would have punched a hole through the cabin wall, then aimed her bloodied first at Neryn's face. Though that woman had been dead for years, Dargah was now dangerous in different ways. She let out a long, thoughtful hum. "So, you think Erjunn never has a *single* lustful thought about his consort?"

A blush crept up Neryn's neck. "That is a crude simplification of the a relationship between—"

"How do your holy books describe it, Counselor? Surely you have it memorized. Recite it to me. Maybe the dirty green whore will learn something."

"That is an odious word," he muttered.

"'Dirty', 'green', or 'whore'?"

Shaking his head, he quoted, "'Mockers who voice their thoughts prove themselves fools.'"

Dargah smiled with sharp teeth, her eyes sparkling with cruel pride. "*The Path of the Wind*, chapter five. Poem one, line twelve."

The attribution rattled Neryn, but he swallowed a retort, instead forcing himself to say, "That is so. How does it come to pass that a half-orc memorizes Erjunn's holy book?"

"I was seventeen. When I was training for the Games that year, I broke my ankle. While I was recovering,

I spent more time lying around than I could handle. So I read. Trashy novels, holy books, family recipes. My brother's diary. Anything I could get my hands on. Orcs are not illiterate, Neryn."

"I never implied they were." He narrowed his eyes. "If you are familiar with the text, then you already *know* the chapter about the conception of the spring."

Her voice dripping with false sweetness, she chirped, "Of course I do. But maybe I just wanted to hear the words out of your pretty mouth, Counselor!"

He replied with a stony scowl.

Switching to the monotone of an uninspired priest, she intoned. "'For indeed, Erjunn looked upon the form of Dehlkia and loved her sweetness and her fullness of beauty. She welcomed his affection, and responded in kind. In due time, the goddess, heavy with new life, cried out in her pains. And she brought forth, after the season of ice and snow, the daughter called Spring, who restores hope and beauty to all which Winter made barren.'"

"Your recitation is a credit to Erjunn," he noted, his tone laced with reluctance.

"If your god himself enjoyed a woman's body, why is it forbidden for you?"

Neryn slapped his open palms down on the table, exasperated. "He joined with her not for his own pleasure but for the blessing his child would be to all peoples! Besides, if you are as well-read as you imply, then you know there are at least two ancient sources that suggest Dehlkia *seduced* Erjunn, deceiving him into fathering her daughter, making him a *victim* of her wiles."

That smirk was still there as she nodded. "Two *elvish* sources, yes. We tell the story a bit differently. Every year, at harvest time, the god Kaylor comes before Dehlkia, determined to share her bed. He paints the trees in brilliant shades of fire to impress her, but she wisely knows that Kaylor's powers of flame and heat, unchecked in the throes of lovemaking, would destroy her. So, without fail, she chooses her other suitor, Erjunn, as faithful as he is gentle... let me see if I can remember exactly how it goes..." She slowly circled the room until she stood behind his chair. Her voice dropped to a purr poorly suited to the recitation of a sacred text. "'And then, the mighty god Erjunn looked upon the beautiful form of Dehlkia with love in his heart and a great aching in his loins.'"

Neryn shifted in his seat, still staring straight ahead.

"In her heart, too, desire had taken root, and she appealed to the god of wind, saying 'Lie with me. Worship my body with your own, for I yearn to feel your caresses.'"

Suddenly, the room was too warm for Neryn's comfort.

"'Yet I am no tender bud, to be blown away with the barest breeze,'" Dargah continued, her lips close to his ear. When he felt the heat of her body through his thin tunic, he understood.

This was a test.

It was a trap, laid by a brazen, wayward daughter of the orcs! But he would not be ensnared. Instead, he would use it as another opportunity to prove himself true to Erjunn, to place his body's responses—primal and unwelcome—on a metaphorical pyre and destroy them.

"'Treat me not as a fragile blossom. My softest bud blooms for you alone, my lover, but oh, I am no rose. I am a clinging vine, I am the thorn of the bush, I am the sturdy root, and I am the broadest tree. Blow upon me, god of the wind, and rustle my leaves with your breath.'" She walked with swaying steps away from him, placing her hands on the table and sitting down again.

He searched for some kind of twisted sincerity in her inky eyes, but he found only a calculated ruthlessness there.

She knew *exactly* what she was doing to him.

"'Shake me until my fruits are bruised, until your mouth is filled with the luscious taste of them. Let the trembling of our bodies, joined in breathless ecstasy, shake the earth. May the mountains quake and even the stars above rattle with the force of our union. And when you, my beloved, spill your precious seed into my—'"

With a sizable amount of effort, Neryn managed to break eye contact. "Ah! Yes! So, our books agree on that particular point, but for a slight difference in details," he interrupted, too loudly. "You are well-versed in... theological nuance."

With her spiteful enchantment broken, the seductress vanished. Dargah plopped herself down on the chair and propped her chin in one hand. "That surprises you?"

"Pleasantly," he admitted, still guarded. "It means that I can expect reasonable conversation henceforth, perhaps?"

"Not if you keep nattering on about your Disciple."

The burgeoning sense of arousal Dargah had been nurturing dissolved immediately into scorn, and a different kind of heat flushed his face. "Surely you are not so petty as to insult my beliefs?"

"Of course not. It's just that I've never read a verse in *The Path of the Wind* requiring Erjunn's followers to take mates."

Neryn sniffed. "And why would you have? That book was written when the world was new and magic was pure. There was no need to discuss what was naturally taking place. *The Wind Walker* was written after my people began to forget who they were, and joined with humans and orcs, and *that* is from whence the Disciple takes his directives."

"I've only known that text to be apocryphal," Dargah murmured. "The elves I consider friends won't even acknowledge it."

"The elves *you* consider friends," he sneered, "are the ones who most desperately need it. They, too forget themselves. The book reminds us of our duties to Erjunn, to bring a pure generation into the world, to do everything within our means to make things as they once were."

"How does that make you any better than a Zealot? Maybe you don't demand the death of people unlike you, but you'll sure as hell shut us out anyway you can, won't you?"

He responded with a cold smile and a serenity designed to infuriate her. "I am oathbound to keep my bloodline pure. I consider the obligation nothing short of an honor."

Interlude II:

Of Crimes and Community

Nineteen Years Ago

Elpida said nothing at first, her heart in her throat, as she picked her way over fallen branches and thick moss to follow the child.

"No mama," the girl announced, pointing to the tent.

Elpida could hardly breathe as she crept towards the campsite. Her maternal instincts raged for her to snatch the child and *run*. "Shh, shh, I see, sweetheart," she soothed, stretching out her arms for the girl. Instead of running to her, the child inched closer to the tent. "No, no, baby, don't...it's not safe," Elpida pleaded. She breathed a grateful sigh of relief when the girl paused, then walked back towards her and took Elpida's hand in her small, plump one.

"No mama," she repeated sadly.

With very little coaxing, Elpida was able to lead the confused girl back into the town, and straight to the home of Provost Hector Savvas.

"You will want to take a few reliable men to help you examine an abandoned campsite across the river," Elpida said by way of greeting.

The portly man squinted up at her. "If you're to be waking me with bad news," he mumbled, "Ye could 'ave at least brought me a bit of breakfast first."

"It's urgent," Elpida pressed. "Gather some men and meet me at the bridge. I'm going to get this wee one something to eat." She cast a wry glance at the older man. "And I will pick something up for you, too."

"Be there quick as I can, missus," he told Elpida, stealing another glance at the unfamiliar little girl.

Adelfi's Inn was not far from the sheriff's house, and so Elpida took her sleeping baby and the foundling there for a quick meal. Tobith Adelfi smiled at the girl as he presented them with a basket full of sausage hand pies - enough to satisfy all the townsmen who were already being pulled from their warm beds. His wife Kalos, nursing their own daughter at the moment, exchanged a glance with Elpida. "My brother gave us some clothing his son grew out of, and it's all still far too big for Ioanie. I think they'll fit our little princess here." She disappeared around the corner, then reappeared with a smile and an armful of soft tunics.

Elpida thanked her, then encouraged the girl to follow her back towards the forest.

Chapter Fourteen:

Of Faith and Fear

When Dargah did not respond to his coldness with the heat he expected, Neryn busied himself by tidying the table, then announced, "It is now dark, and the weather does not bode well for you to return safely to Lindenvale, and the only inn between here and there is disreputable at best. You are stubborn enough, I gather, to attempt the journey anyway, but should reason prevail, there is a private bedroom past the communal sleeping quarters. You may spend the night there."

"I'm an abomination to society, but you and I can sleep under the same roof?" *There* was the spark he anticipated, the embers flickering to life in her eyes. "Counselor, are you trying to flirt?"

"Neryn. My name is Neryn. The title 'Counselor' sounds profane on your lips," he snapped.

"Neryn Sunstorm." She rolled the syllables around on her tongue, savoring the discomfort radiating from the elf. "You know, there's an ancient orcish word that sounds a lot like your name. *Narin.* It means 'fragile'. And, speaking of old tongues, what is it that you keep calling me? *Ifrunn?*"

He finished the last bite of his meal and wiped his mouth. "In one of the older western dialects, it translates to 'hell-cat'."

She actually laughed. "I've been called worse."

"Of that I have no doubt."

They stared at each other across the table for a moment, both lost in thought.

"What *would* the Disciple do if he found a female here? A female half-blood?" Dargah asked, a threat dancing with curiosity. "In fact, how do you know that he doesn't already know?"

"He does not. He will not."

"But—"

Neryn sighed and pinched the bridge of his nose, the same way Alvyx did when his patience grew thin. "*Please,* spare us both any further frustration and just get some rest."

"…What would happen?"

"Such a thing is so unthinkable that I cannot even imagine the consequences."

Dargah hesitated; she had no desire to remain in the lodge overnight. Neryn kept his promise, she ought not put him in further danger, even if the idea of the broad-shouldered elf, knock-kneed and sniveling before his all-powerful Disciple, was enticing. "A little rain won't hurt. If I leave now, and make it to the inn—"

"I told you, it is not a reputable establishment."

She didn't bear the tusks of an orc, but Dargah's wicked grin was no less a warning sign. "That shouldn't be a deterrent for someone like me, though, right?"

"Oh, stop," he scoffed.

"You can't have it both ways, Neryn. I can't be a horrible, repulsive, gods-damned creature *and* someone that you feel deserves protection. Now, I can leave right away if you lend me some supplies—a lantern and something more substantial to eat than a piece of fruit—"

Neryn resorted to a weary plea. "For this, the briefest of moments, *ifrunn*, I am at your mercy. Please grace me with your silence. Go and rest. I am growing tired of… " Neryn paused, looked directly at her for a moment, and then, seeing her tense, he murmured. "Of everything. Of all of this," he concluded, mostly to himself.

A wave of exhaustion hit Dargah just then, and the journey back home, in the dark, in the rain, suddenly seemed as impossible as Neryn claimed. She allowed herself a nod in response, and took a step toward the bedroom. Then she stopped and asked, "Do you love her? Orlaeth, I mean."

"Feelings of love are irrelevant," he said, but she noticed that his voice had lost its acidic bite. "I pledged to her family that I would care for her and protect her from harm. And I would have, choosing my own defeat if it guaranteed her safety. In a way, perhaps I have done just that." He looked her way, the fire casting flecks of gold on his bronze skin. "I would have been kind to her, *ifrunn*. Know that. I would have provided her everything she needed."

"Except freedom."

He had to look away; her words rang too true.

*

Dargah placed a lantern on the bedside table and noted her surroundings. Less spartan than the main room, but not much more welcoming. The bed, at least, looked comfortable, and that was all that mattered at the moment. She stripped off her stained clothing and released her hair from its braid. For a long moment, she reveled in the perverse pettiness of simply existing as a half-breed woman, lounging completely naked in such a hallowed place. After she was done gloating, she pawed around in the wardrobe, looking for something to wear. She found a tunic matching Neryn's. Several of them, actually. It was probably standard wear for purification parties and whatnot. It was soft, pristinely white, and gently scented with lavender and lemon. She shamelessly buried her face in it, luxuriating in the softness and inviting scent, then slipped it on. She crept back out of the room with her clothing, planning to drape it over the bench by the hearth.

Neryn was still seated. He did not appear to notice as she spread out her bodice, blouse, and leggings, nor when she turned again to point to his lyre.

"Will you play?"

He started. "What? Oh. No. I am unable to attend the nightfall vigil due to the ritual mourning. I will spend additional time in silent meditation this evening instead."

"You only play for your god?"

"That is what I was trained to do, yes."

"And you only do the things you were trained to do?"

"I told you. Rules and regulations—"

"Do you ever have fun?"

"By 'fun,' are you asking if I engage in foolish play, or are you asking if I enjoy my role here?"

Dargah shook her head. "If you have to ask, then I guess the answer is no. Never mind." When she moved to return to the bedroom, he rose.

"I cherish what I do. My father taught me how to play, and at a young age, I began to serve during the daybreak vigil. I feel humbled to use my gifts to honor my god."

"I'd never use the word 'humbled' to describe you," she muttered, leaning against the doorframe.

When he answered her, his voice was noticeably softer. "When I compose a new psalm, I feel that Erjunn is whispering in the wind to me, telling me which notes to play, and when. I am never more at peace than when I feel connected with him in this way."

Dargah felt her lips tilt upward in spite of herself. "I think my brother is like that sometimes. It's almost like the heartbeat of Dehlkia herself is trapped inside his head, and the only way he can release it is to beat that drum."

"He plays to honor the goddess? I would have assumed that his repertoire was somewhat bawdier," admitted Neryn.

"His taste is rather eclectic. Have you ever heard 'The Ballad of the Orcish Fishwife'?"

"I have not."

"I advise that you keep it that way."

"Good night, Dargah." He had already turned back to the hearth when she slipped out of sight.

*

"Now that you know I have fulfilled my oath to Orlaeth, there is no need for you to remain here any longer. If you head due south and travel parallel to the main road, you will arrive a mile or so outside of Lindenvale, but you will not risk being seen by any of the Remnant."

"Well, good gods-damned morning to you, too, sunshine," Dargah grumbled. She'd just woken up, her elvish tunic askew and her hair in her face. Neryn stood in the hallway, the rising sun casting him in silhouette. She'd been certain she locked her door the previous night, but perhaps she'd been wrong. He hadn't been watching her, had he? Waiting for his chance to smother her in her sleep? She pushed her dark waves out of her eyes.

"The rain has ceased," he went on, "so your journey should be an easy one. I will provide rations and extra clothing if you are in need. Perhaps you will be kind enough to give my regards to Orlaeth." He placed her now-dry clothing on the table close to the door, avoiding entering the room while she was in bed.

"Can I maybe get something to eat first?"

"Very well." He left her to get dressed.

Neryn had prepared a bowl of fruit and was heating a small pot of porridge in the hearth. Dargah had forgotten for a moment that she wouldn't be getting bacon and eggs or even bread with sweet cream from the strictly plant-based coffers of a Remnant pantry. Still, even a bowl of that sad, beige mush would fill her empty belly. "Thank you."

Neryn sniffed.

"I didn't mean to hurt your feelings last night," admitted Dargah, tapping her fingers against a fat pear. "Even though you deserve it because you're a pompous ass."

"My feelings do not matter," he responded, gliding over her insult. "What matters is that you are disrespecting and treating with contempt something that is an essential part of who I am."

"Essential part of who you are...like your heritage? But not *my* heritage." Dargah was quiet for a moment. "Dehlkia has never called upon me to win others to her cause. Does Erjunn need you to defend him?"

"Of course not! He is above any such—"

"Then why does the Disciple?"

Neryn pulled the porridge out of the fire and stirred it. "Because there will always be people like you who either cannot or *will* not understand the great burden and strain that is put on him daily. Is that not so of other mortal leaders, regardless of field? There will always be people who question his decisions, asking if they are truly guided by Erjunn. But you cannot *see* faith, Dargah. That is what makes it faith."

"I don't question your *faith*, Neryn. I'm questioning this leader of yours. I asked you last night, and I'll ask you again—what happened with Orlaeth? Why would your Disciple, in his gods-given wisdom, mate a robust young male with a weak, scared little girl who has nothing even resembling childbearing hips?"

Neryn's face reddened, but his tone was resolute. "She is not weak." He placed a bowl of porridge in front of her, then took one for himself.

Dargah snorted. "Of course she's not. But her choice to run off would be seen as cowardice or even treason by your Disciple, wouldn't it? Sinful. Disobedient." She leaned closer to him in earnest. "If you hadn't convinced him she died, what would have happened to her for leaving you?"

"I already told the Disciple that I would take her to wife, even if she had betrayed me." Neryn watched several blueberries slowly slip beneath the surface of his porridge. "But that would not negate the consequences of her actions. As far as I am aware, such a thing has only happened once. It was before my birth. A male—Gewarth Wintersky—rejected the wife chosen for him. He openly expressed a preference for her sister, who was, by many accounts, the more appealing of the two." Neryn refused to meet Dargah's curious stare. "In the end, both women were given to others, and Gewarth... he was disciplined."

"How?"

Neryn tensed. "His eyes were... *removed*... by the rejected woman's new mate. Then he was sent into the wilderness to atone for his lustful heart and rebelliousness."

Dargah drew in her breath. "Gods. He didn't survive, did he?"

"No. And his body was burned without prayer." Neryn took a shallow breath. "I imagine that if Orlaeth had either returned on her own or if I had brought her back, she would have been disciplined in a similarly symbolic fashion. Unless I could have convinced the Disciple that she had been abducted. Another lie to keep her blood from being spilled."

"And you would have done that, wouldn't you? Because the alternative is unthinkable." She shook her head. "This 'discipline' is… Neryn, the rest of Argodoth would call it *torture*. Except in the kingdom of Inbar, of course. And among some of the Northern dwarves. Regardless…" Her hand reached out, then pulled back. She put her hands in her lap, looking rather like a scolded child. "No more about the Disciple, Neryn. Tell me what *you* believe. Tell me about Erjunn. I know you know his holy book. Why did you ask Orleath about her copywork? What secret does she keep?"

Chapter Fifteen:

Of Crushes and Cruelty

"Well?"

Charis rested her chin on her hands and stared at Rinah with wolfish intensity. The older girl glanced up from the potatoes she was chopping and waited for Charis to continue. Orlaeth had offered to help prepare lunch, but Rinah had shooed her away, and now the elf was seated in Alvyx's chair, poring over a book.

"Well, what?"

"Well, aren't you going to tell me how things are going?" Charis practically wriggled with delight. "With *Bram?*"

"Nothing's going on." She scooped the potatoes into a heavy pot, then started mincing garlic. "He visits me sometimes."

"And you think that's *nothing?*"

Rinah allowed herself a small smile. "Well, no. I'm just afraid to get my hopes up. Miss Vigga *did* tell me that he's kind of a flirt."

"Well, I haven't seen him flirting with anyone but you," Charis noted. "And don't tell me you're still stuck on Erol."

Rinah shook her head. Erol Anomia was a hard-working farmhand who often helped pick fruit at an orchard just outside Lindenvale. He was a little older than the girls, soft-spoken, and disarmingly sweet-natured. Last summer, Rinah had taken a liking to his gentle smile and made it a point to visit the orchard as frequently as she could. Unfortunately, Erol was far too reserved to respond to any of Rinah's equally shy coquetry, and after three months of getting absolutely nowhere, she had given him up as a lost cause. "No, I'm not, but my pride *was* a little wounded," she admitted.

"The poor darling, I think he didn't even realize you were flirting with him. Men can be a little dense sometimes." She perked up. "But as far as I know, he's still unmarried. If things with Bram fizzle, you've still got a chance with Erol. Maybe if you unlaced your bodice a bit and pretended to faint onto his apple cart, he would finally notice you."

Rinah laughed so hard that she snorted. "And so would everyone else."

"At least it would increase your chances of catching someone's eye!" Charis giggled. "But I promise, I won't tease you about Bram if it bothers you."

"It doesn't," Rinah admitted. "After all, he *did* seem upset when I couldn't visit with him yesterday."

"Of course, he was! He *likes* you! If he hasn't made things official yet, maybe it's because he's a little intimidated by Alvyx. Your papa *is* a bit odd."

"I don't think that's it."

"But then again, lots of people use the festivals during Adorations to make their intentions known," Charis said dreamily. "Maybe he's just waiting for the right moment!"

Rinah's grin turned naughty. "So, will you be consuming all of Galen's free time at the festival, or will you let him speak with a few other lucky girls?"

"Galen can do as he wishes. He is his own person. At least until we're married. Then, I'm in charge. Right?"

"Oh, is *that* how it works?" Rinah's eyes danced as she laughed.

"Gods, I hope so."

Neryn wondered if Dargah's contrite, curious tone was just an act. Still, he told her, "Over the past few months, the Disciple has begun to share with his inner circle—his twelve advisors, myself included—teachings for which I cannot find references in either text. Now, to be certain, he has every right to expound upon the principles of our faith, as does any religious leader…"

"But?" Dargah prompted.

"But he has been alluding to secret knowledge being revealed to him by the will of Erjunn. I do not necessarily doubt this, but I am convinced that these revelations have something to do with the archival documentation that he has assigned to Maolyr Silverwillow and Orlaeth."

"Orlaeth's father? Then why not ask him?"

Neryn gave her a withering look. "Truly, *ifrunn*, do you have *no* concept of decorum? Maolyr is not only my elder, but was very nearly my father-in-law. To approach him with concerns like these…"

"Do you genuinely think the Disciple is keeping secrets from you? From your whole community?"

"I had hoped that Orlaeth might help me make sense of things. I have always believed that she has wisdom that neither her parents nor the Disciple ever acknowledged. It is written in her eyes. I should have spoken to her the night of our dinner. If I would have done so, perhaps I might have realized how deeply distressed she was about our engagement. I do not know how I would have resolved the problem, but at least I could have—"

Dargah interrupted, no longer interested in hearing about Orlaeth. "Most leaders would appreciate someone caring for the people's best interest… if you present your thoughts that way, perhaps the Disciple will be open to hearing them?"

"You seem to think I am his personal attendant and spend hours a day at his side," Neryn said with the faintest huff of laughter.

"You don't?"

"I spend the majority of my day in prayer and meditation. I rehearse. I plan out our morning, midday, and evening services. And I serve the same ways that all of my brothers and sisters do. I, too, work in our gardens. I make repairs to the cabins when necessary. I train younger males in the arts of elemental magic. I myself am being trained in diplomacy. And I do *not* impose upon the Disciple to satisfy my own curiosity."

"And what will you do with all of the research Orlaeth has given you?"

He made his confession with a dismissive shrug. "I had not thought ahead that far. I had hoped that I have been concerned over nothing at all. That I was being overcautious."

276

She raised an eyebrow.

"I had also hoped to find fresh inspiration for psalms of praise in those writings," he added quickly. "As an artist, I appreciate the mental stimulation of such novelties." Dargah's lips curved into a smile, and Neryn wondered why her expression brought a sudden heat to his chest.

"I think there is something inside you that *wants* to ask the questions."

This conversation had gotten too intimate, too dangerous. "That is not a part of myself that I nurture."

"I have never read any text teaching that Erjunn condemns curiosity. Or even uncertainty. Why do you feel the need to quiet those things in your own mind? Help me understand."

Without a hint of mockery or scorn, he answered, "I do not know if you can."

Dargah's eyes remained trained on his face. He noticed they were so black that they seemed to swallow the light. "Why do you hate me?"

The question struck him like a physical blow. "I do not hate you," he responded, his face clouded with confusion.

"Yes, you do. Half-orcs, I mean. Half-breeds in general. Is it because, by being alive, we're somehow committing some kind of crime? It's not like I haven't heard *that* before."

"It is… more complicated than that."

Dargah raised her eyebrows as if to say, 'Try me.'

"One of the tenets addressed in *The Wind Walker* is the idea of sacrificing one's own desires for the good of others. That includes being willing to reject the idea of romantic love in favor of a biologically suitable mate to further one's pedigree and raise future mages. Elves who have chosen to mate with humans, orcs, or dwarves, or not to mate at all, have shown that they care more about their own feelings, their own physical pleasures, than they do for the health of the community at large. I find it… upsetting."

"But not all elves believe that."

"No. Which is why we have distanced ourselves from them. We... *I* am troubled that Erjunn's own people would turn their backs on him, would forgo serving him as dedicated vessels with pure lives, in order to satisfy their own carnal desires…"

"Shall I remind you yet again that Erjunn regularly indulges his carnal desires with Dehlkia?"

Neryn gave her a sour glare, masking his dread of another one of her recitations from the holy book. His dreams the previous night had been haunted by her dark eyes and her breathy voice, and he had woken up more than once, his heart racing and a greedy rumble in his throat. He'd spent an extra half-hour in prayer, repenting of the deplorable scene played out by his subconscious. "Should *I* lie with a woman, the seasons would not change.

Worshiping a god with base, wanton sexual escapades? Blasphemous."

"Remind me never to invite you to a Dehlkian Harvest Festival," Dargah said with a smirk.

"Should the opportunity arise, I will decline," he assured her.

Slowly, the glint faded from Dargah's eyes. "I really am sorry about Orlaeth."

"What do you mean?"

"Well, despite the fact that you're about as expressive as a bag of rocks, I'm assuming you *do* have feelings. Aside from arrogance and irritation, I mean. Hearing that someone you care so much about basically wants nothing to do with you..." She offered him a small but authentic smile. "It can hurt."

"Are you apologizing on behalf of Orlaeth's lack of physical attraction to me?"

Dargah looked baffled for a second, then shrugged. "No? Um… I guess I'm telling you *I* feel bad for *you* feeling bad."

"I do not 'feel bad.'" Neryn's face was calm, but a tiny splinter of doubt drove itself into his mind. Was Orlaeth truly disgusted by him? He had thought little of it before, assuming that she simply feared the inevitable pregnancy and childbirth that came with marriage—not uncommon fears as both were riskier for elves than for other races. But was it, in fact, *Neryn* whom she fled? Specifically? He allowed himself to ask, as casually as he could, "Has she mentioned a dislike for me? Does she find me undesirable?"

"I haven't known Orlaeth long enough for her to complain about you, Neryn, or say literally anything about you at all, up until you showed up in town. And, once you did, all she said was that you were true to your word."

"Oh."

"I'm sure it won't be long before your Disciple matches you up with a nice, obedient, fertile wife," she assured him. "Then you can make all the magical babies you want."

"Do not speak so callously! Raising children is a blessing and a privilege," he retorted. "Especially for elves. Unlike *your* people, our women do not conceive easily. They often struggle during childbirth. To have more than one child is quite often a miracle for many of us. Some females never fully recover from the strain. So I will thank you not to mock my people in such a manner."

"Yes, orc females are known for being fertile, but no one ever talks about what happens when—" She stopped and shook her head. No. Neryn hadn't earned the privilege of hearing about *that*, either. "Regardless, I'm sorry about your situation."

"You do not have to apologize for the fact that—"

"Let me. *Let me*, all right?" Dargah interrupted, raising her voice. "Let a stranger have just the smallest amount of pity, of compassion, because things have clearly not turned out the way they maybe should have for you. I'm sorry because, even though you did the right thing, it means you're ending up alone, which is something you obviously don't want."

"I am not 'ending up alone.' I will have a mate, in time. My situation is not permanent."

Enough was enough. Dargah shattered the veneer of civility she'd allowed. "You're too damn proud to accept sympathy, aren't you? Or is it just because it's coming from someone like me? Is that it? Erjunn forbid you accept a scrap of pity from someone so far beneath you. I should be saving all that pity up for myself, shouldn't I?"

"I need sympathy from no one," he said sharply. "Sympathy changes *nothing*. Sympathy cannot bring the dead to life, cannot erase poor decisions. Sympathy cannot take back the things my father said to—" This time, it was his turn to stop short, his own fire extinguished. Then, he turned dead eyes on her. "You should go. *Now*."

Dargah's face registered confusion, then fury. She rose, her body shaking. "Gods Above and Below, Neryn! You obviously had a chip on your shoulder and your head up your own arrogant ass long before Oraleth left you, and she was smart enough to realize it. No wonder she bolted!"

Neryn's eyes narrowed into slits as he, too, stood. "You call me arrogant. And yet *you* are a female brazen enough to wield the authority and work of a male. You view your potential mates as *conquests*, not partners. You mock my god and my people, yet you cannot even bring yourself to acknowledge *either* of your ancestral spirits with anything even close to honor." His eyes flashed white briefly, and he wrestled with his magic. Pushing it down within himself, he spat, "You are an *infection* on the earth. You and the thousands like you are *pollution,* and for every one of you that is born squalling and infirm and utterly devoid of magic, the world is another breath closer to death, closer to losing everything pure and purposeful in it!" He heaved a breath. "Get out."

"Neryn—!"

"If you do not leave, I swear by Erjunn, you will suffer, either by the hand of the Disciple or by my own. Get out *now*."

*

The emptiness in Neryn's eyes and the chill in his words stirred Dargah's rage. In spite of the patience she'd cultivated over the years, right now, she yearned to rake her nails across his face and paint that contemptuous sneer with his own blood. She could not control the wind, no, but she could control her body. Every muscle was honed, every nerve taut. Her entire life had been spent teaching her body to obey her commands and never the other way around. There was not a shred of doubt in her mind that she could pounce on him and tear out his throat before he could summon even a light breeze.

But that would undermine everything she'd been trying to prove.

In a breath, she was gone, the door banging violently behind her.

*

Neryn's entire being trembled.

It trembled like it did when he was eight years old, and he'd gone too deep into the woods, tempted by the idea of adventure. He'd fallen, torn his tunic. The berries his mother had requested were now a dark stain on the ground, trampled by his clumsiness, and the basket was broken, too.

It trembled like it did when he returned home, dirty, ashamed, empty-handed.

Like when he saw his mother's disappointed frown.

Like when his father went outside and stripped a tree branch of its bark.

Trembling, Neryn stared blankly into his cold porridge, his eyes blurring with unspent grief.

it wasn't her fault it wasn't her fault

his anger wasn't Dargah's fault

And he needed to tell her that.

He flung open the door so fiercely that the hinges shrieked and broke.

But she'd already disappeared.

*

Stumbling over roots and bushes, Dargah's blind rage carried her almost two gloomy miles before she realized that she wasn't sure where she was. Every so often, the sun peeked out from behind its cloudy cloak, giving Dargah a glimpse of encouragement, and she eased her breakneck pace, allowing herself to breathe.

As if in protest, however, her mind refused to slow down. Against her own will, it replayed the hideous things Neryn had said to her. About her. About people like her. White-hot anger spilled down her cheeks in salty rivers.

She'd grown up knowing that her parents favored their orcish ancestry over their human blood. Most half-orcs did, regardless of their heritage. Rare was the half-orc who could pass for any other race, so it made sense for all of them to lean into their Dehlkian roots. Surrounded by so many others like her, Dargah had never grown up seeing herself as anything other than orcish. Her human ancestry had made no difference in the Dehlkian Games; as long as she could bleed and draw blood, her efforts were applauded. Even in Lindenvale, there were so few pure-bloods of any kind that her mixed genealogy seemed irrelevant. As long as she could heft a sledgehammer, Vigga Ilsted was happy to have her on board. And as long as her coin was genuine, Ioanie Adelfi was willing to rent her a room.

Dargah had always been vaguely aware of groups like the Remnant. Back home, they were very rare and kept to themselves, and most held court in the kingdom of Inbar. They were isolated. Easy to ignore. Their members didn't burst into taverns looking for runaway brides.

She gritted her teeth. Orlaeth had insisted that Neryn was a good, kind man, but Dargah had seen little evidence of it. While he had kept his promise to lie to the Disciple on Orlaeth's behalf, Dargah couldn't decide if the act was a noble sacrifice or a coward's gambit. On one hand, she was grateful that her new friend was safe. On the other, seeing Neryn lie so effortlessly to his spiritual leader was disconcerting. He did it almost too well. And, while he did invite her into the safety of his cabin, he turned around to threaten and insult her.

She sighed. She *had* threatened his life first, she admitted to herself. Still, threats and antagonism were second nature to her. She'd been a prizefighter, for Dehlkia's sake! But such behavior seemed ill-advised for a trusted counselor of a beloved spiritual leader, she reflected, making Neryn's behavior less excusable than her own.

She'd tell Rinah that Orlaeth was safe and nothing more.

*

"You know, you *can* hit an anvil too hard."

Vigga's scolding forced Dargah to stop working. She released her grip on the sledgehammer and stretched, sweat streaking her face and clothing. Only then did she realize how tense she'd been. Her fingers were twisted into claws, and her shoulders ached.

"Who pissed *you* off?" asked the wise old blacksmith.

Dargah shook her head. "It's nothing I want to talk about."

"Well, my property does not exist for you to take out your orcish rage upon it," snorted Vigga. "Cool off for a few minutes. Take a walk to Adelfi's. Bring me back something to eat." Dargah opened her mouth to protest, but Vigga shook her head and pointed north, to the inn. "Tell her you're willing to wait for bread fresh out of the ovens. I don't want this morning's leftovers."

The clanging and thumping of her fellow apprentices, minus Bram, who had not shown up for work that day, faded as Dargah made her way to Adelfi's. She wiped her forehead and rubbed her eyes. She'd returned to Lindenvale in the early morning hours, her restless flight fueled by anger and adrenaline and illuminated by a full moon and a cloudless sky - and the lantern she'd snatched from the cabin as she left. She hadn't slept upon her return; instead, she took the time to send word to Rinah that they needn't worry about Orlaeth, then to Orlaeth that Neryn had kept his word. After completing her task in full, she dragged herself to the forge, still fighting a tired, angry fog.

Adelfi's Inn was bustling; it was the hottest part of the afternoon, and anyone who labored outdoors would be seeking shade and a hearty meal. Most farmhands and orchard workers were fed by the farmers and their spouses, who had pots of stew perpetually boiling to serve them in shifts. Ioanie's clientele tended instead to be the messenger boys, the nearby tradesmen, and the merchants passing through Lindenvale. When Dargah finally caught Ioanie's eye, all she said was "Vigga," and the younger girl nodded. In minutes, she'd wrapped up a thick slab of roasted pork and two large, buttered rolls, exchanging them for Dargah's coin.

"Runo told me he didn't know if you were feeling better yet. I must have missed you leaving this morning," Ioanie said by way of opening. It was clear that she had no idea about the incident with Neryn.

"Yeah, I'm great now. If he's working later, tell him I'm fine, and so is Orlaeth."

"Who?"

"It's a long story. And he's not supposed to talk about it. So I'm sure he'll tell you everything."

Dargah allowed herself a brief rest at the courtyard fountain outside Adelfi's. Gods, the humidity of this place was brutal. Heat, she could handle. She'd grown up in a desert, after all. But the slums of Gora-Vekiri had been arid. None of this walking outside and feeling as though you were drowning in someone else's sweat. Dargah closed her eyes and took a few deep breaths. She was no longer the tinderbox she'd been in the ring. She'd left behind that woman when she left home, not long after Parviz had dropped her. But she couldn't shake the indignation that Neryn's words had stirred within her. She almost laughed. The Dargah of the Games, the Champion, would not have hesitated to leap at him, tearing at his mouth for saying such cruel things, clawing at his eyes for seeing her as a barbarian.

Dargah of Lindenvale was not a barbarian.

She soothed herself with the reminder that now, no member of the Remnant had any reason to visit Lindenvale.

Unless another runaway bride turned up, of course. From the way both Orlaeth and Neryn described the women of Dirgil, that seemed unlikely.

Dargah would have to leave them to their fate.

Chapter Sixteen:

Of Sorrows and Seduction

The position of the moon told him dawn was not far off, but Neryn had not slept that night. He'd been relieved to return to the main camp at dusk, free at last from that woman's piercing gaze and infernal line of questioning. He'd sung at Orlaeth's memorial, just loud enough to be heard over the wails of her distraught mother. Maolyr had comforted his wife, reminding her in gentle tones that such a display of hopeless grief was undignified and shallow.

Neryn had wept just like that when he and Orlaeth had discovered his mother dying on the cabin floor. And when the older women of Dirgil came to take her body to prepare it for the pyre, Orlaeth had cast her own discomfort aside and let Neryn soak her gown with his tears, her narrow frame convulsing with his sobs. Orlaeth had not reminded him to be dignified. She had let him release his grief, let it splash onto her, let it make everything ugly and grim for a time, until Neryn was ready to cloak his selfish, childish feelings with a young man's unbowed, unbent pride.

He hadn't looked back since.

As he watched the stars begin to wink out, he felt a stab of regret. He hoped with all his heart that the tragic news would not send Aine into early labor. The last thing her family needed would be a premature babe and a sickly mother. He wondered if there was a way he could somehow let them know the truth without implicating himself. The sun had begun to rise before he could figure something out, and he took a moment to meditate in Erjunn's presence before he dressed and made his way to the temple for the daybreak vigil.

He hadn't needed to burn the tunic Dargah had slept in, but he made sure to scrub it, along with the bedding, in the stream outside the cabin. Its lavender scent had mixed with whatever fragrant orcish oils she was wearing, and he couldn't risk anyone asking any questions. Once he was certain her perfume was undetectable, he hung the tunic to dry and made a final sweep of the cabin just to ensure that no trace of his unwelcome guest remained.

No, nothing physical was there. Only the bitter taste of the words he'd spoken and the memory of the sheer loathing in her eyes.

Half an hour later, Neryn approached the altar of Erjunn without his customary tranquility. Instead, he was so lost in thought that he nearly walked past it without lifting his hands skyward—an affront to the god and to the Disciple alike.

"Greetings, my friend!" Tiarnán said solemnly.

Neryn arranged his face in its usual placid lines and nodded. They took their seats behind the Disciple, who seemed pleased to have all his counselors again on the dais with him.

When you are given an opportunity to speak, use the wind in your lungs, the air I have given, to speak truth and to speak kindness. Speak to draw others toward you, and not to spurn them. As I am the god of peace, I charge you to create peace with your words.

"Chapter three, poem five," Neryn murmured to himself. Before he could contemplate the verse, the Disciple gestured for him to greet the day with a song.

He could do nothing but smile and obey.

*

"Did you sleep at all, sweetheart?"

Bram's playful teasing irked Rinah this morning because she knew *exactly* how awful she looked. She was happy about his early visit, but she'd had a fitful sleep the night before. She couldn't remember having any nightmares, but she'd fared poorly nonetheless.

She pounded mint leaves into a smear of green with her pestle and said, with uncharacteristic tartness, "Are you going to help or not?" She pointed to a basket of dried calendula petals next to his chair. He passed it to her and raised an eyebrow at Alvyx, who sipped his tea and turned the page in his book.

Rinah pulverized some of the petals, blending them with the mint. She carefully poured a measure of melted beeswax and oil into a tin, then added the mint and flowers. After mixing it thoroughly, she set it aside to cool and set. She repeated the process with several more tins until Bram finally asked, "What are you making? Smells nice."

"Just an all-purpose salve," she answered idly as she continued to weigh the ingredients.

"Oh." He paused. "Hey, where's that quiet blonde lady? Your elf friend?"

"Orlaeth. And she's at work. Mr. Naoum hired her to help in the library. She won't be staying with us much longer. There's a room available at Bronte's boarding house. It's nothing fancy, but it's affordable, and Orlaeth doesn't seem to mind."

"And," Alvyx piped up from behind his book, "She is always welcome to visit whenever she likes."

Bram nodded. "Good for her. You two are really great people, you know that? Back home, no one has any kindness left in 'em."

"Is that so?" Rinah couldn't tell if her papa's tone was asking Bram to expound on his statement or rescind it.

"Yeah. People were pretty rough on me there. I mean, you know, I'm not a perfect person, but I try to do the right thing. Some folks just can't see that."

Feeling a prickle of discomfort, Rinah decided to change the subject. "This batch is done," she announced. "Just two more to go, and I still have a week left before the Adoration."

"I'm looking forward to it," said Bram. "The food and the dancing!"

"Ha! For everyone but me," Rinah laughed, wiping her oily hands on a cloth.

"Why is that?"

"I've always been a little clumsy," she admitted.

"Oh, how my feet always ache after the festival," Alvyx said mournfully. "Dancing with the prettiest girl in Lindenvale has its downside. Fortunately for me, Rinah's mint salve works like a dream, and my poor, trod-upon toes felt better in no time."

With a smile, Rinah tossed the dirty cloth his way. "You're terrible!" Alvyx laughed as he took a final sip of his tea.

The rest of the morning was spent with Bram assisting Rinah pour candles. After setting them aside to cool, she organized the area, placing the fruit bowl back in the center of the table and returning her tools to her workspace.

"So neat and tidy," Bram said. "Hey, I'm starving. Dargah's little brother works as a cook at the inn down the road, right? Adelfi's?" He hung an empty basket on a hook, then moved it to the table, then back to the hook again. "Let's go eat there."

"Yes, his name's Runo. And I would love to," Rinah said, wiping her hands of oil, "but I still have a lot to do. Papa and I need to get to the orchard, and—"

Alvyx snorted. "What you *need* to do is relax and enjoy a nice meal with your gentleman caller."

Rinah grabbed a tin from the table. "I *did* promise Runo some of this. He keeps scalding his hands. All right. I can't stay too long, but let's go."

"Can I treat you, too, Mr. Autumnsong?"

Alvyx didn't look up from his novel. "Awfully busy, don't have the time." Rinah noticed his cheeky grin hiding behind the pages.

Bram hopped to his feet and offered his elbow to Rinah as though she were a fine lady. With her on his arm, they strode the half-mile toward Adelfi's Inn and whatever it was that Runo had whipped up for lunch.

*

303

It was indeed Runo who greeted Rinah and Bram as they arrived at Adelfi's, offering them each a mug of ale. Rinah declined, and she and Bram seated themselves at the counter.

"Magnificent!" Runo exclaimed joyfully when she handed him the balm.

"Her stuff's that good, isn't it?" Bram boasted.

"Yeah! Well, yes, but also, I appreciate that you remembered!" Runo told Rinah. "Oh, and Dargah told me to thank you for the flowers if I see you before she does. So, thank you for the flowers."

Rinah laughed. "I'm so glad she liked them!" Seeing the befuddled look on Bram's face, she added, "So, it's an old Ayusan custom to "speak" with flowers—it's not really popular anymore, but I think it's clever. There's a whole book on it, actually. Almost every flower native to

Ayusa means something. And, depending on the color, the meaning might change."

"Nah, we never did anything like that. Sounds complicated."

"Well, I'm sure it would be if I tried to memorize it all. But I have the book at home. So I sent Dargah blue hyacinth flowers, which stand for faithfulness, and hyssop, which stands for sacrifice."

"Why, though?"

Rinah's smile drooped a bit. "She did a very selfless thing for Orlaeth a little while ago, and it meant a lot to me. So I was just showing my gratitude, that's all."

"They smell nice. I've been meaning to get out and buy her a vase. She's got them in an ale mug right now…which I kind of need back," Runo said sheepishly.

"Oh! Wait! Her birthday's coming up! We could pool our money and get her a really nice one. Do you want to go to a pottery shop with me tomorrow? Orlaeth found the most beautiful pot for her plant the other day. Well, my plant. Her plant at my house."

"I'd like that, Rinah."

Bram tried to ignore the softness in Runo's smile and announced, "I didn't even know orcs liked flowers."

"Well... I mean, everyone likes pretty things. Don't dwarves?" Runo asked.

"Sure, but we prefer beauty that lasts." He held up his wrist, around which was a hefty bronze band, etched with characters Rinah couldn't identify. "Flowers are dead in a day. But this could outlast *me*, even."

"Imagine that." Rinah noticed the tension building on Runo's face and let out a nervous breath when he added, "That's some nice craftsmanship. But metal and gemstones aren't a part of how we worship the goddesses. Or express gratitude."

306

"Hence, the flowers," Rinah concluded tidily. To head off any additional bickering, she said, "Runo, what should we get today?"

Runo threw a towel over one shoulder. "Ioanie's got potato soup bubbling back there, and I'm about to pull some hand pies out of the oven."

"What kind?"

"Umma's recipe," Runo said with a knowing smile.

"My favorite!" Rinah clapped, delighted as a child. To Bram, she said, "Runo makes these delicious, fluffy flatbreads, and then he puts chicken and spices and—"

"I know what a hand pie is, Rinah," he said lightly.

She quieted. "Of course you do. I just meant that, well... he puts dill and cilantro in the dough... it's traditional in Granaat. I never had it that way before, so I guess I assumed you hadn't, either."

"I'm fairly well-traveled. I've tried pretty much everything Argodoth has to offer, so yes, I've had hand pies with cilantro and dill doughs." He snickered to himself, waiting for Rinah to mention his clever play on words.

She didn't. Runo glared. Bram shrugged. Not everyone appreciated his sense of humor.

Rinah couldn't tell if the gnawing in her stomach was from hunger or from the faint trace of disappointment she saw in Bram's face when he looked at her. Runo seemed to sense the change in her mood. He leaned forward with his signature toothy grin and said, "No charge today."

Bram raised his eyebrows. "That's mighty generous of you!"

Runo flicked a glance his way as archly as Dargah would have as he swaggered back into the kitchens. "No charge for the *lady*."

For years, Neryn had held the honor of leading the dawn veneration of Erjunn every day, with few exceptions. Before first light, he was already dressed, neatly groomed, and standing in front of the altar the elders had built decades before. It had been erected on the highest point in Dirgil, which, seeing as how the village was close to marshland, was not particularly high. Soon after, a temple was built to house the altar. It was simple, with an open framework that allowed the elements free rein over the services. It often meant, of course, that the community gathered in the pouring rain or the haze of early morning fog, but the Disciple's expectation remained the same.

Daybreak was the time to worship, at least for the men.

By the time the sun appeared on the horizon, the men of the Remnant were to be prepared to greet the day in adoration of their god. Neryn would open with a hymn he'd written, and the men would join him. The Disciple would then recite scriptures and admonish or encourage the men on the finer points of their faith, and remind them of business that needed tending in Dirgil. Neryn would close the hour-long service with another hymn, then retire to break his fast and prepare for the midday service, which included the women and children.

This morning should have been no different. And it wasn't, at first. After he sang, Neryn took his seat behind the Disciple as he shared his fifth consecutive message about purity. Neryn fought the frown that tried to twist his face. There were far more important issues to address at the moment! Some of the student mages were not progressing in their studies; the harvest was somewhat smaller than last year's, and the women and children would need to increase their time foraging before the rainy season set in; three cabins needed repairs before then as well.

But the Disciple hadn't mentioned any of that, not at the daybreak services, meetings with his advisory council, or in private discussions with his trusted aides. Purity was an essential aspect of service to Erjunn; Neryn wouldn't deny that, but there were other requirements of his followers as well. Creating and nurturing peaceful relationships with others, for example. Caring for nature and treating the land with respect and mindfulness. Faithfulness to one's mate and the appropriate treatment of one's children. Self-discipline with the goal of becoming more like the gentle, patient god of the air. All of these aspects of worship should be addressed regularly to keep them front-of-mind for Erjunn's followers.

And yet, instead, they'd received nearly a week of lectures about purity. As the Remnant's sole publicly-jilted-yet-perpetually-unruffled bridegroom, *he* didn't need to be reminded about the value of chastity. Before he could congratulate himself for his supreme discretion and divinely inspired restraint, however, a buried memory flickered to life in his mind like a flash of lightning in a starless sky.

"Worship my body with your own, for I yearn to feel your caresses."

The way her lips—lush and full and as scarlet as sin—formed those words.

"Blow upon me, god of the wind, and rustle my leaves with your breath."

The way her eyes taunted him, half-amused, like she was a cat observing her hapless prey.

"Shake me until my fruits are bruised, until your mouth is filled with the sweet taste of them."

The way her voice melted into a throaty purr and the curious ache it stirred inside him.

"Let the trembling of our bodies, joined in breathless ecstasy, shake the earth."

The way he woke in the dead of night, gasping, from dreams of her mouth hot on his skin and her naked legs wrapped around his waist. The way she looked in his rumpled tunic that morning, her hair splayed out like spilled ink on the pillow.

And the fearful shame that had overtaken him once she'd gone, the chagrin of causing anger with such harsh words, the recognition of his own deceit finally sinking into his brain, the distressing flow of desire pumping through his body when he woke from those dreams—

"... yet we triumph over these base and primitive desires as true servants of our god, strengthened by him and inspired by him, do we not?"

The men loudly rumbled their agreement. Neryn winced as though he'd been struck. He hadn't realized his thoughts had drifted, and the Disciple's sharp words dragged him back to higher ground.

And yet...

Three hundred and seventeen men sat in front of him, and eleven more with him on the dias, silently nodding as the Disciple spoke, weaving physical chastity and purity of the blood into a single concept. How many of them, Neryn wondered, presented grave faces to the world but were actually entertaining thoughts of their wives? Of caressing them, of kissing them, of the softness of their skin and the sweetness of their words? How many of them would return home from this very meeting and be greeted by wives with lustful eyes, wives drawing them into loving arms and—

Neryn sighed so heavily that Tiarnán looked his way, concerned. He forced an apologetic smile, then tried to pay attention to the message.

The Disciple had always taught that the ultimate—and only—goal of an intimate encounter was to produce a new generation of elves to venerate Erjunn and preserve their precious mages' blood. Therefore, it was important for a male to be familiar with his wife's cycle to know when she was most likely to conceive. Once that happened, naturally, there would be no intimacy at all until several months after the birth to ensure that her body could recover properly before her next pregnancy. And it was, of course, the husband's job to disregard his urges, should he experience any, during this time. Their wives often sacrificed their health to bring children into the world. The *least* a good husband could do, the Disciple insisted, was to silence the selfish yearnings of his own imperfect body.

Imperfect bodies, even as pure-blooded mages. And what of those with mixed blood? How corrupt were *their* bodies? How unredeemable *their* souls? Neryn considered this until Dargah's question echoed in his mind: *"Why do you hate me?"*

When he'd looked into her face at that moment, hearing those softly-spoken words, he didn't see a she-devil or a brawler, or a heathen, or anything else he was supposed to see. He saw a weary young woman too tired to hide the disgust in her eyes.

Hate was a strong word. In fact, it didn't appear a single time in the entire text of *The Path of the Wind*. The book centered around Erjunn's love for his children and, to a lesser degree, his love for his consort. It focused on his tenderness toward the earth and his expectation that his followers treat it with reverence. It spoke of careful management of one's emotions and actions, frequently reminding readers that actions cannot be undone and emotions are temporary. It encouraged elves to care for their bodies and taught them how to live long, healthy lives. It shared Erjunn's desires that his children would live harmoniously with each other and worship him joyfully, sharing their gifts and abilities with the entire community. And yes, it spoke frequently of the importance of faithfulness and loyalty to one's mate and family, of the need to avoid habits that did not come into alignment with Erjunn's own nature.

But neither the word hate nor any akin to it appeared in the book.

Why did he hate Dargah?

He didn't, he had insisted.

Yet the disappointment in her eyes had remained.

Chapter Seventeen:

Of Empathy and Exploitation

Orlaeth had never before been struck by such a strong and unmistakable dread. It felt like ice in her stomach, slowly climbing up her insides until it clawed at her throat. She sat on the shabby bed in her room, the flame of a single candle dancing across the ceiling, and she prayed.

She did not pray the way she had been taught. She prayed in the Old Tongue, words spilling out of her and sliding down the walls like liquid echoes. She begged Erjunn for his revelation to be made clear. The icy anxiety circled her neck and squeezed, and a single thought filled her mind.

Death.

Mist surrounded the image as though she was peering through a thick fog, hovering on the moors. She only saw flashes of fabric, of flesh, and then, a surge of bone-deep terror swallowed everything whole.

Orlaeth sobbed, even as her eyes, open wide, saw nothing. She could not bear the burden of these feelings, these images, these unclear promises. Her hand flew to her chest as if to try and defend herself against the despair brooding inside her. At that moment, her fingers touched the pendant Neryn had given her on her last night in Dirgil, and the fear began to fade.

*

Rinah sat alone in her garden. The sun flirted with the clouds and peeked out every so often, sending haphazard golden rays into the bushes. Orlaeth's tansy had been transferred to an ornamental pot on which she'd asked the potter to inscribe the elvish word *camydahl*. The elf had carefully placed it as far from the house as possible, while still keeping it out of the shade. Rinah had plucked several of the blooms, wondering if she might use them, dried, in some kind of tincture or poultice. She would have to experiment. The tansy seemed happy, and the rest of Rinah's flowers seemed happy.

Rinah was not happy.

Yesterday, Bram had promised to help her and Alvyx finish up the last few batches of soap for her stall at the festival, but he hadn't shown up on time. Hours after she'd finished, he stopped by and asked if she'd like to play some card games with him at the Screaming Siren. She'd declined and reluctantly agreed to meet today instead, hoping to smooth out whatever tension had begun to develop between them. She nibbled on the scone Alvyx had forced on her when he left to help the Soters repair their wagon after lunch.

Rinah hadn't been able to eat a thing, and even the sweet, tender scone felt like sawdust in her mouth. She set it aside and waited, hugging herself and trying hard to be patient.

It wasn't long before she heard Bram's distinct gait shuffling through the grass behind her. She turned.

"Hey, pretty girl," he said with a smile.

She returned the expression, but the tension in her chest faded only somewhat. "Come," she invited, making room for him on the wooden bench.

"Don't mind if I do," he replied, sitting close to her.

Rinah had run herself ragged the night before, thinking of a dozen different ways to begin the conversation. After a deep breath, she opened with, "I'm worried about you."

"Why is that, sugar?"

"You've seemed a little out-of-sorts the past few days. I don't know, it's like you're not really enjoying yourself as much as when you first came into town." There, that didn't sound bad. Not an accusation. A concern.

"Well, even *I* can't be perky and bright every day," he said with a laugh that sounded forced. He looked away. "Doesn't help getting bad news from back home."

"Oh, no! What's wrong? Is someone ill? Your mother?"

"No, no, it's nothing like that." His jaw tightened, and his blue eyes looked watery. "It's just... y'see, my Farfi—that's what we call my father's father—my Farfi was supposed to get me all set up with my inheritance when I turn thirty. I was gonna go home, just for a visit, after my birthday next month. But… I don't know, I guess there's something wrong with the records, 'cause the man in charge of the funds sent me a message saying they had to cancel the meeting."

Rinah gasped. "Why?"

Bram shook his head. "No idea. Farfi's a hard man, a real stern man. For all I know, he decided he doesn't like me anymore and changed his mind."

"No! That's *your* inheritance!" Rinah cried.

He hung his head. "Not anymore, it looks like."

Rinah threw her arms around him and said, "I'm so sorry. But at least you're able to earn some money at the forge while you contest your grandfather's decision, right?"

He scowled. "Do you know how long I'd have to work at Vigga's to earn even a quarter of what I was supposed to get?"

She withdrew. "A long time, I'd imagine."

"*Years.*" He rubbed his eyes, and Rinah suspected that he was wiping away tears. "How'm I supposed to settle down with a girl and have a family on that kind of pay?"

Her heart fluttered. "Is that what you want to do?" she asked softly. "Settle down and get married?"

He took her hand and squeezed it. "'Course I do." He gave her a dimpled smile and then kissed her hand.

A rush of delight flooded her. She'd been wondering if he'd lost interest in her, but it was just the opposite! Imagine if *she* got married before Charis did! No, no, that wasn't the right way to think. It wasn't a competition. But no—no, she and Bram weren't even courting. He'd never even made his intentions known. Or had he? Did he talk to Alvyx when she wasn't around? Did he ask for her hand? Was that even a thing anymore? Was she too old-fashioned?

Bram's arms moved to encircle her, and he kissed her cheek. He pulled her into his lap and hugged her tighter. His hand slid from her back down to her hip, and he squeezed her flesh through the thin wool of her skirts. She gasped.

"You really are a pretty thing," he murmured in her ear. He squeezed again, a bit harder. "I like this."

This time, she let out a laugh and a little squeal. "Don't, Bram! I'm ticklish!"

He chuckled. "You're not gonna be loud, are you?"

"What?"

He shook his head and forced her out of his lap. "Did you want to go inside? That's fine."

Rinah stood quickly, rearranging her clothing. "For what? Lunch? I can get you something to eat if you want." She glanced back at Bram and noticed, her hope drooping, that he'd slipped a hand down his trousers.

"Come here. I got a better idea." He placed his other hand heavily on her shoulder, the pressure enough to buckle her knees, and it was only then that Rinah fully understood the gravity of her situation.

"Bram!" she pulled away from him. "Not here. Not—"

"You know the neighbors can't see a thing over that stone wall you've got."

Her face grew hot. "It—it's not about someone seeing," she stammered.

"I doubt they'll hear anything either, so long as you're not a screamer."

"I wanted you to come here to *talk*," she tried.

"You wanted me here when you knew your papa would be out. It's not exactly like I could take you to my room at Vigga's, right?" He made a disgusted face and rolled his eyes. His hand was still moving inside his pants.

"I'm really sorry if..." Rinah's mind went blank for a moment. "But Papa's going to be home shortly. If he caught us—doing anything—he'd skin us alive!" He wouldn't, of course, but Bram didn't know that.

He gave her a lazy smile. An invitation.

She liked him. She did. Vigga said that Bram was a flirt. Rinah trusted Vigga, but maybe Vigga was judging her nephew too harshly. Family always does that, don't they? Rinah liked the way she felt when he looked at her, most of the time. "When you... Were you talking about me? When you said..."

"When I was talking about settling down?"

She nodded.

"Who else would I be talking about?" He crooked a finger at her, beckoning her back into his lap. A rush of emotion swirled up inside her again, a million pinpricks that tickled the inside of her skin. She took a step forward. He reached out to grab her skirt, jerking her again toward him. Toward the angry-looking, ruddy-pink shaft he'd pulled out of his trousers.

"Bram," Rinah gasped, yanking her skirt out of his grip. "Oh, my *gods*—" She stumbled backward, quickly righting herself.

He simply grinned. "I know," he said, as though excusing her shock as commonplace. "Half-dwarf, remember?"

She giggled nervously, hating the sound of her own voice. "I'm sorry. You just caught me a little off-guard."

Rinah stood, contrite as a schoolchild who'd misplaced her book, awaiting a scolding.

He stared at her for a few seconds, his jaw working. "The good girl act is getting old, Rinah. I don't like playing games."

She took another step back. "It isn't a game! I'm sorry! I just... I wasn't ready for this, you know, right *now*." Her eyes scanned the path in front of the cottage, desperate for a distraction.

He shook his head as he pulled up his pants. "I probably should have tried something a little more romantic, huh? I was hoping you'd be the kind of girl I could throw down in a barn and have a good time with, you know? Like an actual roll in the hay."

"I don't think I'm that kind of girl," she uttered, red-faced. "I didn't realize I gave that impression."

He shrugged. "Well, I guess this wasn't my best effort. I'll try harder next time. Do you at least have something I can use to take care of this?" He gestured to his tented trousers. "I've gotta go back to work."

"...Something...? Oh... um, yes." She scurried to the basket of laundry she'd taken from the line earlier and, still looking away, offered him a washcloth.

"Sure you don't wanna help?" he asked with a smirk.

"I don't think I can handle you," she said with complete honesty.

He chuckled and disappeared behind a tree.

Rinah took the rest of the laundry into the cottage, locked the door, and cried.

*

The Remnant's Suppliant Prime hadn't been sleeping well.

Actually, he hadn't been sleeping *at all*, and even the Disciple had noticed that Neryn now lacked the brisk confidence that had become his defining trait. He hadn't offered any excuses to his leader, simply apologizing for appearing unwell.

Neryn declined Tiarnán's request to sit with him at the communal meal, instead taking only a wheat cake and an apple from the table, then retiring to his cabin.

He sat at his desk, glaring at the blank leaf of paper before him. Taunting him. Daring him to create something—anything—to honor his god. A poem. A song. A declaration.

But nothing came to him.

He broke the cake in half and idly chewed on the larger piece. What in the name of the Gods Above and

Below was going on in his head? Free from the Disciple's melodious litany of warnings and worries, Neryn's thoughts were again his own, and he tried to sort through them.

First, he missed Orlaeth. They had been so close as children. Although they interacted less often as they grew older, it didn't change the fact that he keenly felt her absence. No one had chosen to leave the Remnant in decades. The only farewells had been for a few elderly men and one widow, eight stillborn children and, five times, their mothers with them. He would never have expected Orlaeth to be the one who broke tradition to strike out on her own.

Second, of course, was the fact that he faced the grieving Silverwillow family daily, bound with invisible ties to keep Orlaeth's new life a secret. Mother Aine had taken to bed the day he'd returned, and the village's midwives told her not to lift a finger—not even to cook— until the child came. The promise of the new baby cheered her, but little else did in the wake of Orlaeth's disappearance.

And third, which should probably have been first, was the problem of Dargah.

Neryn stood, stretched, and dropped himself into his bed, fully clothed. It wasn't *just* the dreams he'd been having. Even more compelling than the remembrance of her captivating, scarred face and her powerful body were the words she'd spoken to him. The questions she'd asked. The challenges she'd posed.

A strange warmth pulsed in his chest.

No.

Not in it. *On* it.

Neryn sat upright, pulling his necklace from its hiding place beneath his tunic. Its charm, the twin of which he'd given to Orlaeth, was throbbing with an urgent, reddish glow. Startled, he dropped it. He'd had the charm for nearly twenty-five years, since the day their mothers had taken them to sell their handmade wares in Sterlingshire, and it had never done anything like this.

*

That day, Neryn felt particularly daring, and he somehow convinced little Orlaeth to explore the market with him—out of the sight of their mothers. They wandered from stall to stall, amazed by the seemingly endless variety of spices, textiles, ceramics, toys, prepared foods, and crafts surrounding them. While Neryn could have stayed for hours and not grown bored, Orlaeth quickly became tired. "It's pretty here, but my head hurts," she whispered. "The sounds hurt my head."

Neryn ducked into a brightly colored tent, dragging the small girl with him. The heavy canvas muffled the noises of the bazaar, and it was cooler inside, too. He watched Oralaeth closely, half-afraid she was genuinely hurt and half-excited they were sharing an adventure together.

It was then that he heard a voice, a kind, motherly voice, haltingly questioning him in the Common Tongue. "Little man, what do you do in my tent?"

Neryn whirled in a panic and looked upward into a softly rounded orcish face. He gasped, dropped to the floor, and started to retreat, entreating Orlaeth to follow.

"No, no, little man," the orcish woman said, gently pulling him back into the tent.

Neryn squeezed his eyes shut. He would probably die now. If the orc didn't do something terrible, like eat him or sacrifice him to her god, then the best scenario was her keeping them here forever to be her puppets or her slaves or—

"The girl is…ah, weary, yes?" The orc leaned down and offered Orlaeth a cup of cold water.

Neryn nearly told her not to take it, that surely it was poisoned or cursed, but she simply reached up, her lips stretching into a grateful smile. "Thank you, madam," she said in her most polite voice.

As Orlaeth drank, the orc hauled a large trunk toward them and sat heavily upon it, watching them. When Neryn dared to take his eyes off their captor, he noticed that the tent was full of dusty old books and jars of dried leaves and flowers. A thin ribbon of smoke curled up from a censer, and an unfamiliar fragrance wafted his way. In spite of his worry, he closed his eyes and let the scent envelop him. The wildflowers that sprang up around Dirgil were pretty, and they smelled of freshness and spring. Not so, this strange, beautiful, heavy aroma. It smelled of night and the crescent moon, of ancient manuscripts as yet undiscovered, of Dehlkian earth, rich and fertile, of sand and musk and sky, of treasures hidden since the beginning of time. When he opened his eyes, the orc woman was smiling.

"Little man, you need rest?"

Neryn shook his head.

"No mistake," she said finally, "that you come here. *Mojhaze*, is the word in my home. Destiny. Happy destiny. I have something special. I wait—waiting for goddess to tell me when to be using. Today, she speaks!" She rose and puttered around the jars and tins, moving aside boxes and books, while the heaviness of the incense continued to fill his lungs. "Yes!"

In her hand, she held a pair of charms, each no larger than Orlaeth's thumb. Neryn peered at the highly polished stones, cream-colored and smooth, almost like quail eggs. He looked up at the orc, confused. She nodded as she slipped each charm onto its own thin cord, deposited them both into a dusty velvet bag, and pressed the bag into Neryn's small hand.

"No, please, madam, I am not allowed to have this," he protested. If his father knew he'd been talking to an orc—a half-orc, whatever she was—he'd be punished severely. Neryn didn't even want to imagine what might happen if it was discovered that he'd accepted a *gift* from one.

The woman placed one green finger to her mouth. "Shh. Yes, little man. The goddess told me. I obey her because I love her. When I find magic, I share."

Neryn guessed that it would take more time than he had to explain that he did not worship Dehlkia. His mother and Orlaeth's were probably terrified or furious by now, and the only thought in his head was to get out of the tent and get his friend where they could be safe.

*But you **are** safe here, sweet boy. With me. Always.*

Neryn paused just long enough to see if it was the lady orc who'd spoken the soft, comforting words.

It wasn't. She had already turned back to her jars and books.

Without another sound, he grabbed Orlaeth's hand and shimmied back under the side of the tent, trying to prepare for the punishment he knew was waiting for him.

*

Neryn hunched over his pendant and watched it glow.

What kind of magic was this? Was it dwarven? Perhaps a mage of Kaylor had fashioned this; that would explain the warmth. But... No, this magic felt different. It didn't feel quite right. But it also didn't feel wrong. Gingerly, he picked it up and allowed it to rest in the palm of his hand.

In a heartbeat, he felt chilling fingers grip his throat. Fear and confusion tumbled over each other in his mind. The sensation of bracingly cold water trickled from the top of his spine all the way down to his feet. His stomach lurched, as though he had to vomit, and a violent shudder rocked his entire body.

He dropped the charm, and the sickness lifted. But the fiery glow did not disappear, and Neryn understood, somehow, that he needed to get to Orlaeth.

Now.

Chapter Eighteen:

Of Diversions and Depravity

The Adoration of Ayusa was always held during the longest days of summer with its peak on the solstice, rain or shine. The morning of the festival hinted at a hot, sunny, cloudless day ahead. Excitement floated in the air from the often-soggy west bank of the Linden River all the way up to the temple of Erjunn, which rested peacefully atop a gentle slope.

Brilliantly colored canvas tents and pavilions had been erected along the town's main road and the riverwalk. A handful of Lindenvale's finest artisans were invited to sell their items in the town square, their stalls arranged around the central fountain. The statue of Ayusa atop the fountain's highest tier seemed especially beatific today, as though the goddess herself approved of the craftsmanship on display. When the afternoon heat began to fade, the stalls in the square would be replaced with dozens of couples and families dancing to traditional music, anticipating the rich delights and beauty of the long summer days ahead.

Although Rinah's wares did not entitle her to a coveted space in the town square, she had been quite pleased to be assigned a beautiful, shady lot close to the river. She unpacked the candles, balms, oils, creams, lotions, tinctures, and teas that she and her papa had prepared and tried to focus on making her stall look appealing rather than on what had happened the day before.

After Bram had gone back to work, Rinah wept for nearly an hour, then crawled into her loft bed. There, wedged between the mattress and the wall, she found her old doll. Eutha was a well-loved, raggedy thing with black yarn for hair and two glossy buttons for eyes. Charis's mother had given it to her on the day Alvyx had selected for Rinah's fourth birthday celebration. He had joked with her when she was older that he had chosen a spring birthday because her personality seemed to reflect the star signs of the mild season—the watchful rabbit, the gentle dove, and the clever fox.

Now, the button eyes were dull, and the yarn had gotten tangled and been trimmed all the way up to her chin. Her pretty pink dress had been stained and washed so many times that the delicate rosebud pattern on the fabric was hardly visible anymore.

Rinah took the doll into her arms and squeezed it tightly. The doll was Elpida, tender and nurturing. And Charis, sweet and playful. And Dargah, strong and brave. And Orlaeth, insightful and poised.

And the doll was Rinah... simple-minded and ashamed.

Why hadn't she had a little bit of fun with Bram? She liked him a great deal, and he was handsome. And he wanted her, too. He said he wanted to marry her. But Rinah had never done much with boys before. And Bram was hardly a boy but a man of almost thirty! Once, when she was thirteen, an older boy had noticed the new swell of her hips and rear, and had groped her, praising her thick figure. At fifteen, she'd developed a mutual crush on a half-elf boy from across the river; they were caught kissing behind a barn and his parents put a stop to the relationship that hadn't even started. And when she was sixteen, she'd untied her bodice and pulled down her chemise for the son of a merchant passing through town. He was so nice to look at, and he said the loveliest things to her, but she'd changed her mind about being intimate when she realized that he'd be leaving in just a few days. She'd seen him almost naked, and she remembered with a blush that she'd liked what she saw. But that boy hadn't done anything to her without asking. Granted, he was as inexperienced as she was, and he didn't get much farther than asking to touch her breasts (she had said no, thank you, and preferred that he just look at them). The experience hadn't frightened her. It had been a little awkward, to be sure, but she never felt unsafe.

Bram wasn't shy. And his intensity *was* a little frightening. She wanted to at least try to feel relaxed and excited the first time she made love. Was that really what Bram had wanted? To make love? No, she didn't think so. She hadn't felt relaxed at all. She had felt excited, though it was the kind of excitement that filled her body with urgency, but her mind with worry.

"Child, we have ten dozen muffins to bake tonight! Why are you not preparing the batter already?" Alvyx's good-natured rebuke drifted up to her loft, and Rinah started. She hadn't even heard him come in.

"I can't believe I forgot!" she cried, scrambling down the ladder. "There's too much to do." She began to line ingredients up on the table. "Do we have enough flour? I can run to the mill."

Alvyx placed gentle hands on her shoulders. "It's all right, dearheart. Just breathe." Rinah tried. Tears stung at her eyes, and her papa asked, "What's wrong?"

"It's my cycle, that's all," she lied.

He gave her a quick hug. "Well, then let's get you a cup of raspberry leaf tea, and then you can go right back up and finish your nap. The muffins can wait a bit longer."

*

For pious orcs, the autumn and spring celebrations were the highest holy times of the year. But that didn't keep Dargah from anticipating the Adoration of Ayusa with relish. Vigga closed down the forge and proudly took her place as one of seven honored artisans in the town square, displaying daggers, decorative pieces, religious decor, and other projects she'd worked on when not making custom orders.

While Ioanie certainly couldn't shut down the inn, on account of it being full to bursting with out-of-town guests, she celebrated in her own way. Runo was relieved of kitchen duty for a few hours to play his drum with a band of traveling musicians, much to the delight of Adelfi's patrons. Then, he was dismissed to enjoy his first Ayusan celebration in Lindenvale.

Rinah pushed every single second of yesterday's encounter with Bram out of her head as she placed freshly cut pink roses—a sign of cheer and friendship—on the table. She knew they would be wilted by the end of the day, but right now, she needed the simple peace their beauty provided.

Her papa, with his baskets of muffins and scones, was not far, grouped with sellers of all manner of foodstuffs. Surrounding him were purveyors of smoked and salted meats, pickled vegetables, fresh and candied fruits, cheese, wildflower honey, wine, roasted almonds, herb-infused oils, compotes and jams, hand pies, and the flakiest, most divine Dehlkian pistachio-and-honey tartlets that Rinah had ever tasted. She'd eaten three for breakfast and debated having one for a snack.

Then maybe another for supper.

*

Dargah lost herself in the sounds and scents of the festival. She had considered asking Orlaeth to join her, but Rinah had quietly pulled her aside and hinted that their new friend was unlikely to enjoy the crowds and atmosphere of the celebration. Perhaps she'd prefer a thoughtful souvenir of some kind instead.

And so, Dargah kept that in the back of her mind as she perused the stalls, following her nose from one pastry cart to the next. She would have gladly gobbled a treat from every single vendor she saw, but, beaming with virtue and self-control, she selected only a slice of lemon cake, bursting with bright citrus flavors and decorated with candied orange peel. It was delicious and well worth her coin. That was *one* good thing she'd learned from Parviz: *pace yourself.* In the ring, at the table, with your money.

Never in bed, of course, but that went without saying.

*

"Gods, *no.*"

From atop the Disciple's horse, Neryn balked at the throng of revelers surrounding Lindenvale. His first reaction should have been disdain; so many half-breeds and patchworks were gathered here, their very presence an insult to the gods. Instead, he fought a wave of panic that threatened to drown him. He hadn't realized that so many visitors would be descending on the town like a swarm of cicadas for the summer festival. How would he find Orlaeth now? There would be no way for him to safely get through the crowds on horseback; Tempest, the Disciple's mount, was an anxious creature, already flat-eared and breathing heavily. He could not be trusted to remain docile in this environment.

Neryn dragged the horse to the nearest stable, placating him with soothing words and the last of his own rations. Then, he took a deep breath and plunged into the sea of abominations, hybrids, and sinners, feeling more like one of them than he cared to admit.

Orlaeth had remained motionless on her floor for almost a full day after crying out to her god. She was awake and conscious but could not bring herself to eat or properly rest. The chill that had seized her had lessened greatly, but alongside it was now a low murmur, a dull, aching warning that reminded her of a wasps' nest. She knew that it meant something, that this experience had to be understood, interpreted, but the possibilities were endless, and she did not know where to begin. And she was tired; her bones were tired all the way to the marrow.

*

The last person Dargah expected to see among the festival's dwindling crowds was Neryn Sunstorm. But that's exactly who she witnessed gliding through the thinning mob with a determined stride and an expression of agitation on his face.

Her gut reaction was one of seething resentment, but it was swiftly replaced by concern for Orlaeth. Had Neryn's lie been discovered? Over a month had passed since he'd unceremoniously ejected Dargah from the lodge; that was surely enough time for news about Orlaeth to have meandered its way up to Dirgil. Perhaps Tiarnán had seen her, after all, and decided to come clean to the Disciple. Dargah's pride wrestled with her compassion, and she suddenly found herself standing right in front of the Remnant's Suppliant Prime, demanding to know, "Is Orlaeth in danger?"

Neryn didn't react the way she'd expected. Instead of a cold sneer or sharp word, he met Dargah's hard stare with undisguised alarm. "I fear that she might be. Where can I find her?"

"I assume she's at her boarding house," she said as she ushered him through the throng of revelers. She cut through the town square and led him down a side street.

"She lives alone?" Neryn asked.

"She's more independent than you think," snapped Dargah, breezing past a cobbler's cart.

"It is not her independence with which I am concerned," he said, "but her health."

Dargah's heart sank when she heard the worry in his voice. Orlaeth was a frail-looking woman, yes, and she was withdrawn, but Dargah hadn't thought that she might have some kind of illness or condition that could put her in harm's way. She broke into a run.

Neryn kept pace with her, and in minutes, they arrived outside Bronte's boarding house. "Here?" he asked.

Dargah thought she detected a hint of disgust in his voice but decided that now was not the time to discuss the home's shabby decor. She pushed open the front door, then hurried down the hall to the third door on the right and banged on it with an urgency that she felt in her blood. Neryn called Orlaeth's name, but there was no answer.

"Hey! Hey! You two should be out enjoying the festival, not harassing my boarders!"

Dargah turned to see a slender, elderly man shuffling out of one of the rooms, his face wrinkled with irritation. Neryn pounded at the door again. When only silence responded, his magic, perhaps of its own accord, blasted the door into a shower of splinters, revealing the cold, limp form of Orlaeth sprawled on the floor.

*

Orlaeth was vaguely aware of strong arms embracing her. She thought she heard a familiar voice cry out for help. She blinked once, twice, and saw only a haze of colors. She closed her eyes again, felt warmth and pressure and a steady heartbeat against her ear, then a calloused hand patting at her cheeks. She tried to speak, but her lips couldn't quite form the words the way her brain wanted them to.

"What happened?" That was Dargah's voice, tense but garbled as though she was speaking underwater.

"Orlaeth! Wake up. Wake up!" The fog slowly dissolved from her senses, and she breathed in the scent of sweat-drenched hyssop. Neryn!

She struggled to open her eyes again, but when she did, the blurry faces of her oldest friend and her newest came into focus, both drawn with worry. She realized she'd been placed on her bed, and her shivering body had been swaddled in a thick, wool blanket. The rim of a cup was placed to her lips, and cool water soothed her dry mouth and throat. Someone pressed a damp washcloth to her forehead. She took a ragged breath, then spoke.

*

The festival showed signs of winding down, and Rinah did, too. She'd sold every last bottle of her orange blossom perfume, her whole collection of salves and balms, and several candles. Not wanting to bring anything home, she simply gave away the few items that remained. She and the vendor next to her, a visitor from Sterlingshire named Nikola, had enjoyed pleasant conversation all day, and they'd ended up trading wares. In exchange for a jar of peony-scented face cream, Rinah received a corded bracelet, strung with sparkling glass beads the color of the ocean. Both she and her new friend believed they had received the better end of the deal.

As tokens of cheer and friendship, Rinah passed out the pink roses, which held up surprisingly well in the heat, to her fellow vendors. The music was still lively, but the crowds had begun to thin as parents hefted sleepy children in their arms and elderly couples complained of weary joints.

Rinah secured her new bracelet around her wrist and, waving good night to her fellow revelers, wound her way through the streets back to her cottage. Alvyx, too, had left early—as soon as he'd sold his final scone. He wanted to spend the rest of the evening with Nell and jokingly told her not to wait up for him. She was beginning to think that Nell had changed her mind about becoming friends. And why hadn't Nell come to the festival with her children? Perhaps they did not worship Ayusa.

The cheerful sounds of music, good-natured heckling, and laughter began to fade as she neared her cottage. Her feet were sore, and she decided to treat her toes to a soak in a basin of warm water and calendula oil before bed. When she heard approaching footsteps, she knew her plans would have to wait.

*

"Rinah."

Dargah and Neryn exchanged a glance over Orlaeth's still-trembling body. "What about her?" the half-orc asked.

"Rinah," Orlaeth repeated. She was beginning to understand. Tears began to seep from her eyes.

"We're here to take care of *you*," Dargah insisted.

Orlaeth forced herself to sit, knocking the cup out of Neryn's hand. "Rinah!"

"What's going on?"

"I wish I knew," Neryn said. Only then did Dargah notice the charm around his neck. It glowed a dull, dim red. Surely that had to have something to do with all this, didn't it? It was weird, and this situation was weird. That was enough of a connection for Dargah.

With a determination that belied her fragile body, Orlaeth pushed her way out of the blanket like a moth emerging from a cocoon and stood shakily, refusing Neryn's offer of assistance. *"Rinah is going to die."*

*

Makoa had taken a break from his patrol and was settling into a tuft of tree moss when a male voice startled him.

"Shame on you. Didn't save me a dance, pretty girl."

Then, he heard a woman's voice. Was it *her* voice? The woman he'd seen in the moonlight, weeks before?

"Bram, I didn't dance with *anyone*," she replied with a faint laugh. "I hardly left my booth."

"I've been thinking," the male voice rumbled, "that I'd really like to finish what we started yesterday. It's dark and kinda romantic, so maybe you can invite me in now."

The woman's reply came slowly. "I-I don't think that would be a good idea."

Makoa tensed. Something didn't feel right.

Bram huffed, "So you *are* a tease."

Makoa rose and silently padded to the edge of the garden's mossy patch. Unprotected by wards, he was still safely out of view. He stood in the shadows; even his brilliant orange wings were hidden from the couple standing at the cottage door.

"I'm not! How am I teasing you?"

The woman—yes, it *was* the same one he'd happened upon earlier in the summer; he could tell by her figure and her thick, curly hair—was standing with her back to the door, her hand hovering over the handle. The man, only a few inches taller than her but much broader, was angled toward her as he murmured, "You got me all hot and ready to go, moaning like you were a bitch in heat.

Then, you just up and walked away like you didn't have a care in the world. In my book, that's a tease."

The lantern above the door illuminated the blush that flooded her cheeks. She glowed pink as her voice broke. "I just wanted to talk! You're the one who—"

"How about a little of your papa's blackberry wine? Is it as good as Adelfi's?"

Bram's request seemed to throw Rinah. "Uh, well, some people say so." She hesitated, her eyes flickering to the cobblestone path, then back to the man's face. "But you already had some wine during the festival. Didn't you?"

"A tease and a *nag*, too!" Bram said, throwing his arms wide as though speaking to an audience. He shook his head, scratching as the blonde bristles on his chin. "I can't live with a woman like that."

"But yesterday, you wanted to marry me!"

In spite of his criticism, he leaned in closer to her, bracketing her shoulders with his thick hands. "Rinah, tell me something. Say I *did* marry you. With the way you're teasing me, how do I know the next time I'm outta town, you're not getting cozy with one of the neighbors, huh?"

"What makes you think I would do something like that?" she cried, her voice thick with disgust.

"It's what girls like you do. Trust me, I know. I'm not gonna get burned again. But I like you, Rinah, and I want to be able to trust you. To *love* you."

Rinah was quiet for several seconds. Then, she stated, her voice dull, "The cottage is still a terrible mess from all my cooking and crafting. Would it be all right if I brought some wine out here for you instead?"

A grin split Bram's face. His voice was a soft rumble as he toyed with the ribbon on her bodice. "Yeah, sugar. That's great."

She escaped into the cottage, but Bram stuck out his foot, keeping the door from closing. A moment later, she reappeared with a wooden cup and a bottle in her hands.

Bram chuckled lightly. "Maybe you're a nice girl after all." He took the bottle, filled his cup, then set the bottle on the window ledge behind her. He wrapped one arm around her waist and nuzzled her hair. "Sweetheart, listen. You're always taking care of other people, you know? Like taking that balm to the orc kid and the flowers for his sister. When does someone get to take care of you, huh? That's all I want." He kissed her cheek.

She stiffened. "Runo. 'The orc kid' is my friend. His name is *Runo*. I've told you."

"He has a crush on you, you know that?"

She shook her head slightly.

"You're leading him on, too, huh?"

Her eyes widened. "No! I'm not leading anyone on!"

Bram put his fingers to her lips. "Shh, it's not like I blame him. You're so pretty, and so sweet..." His fingers traced the shape of her lips, then slid down her neck and rested on her breast.

Makoa could see her pulse fluttering in her neck.

"Bram." Rinah attempted to slip out of his grip, but he held her even closer, wine sloshing out of his cup. "I'm tired. Really. I've been on my feet all day. Can we please just say good night?"

"You're just gonna visit with your skinny little green boyfriend when I leave," he accused with a huff.

Rinah's face darkened, indignation briefly overtaking her timidity. "Bram, just stop it! You sound ridiculous."

Magic flashed as Makoa's hand twitched to drum up a defensive ward around the woman. He mentally tore through the spells and enchantments in his limited repertoire, ultimately realizing that magic was not going to solve this problem. He'd never used those wards on a *person* before, only his home and himself. His magic might not work correctly or, worse, it could hurt her. He balled his fists in frustration, allowing the gleam of power to ebb until it disappeared.

"Ooh, there's a little bit of fire in you after all!" Bram chuckled and pressed his lips to her neck. He downed the wine, then spluttered a cough. "No offense to your papa, but Old Man Adelfi's is definitely better." He chucked the empty cup into the trees, still coughing. When he recovered, he announced, "I think I know what's going on. You're just afraid. It's your first time, right? I get it."

"No! I mean, yes, but that has nothing to do with—look, I tried to be nice! I'm sorry, but, please, I—I can't do this. You have to leave. I *need* you to leave!" With determination in her eyes, Rinah put her hands on his chest and pushed as hard as she could. "Please, just go away!"

Her resistance earned her a backhanded blow so powerful she tumbled to the ground. Shock stole her voice, and she stared up at him, aghast.

"Why the hell did you make me do that?" Bram asked, taking a step toward her. "Now your pretty face is gonna be all bruised. Damn it!" Breathing heavily, he picked up the bottle and hurled it against the ledge. It shattered in a rain of glass and purple wine, and Rinah gasped, covering her head.

Makoa's heart raced. This was not right. What was he supposed to do? What was he *allowed* to do?

Hands raised in protest, Rinah clambered to her feet and tried to back away from Bram. She tripped over her skirt. It tore, and she collapsed again.

He crouched down in front of her, grabbed her arm, and whispered, his voice hoarse, "I hope you're gonna play nice now, sweetheart, and give me what we both want, yeah?" He coughed and spat on the ground. Without taking his eyes off her, he pulled a narrow blade from inside his boot. He placed the tip a breath away from her chin. "I don't like having to get mean."

Makoa saw red. In a silent blink of furious, brilliant energy, he made a decision he'd never made before.

Chapter Nineteen:

Of Rescue and Resourcefulness

Here, in her precious garden, where she felt most alive and most at home, Rinah now knew terror. Everything was happening too fast, but in her mind, each second that ticked away was unbearably long. She tried to make sense of Bram's stale breath in her face, the glint of the dagger he'd flashed, the fear knocking between her ribs. She couldn't run to the nearest neighbor. She wasn't fast enough. And the stone wall was too high for her to easily climb. The only option was the forest beyond her garden. He wouldn't be able to find her in its darkness, but she wouldn't get very far without any light, either. She had no escape, and no weapon but her voice.

"You don't need to use that. Please put it away," was all she could say, unable to take her eyes off the knife. "I'm sorry I upset you. You're scaring me. Bram, *please.*"

Bram leaned forward and flicked the dagger up her bodice, slicing through the laces. He then pulled her to her feet, kissed her roughly, and spun her away from the cottage. Pushing her through the garden, past her beloved roses, her peonies, her herbs, and her ferns, he forced her to her knees.

"I don't think she's interested in you."

Rinah froze, eyes wide. That voice didn't belong to Papa, returning from his late-night rendezvous. Oh, gods, was someone *watching* them? Embarrassment joined the fear flooding her body.

Bram tensed, his grip on Rinah's arm still crushing, and coughed through a string of filthy dwarven curses. He turned to see the intruder.

The man's silhouette in the moonlight was tall—a good deal taller than Bram. It was also evident, even in shadow, that he had a lean, athletic build. Bram did not.

"Who in the seven hells are you to be interrupting me and my girl?" Bram shouted.

"And who in the seven hells are you to be treating a lady like that?" The man's voice was sure and steady, but Rinah didn't recognize it.

"A lady?" Bram laughed. "Go home, little boy." He shook Rinah, and she couldn't hold back a whimper. "Unless you wanna watch? I don't mind an audience."

Makoa felt a surge of adrenaline as he took a single step toward the dwarf. "If you touch her again—"

Shoving Rinah to the ground behind him, Bram stood as tall as he could and mirrored Makoa's stance. "You don't tell me what to do, nasty little scrubling." He balled one hand into a fist, trying to size up his opponent in the dark. With the other hand, he tightened his grip on the dagger. His shoulders began to shake.

Hunched over, trying to cover her breasts, Rinah risked a glance toward the interloper. Meeting her gaze, Makoa's resolve strengthened. Through his chest seared another surge of protectiveness. Pride. He was hardly listening to himself as the words tumbled from his mouth. "If you touch her again, I swear I'll kill you."

Bram swore again, doubled over, and let out a groan. He took a few steps forward, then fell facedown in the dirt, slurring garbled curses. He raked his fingers across his throat, then vomited.

Makoa waited for him to rise, to lumber toward him, swinging angry fists, cussing, and spitting. But he just lay there writhing, his face twisted in agony.

With a kind of hazy detachment, Rinah watched Bram gag and squirm, his eyes watering as he dragged clawed fingers through the dirt. When his thrashing slowed and his groans turned to whimpers, and with one hand still straining to cover her breasts, she picked up the dagger he'd dropped. Then, she stood up and stepped past the body of her attacker to face Makoa. "Did you know that, if consumed, the leaves and flowers of the common tansy can cause severe intestinal distress?"

"Now I do," the faerie noted, glancing at the glinting dagger. "In the wine?"

"In the cup," she corrected. She stashed the knife in her pocket. "More than enough to keep his guts occupied for a while. I wasn't sure it would take effect fast enough, so... thank you."

Makoa felt a grin spread stupidly across his face.

"So, what's your name, friend?" Rinah answered his smile with a sigh. "And how long have you been standing naked in my garden?"

*

Dargah tore through the streets of Lindenvale. On her heels was Neryn, Orlaeth in his arms. Dargah probably had less of an idea about what was going on than either of the elves did, but she didn't care. If there was even a chance that Rinah was in danger—the sound of her name gave her pause long enough to turn her head, and she saw her brother leaving a crowd of his friends, holding a half-eaten pastry, leaping over stalls, and dodging carts on his way to her. Before he could form a question, she was gone again, hoping he had the good sense to leave her to her mission.

It was Runo, though, so he didn't.

Several minutes later, the four of them found themselves in front of Rinah's garden, where she appeared to be having a friendly conversation with a naked man.

*

"Rinah!"

Dargah's cry startled them both, and, to her dismay, Rinah watched Makoa all but disappear in a flash of light. A pair of orange wings flitted away and vanished between the shadows of the forest. What in the world...?

In a rush, her friends surrounded her.

"Are you all right? You're not hurt?"

374

"You're alive! Thank the gods."

"What happened?"

Seeing her four would-be rescuers with concern and fear written on their faces, Rinah's fragile confidence crumpled and she allowed her tears to fall. Dargah swooped in to embrace her, and Rinah could tell she was also checking for injuries. "What's going on? What is Neryn doing here?" Rinah asked through sobs. "What is *everyone* doing here?"

It was Runo who, still holding his half-eaten tart, took her hand and calmly ushered everyone into the cottage. Dargah draped Rinah in a shawl, then lit all the lanterns and candles she could find. Neryn carefully deposited Orlaeth, who was now alert, in Alvyx's chair. Runo poked around for a kettle and some packets of tea leaves, then found where the mugs were stored. Once they had all arranged themselves inside, Rinah uttered, "Bram."

Dargah's dagger appeared in her hand. "Where is he?"

Rinah looked at her, tears rolling down her cheeks. "I think he's still outside. Out back."

Without wasting her breath on threats, Dargah left.

Neryn didn't seem to know what was going on, but he murmured to Runo, "Keep the ladies safe," then followed Dargah into the night.

The boy placed the kettle on the hearth as serenely as though he were entertaining a group of grandmothers. "Chamomile tea or mint?"

*

The anger Dargah had felt when Neryn called her an infection—a *pollution*—was hardly a spark compared to what boiled in her veins now. She scanned the garden for her prey. All she needed was the faint gleam from the cottage lantern to find him. She sheathed her dagger. She wouldn't need it to wring the life out of that bastard.

Dargah saw a flicker of movement behind a tree.

There he was. *Hiding.*

She sprang.

Bram cried out as she tackled him, and they crashed into the bushes. She pulled him to his feet by his collar. He reeked of vomit and wine, his face flushed and blotchy. She said nothing as he flailed, protesting her harsh treatment of him.

"Dargah."

She heard Neryn's voice but didn't turn. She watched terror fill Bram's pale blue eyes as he coughed and groaned, flecks of red staining his beard. Something fierce and wild and ancient in her blood luxuriated in his fear, delighted in seeing it slip down his face in rivulets of sweat. Her heart beat in time to his panicked, staccato breathing.

"*Dargah.* Of what crime is this man accused?"

Neryn spoke calmly, with authority and a clarity that sliced through the blaze of anger in Dargah's brain. With some difficulty, she restrained the lioness inside her, dragged Bram toward Neryn, then flung him at the elf's feet. He tried to right himself, scratching at his neck and chest. She looked at Neryn as though seeing an opponent in the ring. If she had to dispatch Bram, and then the elf, she would, without hesitation.

"Call him a man if you like, but he's a monster." She boldly met his glare but dropped her voice to a disgusted hiss. "He attacked Rinah."

Neryn's temper flared hot enough to make his chest ache, but he would not allow Dargah to see him lose his composure again. He looked down at Bram, icy disdain written on his features. "And what is your response to this accusation?"

In what could only be a last-ditch effort to defend himself, Bram spat, "Is that what she told you? Dumb bitch. I didn't do anything! I barely touched her."

"She didn't give herself that black eye," Dargah hissed.

"...I barely touched her," the half-dwarf repeated.

"Is that so?"

Bram looked up at Neryn, a glimmer of hope in his bloodshot eyes. "Yeah."

"Then I," said the elf, his eyes pearl white, "shall barely touch you."

*

"What happened, exactly?" Runo asked, stirring honey into Rinah's tea. Orlaeth discreetly pulled the other mug away from him before he could do the same to hers.

"I was going to ask you the same thing," Rinah said. Her voice was still shaking. Her body was still shaking. "Why are you all here?"

Runo finally picked up the pastry he'd been neglecting and put the rest of it into his mouth. "I'm not the person to ask. I was at the festival with Xinny and Galen and a few of his friends from the garrison, and I saw Dargah tearing through the square like she was being chased by some horrible monster or something. And, turns out, I was kind of right because all of a sudden, there went Neryn, running in the same direction, holding Orlaeth like she weighed less than a sack of flour. No one stopped to tell me anything, so I just followed everyone here." He raised his eyebrows and nodded at Orlaeth. "Maybe *you* can fill us both in?" Then he began to rummage around the kitchen.

Orlaeth, making herself immediately useful, located a tin of ointment and gently applied it to Rinah's broken skin. She thought for a moment, then said, "I do not know

380

exactly what happened. What I remember is that I was in prayer, as I felt deeply troubled. That is not the correct word for it, but I do not think the word exists in the Common Tongue. I felt as though I were carrying the weight of another person's emotions. Fear. Stabbing fear. And a terrible cold. Like I would never feel heat again." She placed a delicate hand on her chest. "Then this strange charm began to glow and grow warm. I recall little else until your sister and Neryn appeared."

Rinah watched Orlaeth's fingers dance around the pendant. Something about it was comforting. Familiar. She quieted her mind, trying to pull up the memory that might match what she was feeling. It wasn't a single memory, or even a collection of memories she decided, but a *person*. Oddly, it reminded her of Papa.

"…and then we were returned to our mothers, both of whom beat us soundly upon our arrival," Orlaeth was saying to Runo.

"That answers exactly zero of my questions, Orlaeth," he replied.

"I theorize that this pendant and its twin are some kind of charmed communication device. They could be linked empathically, somehow, but I do not know of any spell or incantation within the realm of elemental magic that could be used in such a way. Perhaps it was activated by my distress, and it notified Neryn. Or it transferred my emotional state to him."

"So, in summary: Your magic telepathic necklace told your ex-boyfriend to come here because you were stressed out."

"Then, I had a vision of Rinah's death at Bram's hand."

Before anyone could say another word, something exploded outside the window.

Chapter Twenty:

Of Chaos and Confusion

Dargah watched, slack-jawed, as Bram hurtled through the air, graceless as a salmon leaping out of water, then crashed against a tree with a sickening thud. Without even a whimper, he collapsed in a heap. Leaves fluttered around him, and above, a very angry owl voiced her displeasure at being disturbed. Dargah was quiet for too long, then asked Neryn. "Is he dead?"

"Of course not. He will need to be held accountable for his actions. I assume there is some type of justice system in your town?"

"There is. But I have a better idea."

*

For the second time that day, Dargah found herself banging on a door, only to be met by stillness within. She could open the forge herself and simply dump Bram inside; she had a key, after all. But this situation was too significant not to involve Vigga directly. Dargah shouted toward the smith's window, demanding she come downstairs.

The soft glow of a candle appeared behind the shutters. Dargah glanced at Neryn, standing still as a statue with Bram's bulk slung over his shoulder. As soon as the bleary-eyed Vigga cracked open the door, he announced, "I beg your pardon, madame," pushed past her and, with a wet thump, dropped her nephew on the dirt floor.

"What the hell is going on here?" the half-dwarf cried.

Dargah followed Neryn inside, then turned to Vigga, unable to hide the pain and anger in her voice. "You tell me!" she snapped. "Your 'charming' nephew just tried to rape my best friend. Was *this* the kind of trouble he caused back home?"

Vigga's florid face paled. "Oh, gods." She looked down at Bram, his hair damp with sweat, his mouth bloodied, and his face purple with bruises. Twigs were snarled in his hair, and his brand-new, expertly tailored clothing was thoroughly soiled.

She kicked him.

"You bastard," she hissed. Then she kicked him again.

"Madame," Neryn said, stepping forward. "Please, refrain from causing further injury! He must live long enough to face the consequences of his assault."

"These *are* the consequences!" Vigga growled, kicking him a third time. She stalked over to a table and immediately started penning a letter. "Been in town barely a month, and he's already showing his true colors!" Her writing looked like angry claw marks on the page.

Dargah seethed. "So this is nothing new for him?"

"Quite the opposite." Vigga looked up. "The reason his mother sent him here was because he was 'courting' two young women in Black Lake—cousins, no less—and both have accused him of fathering their unborn children. He was supposed to stay here, *behaving himself*, until things blew over back there, and their families could figure things out."

"That is deplorable!" sputtered Neryn.

"What's deplorable is *me* agreeing to this whole ridiculous plan," Vigga confessed, still scribbling. "I should have known he'd go after someone like Rinah. I warned her, but I didn't realize he'd gotten so close."

Dargah had come to adore Vigga as a mentor and friend, but this was unforgivable. She looked down at the half-dwarf, her face darkened by anger. "No. You told her he was a flirt. *I'm* a flirt, Vigga. He's a wolf. A *monster*."

"He is a traitor to his sex," Neryn added firmly. "This kind of behavior is shameful."

Vigga finally paused to take in Neryn's stature, his eloquence, and his vomit-drenched hair. "Who the hell is this?"

"He's a musician," replied Dargah dismissively. "What are you going to do now?"

"I'm leaving him in his own filth for the night, then sending him home at the crack of dawn. I'm telling my sister that he's no longer welcome here."

"What makes you sure he'll stay away?"

"Money, honey," Vigga sneered, rubbing her fingers together. "I happen to know that his grandfather, Farfi, has recently become aware of what he did in Black Lake, and he's changed his mind about Bram's inheritance. The boy turns thirty next month, and if he'd been able to keep it in his pants, he would have been set for *life*—the estate, a dairy farm, two orchards, and a mill. But Farfi's first wife left him years ago, and understandably, he refuses to reward a rakehell like this. Good on him, I say. At least someone in that family has a moral compass. Everything will probably go to his younger cousin. So just like that"—she snapped her fingers—"Bram gets nothing. All he has to his name right now are the clothes his mother bought him? To top it all off, he was a horrible apprentice, too. Gods, if I tell Farfi what he tried with Rinah, that boy won't even have the shirt on his back."

Neryn's tone was respectful but his expression was grim. "While this is a satisfactory solution for you, madame, it will also be necessary to make amends to Miss Autumnsong," he announced sternly. "It is clear that you did not have ill intentions, but you withheld information that might have led her to avoid Bram from the start, thus preventing this attack altogether."

Vigga's eyes flashed fire, then went dim. Dargah was surprised to see her lower her head, chastened. "I can't deny that." At her words, Neryn nodded his approval, then stepped outside the forge. Vigga nudged Bram with her foot and muttered, "Not that I care, but will he be all right? He looks terrible."

"He'll live." Dargah reached into the pouch strapped to her belt and offered Vigga its contents. "Here. It's not much, but see that it goes to those women—for their babies. Gods know they won't get a coin out of Bram now."

Vigga looked at the coins in her palm in quiet appreciation. "You're a good woman, Dargah."

"I just would have spent it on something useless at the Adoration," she insisted. "The orcish vendors' prices are outrageous come autumn."

"You *could* use a new oilskin cloak," Vigga noted. "After five years, you're still never prepared for heavy rain." When Dargah just shrugged, she added, "Thank you. And I'm sorry. I truly am."

"I know. Make sure Rinah does, too."

*

Dargah was surprised to see that Neryn had waited for her outside. She hadn't commented on his display of power or his disgust with Bram's behavior, and she didn't know what to say right now, either, so she asked, "Is that something that you do often in Dirgil?"

"Hm?"

"Throw men like Bram into trees. Magically."

"No."

She waited for him to elaborate. When he didn't, she pressed, "Well, what made you decide to do it here?"

"The principle of it," he said. "He intentionally caused physical harm and emotional upset to a young woman. Regardless of whether I knew the woman personally, the behavior he displayed was vulgar and offensive by any reasonable standard."

"Ah."

"And, in this particular case, he caused offense and injury to a woman who has befriended someone for whom I care deeply. I suppose I felt it necessary to dole out some form of justice." Without letting Dargah reply, he went on, "I am aware that you consider my lifestyle narrow-minded and the role of women irrationally limited within the Remnant, but understand that when I am given a mate, I will allow *no* harm to come to her. Should she be regarded as in any way inferior to me, should another male treat her inappropriately, should even my own kin speak ill of her, then I will do to him no less than I did to Rinah's assailant. *No* female should be treated thusly, least of all one whom I am a protector."

Dargah was astonished into silence. Unsurprisingly, Neyrn capitalized on that.

"I realize I took from you the opportunity to wreak your own vengeance upon him, and that was perhaps selfish of me. However, I also realized that, due to your closeness to the situation and your loyalty to Rinah, you were more likely to kill him than I was, and I considered it important for him to receive justice beyond mere physical pain for his cruelty. I would *never* intentionally end a life."

"Uh, no, it's fine," she said faintly. After a moment, she asked, "What *are* you doing in Lindenvale tonight, anyway?"

"I am not certain. I believe that I was summoned by a kind of magic I cannot identify. Somehow, I knew that Orlaeth was unwell and that I had to be here. That is all."

"So you just… up and left Dirgil? Alone?"

"Yes, and I stole a horse in order to arrive here in all due haste. I only regret that I might need to fabricate another lie to appease the Disciple."

He did not sound as regretful as she would have expected. Or at all. She couldn't tell, but in the darkness, it sounded like he was smirking.

"So, do you and Orlaeth have some kind of magic link or bond? Is it an elf thing? A betrothal thing?"

"No such bond exists among users of elemental magic, mates or no. And, besides," he added gruffly, "after my return to Dirgil, Disciple has declared our betrothal invalid on account of Orlaeth's 'death'."

"Oh. So you're on the market again?"

A haughty sniff. "You make it sound as though finding an appropriate bride is nothing more complicated than selecting a choice vegetable from the harvest."

Dargah was too tired to be drawn into another debate about the merits of arranged marriage. "Well, Neryn, I hope you find The One among all the lesser turnips and squash," was all she said.

*

It wasn't long before they arrived back at Rinah's cottage. Despite the late hour, light blazed within, and Dargah even thought she smelled something baking.

"Good evening!" said Runo as they entered. The consummate host, he presented them with a plate of warm oat cakes, then added, "Damn, Neryn, you're *gross*."

In the light, Dargah could now see how thoroughly the elf's pristine tunic was saturated with Bram's vomit and other stains that might have been made by any number of things. "Be nice," she chided her brother, surprising herself. "We dropped Bram off at the forge, and Neryn's clothing was collateral damage."

Rinah spoke up, "You can change into my papa's robe. But maybe wash up first, out back."

"There is a lovely stream just outside the stone wall," added Orlaeth.

Neryn looked between Orlaeth and Rinah, asking them both, "Are you all right?"

Orlaeth inclined her head, and Rinah burrowed further into her shawl as she said, "Not yet. But I think I will be. Thank you for your help."

He nodded and took the offered robe, closing the door behind him.

"Now, girls," said Runo, clapping his hands once. "Who wants the honor of explaining what the hell is happening here tonight?"

*

Makoa's frantic heartbeat hadn't slowed since he fled from the people entering the garden. It had been so close. Perhaps they hadn't gotten a good look at him in the darkness. How could they? The only one who *had* seen him up close was the brute who'd been hurled into the tree. That was pretty spectacular to watch. And maybe the impact knocked his brain around enough that he wouldn't remember a thing. That would be good.

Using wards to keep himself unseen this time, Makoa dared to approach the cottage. He landed carefully on a windowsill, peeking inside. The woman, Rinah, sat on a sofa, holding a cup of tea. The skinny, pale girl—an elf, Makoa could tell—was talking with her. Two half-orcs, one male and a taller female, sat at the table, eating some kind of delicious-smelling food. At the sound of the door opening, Makoa reflexively flattened himself against the window pane, holding his breath.

The imposing male elf came around the house and through the garden, careful not to damage any more vegetation. The elf neared the water, turned this way and that, apparently concerned that either there were additional would-be attackers nearby, or… oh. Wait. He was preparing to clean himself up and was just checking for prying eyes.

Makoa never understood the modesty embraced by the Created races. But the elf needn't worry. All of Makoa's interest was focused on the scene playing out inside the cottage. He couldn't quite hear what was being said, but to his surprise, Rinah stood up and marched out the door with a lantern, walking into her garden, towards the dark of the forest.

She stood for a moment, then called out, "Hello? The… uh, person who helped me? Whoever you are, please come back if you're out there. I want to thank you." She peered into the night with hope on her face. "My friends didn't mean to scare you off."

And that's when, to his horror and shame, Makoa saw the bruise already forming on her cheek. He should have done something sooner. He decided that he'd introduce himself, rules be damned. He'd just apologize, make sure she would recover, and be on his way, but he would be a bit more subtle this time.

He fluttered behind a bush, took a deep breath, and shifted. Before he could get Rinah's attention, he heard a voice from inside the cottage shout, "Oh, my gods, the naked guy is back!"

Chapter Twenty-One:

Of Magic and Misfits

As Dargah watched from the window, Rinah turned, saw the figure in the bushes, and cried out. In seconds, Runo was at her side with a butcher's knife and a skillet, and even Neryn, from beyond the garden, began yelling vague threats and splashing around—somehow, also threateningly. Dargah looked at Orlaeth. "Just, uh… stay there," Dargah ordered.

Orlaeth sipped her tea.

Then Dargah grabbed Alvyx's rarely used walking stick and barrelled out the door.

"It's just me! Don't be scared!" a male voice pleaded from behind the bush.

Rinah screamed again.

"There!" Runo cried out, pointing with the knife to the figure in the bushes. He danced back and forth on the tips of his toes, swinging the blade. "Come out and fight like a man, you knave!"

Dargah charged through the garden, wielding the stick like a spear.

"Stop! Please! I mean you no harm!" the figure shrieked. "I'm a friend!"

Neryn continued to splash threateningly.

"Wait! That's him!" Rinah gasped. "That's him! I recognize his voice!"

Dargah halted, her arm still in prime stabbing position. "And who is *he?*" she asked, her eyes fixed on the tall, male silhouette.

"Hi, I'm Makoa!" the voice replied cheerily from the shadows. "Can I have some pants?"

*

Momentarily, the group was gathered back inside the cottage. Orlaeth had finished her tea and sat on the sofa, wondering when it would be appropriate to ask for another cup. She watched Rinah's dried herbs sway in the breeze ushered in by the open door. Runo tidied the kitchen. Rinah was in Alvyx's chair, wrapped again in her shawl. A damp Neryn stood awkwardly in the corner. And the stranger who called himself Makoa, after receiving a pair of Alvyx's trousers, which fit him about as well as his robe fit Neryn, took a seat at the table.

As all eyes focused on the pale, orange-haired boy, Dargah spoke. "What in the high and holy marriage bed of the goddess is going on?"

"I *think* I share the sentiment," Neryn added.

"Why is everyone in my house?" Rinah wanted to know.

"Where did *you* come from, Carrots?" Runo quizzed Makoa.

It probably wasn't the best time, she realized, but Orlaeth asked, "May I have another cup of tea?" Runo obliged.

"Look," Dargah said. "If we put all our stories together, we might be able to figure out what is happening right now."

Rinah stared into her half-full mug and, with some difficulty, recalled the events of the night. Her eyes darted to Makoa as she concluded. ...and that's when you showed up."

"Am I to understand that Carrots was naked then, as well?" Runo asked. "Is that a thing here? I have never been invited to 'naked night' at the cottage."

Makoa looked a bit sheepish. "Yeah, but it wasn't on purpose."

"How can you *accidentally* be *naked*?" Runo cried.

Dargah had to side with her brother on this one and raised an eyebrow at them both. Makoa appeared to be deep in thought, weighing his words carefully. Then, as though each syllable caused him physical pain, he stated, "I don't wear any clothes in my true form, so when I shifted, I was.... also not wearing any clothes."

If Dargah was honest with herself, she was probably better off not knowing. But she heard herself repeating, "True form?"

Makoa looked from face to face, his amber eyes bright. Pleading. Hopeful. Afraid. "Uh, so... I'm an earthborn faerie."

Silence swallowed the room.

Runo broke it, his tone challenging. "What the hell is an earthborn faerie?"

"A faerie that wasn't created from the body of the Unseen One thousands of years ago like all the other Guardians were. I was... you know, made the other way. Like you were made, I'm guessing?"

Runo rolled his eyes. "Not that I believe you, but you being a faerie only explains why you're naked, not why you were naked in *Rinah's garden*."

"Show him," Rinah begged Makoa. "Can you?"

Makoa's apprehension melted into confidence at her request. In seconds, a pair of gently fluttering orange wings sat perched atop the chair.

Eyes wide, Runo inched closer to examine what might be attached to the wings. "He's naked," he confirmed. "Definitely a naked faerie."

Before Runo finished speaking, Makoa was again seated in the chair, hurrying to cover himself with Alvyx's pants and pushing his shaggy hair out of his eyes.

"Can it be that magical amulets are the *least* interesting topic of the evening?" Neryn mused.

Makoa appealed to Rinah alone. "I guess, in retrospect, I should have anticipated being naked, but, um, I've never shifted before and that wasn't exactly front-of-mind at the moment. And I guess maybe we're even now because once, I saw you naked, too."

Rinah spat her tea. "*What?*"

Dargah bared her teeth. *What* was *it with creepy men this week?*

"It was an accident," Makoa insisted quickly. "I swear it was! It was a few weeks ago. I'm still kind of new to patrolling this area, and I saw how wonderful your garden was, so I decided to take a break here. It was so late I didn't think anyone was awake, but then you came by and—"

Rinah's eyes widened. "Bathed in the stream," she finished. "I… I never do that sort of thing. I *bathe*, I mean, but in the bathhouses. I'm not—I mean, I don't just walk around naked in the garden all the time. Who does that?" She flushed violently, again avoiding everyone's stare and crossing her arms over her bosom. "But that night was just so peaceful—and no one could see, and it was dark out, and I—" She covered her face with a hand. "What are the odds that a *faerie* was watching me?" she murmured.

"Oh, don't be embarrassed. You're beautiful. Your body is beautiful," Makoa assured her brightly. "What I saw of it."

"Sir, there will be none of this!" exclaimed Runo. Even Neryn cleared his throat rather aggressively.

Rinah just stared, still crimson with shame. "Exactly how *much* did you see—"

"Not a lot," Makoa continued, panicked. "I... there was almost no light, but I saw—I saw how your, uh... shape... is different? Faerie women are not... They aren't made like... like *you* are." He gestured feebly with his hands, then threw them up in defeat. "It was only a moment. I... I didn't stay and watch or anything. I'm really sorry." He, too, reddened and looked away.

Rinah sputtered a nervous laugh, "Oh! Well, I didn't see a lot either tonight. Not that there wasn't a lot to see. That is to say, I'm sure there is. I mean, I wouldn't know, of course, but I assume there's more to see than what I saw. You're quite… tall."

Dargah was rarely at a loss for words. But this—watching these two stumble over themselves, apologizing for mutual accidental nudity—yes, this was one of those times. Fortunately, Runo blurted, "All right, now that we're all *incredibly* uncomfortable, let's move on. So, hurray! The naked faerie rescues the damsel in distress—"

At that very moment, Alvyx Autumnsong, brushing feathers from his shoulders, walked in on the ragtag posse assembled in his tiny cottage. A reverent and slightly fearful hush fell over the room. For a moment, no one breathed.

"Daughter," he said slowly. "It is very, very late at night. There are two unfamiliar males in my house, both of whom are minimally dressed in articles of *my* clothing. I would like an explanation. First, however, I would like to express to Orlaeth and Dargah that it is a pleasure to see them both again, and I would also like to extend my personal thanks to Runo for wearing what appear to be his own clothes at the moment."

"My pleasure, Papa Alvyx," Runo said with a firm nod.

Rinah took a deep breath and stood up. She gestured first to Neryn. "Papa, this is Orlaeth's former betrothed, Neryn Sunstorm."

The elf stood respectfully, holding the robe closed. "Long life and Erjunn's many blessings upon you, sir. I am honored to meet you."

"And this is Makoa." Rinah gave him a helpless glance. Was she supposed to leave it at that, or…?

"Good evening, sir. I'm an earthborn faerie from Duskweaver Colony."

Alvyx's expression remained unchanged. "Huh."

Makoa hopped up from the chair and, with a friendly smile, extended his hand to Alvyx. "This—humans do this, right? This is a human thing?"

Alvyx shook it. "It is, my boy. A pleasure to meet you both. I will now ask again for an explanation. Hopefully, one that includes the reason for the injury on my child's face."

Escaping the rising tension inside, Rinah led her papa out into the garden and closed the door behind her. Her friends were going to just have to chat amongst themselves until she returned, and hopefully, none of them would kill each other in the meantime.

*

"Before I say anything," Rinah began, her hands folded contritely, "I need you to know that... the situation has been *handled*."

Alvyx sat, raising his eyebrows. She took that as an indication to proceed.

"Tonight, after I left the festival, Bram showed up and—"

Alvyx sprang to his feet. "Gods damn it, Rinah, if that boy—"

She placed her hands on his shoulders and encouraged him to sit back down. "Please, let me finish! I promise, you'll understand why there are two strange men in the house." She spat out the whole story again, unable to meet his gaze.

Alvyx's indignation flared, and the air around him shuddered like a thunderbolt. "Oh, my girl. My dear girl, I am so sorry." He folded her into his arms.

For several minutes, Rinah allowed herself to feel the shame, the anger, the fear, the pain and confusion that Bram caused her just hours ago. She should have told him before tonight that things were over. She should have told him that no, she hadn't had a man before, not that way, and she didn't want *him* that way either, not yet and maybe not ever, and that he had to stop pestering her about it. She should have hidden inside the cottage when she thought she heard him coming. She should have moved faster, fought harder. Kicked him. Bit him. Screamed louder. She should have taken Vigga's advice to heart. She should have spoken up for herself over dinner at Adelfi's when he made her feel ashamed of getting excited about Runo's cooking. She should have told him that she wanted to spend time getting to know Orlaeth, too, and not just him. She should have been smart enough to see all of this coming. Why hadn't she been? Or did she see it all, and just… ignore it?

"Forgive me, Rinah, if it's insensitive of me, but I need to know. Did he—"

"No." Her breath rattled, then she laughed. "You know what ended up saving me? Your allergies." In response to his confused grunt, she explained how, remembering his reaction to the tansy plant, she laced Bram's cup with its crushed, dried buds, which she'd saved at Orlaeth's urging.

Alvyx caught her up in another tight hug. "I hope he choked."

"He didn't get sick right away, and while he was… doing what he was doing to me, Makoa showed up out of nowhere and tried to scare him off. And then everyone else just kind of appeared, and I didn't see it, but I think maybe Bram got thrown into a tree?"

"Yes, the oak out back is cracked, almost in two. I wondered about that."

"Dargah and Neryn dragged him to the forge. And Vigga is sending him home. So, I guess that's that."

He kissed her forehead. "No, that is *not* that. Rinah, I am very, very sorry this happened to you. And I also very much regret encouraging the two of you to spend time together. He seemed like a decent boy to me, and you seemed to like him… I should have realized that he wasn't who he claimed to be."

"It's my own fault," she muttered, wiping her nose on her shawl. "I kind of thought he was starting to act a little different, kind of impatient with me, but—"

"Rinah." Alvyx's note held a warning tone that frightened her almost as much as Bram's attack had, and she flinched. He said her name again, gently, and took her hand. "No, my girl. It's not your fault."

The tears welled up again. "But I flirted with him, and I kept seeing him, even after Vigga told me that I should be careful. I *did* like him. I wanted him to like me, too, and I thought he did!"

"Child, if a clever, determined raccoon climbs up and steals an egg from a bird's nest, do we blame the egg for being stolen?"

"But I don't want to be an egg! I don't want to be a sweet, little girl!" shouted Rinah. "I want to be strong, and I want to be smart, and I don't want to ever feel this stupid again. I want to be able to be the *raccoon* if I have to." Her skin felt flushed and hot. "If the tansy hadn't worked, or if Makoa hadn't shown up, I'd be dead right now!"

"Rinah, you don't know that."

"Orlaeth does."

Alvyx let out a breath, closed his eyes, and let his head droop onto his chest. When he looked back at his daughter, he half-smiled. "She's a seer, isn't she?"

"Maybe. I don't know. She definitely looks at the world differently than most people do. She's very religious.

She's perceptive. Maybe she just figured Bram out before I did and was convinced of the worst possible outcome."

"Well, you didn't die. And you have five young people here who care very much about you. Let that be the good that you take from tonight."

He let her sniffle a bit longer, let her lean on his shoulder, and sang to her the old nursery songs he had sung when she first came to him, as confused and afraid as she was right now. Back then, when she shrank into herself with terror or worry, he would gently hold her until she was his beloved Rinah again, all sweetness and softness and hope. But tonight, he would begin to forge her into something new entirely. Something with an edge He owed it to her.

"Daughter, it's time I told you the truth."

*

417

When Rinah and Alvyx stepped back into the cottage, Runo was saying, "…but I'm sort of still stuck on the magic telepathic necklace thing."

"Yes, we need to figure this part out," Dargah agreed, reaching out to squeeze Rinah's hand and offer a comforting smile. Rinah did not smile back.

They all listened as Orlaeth explained about the mysterious charms and her strange vision. Then, Neryn told them about his own experience and the need to get to Lindenvale as fast as he could.

Runo turned to the elf. "Did I hear you correctly? You not only stole a horse, but you stole the *Disciple's* horse?"

"Yes," stated Neryn, who had given up trying to keep Alvyx's robe tied shut. He sat in a chair, his lower half hidden by the table cloth. For modesty's sake, of course. Dargah found herself somewhat disappointed, as Neryn's calves had been providing a worthwhile distraction from the evening's troubling events.

Runo appeared equal parts appalled and elated. "You're a horse thief! And how are you going to explain—"

"I will inform the Disciple that I was unable to sleep and took a walk around the compound to clear my head. As I was doing so, I heard unfamiliar and suspicious sounds. I followed them to the stable and happened upon a thief in the process of absconding with Tempest. I pursued, eventually cornering the culprit and returning the animal to its true owner. It is a convincing story, as all of the Remnant already believes that Orlaeth was abducted by some mysterious villains. If they had succeeded in that, why would they not return for other valuables?"

Dargah exchanged a glance with Runo. "You're getting too comfortable with this little white lie thing, my man," he murmured to the elf.

"The truth would result in the discovery of Orlaeth here and her subsequent death, as well as my own, at the hands of our people," Neryn responded sharply. "Would you prefer that? It gives me no pleasure to deceive my spiritual leader."

"Well, my goodness, there are a lot of things I'm learning about just now," Alvyx announced. "But, if I may ask, do either of you have your pendants with you at the moment?" When the elves handed them over, Alvyx smoothed his hands over the stones. Then he whispered something unintelligible to them. When he opened his hands, both of the charms glowed green for the briefest moment, then returned to their soft, eggshell white. "There we go. They've been reset."

"But what *are* they?"

Alvyx chuckled. "They're properly called Empathy Stones, but I've heard them referred to as soulstones, lovers' charms... You don't see them so much anymore, but when my grandfather was a young man, sweethearts would use them to share their most private feelings. They can only be created in pairs. When the charms are held at the same time by both partners, they can convey one's emotional state to each other over a great distance."

"How does one acquire these stones?"

"Are they attuned to their specific owners?"

"How are they made?"

"*How do you know this?*"

Rinah exchanged a glance with Alvyx. When she nodded, he said, "Those pendants were enchanted using rogue magic. Magic that no longer belongs to a mage. It's harvested and used by druids... like me."

Only Orlaeth nodded to herself. The scent, almost undetectable, that she associated with the Autumnsong cottage, was the same one she'd smelled when the orc woman had given Neryn those pendants. It was the fragrance of rogue magic. She chastised herself for not realizing it sooner.

Dargah leaped to her feet. First Vigga's admission of guilt, and now *this*? Merry and absent-minded Alvyx Autunsong, baker of pastries and healer of headaches, was practicing forbidden magic? She'd be laughing if his confession wasn't so reckless. She ran a hand over her face, muffling a curse, and said to Rinah, "So, the entire time I've known you, your father has been engaging in very dangerous and very illegal magic. Magic that has been forbidden specifically because it can kill you. And everyone else around you!"

"Hey," Runo said, his hand on her arm. "Hey, don't. Not now."

Rinah stiffened.

"You may address your concerns to me, Dargah," Alvyx said evenly.

"You're putting Rinah in danger! You're putting *all* of us in danger!" she snapped, slamming both fists on the table. This time, Neryn's hand found its way to her other shoulder.

"*Ifrunn.* I heard Bram's excuse, unreasonable as it was," he murmured to her. "*You* must hear *his*." Then his flickering eyes focused on Alvyx. "Though it may be equally unreasonable."

Realizing that Alvyx would follow Bram headfirst into the tree if Neryn deemed it morally necessary, Dargah was soothed. She held her tongue, but fixed an angry glare at her dear friend's papa.

"If I truly thought my daughter was in danger, do you think I would continue to practice my craft? The druidic arts *can* be deadly, yes. But so can elemental magic!

Now, listen to me before you work yourselves up. The gift of 'recycling magic,' if you will, has been in Argodoth for centuries, and all this ridiculous fear over it isn't going to make it go away. Fate has given me Rinah, and so it is through her that this legacy will continue."

"Also, I just learned he can turn into an owl," Rinah added, her voice small but hopeful.

"Lemme see!" demanded Runo.

"Certainly not. My gifts are not a party trick!"

Runo pouted. "Makoa showed us his party trick!"

"No." Alvyx set his lips in a thin line.

"My true form isn't a party trick!" Makoa objected. "I'm not even allowed to go to parties!"

"See? Papa's being responsible! A careless person would have shown off!" Rinah exclaimed. Then her face hardened. "And he is going to train me, too. I should be able to protect myself. After what happened tonight…"

It was Makoa who spoke next, his words measured and deliberate. "You *did* protect yourself. You didn't need any of us. Not really." He turned an admiring smile on her. "If I think about it, my own life is as unnatural as rogue magic seems to be. Faeries aren't supposed to be *born*. But here I am, and I guess I'm doing all right. Is there a chance it might not be as awful as everyone claims it is?"

"It's been outlawed for centuries," Dargah cried.

"Do you really think that means it hasn't been practiced? That a ban on something so beautiful and so precious could truly be successful?" Alvyx asked her, his tone growing gentler.

"We've all heard the stories," Runo protested, taking up his sister's cause. "Even if you live in a cave, you know about Lady Akeldama and her sister…"

Rinah winced. Of all the stories about rogue magic to mention, Akeldama's was by far the most infamous. Six hundred years ago, she and her twin sister Kasdeya were born to the rulers of Peruuz, in Dehlkia. At the time, leadership was still passed from parent to child, but birth order had nothing to do with inheritance. While the eldest typically took the throne, the reigning emperor and empress could choose any of their brood to rule after them. With orcish families typically being quite large, disputes over the throne were common, and sometimes bloody. Having just the two daughters, the girls' parents determined that the younger, Kasdeya, should ultimately lead Peruuz. Infuriated at what she took as a slight, Akeldama sought an assassin to dispatch her sister. Wisely fearing retribution, even the bravest warriors refused her. Except for one.

Half-orc and half-everything else, Sammot Raseri was bold enough to openly approach Kasdeya during her installment as Empress. In the sight of the entire royal family, visiting dignitaries, and commoners alike, he released his rogue magic and, unpredictable as it was, it ended the lives of everyone in the room, including Akeldama. Those beyond the throne room were spared, but devastated by the loss. Many never recovered from the shock. But the mage's body was never found. Old orcish tales whisper that the goddess forbade him from entering the Other Realm, and he still roams the land as a haunt, regretting that, although he received his payment before the deed had been done, he was unable to enjoy his profits.

It wasn't long after that the use of rogue magic was deemed the highest form of treason in Dehlkia. Within fifty years, the rest of Argodoth had followed suit, worried that druidic assassins lurked behind every palace door, brewing rebellion and nurturing anarchy.

"Paranoia drove us underground," Alvyx replied. "And common sense will, someday, allow us to rise again. But for now, I practice in secret. You know me, Dargah. I harbor no desire to use my gifts to harm." The half-orc looked as though she were about to protest again, but he continued, "Hear me. Please. Rogue magic and elemental magic differ in one crucial way. Elemental magic relies on the physical strength of its user. A sickly man, no matter how well-trained, is a poor elemental mage. But rogue magic, now that—*that* is a different creature! It is tied to the *emotional* fortitude of its user. Only the strong of mind can control it. The foolish can barely sense it, much less understand it. 'Unnatural' you may say, but I say it is the gods' gift. A way for the impurely-born to possess magic of their own. Compensation, if you will, for being born 'less than'." He looked squarely at Neryn, as though the elf's appearance alone made him guilty of persecution.

It was Orlaeth who, seemingly unfazed by the night's endless revelations, cocked her head and glanced around the room. "Are there any other life-threatening secrets clamoring for utterance this evening?"

"I wore a women's corset once," Runo volunteered.

"*Life-threatening*," repeated Neryn.

"I almost couldn't breathe. I could have died."

"Aren't *all* corsets women's corsets?" asked Rinah.

"I can tell that you, little lady, have never been to the tavern at Lavender Wells," Runo said with a wink.

Dargah shook her head. "Stop it! This isn't a joke. Just *knowing* that Alvyx practices rogue magic puts all of us in the line of fire. You *know* that Zealots still sweep through border towns after every Adoration, ears to the ground for death mages."

"It is a holy rite for them, an ancient custom that is more habitual than anything else." Neryn noted. "I cannot recall hearing of a true druid being taken in over two hundred years. Is that accurate, Orlaeth?"

She seemed to process his question, skimming through endless tomes locked in her mind. "A male half-dwarf was found to be practicing the art two-hundred-and-nineteen years ago in a village on the border of Kaylor and Dehlkia. He was put to death by stoning after a prolonged trial. To my knowledge, that is the most recent incident."

"Well, they'll never find Papa," Rinah said with unusual harshness.

"Considering Miss Autumnsong's injuries, the lateness of the hour, and my own need to take my leave shortly, this might be a discussion best saved for another time," Neryn suggested. "But you have my vow that I will never breathe a word of this to anyone."

Dargah whirled on him. "You! *You,* of all people, I'd expect to be leading the charge against rogue mages! Aren't they the ultimate slap in the face of the gods? Not *only* do they have mixed blood, but—but they…" Confused by the elf's contrite expression, she faltered, then turned to Alvyx and Rinah. "Look. I couldn't possibly care less that you're doing something *illegal*," she told them. "I just hate the idea of you risking so much for—for what, exactly? What's the point?"

"For the sake of tradition. Of history. Of remembering and honoring the mages who came before us. For keeping a bit of them alive inside of us long after their souls depart. We do this for the greater good, ultimately. For the hope that still lives within me, that my gift will not be considered a crime forever." Alvyx's tone was soft and thoughtful. "And also, it satisfies the rebellious streak I never outgrew."

Dargah sighed. "I guess everyone's shown their hands tonight. Now we're stuck with each other for good."

"What are you saying?"

"Neryn, you're a full-blooded elf-prince... magistrate—"

He straightened a bit. "Counselor and Suppliant Prime."

"—high-and-mighty advisor, lying to your leader and spending time with grubby peasants like us. Plus, now you're a horse thief, I guess."

"Horse thief! Horse thief!" Runo cheered.

"I will be returning the horse to its rightful owner within a reasonable timeframe."

Runo sulked.

"And Makoa—he's not supposed to exist. I mean, we're not supposed to *know* he exists. He's not even a normal Guardian. Which you did a great job with tonight, Makoa, the guarding thing, so thank you. Alvyx practices a very secret, very *forbidden* magic that, if used incorrectly, can kill him. Or us. At the very least, makes them liable to attract the wrong kind of attention from Zealots. And now Rinah's going along for the ride."

"Papa is very responsible!" Rinah protested again.

"How responsible is it to spill a secret like that in a room half-filled with strangers?" Neryn queried.

Squelching her appreciation for his comment, Dargah continued. "And Runo is…" He turned his puppy eyes on her. Dargah resisted. "Runo is a runaway, I guess. And since I didn't send him home, I suppose that means *I'm* harboring a refugee or something. And Orlaeth… Orlaeth is *dead*. So. I guess we've all got secrets."

"Running away isn't a *secret*, really. It's a lifestyle choice."

"Shut up, Runo," said Neryn.

"Nothing that was said tonight leaves this room." All eyes turned to her, and Dargah lifted her chin confidently. "*Nothing.* We're in potential danger, one way or another. So we all need to watch each other's backs."

"Ooh, we're like a *secret club!*" Runo shouted, jumping up from his chair.

Rinah's eyes darted to the open windows. "Not anymore, we aren't. My gods, you're loud."

"A guild!" he continued. "Like a real guild! We already have a code of conduct: Keep each other's secrets and keep each other safe!"

"That's not a guild! That's just what normal people do to take care of each other," Dargah groaned.

"But!" Runo lifted a scone into the air as if proposing a toast. "But *we*, my beautiful and brawny spinster of a sister—we are *not* normal people!"

Part Two

Chapter Twenty-Two:

Of Charms and Changes

A damp blanket of heat hung over Lindenvale, slowing the typical bustle of daily life to a listless crawl. Here and there, an overworked bumblebee fell asleep inside a flower. Doors and windows had been flung open as families prayed for the slightest draft to flow through their houses. Most everyone struggled through the day, desperate for moonrise and the blessed relief of cooler evening air.

Rinah Autumnsong, too, awaited sunset, but it was not for the peaceful calm of a refreshing twilight breeze. She was expecting a night-time visitor.

Before Makoa left for his colony on the night of Bram's attack, Alvyx had invited him—and all of his daughter's "saviors"—to weekly suppers at the cottage. To keep an eye on him, of course, he added playfully. Neryn politely refused, as he would need to return to Dirgil. Orlaeth accepted, with the understanding that at least part of the meal would be free of animal products. Runo and Dargah accepted because they were both too smart to pass up a free meal, and they enjoyed the sense of family they felt at the Autumnsong cottage. Ultimately, the fear of forbidden magic didn't change that.

And Makoa—he'd accepted because he had nothing better to do.

It had been so blisteringly hot lately that neither Alvyx nor Rinah could bring themselves to stoke the hearth to bake or roast. They'd settled for simpler meals of juicy fruit, crisp vegetables, and cheese, and that was what would be on the menu again this evening.

At last, dusk fell in a lavender-blue haze, and Rinah found herself growing anxious as she sat on the iron garden bench. She toyed with the linen shirt and soft trousers in her lap. Alvyx's old pants just wouldn't do anymore for Makoa. She had asked Qadira, the local tailor, to use her discretion regarding the cut and style, as long as it was comfortable.

"Rinah?"

Everything inside her body, and her then body itself, leaped at the sound of his whisper. Rinah turned and saw a shadowy figure peeking out from behind a tree.

"Hi," Makoa said.

She grinned in response and presented the new clothes to him. "Surprise! I hope they fit. I had to guess your measurements." He reached out and snatched them up. A moment later, he emerged from behind the tree with a delighted smile. Even an ordinary tunic and trousers couldn't dull his peculiar beauty. "Thank you," he said, fingering the buttons at the cuffs. "This is so nice!"

"I hope it's all right to talk a little before everyone else arrives for supper? Um, just us?"

"Sure!" Makoa plopped himself on one of the benches.

Rinah opened with, "After getting to know you a little better, you're not what I would have expected a faerie to be like."

He tilted his head like a bird. "What did you expect?"

"I don't really know. When I was a little girl, I used to imagine that I had a magic ring that shrank me down to the size of a mouse, and then I went dancing with the faeries at night." She smiled wistfully. "I guess I assumed you'd be more... whimsical."

"Well, for one thing, we don't dance at night. Nighttime is when we usually perform our blood sacrifices." When Rinah's face blanched, Makoa laughed. "I'm kidding. I'm sorry. I shouldn't mess with you. But no, mostly, we sleep at night. Same as you. There's always a few of us from every colony on patrol at night to refresh our wards, but we're just not as interesting as some of the stories, I guess."

"I didn't say you weren't interesting," corrected Rinah. "Just not what I expected."

"I *can* dance at night if you'd like to." He stood swiftly, extending a hand and offering a little bow.

What was this creature, truly? The first night he'd appeared in the shadows, he looked and sounded like a commanding god, a mysterious knight ready to defend her honor. But in the soft glow of lantern light, he was revealed as a pale, tattooed, lean young man with flaming orange hair and a smile a little too big for his face. He looked so much younger than he'd sounded in that moment he'd first spoken—the moment that, admittedly, made Rinah want to weep with relief.

"I'm too clumsy," she laughed, waving his hand away. "I'll step on your feet and break your toes."

"Whew. Good. I don't actually know how to dance, either. We can maybe not dance together another time, then?"

"I'd be honored," she giggled. "I suppose, at some point, I should invite you in for a proper tea. One where everyone has clothes on, start to finish. Could you manage that?"

"That kind of tea is an afternoon thing, isn't it? I can't come visit during the day," he said, a bit forlornly. "To be honest, I'm not supposed to be here at night, either."

"But you said you patrol this area at night."

"By here, I mean *here*. With you."

"Me… personally?" She pitched her voice to sound only the slightest bit curious.

"Uh, you know, with any of the Created races." He looked away. "There's kind of a code of conduct the Guardians follow. We're just supposed to protect the land and the important stuff, right? Drakes make sure that people aren't getting greedy mining for ores and gemstones. Nixies make sure that lakes and rivers stay clean. Golems make sure that the land isn't overworked.

Faeries protect the forest. And, the thing is, none of *you* are supposed to ever see any of *us*."

"Then… why…?" Rinah tried to arrange her thoughts. "Why did you let me see you that night? Let all of us see you? Could you get in trouble or something?"

"You needed help."

"I would have been all right, though, because of the tansy—"

"I didn't know about the tansy."

Rinah knew that Alvyx would be calling them inside shortly. She hurried on. "Can all Guardian races shift? There's so many stories about you, but I don't know which ones are true. Maybe none of them are."

"We can all shift. This body is kind of the standard—we all wind up looking kind of human-ish. We've all got these wards on our skin. They're used to

444

defend our homes and they allow us to go unseen by anyone Created." He lifted his sleeves to point out the detailed tattoos on his arms. "They don't disappear when we shift, but they don't work anymore, either. We can't access our magic in these bodies, so it's kind of pointless."

"Except when you're rescuing helpless women, who aren't really helpless at all?"

Makoa placed a finger over her lips, and her cheeks warmed. "My turn to ask a question," he announced. "How are your lessons coming along?"

Rinah forced a smile. Learning that her papa was a rogue mage hadn't been as shocking to her as it had been to her friends. The signs had been there all along, she realized—Alvyx's odd, middle-of-the-night treks into the forest and the vaguely mysterious old journal he still thought she didn't know about, for starters. Still, she had been reluctant to learn the art. Dargah was right; it might put her friends in danger. But Papa had insisted. If he'd have taught her earlier, she would have been able to throw Bram into a tree herself. He reasoned that, even if she spent years training with the men of the garrison, she'd never have the kind of physical strength to defend herself like Dargah could. Rogue magic could not only keep her safe, but she could use it to keep others safe, too. That was what had finally convinced Rinah—the promise that she could have a resource in addition to her medical knowledge, to help people in need. "I have a lot to learn," she admitted.

Just then, Alvyx rapped on the window. "If you two don't come in, Runo is going to eat everything himself!"

Dargah, Runo, and Orlaeth had arrived, unnoticed by Rinah, and were already choosing their favorites from the spread on the table. Makoa pointed to each snack he hadn't seen before, asking Rinah about it. "Those almonds have been seasoned with salt and garlic. They're savory. And this is groundnut paste. I like to dip vegetables in it. Or have it on a biscuit, with blueberry preserves. What do faeries usually eat, anyway?"

"Whatever we find. But when your stomach is the size of a pea, you don't need much."

"So your whole colony could survive on, say, a single onion?" Runo appeared unreasonably intrigued by this.

"We *could*... but... why would we?" Makoa spat out his tongue in disgust.

"Has anyone heard from Neryn recently?" Alvyx asked as the group settled into their customary seats—Dargah, Makoa, Rinah, and himself at the table, Orlaeth in the armchair, and Runo sprawled across the sofa.

"It's not like he can mosey on down here wherever he wants," Dargah said, breaking an apple in half. "He's got all kinds of important things to do, like reminding everyone else how unimportant they are."

"That is unkind," Orlaeth stated. "It is also untrue."

Dargah looked up from her meal. "He might be sweet as pie to you, but you don't know the things he said to me, Orlaeth. You don't know how hard he tried to make me feel disgusting just by being alive."

Alvyx replied calmly, "Counselor Sunstorm will always be welcome in this home for the kindness he has done for Rinah—and for Orlaeth. That does not excuse anything improper he has said to you. However, should he take us up on the offer to join us, at any time, I hope that you can treat him with civility for the length of one meal, at least. And that he can do the same."

"I'm willing to play nice if he is," she replied, drowning the apple in a dish of nut paste.

"Speaking of playing, Ioanie told me that those play-actors from Granaat, y'know, the ones who performed at Ayusa's Adoration? They're coming back in autumn!"

448

Runo crowed. "You should come, Makoa! The Adoration of Dehlkia is the biggest, most beautiful celebration there is."

"You haven't even seen it here yet," laughed Rinah.

"I'll see what I can do," the faerie said, mimicking Dargah's treatment of the apple. He bit into it with a messy crunch. "Oh, this *is* good!"

"It's even better with honey," she told him, drizzling some on both their apples.

"Everything is," agreed Runo.

*

The rest of the evening passed with little fanfare. Orlaeth excused herself early, as usual, as she rose before dawn to meditate and pray and retired before the others. Runo leaped to his feet and gallantly offered to walk her home. Dargah followed soon after, reluctantly apologizing to Rinah for her comment about Neryn. And then Alvyx settled back in his chair. "Will you read, my dear?' he asked his daughter with a yawn.

"Of course. What would you like?"

"Let Makoa choose something."

The faerie pointed to a random book on the shelf. "That one."

Rinah pulled it, then broke into a smile. "Elpida gave me this for my fifth birthday. Do you remember?" She showed the cover to Alvyx, who smiled. "You read from it to me every night for years."

"Long, long after you learned how to read all by yourself," he chuckled.

Makoa perched on the sofa, not touching Rinah as he did so. "Is it a good book?"

"You can decide for yourself," Rinah offered. "'A long time ago, when the world was new, and the Gods

Below were as yet unborn, Unseen One wandered the lifeless mists of Argodoth. He called forth the waters, and the essence of Ayusa arose from the deep. The Unseen One crafted her body from seafoam and starlight and gave her the moon for a lover. Ever-changing and relentless as the tide, Ayusa was nothing like her fellow gods. Dehlkia crafted her people from clay and fertile soil; Kaylor's were hewn from rock and gemstone; Erjunn's were formed from the crystals that gather where clouds kiss the sky; Ayusa had no interest in creating a people until she learned that they would worship her. She dabbled in sand and saltwater, cobbling humans together in her own image—lean of torso and long of limb, with serpentine tails and hair like snakes. Realizing that they could rule the sea but never dwell on land, she cast them back onto the shore and split their tails, leaving them with two legs and an endless desire to return to the oceans in which they were born. Ayusa ignored her children for an age, ashamed that they seemed in every way less than the children of the other gods. They were clumsy where the elves were graceful, fearful where the orcs were bold, and foolish where the dwarves were cunning. Ayusa did not understand that the other gods had poured their own gifts into their children. Where Erjunn sought peace among his people, Ayusa cared little about how humans behaved, as long as she received their worship. Where Kaylor was stubborn and fierce, teaching his children about courage and resourcefulness, Ayusa was mellow and changeable. Where Dehlkia was sensual and grounded, teaching her children about family and community, Ayusa was childlike and fanciful. She loved beautiful things, and so when she finally deigned to walk among her creations, she taught them about art. Sculpture, painting and poetry, dance and weaving, and drawing. Every gift she gave her people, she gave so that it would inevitably return to her in the form of something she could see, or hear, or touch and enjoy. Ayusa's vanity would lead her to sorrow. As the other gods taught their peoples how to grow crops, care for animals, or work in partnership with the natural world, Ayusa simply wanted beauty. And so, while humans became the finest artisans in all of Argodoth, working with wood and metal and glass and stone, they did not learn how to care for themselves, the land, or each other.

"The Unseen One was deeply disappointed that humans had been left to fend for themselves, and so he tore from Ayusa her lover, placing the moon forever out of her reach. And that is why, even today, the moon draws the sea and tells the tides when to ebb and when to flow. It is Ayusa responding to the calling of her beloved but unable to feel his embrace. To ensure that humans survived, the Unseen One asked the other gods to send some of their children into Ayusa's lands, that they would do what the goddess had failed to do—teach them practical skills about farming and livestock and building. The result was that humans indeed learned how to build a civilization on more than beauty alone, and they welcomed the customs and cultures of other people into Ayusa. Because of this, because of the humans' embrace of and partnering with elves, orcs, and dwarves, Ayusa's people have fewer mages among them. Her punishment continues to this day, but she is proud and unbroken. She yet reaches for her lover nightly and watches, unaffected, as water magic fades from Argodoth. But her people still create art so beautiful, it stirs the soul and leads to tears—saltwater, like Ayusa's seas—and brings about emotion and passion and change. Her mark is left on the world, regardless of her vanity, and so, in the end, her influence remains. It is said that Ayusa's vanity still runs in the veins of humans, most often seen in young women who view themselves as art to be admired and never made to work.'" Rinah closed the book, realizing only then that her papa was softly snoring in his chair.

"Not you, though," Makoa said quietly to her, eying the sleeping man.

"Not me what?"

"Not you, you're not a vain human."

Rinah smiled at what she assumed was supposed to be a compliment. "Well, first of all, I'm not actually a pure-blooded human. I don't know my heritage. And second, yes, unfortunately, I *am* vain."

He shifted to sit a bit closer, still not touching her. "How?"

She hugged her knees to her chest and rested her head against the back of the sofa. "That's kind of what got me into trouble with Bram in the first place," she admitted. She couldn't look at Makoa, so she just focused on the flickering lantern above her. "When he first showed up in town, he seemed interested in me right away. And I was sort of surprised. I mean, I think he's handsome and he was so friendly, and the fact that he wanted to get to know *me* more than anyone else... It made me feel special. I wanted to hold on to that feeling, so..." Rinah paused, then took a deep breath. Not a day had passed that she'd not experienced a flash of humiliation, remembering how Bram had cruelly betrayed her trust. "So I sort of ignored the other feelings. The bad ones. The disrespect I felt when he talked down to me like I didn't know anything. The embarrassment when he"—she closed her eyes—"tried to make me do things I didn't want to do. I was so excited to be wanted and admired that I stopped... *thinking*." She dared a glance at Makoa, and he was closer still, clear amber eyes wide with emotion. It was then that she realized how easy it had been to spill her thoughts to him, like she'd known him for years.

He said, "I don't think that wanting to feel special is the same thing as being vain. I don't know everything about humans, but that kind of seems normal to me, to want that."

"How long have you studied humans? And do you usually do it by watching women bathing by moonlight?" she asked with a soft laugh.

He went red. "First of all, I apologized for that. And second, no, I don't. And third... I'm not *supposed* to study them at all."

"You said you're not supposed to *show* yourself," she reminded him.

"Yeah." He snuck another glance at Alvyx, then flipped his focus back to her. "So why would Bram treat you like you don't know anything? You know lots of things. Last week, you taught me about all the different earthworms in your garden."

Rinah had to clap a hand over her laugh to keep from waking her papa. "That's not really what I meant, but I'm glad you enjoyed it. Earthworms are deeply underappreciated creatures. What I *should* have said is that the way he talked to me made me feel like I wasn't capable of thinking for myself."

"I'm sorry he did that to you."

"Me, too."

"I should leave," Makoa eventually said, not standing up.

"And I should try to get some sleep," Rinah agreed, unmoving.

They sat in a calm, comfortable silence for a while, then Rinah asked, "Did you mean it?"

"Mean what?"

"You told Bram that if he touched me again, you'd kill him. But you're not allowed to do something like that as a Guardian, are you? You don't have that kind of power. You were just trying to scare him."

He stood and stretched. "As a Guardian, my only duty is to protect the valuable and the irreplaceable." He gave her a smile. "See you next week." He performed his dazzling disappearing act, and his clothes crumpled to the floor. A pair of sunset-orange wings glided out through the window. Rinah began to clear the table, pretending she didn't notice her own flushed skin or racing heartbeat.

*

To outsiders, it seemed that Orlaeth enjoyed her work at the library to a concerning degree. She performed her copywriting with tremendous speed and accuracy, with minimal requests for assistance or clarification. While Mr. Naoum's quaint library was not as deathly silent as the archival room in Dirgil or the Cloisters in Reefside, it possessed a similar atmosphere, one in which guests felt it necessary to speak in soft, gentle tones, to treat the books and scrolls with reverence, and to refrain from disturbing any other visitors with small talk or boisterous greetings.

It was as close to the promised peace of the Other Realm as Orlaeth was going to find in Ayusa. Every time she saw Rinah—every single time—Orlaeth made sure to mention that she was humbled and grateful that Rinah had been willing to ask Mr. Naoum to hire a complete stranger.

Her time at the library was fulfilling and enriching and provided the structure and routine she craved.

Today, she had finished her most ambitious assignment to date—a copy of the earliest-known genealogy chart of Kaylor's nine original tribes. The papers were delicate and faded; she had to cross-reference many of the dates for accuracy. The project had taken her three weeks, and she had delighted in every minute of it, often requesting to remain in the library to work long after Mr. Naoum had locked the door and gone home to bed.

And during these nights, when the room was cool and dark, and her lanterns flickered eerily, Orlaeth would close her eyes and invoke memories of her father.

Maolyr Silverwillow was a soft-spoken and gentle man. He was brave, too, remarkably brave, for even suggesting to the Disciple that his little girl, so gifted with such a steady hand and keen eyes, might accompany him—only sometimes, of course—as he traveled Argodoth, searching for the materials and resources that the Disciple requested.

Perhaps Kaedryn could sense that Maolyr was willing to resign from his role if his precious daughter was not permitted to assist him. Perhaps, for a brief moment, the Disciple chose to ignore the fact that Orlaeth was a female, for after he saw her work, he could not deny its excellence. Or, perhaps, sweet Erjunn had whispered in his ear that this time with her father would be critical in allowing Orlaeth to reach her full potential in serving her Disciple and her future mate, whoever he may be.

Regardless, Maolyr's impossible wish was granted, and his too-small daughter, with her too-large eyes, would follow him to study collections in every corner of Argodoth, but most often, to the Archives located in the Ayusan capital of Reefside. There, Orlaeth disappeared into the Cloisters, a branch of the Archives managed solely by water mage acolytes and containing documentation irrelevant to Maolyr's assignments. On some days, he would take his child to the Sisters there, asking permission for her to sit and read while he worked elsewhere. Males were not permitted in the heart of the Cloisters, so if research did have to be done there, Orlaeth would have to perform it on her own anyway.

Oh, how she had loved the ladies in Reefside! A few of them, like fussing mother hens, had taken her under their collective wing, sitting with her and letting her ask them everything she wanted about anything she wanted. They did not ask her to keep quiet or mind her posture or walk with silent footsteps. They allowed her to read any book, any scroll, any parchment that caught her fancy. And one of the ladies, the one whom she had come to adore like the favorite aunt she never had, presented her with a book she had prayed for, silently, of course, each and every day since she'd turned six years old—*The Education and Training of Wind Mages: Spells, Incantations, and Enchantments.*

She had been given an invaluable gift. Orlaeth had spent days reading and rereading, devouring the knowledge therein as though it were a feast, and she, a starving beggar. The only thing she must remember, the beautiful-eyed Sister had told her, was that she must keep all the knowledge inside her brain and never let anyone—not even her father—know it lived there. Orlaeth had promised, promised on her life, promised on her future husband's life, promised on her future children's lives, that she would never let slip the precious, secret knowledge that she'd been given.

And then Orlaeth would open her eyes, the memories fading like a dream upon waking. She would again look around, at the neat stacks and rows of books, at the orderly row of quills and inkwells and styluses and charcoal, lined up perfectly at the edge of Mr. Naoum's desk, at the soft, comfortable chairs that he had spent so much money on, in the hopes that the atmosphere would entice guests to stay longer and perhaps purchase a book.

And Orlaeth would smile. For the first time in her life, Orlaeth Silverwillow felt at home and happy.

Chapter Twenty-Three:

Of Delight and Drudgery

"What is the forest telling you?"

Perched on a fallen log, Rinah closed her eyes and slowed her breathing. She heard the cheery one-note greeting of the cardinal. The rustle of a light breeze through the trees. The crunching of pebbles underneath Alvyx's boots as he circled her. She smelled the wet, earthy scent of the morning's rain and felt the weight of humidity settling in her hair. And there, the distinct, musky odor of fox droppings—she hoped Alvyx hadn't stepped in a fresh pile. She felt the wind picking up a bit, felt its damp caress on her face. Felt the rough bark of the log flaking beneath her hands.

She waited.

And waited.

There it was, just underneath the sounds of the birds and the wind—the sound of magic. It wasn't audible, not quite. More of a vibration. The thrum of ancient power. The traces of magic left behind when death came to claim the mages.

Magic itself could not die, Alvyx taught her. When a mage died, his power returned to its source—the god or goddess who had gifted it. But traces still existed, leaking from the objects left behind and the people influenced by the magic. It was a part of Argodoth now.

And this pool of leftover magic was the source from which druids drew their strength.

Leeches, the ancient druids were called. Vultures devouring carrion. Half-breeds and patchworks, siphoning and manipulating magic that was never theirs to possess. Many pure-bloods had looked down their noses at those they deemed "grave-digging augurs," openly criticizing them. To protect themselves, even before their art was outlawed, druids rarely practiced their magic in public. In private, however, Alvyx's lessons were long, involved, and informative.

And already, Rinah had learned how to catch rogue magic quicker than the village children could catch colds.

It was different from elemental magic, of course. It had been broken down into its basest form—the power of suggestion—and had lost direct connection with the element it had once ruled. No longer could these fragments of magic call forth windstorms or rain, but they still contained power.

And druids harvested that power. Harnessed it. Shaped it.

Just as a water mage could draw droplets of the ocean with a command, a druid, with enough magic, could wrap it around himself like a cloak and appear to others as he needed to appear. The power of manipulation was strong enough that a well-trained druid's magic could convince even his own body to change according to his will, or rather, the will of the magic. A well-trained, talented druid could take the form of an animal in order to view the world in a new and different way. Or to carry out a secretive mission.

And this, of course, was why they were so dangerous. One could never tell; the squirrel, oddly unafraid of human children, could be a druid. The hawk circling overhead could be, too. Horrifyingly, even the freshly caught, wriggling salmon on the fisherman's pole could be a druid.

One would *hope* he would return to his original form before being tossed into a sizzling pan.

Alvyx was the nephew of a rogue mage who had himself been taught by a grandmother. The beauty of their gift, he had been told, was that pure-bloods could *not* wield it. And that it was, in a way, a service. A recycling of elemental magic into new things, new forms. And why would that not please the gods? Dehlkia was the patroness of rebirth and renewal. Erjunn was the master of wisdom. Ayusa was called the Hand of the Arts, and even the moody Kaylor's teachings urge his followers to carefully steward one's magic, as well as one's surroundings. A druid's magic honors all the gods.

And that, of course, was what terrified those in power—that the gods allowed such magic to exist at all. It was, to many, an abomination. Not unlike half-bloods themselves.

"What is the forest telling you, child?" Alvyx repeated.

An unseen warmth dusted her shoulders, as comforting as the feeling of settling into a cozy bed. A current of excitement brewed just beneath it, the jittery joy of catching up with a long-lost friend. Rinah drew in a sharp breath. "The forest is… greeting me."

"Yes, Rinah. The forest is welcoming you home."

"Papa, I… feel like I belong to it."

"You belong to the forest as much as any wild animal does. You're a part of it. Tell me. Does the magic here want to be a part of you?"

"I think so. Can I ask it?"

"Remember what I taught you."

Rinah took a moment to clear her thoughts. She wanted the magic to feel safe with her. She sent a greeting its way—warmth, the affection in an embrace, the sweetness of honey in a mug of hot tea, the softness of a favorite quilt on a rainy afternoon, the peaceful joy of a holiday with friends.

And the magic responded.

Rinah gasped as she felt it—cautiously at first, then with excitement—flow underneath her skin and into her blood, racing through her body faster than she could blink. It felt like soap bubbles filling her from toes to crown. She couldn't help but giggle as she tried to explain the sensation to Alvyx.

He smiled. "Ah. The magic of a child," he guessed. "Young mages find such delight in their gifts that the first thing they tend to do is use them to make others laugh. A child's magic is innocent, unhindered by so many of the troubles that trip us up as we grow."

Rinah's face fell. "But if a *child's* magic is here... oh, Papa. It feels wrong to claim something so precious."

"It wouldn't be here if it didn't want to be claimed."

She pictured a child mage trying to show off for his friends. She was sure she'd have done the same, had she been born pure-blooded. "Is magic able to... to *think*, like we do? Express emotions?"

Alvyx sat next to her on the log. "In a way. When mages die, sometimes, the magic chooses to stay with its mage for a while. Not inside the corpse, mind you—goodness, that's morbid!—but unseen, as though it is keeping guard. You know that. And, highly skilled druids might even notice it, shimmering just on the edge of their vision, like a cloud in a necropolis or graveyard."

"Which is why people used to accuse druids of being grave robbers or necromancers."

"Some were. Gave us all a bad name." Alvyx forced a grin. "That's a story for another time. As for the magic you just adopted... well, sometimes, magic makes something of a pilgrimage. It returns to the place where it felt most connected with its mage. Like a memorial. That's what I think happened in this case."

"So this is not necessarily where the child died or is buried?" Rinah's relief was evident in her shaky smile. "I don't like the idea of trampling on a child's grave." When she took another look at her surroundings, she noticed things that a child might play with: several colorful rocks, just visible beneath a pile of dried leaves, long, straight sticks and branches that might have been imaginary swords or staffs, and a handful of acorns, not yet gobbled up by hungry wildlife.

"It was recent. Not even a week ago." The magic tried to cheer her, but she couldn't shake the solemnity of the moment. "It was a little human boy, I think, and he had just begun to train. He played here with his friends."

"Magic doesn't often reveal much about its former mage. But sometimes, you can get a sense of them, just by how the magic reacts to you."

In spite of the rogue magic's innocence and the forest's reassuring welcome, Rinah shivered. It felt like she was intruding on something sacred. She stood abruptly. "Can we be finished for today?"

"Yes. Do you want to hold onto this magic, or would you rather release it?"

Rinah hesitated. "It's gentle. It feels… happy. But I don't want to take on any more until I've gotten used to it."

"No, of course not. Sit with these morsels for a bit. Let them get used to you."

Chapter Twenty-Four:

Of Amends and Audacity

Neryn had not been surprised to learn that Dargah had been promoted at the local smithy; now the half-orc was its supervisor. But it was not she who welcomed him into the shop. It was a shorter, broad, leathery-skinned woman who appeared to have dwarf blood. Ah, yes. It was Vigga, the smith whose nephew he had... handled. She looked a bit different in the light of day. Older. Angrier. She gave him the once-over, then cracked a smile.

"The blessed spirit of retribution," she said softly. "At least you smell better than when we last met. What is it you're needing today?"

Neryn unsheathed the simple dagger at his side and presented it to Vigga. "My blade appears to have met a tragic fate," he lamented. "I doubt it can be repaired."

Her lip curled in disdain. Vigga didn't even touch the weapon. "You are correct. First of all, that thing is no better than scrap metal, and second, even if it was decent-quality steel, I couldn't smooth the nicks and chips out without taking some serious length off the blade." She paused to glance at her new supervisor. "And, after all, what good is a man with a stunted blade, eh, Dargah?"

The half-orc raised an eyebrow at Vigga, flicked a glance Neryn's way, then returned to her anvil.

"A new one, then? Will that take long?" he asked.

"I suppose that depends on how much you're willing to pay."

Neryn counted seven coins and dropped them into the woman's rough hand.

"For that kind of investment, it will be done after lunch," she murmured.

"Ah. Lunch. Have you any recommendations on where one might find a good meal in town?"

Vigga stretched, her back aching. "Depends on what you're looking for. Ayusan high society food? Across the river at Lady Tilia's. It's popular but not to my taste. If you're happy with simple fare, there's a few peddlers that sell street food in the square in the afternoon. And Ioanie's place is not far. Turn left as you leave, then about two blocks down toward the river. Can't miss it."

"Adelfi's Inn? Yes, I have visited it before."

"A regular, are you?"

He smiled tersely. "Not yet."

"Are you spending the night with us?" Dargah asked.

Both Vigga and Neryn turned surprised faces her way.

Irritated by the mischievous glint in Vigga's eye, she added, "What I mean is, if you're going to be at Adelfi's this evening anyway, I'll just bring your dagger over when it's done. You don't need to come back to bother us."

"I had planned on leaving this afternoon. But I might be persuaded to rent a room, especially if the food there is as good as you say. Tragically, during my previous visits here, I was unable to stomach a thing." Neryn did not meet Dargah's glare. "Good day, then."

As he left, he heard Dargah hiss, "Don't trust him, Vigga. I know he stood up for Rinah, and I'm grateful he did. But don't trust him."

"Who said anything about trusting him? If he's got coin, he's got coin. I'm not going to turn away a paying customer. Not in this economy. But, to tell you the truth, money doesn't matter. We're making that boy the finest dagger we're capable of." She lowered her voice, forcing Dargah to lean toward her, and Neryn's ears to twitch with embarrassment when he realized he was eavesdropping. "The letter Bram's mother sent me when he arrived home was so scathing, so absolutely *vicious,* that I pinned it next to my bed. That way, the first thing I read every morning reminds me of how I'm apparently ruining her life. It starts the day off right. So, no, maybe I don't trust the elf, but goodness, my girl, I do like the way he does things."

*

"Well, damn. He showed up after all."

Runo followed his sister's line of vision to witness a tall, broad-shouldered male enter the inn. There was no question that it was Neryn Sunstorm. He wore a cloak to conceal his features, but there weren't a lot of people who

479

walked with that kind of stiff-backed confidence. Even while attempting to skulk. Also, who wore a *cloak* in this impossible heat?

"Huh," Runo remarked, wiping down the bar counter.

"He stopped at the forge this morning, too," Dargah answered, swallowing the dregs of her beverage. She pulled a package from her satchel and slapped it on the counter. "This is for him. No charge. I'll be in my room." She eased herself off the stool. "I'm not interested in being insulted today."

Before Dargah could escape, Neryn called her name.

"I don't think my sister wants to talk to you," Runo said, stepping out from behind the bar and placing himself between Neryn and Dargah. He looked up at the elf's face, then gave him a too-friendly smile, all teeth. "I'm happy to get you something to drink. It'd be nice to catch up with you. Where's your buddy, the shorter one? Titania?"

"Tiarnán. And no, thank you. I am not here for social purposes."

"Of course you aren't," agreed Runo in a very Dargah-like tone. "Oh, how nice it would be if somebody just stopped by to say hello to me. No one ever asks me how I am."

"How *are* you?" Neryn asked testily.

Runo radiated excitement as he said, "Fantastic! Last week, Ioanie let me sing again when the guy she had scheduled got sick. It was great! Not the guy getting sick. I mean, dysentery is no joke, but—"

Neryn's eyes darted back to the stairs, but Dargah had taken advantage of her brother's chatty nature and was gone.

"While I am *always* pleased to speak with a fellow musician," Neryn bristled, "I very much need to talk to your sister at the moment."

Runo fidgeted. As an employee of the inn, it was his job to keep his guests happy. And he didn't want to cause any kind of fuss for Miss Ioanie. On the other hand, he knew what kind of bodily havoc his sister, when upset, could wreak with bare hands alone. He opened his mouth to tell Neryn to shove it, but something in the elf's eyes was so desperate that he reconsidered, rapping on the wall to get Dargah's attention.

She returned with a moody frown for Neryn. "You missed the human Zealots. They were here a week and a half ago, lecturing us on the dangers of rogue magic and its practitioners. Too holy to even set foot in this place. You'd have *loved* them."

The elf exercised every ounce of his remaining patience as he asked, through clenched teeth, "May we please speak privately?"

"I'd rather not be alone with you, Neryn."

He reacted as though she'd slapped him. "Have I given you reason to suspect that I would treat you inappropriately?"

She leaned against the wall, crossing her arms. "Oh, I'm not worried for myself. You'd rather gnaw your own fingers off than touch me. I'm worried for *you*, elf. If there are no witnesses, I might be tempted to get in a little target practice." She mimed hurling a dagger at his face.

"I am choosing to ignore that, as what I have to say I will share with no one else."

"Oh. You 'need' me. That's cute." She rolled her eyes and tossed to Runo, "If our pretty friend isn't back down here in five minutes, feel free to send Ikraam up to escort him out."

To the elf, Runo added, "He's courting Ionie, so he's really careful to keep *vermin* outta the place, you know?" He waved at the colossal, tea-sipping orc across the room. Ah, yes, Neryn remembered him. In a stunning display of determination, the wooden chair beneath him managed to bear his weight. The orc met Runo's gaze and then leveled a malevolent stare at Neryn, who, to his credit, simply jerked his chin in greeting. Then, with some amount of caution, he followed Dargah to the second floor, where Ioanie's permanent lodgers stayed.

*

Her small room did not have the stark, bleak atmosphere Neryn had expected. Instead, an oversized, vividly colored quilt covered her bed. Personal effects—her gold rings, a stack of wide bracelets, a small bottle of oil or perfume, and a few coins—were scattered on top of a desk. A copy of *The Path of the Wind*, well-worn and translated, it appeared, into the Old Tongue of the orcs, peeked out from under a pile of neatly folded tunics and chemises. A pitcher, decorated with a brilliant gold and red motif, and matching basin stood on her bedside table. A slightly lopsided bookshelf next to the window held a mug and an elegantly painted vase, and a bouquet of dried flowers hung over her bed. A vibrant trio of potted plants sat on her windowsill, where a weak summer breeze ruffled their leaves.

"It is not fitting that I should be in a female's bedchamber," he murmured, admiring the ferns.

Ignoring him, Dargah did not sit, nor did she offer a seat to Neryn. "Just passing through town?"

"I was sent on business to a village south of here." He attempted a smile. "These days, the Disciple prefers to use me as a messenger boy."

"And the forge is a convenient rest stop? *Talk.*"

"I know that your, ah, visit to Dirgil holds unpleasant memories for us both—"

"Is that your way of apologizing?"

He hesitated.

"I didn't think so. Continue. You've got four and a half minutes."

"I wanted you to see this. It is a copy of what I was required to deliver to an elvish settlement among the villages at Oak Creek."

Neryn handed a scroll to Dargah, who unfurled it and glanced back up at him. "You came all the way to Lindenvale to show me a document I can't read?" She sighed, plopping onto her bed. "If you leave now, you might avoid the wrath of Ikraam."

"*Ifrunn*, can you, for just *once*—" He paused, wrestling with his frustration. Then, in a milder tone, he said, "I *know* you cannot read the language. Allow me to translate."

"Oh, would you? For *me*?" She batted her lashes in the semblance of a damsel in distress.

Neryn read, in the clear, smooth tone that he typically reserved for formal meetings, "Dearest Brothers, the great and glorious god Erjunn, in his endless wisdom, has called us back unto him. To move again with his breath steering us, and his words making right our ways. The time has come for his beloved children to rise up as warriors, as soldiers, and to reestablish Erjunn's domain in the hills and valleys of Argodoth. As the chaff is winnowed from the wholesome wheat, the people of all lands will be shaken and jostled. Only his purest and most devoted children will remain unmoved. Into their hands, he will place the bow and the arrow, the sword and the shield. The men of peace will be called to spill blood, their sons armed with strength and power. Their wives and daughters will cry in anguish as they battle, but their tears and terror shall be assuaged. Indeed, armed with his truth, the children of Erjunn will slay the beasts, and the diluted blood of the mongrels will turn red the rivers of Argodoth. In that day, Erjunn will again see his people united, untouched, and unsullied by the stain of corruption. The blight will be removed from the land with sword and with wind, and hope will be born anew."

"An ancient Zealot decree." Dargah drew her legs up onto the bed and crossed them. "See? Your people aren't the first to revile us, and you won't be the last." She leaned forward. "Did you *really* need to haul yourself here to tell me that? Coulda been a letter."

Apprehension tensing his features, he said, "Dargah, this is not some recently-discovered proclamation from time immemorial. This is a brand-new edict, penned in the Disciple's own hand. He issued it this week!"

"And I suppose you're going to be a part of this monster-hunting venture?"

"Of course not! I do not think that you fully understand the severity of..." Neryn paused, then let out a deep breath. He set the scroll aside and, with the earnestness and awkwardness of a teenaged boy, took one of her hands in both of his. She squirmed and her face twisted in annoyance, but he continued. "Dargah, there is something I need to tell you. I realize I should have told you earlier because it might have been easier for us both had I—"

Footsteps thundered up the stairs. Dargah smirked at Neryn as she withdrew her hand. "You're a little early, dear Ikraam," she announced as she opened the door.

The orc's gently accented tone seemed at odds with his gravelly exterior. "Pardon, Miss Dargah, but I was worried that the elf was being inappropriate. Would you like me to remove him from the premises?"

"The elf has a name," Neryn heard himself announcing into the air, throwing his hands upward in frustration.

"And the elf is going to have *broken arms* if he is taking liberties with Miss Dargah," noted Ikraam, shifting his bulk to fill the entire door frame. There, that was the puffed-up posturing Neryn had expected. Close up, it *was* rather intimidating. Still, he snorted.

"Liberties?" He shook his head, stepping forward. "Sir, that is most certainly *not*—"

Still chatting with Ikraam, Dargah placed a hand on Neryn's chest and shoved him back into the room. "If anyone would be taking liberties, it would be me, but seeing as how we're both fully dressed, and I do *not* look like I'm enjoying myself, I think it's clear that you needn't worry about my virtue."

"*Virtue*," Neryn sniffed incredulously from behind her.

"He still seems like kind of a scrote," Ikraam muttered in Dargah's ear.

"Oh, darling, of course he is. But I can handle this. Thank you, Ikraam. Would you please have my brother send up some food and that package for my guest? I have a feeling this chat is going to last far longer than I'd anticipated."

"If you're sure, Miss Dargah?"

"Yes, Mr. Ikraam." She blew him an airy kiss.

He respectfully dipped his head, but before Dargah closed the door, he shot Neryn a wary glance and pantomimed snapping the elf in two over his knee.

Dargah dropped herself back on the bed, still refusing to offer Neryn a seat. She twisted her hair into a wobbly topknot. "Now, where were we? Oh, yes, you were sweating profusely as you took my hand. I sense some kind of confession is to follow. Were you going to tell me how beautiful my nose is, perhaps?" She turned to the side, showcasing her fine profile. "I've been told it's my best feature."

"I had not noticed." He took a step away from her. "Dargah, the Disciple is my father."

She stared at him for several seconds, her face losing color. "What?"

He hurried on, "Please understand that he is a father by blood alone. I am no closer to him than anyone else is in Dirgil. We are not truly family. We are *colleagues*. Since my mother's passing, his purpose, he has always told me, has been to shepherd the flock. I was but one lamb among so many, and they needed his guidance more than I did."

His mouth was dry, his heart racing. Dargah was right; his hands were damp with sweat. But now, one of his two darkest secrets had been thrust into the light, and both his safety and hers rested on her response.

Absorbing the impact of his confession, Dargah shook her head. When she found her voice, she looked him over and uttered, "I guess he *did* kind of look a little familiar. The eyes. Why the hell didn't you let us know about him earlier? You should have coughed this up the night we all spilled our guts at Rinah's." She crossed her arms and sniffed, "If nothing else, Ruh and I could have shared stories about our childhood, too. We all could have bonded over terrible parents."

Was she making a joke for his benefit or her own? Either way, she took the news far better than he'd anticipated. He'd prepared for a fist in the face or possibly the silent treatment, but Dargah didn't seem the type to hold her tongue. He wet his lips. "I never intended to keep this knowledge a secret or to deceive you. My only interactions with you have been when you were acting as a guard dog, defending Orlaeth or Rinah. What would it have mattered to you or anyone else who my father was in those moments? And after you came to Dirgil and made it so clear how poorly you thought of the Disciple, it seemed unwise of me to admit to having his very blood in my veins. You—you would hate me, too, of course. More than you already do."

Her expression darkened. "I hate *him*."

"Your feelings toward him matter little," he said, sounding as helpless as he felt.

"His bones can feed the wolves!" Dargah cursed. She stood and took measured steps toward Neryn. "I hate him for teaching that my goddess—my beautiful and powerful and *life-giving* goddess—is the queen of whores and a slave to debauchery. I hate him for making Orlaeth feel that she would be better off among strangers than with her own people. And I hate him for turning *you* into something you were never meant to be because it's obvious that you... you were meant to be..." She stood toe-to-toe with him now. Her gaze lingered too long on his mouth. It was hardly fair for a male to have such full, inviting lips. And then, those lips parted.

"Tell me, *ifrunn*, what *was* I meant to be?"

Yours, *of course, my* **Champion.** *He's meant to be yours.*

The words resounded in Dargah's head, but its familiar voice was not her own. A sudden heat swallowed her, the prickling weight of being wrapped in a wool blanket on a hot summer's day, the memory of sun-baked skin, of breathlessness, of blood oaths and blunted blades. She muffled a gasp and moved to the window, willing the panic to fade. "You were meant to be your own person," she managed. "To make mistakes and learn from them. To succeed and to celebrate. To *live*. Like everyone else. It's why I left home and came here. Runo, too."

"I am conflicted. Perhaps this is how Orlaeth felt when she learned she was to be my mate."

"Perhaps."

"To be clear, Dargah, I do not support the goal of this proclamation. I would greatly have preferred to see it torn into a hundred pieces and float away in the river's current than to place it into the hands of another."

She looked at him, her face blank. "That's nice to hear. Surprising, but nice."

His brows drew together. "In spite of what you seem to believe, I do not desire harm of any kind to come to you." Neryn let out a breath. "Or your friends. If any of this is to come to pass, you deserve forewarning."

"So what *is* it you want from me?" she asked, fully recovered from her earlier panic. "Do you want sympathy? Advice? I'm not clear on this."

"This edict troubles me, Dargah, but I cannot discuss it with anyone in Dirgil. They will think me mad, or seditious, or at the very least foolish, but I think… I think I need *someone* to talk to."

She laughed. "You don't even *know* me. Talk to Orlaeth. And, speaking of, why didn't *she* tell us about the Disciple being your father?"

"She is very perceptive—preternaturally so. Surely, you have realized that by now. If she chose to keep the fact to herself, I have to believe there was a reason for it." He shifted a bit, then admitted, "I cherish Orlaeth and always will; but she is prone to share her insight without tact or empathy."

"Just how much empathy are you looking for, Neryn? 'Cause I'm not drowning in it for you at the moment."

He ignored her jab. "I do not need empathy. I need insight from an outsider's perspective."

"And I'm about as far outside the Remnant as you can get. So, you took a detour into town to talk to me about *talking* to me?"

He snorted, again cold and stoic. "I *primarily* came to share with Orlaeth news of her newest sibling. Her mother has borne a baby boy. He has arrived somewhat earlier than expected but is healthy. She is recovering now after a difficult delivery, but she is in good spirits."

"I wondered how her mother would fare after she heard the news," she murmured. Then, with more gusto, she added, "Well, it appears that the breeding program continues to be successful."

"It is not always successful. It was not successful with my own mother."

Dargah's tone softened a bit. "I'm assuming that's not something you want to talk about further?"

"You are correct."

"Fair enough. Let me just get this all clear. You're asking me to be your friend."

"A listening ear. A source of consultation," he corrected sharply. "I do not need *friends*."

"Well, you're in luck because that personality sure as hell isn't going to win you any."

Chapter Twenty-Five:

Of Charity and Choices

"I will consider that a compliment," Neryn announced archly. "Too many men fling their trust to strangers like scattering seed to the wind. I prefer to cultivate trust more carefully. I imagine you are the same way, and that mindset is a gift—to cleave the fine line between intention and implementation with a sharp and unforgiving blade."

"Ah, that reminds me. My brother's bringing up something for you." At that moment, an assertive knock sounded at her door. "A drummer's perfect timing." She opened it to find a curious Runo holding a tray piled high with food and the package she'd left downstairs.

"Hey. You all right?"

"We'll talk later. Thank you."

Runo gave Neryn a casual nod, then pulled the door shut. Dargah handed him the cloth-wrapped parcel. "Here you go. As promised. Worth every cent, and then some."

Neryn unfolded the fabric to reveal a long, slim steel dagger, its polished handle carved from pale linden wood. He said nothing for a moment.

Dargah chewed the inside of her lip. "If you don't like it—"

"This is magnificent," he announced. "Please extend my gratitude to your mistress. Her work is exceptional."

"I would, if she had made it."

"This is *your* work?" When his attention moved to her face, there was no less wonder than when he was looking at the knife. "A remarkable talent."

Feeling an unwelcome warmth in her cheeks, Dargah shrugged. "It's my job. Come on, eat something. You still haven't tried the food here." She pulled apart the warm, crusty loaf of bread and offered half to Neryn. She dipped her own into the savory soup Runo had made. "Mushroom and barley. There's no meat or cream," she assured him.

"Thank you."

It was hard for Dargah not to think of the last meal they'd eaten together, after which Neryn had coldly thrown her out of his cabin.

"You do not owe me this. Neither the food nor the conversation," he said, as though sensing her memories. "I have been unkind."

"I guess I have, too."

"Shall we consider this a fresh start?" A smile began to form on his lips.

"Absolutely not. I can forgive what you said, but not who you are," Dargah said. "I'm willing to listen to you complain solely for what you did for Rinah. And for Orlaeth."

"How is it that you have come to carry a burden of gratitude on Orlaeth's behalf? You cannot know her well enough to do so."

"I don't, really. I just know she is—or was, at least—a desperate woman. Trapped. Afraid, alone. Looking for a way out. *Any* way out."

"It sounds as though you have a similar story to tell," Neryn mused.

"I do. But not to you," she said without malice. "So. Is Runo's cooking good enough to keep you here tonight?"

"Actually, yes," he admitted, savoring the soup. "The seasoning strikes me as inventive and robust."

Dargah looked into the bowl. "Garlic and pepper, you mean?" Gods, this poor boy was missing out on sex *and* the joys of good food? She could pity him for that, perhaps.

"I must not over-indulge." After a few more bites, he set his spoon aside. "Once I completed my delivery in Oak Creek, my plan was to speak *briefly* with you, then pass some time with Oraleth and share the news with her. I

503

wanted to leave Lindenvale before noon." He glanced at the early afternoon sun glinting through the window. "I will need to adjust my schedule, it seems. I had not intended on spending nearly an hour in the bedroom of a—"

"Watch your mouth."

"Woman. The bedroom of a woman."

"Are you *blushing?*"

"I feel warm. Perhaps it is the... pepper."

"By all means, feel free to shed some clothing," laughed Dargah, delighting in his chagrin. She casually removed her own bodice, revealing a sweat-damp linen chemise underneath, tucked into soft, sweat-stained trousers.

"I am not... *that* warm." He turned away.

"Good gods, I'm not *naked*, Neryn," she scoffed. "It *is* hot today, and if you weren't here, I'd be wearing a lot less. Besides, I'm wearing more now than *you* were after your little dip in Rinah's stream." To her gratification, his blush deepened. She pressed even further, pretending to fan herself with her hand. "You do have the most irresistible *knees*, Counselor Sunstorm."

Even the tips of his ears were red.

"*And...* I bet you don't have coin to pay for a room tonight, do you?" She gestured to his dagger. "Spent it all on me—that is to say, the service I rendered." He was *fidgeting*, she observed gleefully. Dargah did not wait for his response but pulled a few coins out of a pouch atop her desk. "Here you go."

His sense of pride overcame his sense of propriety. He huffed, "I cannot accept—"

"I don't know how much you earn as the personal psalmist of a narrow-minded preacher, but I'm guessing I bring in a little more than you do. Go downstairs and tell

Ioanie you need a room for the night. You can leave for Dirgil in the morning." She forced the silver into his hand.

It took him a moment, but for the first time since they had met, Neryn obeyed Dargah. Still, before she shut the door behind him, he said aggressively, "This is not charity! I *will* reimburse you for this coin!"

*

"I don't blame you, Orlaeth."

Dargah splashed some water into her wine and stirred it with her finger. Across from her, the white-haired elf delicately sliced a roasted turnip into six equal portions. Then she cut each of those in half. "For what do you not blame me?"

"For running away from Neryn. Looking at him is one thing, but *listening* to him bluster all day long would be the death of me."

Orlaeth arranged the turnip slices into tidy rows on her plate and tore up a handful of basil leaves, placing two shreds atop each slice. "I did not flee from a marriage with Neryn due to his personality or his appearance. I did so because I could not be the wife he wants and deserves."

"A quiet, obedient female. That's what is expected, right? Of all of the Remnant's women?"

Orlaeth cocked her head. "You must understand that what the Disciple expects of women and what my god expects are not always the same thing. Among the Remnant, however, yes, you are correct. There are no outbursts and no complaining. A gentle demeanor and cooperative attitude are paramount for a female. In fact, anything less is not tolerated. You, for example, would be an atrocious wife. You speak freely, without care for how your words might affect others. You do not dress chastely; your clothing is bright and eye-catching and your figure is not obscured. Your work and hobbies are neither demure nor useful in beautifying the home. None of these traits would be acceptable for Neryn's wife or the wife of any man in the Remnant."

"Well, it's not like I'm rattling the gates, begging the Disciple for a husband, now, am I?" Dargah snorted, crossing her arms. "Besides, I can shoe horses and make plows. That's useful!"

"I do not say this as a form of passing judgment," Orlaeth hurried to add. "Please do not take what I tell you as a complaint or a criticism. Your boldness and sense of justice are qualities that you have used to protect and befriend many in Lindenvale, including myself. I have come to admire you for these very qualities. You see, I, too, fail to meet the standards the Disciple has set for women. I cannot perform the most basic functions of a woman. I cannot love the way a woman should. I cannot… bear life." She paused long enough to chew a piece of turnip. "Cannot? Will not, perhaps. I am no longer certain. In any case, I serve Neryn best by staying away from him. I am worth infinitely more to him as a dead bride than I would be as a living one." She shuddered. "I will not be mated to Neryn or anyone else. I wish to remain celibate."

"Is that… a religious thing? Like a vow to Erjunn?" Dargah had heard of dwarf maidens being sequestered and "betrothed" to their god Kaylor for a period of time, but that was only to increase their perceived value and draw potential suitors.

"It is not. It is a personal decision, one that I was unable to make as a part of the Remnant," Orlaeth said. Then, her tone turned scolding. "Rinah told me only recently that you followed Neryn and Tiarnán back home to ensure that my secret was kept. For that, I am thankful, but I must tell you that your actions were foolish and dangerous."

"That's what Neryn said."

"You further spoke with him?"

Dargah contemplated sharing her experience at the lodge but said instead, "A little. But we didn't agree on much. He's not a lot of fun."

"It is rather bold of you to assume that his upbringing afforded him the same freedoms yours has, is it not?"

Chastened, Dargah looked away. "Well... he did tell me about his mother." She wrinkled her face. "But being the *Disciple's* son? Might explain why he's so damn uptight all the time. I would be, too."

"For as long as I can remember, Neryn has been held to a very high standard. Higher even than men twice and thrice his age, and not just by the Disciple but by all of the Remnant. None of us—none of the children escaped discipline when we erred, but his admonishment was always public and always harsher than our laws required.

Now knowing this, I believe you can understand why he has grown into a cautious man."

"Did he ever stand up to the Disciple, disagree with him?" Orlaeth shook her head. "Would he receive some kind of punishment, even now as an adult?"

"I have no doubt that he would," the elf replied with sadness.

"What exactly would he do if he learned that his son lied about your death?"

The remaining color drained from Orlaeth's delicate features, but before she could answer, Neryn himself approached the table. He offered a respectful nod and said, "Greetings. Please excuse my interruption, ladies, but I was hoping I could speak with Orlaeth. The worst of the afternoon heat has passed, and I thought you might enjoy a brief walk with me?"

Orlaeth looked up at him, then back at her orderly turnip slices.

He noticed her indecision and added, "I am more than willing to wait until you finish your meal. Once you are done, and if you are amenable, would you please join me by the fountain?"

"Of course. It will be pleasant to pass time with you," Orlaeth said with genuine warmth.

Dargah said nothing, watching him stride elegantly through the tavern, garnering the attention of several young ladies—and a few men—as he walked. She didn't realize Orlaeth was staring as well until the elf murmured, "Do you see the lust in their faces? The desire with which they consume his appearance?" She turned back to Dargah and added, "I do not look upon anyone in that way."

"No?"

Between mouthfuls of turnip, Orlaeth continued. "I can *acknowledge* that a male is aesthetically pleasing, as Neryn is. His features and form are distinctly masculine, and his confidence and demeanor are appealing to many women, regardless of race. And Makoa, too; it is clear to me that he possesses what could be termed a 'boyish charm,' and his body is lean and healthy. His smile is disarming and inviting. And, though he is barely an adult, it could be said your brother even has the potential to—"

"Orlaeth, no."

"Still, such acknowledgment never becomes more than a thought. My body—the feminine part of me—does not respond in any way one might expect it to. I do not long for physical intimacy or a man's touch—anyone's touch. I understand that this is uncommon." Before Dargah could quiz her on the secret sex lives of Remnant-raised elves, Orlaeth noted, "I would be impolite to keep him waiting. Will you please excuse me?"

They might not be destined for each other, but Neryn and Orlaeth were cut from the same awkward cloth, and Dargah was perfectly happy enjoying the rest of her afternoon by herself.

Chapter Twenty-Six:

Of Recompense and Restitution

Rinah spent her afternoon reviewing the day's lessons. She'd felt magic again today, just a tiny spark of it, more fleeting even than the winking of a firefly. But it liked her. She could tell. Alvyx had warned her that druids needed to give magic the time and opportunity to decide what it wanted to do. Most often, it would adjust quickly to its new handler, but sometimes, it didn't want to be bothered. And when that happened, the magic could react badly.

"Always let the magic choose you," he reminded her.

And, earlier that morning, it did. Rinah sat for hours next to the crumbling foundation of an ancient wall, older than Lindenvale or any of its trees. The forest had grown up around it, and even Alvyx didn't know what had once stood here. He only knew it had been put in place by orc mages, using their elemental gifts to stack the stones atop one another. With Alvyx standing a considerable distance away, Rinah hummed to herself. She talked to the stone. She asked about its story. She placed a gentle hand on it, reverently running her fingers across the pits and cracks on its surface. And then a scrap of old, old magic leaped, an invisible passenger, from the cool, gray stone onto her shoulder.

It felt like a pebble had been placed on her arm and rolled around by itself, exploring its new host. It tickled, but Rinah didn't want to laugh for fear of offending it. Still, the magic felt her delight and assured her that it appreciated laughter. The orcs who had poured their gifts into this structure—it had been a stable, the spark shared—were jovial and friendly and exactly the opposite of what many people expected them to be. It liked her, the magic decided, and asked to slip into her soul. It hadn't known a mage in far too long, and it was lonely.

As soon as she felt its weight, she leaped to her feet and called for Alvyx. "It picked me," she gasped. "It was just a little bit, but there were horses here, and they were orcs' horses, so they were absolutely huge and—"

"Isn't it wonderful to get to see those things? I love when the magic tells you its story," he cried, throwing his arms around her and squeezing. "But you must remember—let the magic decide what to do and when to do it. Always. Go on and introduce it to the bit you snagged the other day in the forest. A little mite like that isn't much good on its own. Soon enough, you'll find them some more friends, and then we can work on how to use that magic safely."

Rinah winced. Discharging magic was the most challenging part of her training. Unlike elemental magic, which operated within fairly well-defined parameters and was predictable, rogue magic followed no rules. By its very nature, it was a hodgepodge of leftovers, scraps of elemental magic as well as the blessings, curses, and enchantments that advanced mages could perform. Papa told her that elemental mages were like farmers; they harvested exactly the seeds they had planted. And they got out of it what they put into it, as far as effort and dedication went. But a druidic mage was a forager. One day, he might come upon a trove of rare and delicious mushrooms, another he might find nothing but rotting fruit, regardless of his efforts. It was difficult to control the path of rogue magic. The first time Rinah had adopted a crumb of magic that had been used to curse, she discharged it immediately, leaving a nearby tree bereft of its leaves and earning a stern glare from her papa.

"It felt dirty," she had protested, trying to shake the sense of dread it had awoken in her. "I didn't like it."

"The magic's past does not determine its future under your care," he had reminded her. "Whatever it was used for before it came to you is irrelevant. Magic comes in all flavors. It's not all raspberry cream and lemon cakes."

"Well, this was like burnt toast and overcooked beans," she'd returned.

"Even that kind of magic can find a peaceful home within you. The trick is to give it time to settle, to mingle with the rest of the rogue magic you've accepted."

Rinah had ended their lesson early that day, needing the opportunity to reflect on her papa's words.

What used to be bad didn't have to remain bad if she cared for it properly.

*

"You appear to be healthy, Orlaeth," Neryn began, heading toward the river. "Are you enjoying life here?"

"I am. I find great satisfaction in the work Mr. Naoum provides me. He is a pleasant sort of man, and my tasks are much like those I was given by the Disciple, although I no longer copy religious texts exclusively. Last week, I made four copies of a children's storybook. The tale is nonsensical, filled with talking animals, but it does reinforce the concept of being honest in order to build trust amongst one's associates."

"A valuable lesson indeed. But surely, that is not the only difference between Dirgil and Lindenvale?"

"Of course not." Orlaeth squinted, the water's reflection of the sun too dazzling. "Though I am happy, sometimes, it is difficult here. The food is too rich and heavily seasoned; as you have eaten at the inn, you must agree! And the young people are very loud here. I know they do not mean disrespect, but their parents seem unable to control them."

Neryn offered a half-smile at that. "Unlike *our* parents?"

Orlaeth blinked. "I suppose they could not control us, either, in the end, for I am a runaway, and you are a liar."

"You are well, then, even with the noisy children and the over-seasoned food?"

She slowed to a stop near a wooden bench overlooking the river. They sat. "I have friends here, Neryn. Is that not enough? They express an interest in me beyond my physical well-being alone. Rinah and I share an interest in gardening, and her papa was exceptionally kind in allowing me to stay with them until I could afford my own room. The attendants at the temple of Erjunn here, even those who are not full-blooded, are welcoming and well-versed in the holy texts. I am safe. I am appreciated. Is that not enough to make me happy? I admit, I am still an oddity to some here, true, but I was seen as an oddity in Dirgil, too, even if no one gave voice to such thoughts."

Neryn did not contradict her. "But... truly, you are not lonely here?"

"I am not."

"Then I am pleased. Rinah seems like a good companion for you."

"Very much so, yes. Tending her garden is restorative for me. And I have also found that Runo is a thoughtful young man. He offers a mediocre first impression, but he is kind-hearted and good-natured. He is a hard worker." A small smile played on her lips. "He treats me as though I am an elderly aunt, which I think is his way of showing respect."

"And his sister?" Neryn's raised eyebrow told her more than his words did.

"She is generous, like Rinah. She can be quick to anger but she is just as quick to forgive. She is brave and confident. She goes out of her way to ensure the safety of others. I learned only last week that she followed you to Dirgil for my sake. Please know I had nothing to do with that, and had I been informed beforehand, I would have expressed my disapproval of the idea."

"Mostly, I am embarrassed that she tracked us as far as she did without us realizing it," grumbled Neryn.

"You *should* be embarrassed. You and Tiarnán are competent rangers," Orlaeth chided.

"My mind was not on the journey but the destination," he apologized. "I could not keep from thinking about what I was going to say to the Disciple. And to your family."

Orlaeth's usually smooth expression tightened. "I did not wish to bring them any pain."

"I know."

"Do you bring news of my mother, by chance?"

Neryn smiled at the change of subject. "Yes, happy news! You have a newborn brother. He is named Glanhau. Your sisters are caring for the child while your mother recovers. This birth was not as easy as the rest have been, but her health is quickly improving."

She closed her eyes in a moment of prayer. "Praise Erjunn for his blessings. Thank you. You did not need to come here to tell me this, but it brings me pleasure to hear the words from your own mouth. You have been very kind to me, Neryn."

"I have never had a reason not to be."

In silence, they watched the people around them—sweat-drenched men returning home from the fields and the orchards, messenger boys with endless energy, darting from shop to shop, and homebound mothers lugging fresh produce and whining children. Orlaeth twisted her fingers together, interlocking them and then pulling them apart several times before she spoke. Her words were stiff and halting, her eyes still fixed on the passers-by. "I am sorry that I could not marry you, Neryn. I am grieved that I hurt you."

Carefully, he placed a hand on her arm. When she let it rest there, he said, "I would have done everything in my power to make you happy. Surely you must know this, Orlaeth."

"I do. But it is not within your power to make me happy. My happiness can never be found in marriage and motherhood." Neryn hesitated. "I know that you fear what might happen to your body. All females do, I think, to some degree."

"Neryn, what do you know of intimacy?"

He withdrew his hand. "Why are you asking me this?"

"I would like to know."

"The pleasures of intimacy are a distraction. The search for such pleasure is an addiction. The endless pursuit of fleshly passion is a waste of one's breath and energy. The sole valuable purpose of intimacy is to bear children."

"Those are your father's words, yes. What do you know of the act itself?" She settled her guileless, silvery gaze on his face at last.

Neryn's posture stiffened. A blush crept up his neck, then bloomed on his cheeks. "Orlaeth, *please*. This is not an appropriate topic for a male to discuss with a female, even outside of Dirgil!"

She continued to stare at him, though he turned away. He spoke as though each word was wrested from his lips. "All right. I know that the male organ requires a certain level of, ah, stimulation to perform its function, and it is…Orlaeth, *must* we discuss this?"

"And then what?" she answered, coldly clinical.

"It is fitted into the canal that leads to the womb. So, if the female is experiencing her fertile days, she may conceive a child," he spat miserably.

"This is all you know?"

"What else is there to know? I have gathered that the experience *can* be enjoyable, which is why it is such a dangerous distraction and must be avoided whenever possible."

"Then you are not aware of the potential for pain or discomfort for the female during sexual congress? Or how a female's body must be prepared for the act, both physically and mentally, in order to avoid injury?"

"No," he uttered. "I supposed those things... sorted themselves out. After all, there are always children and infants among us, are there not?"

"Has anyone ever told you that a female might not *want* to engage in intercourse?"

"If that were the case, she should consider it her duty to Erjunn, the same way males do." Suddenly cynical, he snorted, "With whom did you discuss such things? *Dargah?* It would not surprise me if a half-orc told you that—"

"Neryn, what do you think happened to Rinah on the night you arrived here? The night of my affliction?"

He swallowed hard. "I understand that Bram had expected Rinah to satisfy his sexual desires, in spite of her refusal. His actions were vile. Unspeakable."

Orlaeth nodded serenely. "Now, perhaps you better understand the husbands of the Remnant."

He knit his brows together as though trying to interpret her cryptic statement. "Such conduct would be reprehensible, and would dishonor Erjunn! I refuse to believe that any of our men would behave so callously!"

"They have no need to, brother, because the women are daily reminded of their duty, and they obey, even if their sentiments are the same as Rinah's."

"*All* are expected to obey," Neryn protested, "male and female alike."

"Obey whom? Obey what?"

529

"The commands of Erjunn." He sounded suspicious, as if he expected a trap.

She had none to spring upon him. She only had the truth. "And yet I obeyed the command of Erjunn when I left. I am called to serve as your mate, and I am called to leave Dirgil. How can both be the will of Erjunn? I know what our god expects of me. It is not what your father expected of me. And I can choose to follow only Erjunn or Kaedryn Sunstorm, not both. You know my path. You know what I am."

"I only wish you could have been able to tell the Disciple."

"Had I done so, we both know he would have dismissed me—or worse—before I had even finished saying my piece. But if *you* had told him, perhaps—"

Neryn stood, his voice low as he tried to remain calm. "You know very well that I have no influence with him. None. I never have. He is just as likely to punish me as he is to mock me, should I approach him with the idea that… that a *woman*—"

"Erjunn speaks to me often, Neryn. Even now, I hear him."

Neryn knew his tone was too sharp. "What else does he say, Orlaeth?"

"Nothing that I am able to reveal right now, and nothing that I understand in full."

"Of course not. I wish he would not speak to you in dreamlike visions and indecipherable riddles," he muttered, taking his seat.

"Do you believe that your father hears his voice? That he has followed Erjunn's guidance, and done well as a leader these past thirty years?"

"I still do not understand now all of this is related! Besides, my opinion is irrelevant."

"And yet I seek it."

"I want to believe that he does. I want to believe that, in every decision he makes, he accomplishes nothing short of pleasing our god. What does any of this have to do with—"

Orlaeth had spent much time listening to discussions and arguments around her these past several weeks, from things as significant as the sale or purchase of land or businesses to things as inconsequential as how to style one's hair. She was learning, albeit slowly, that the straightforward approach—her favored and only method of communication—did not always achieve the desired result. She had been considering how best to confess her thoughts to Neryn for a very long time, in the event that he returned. Erjunn had revealed to her that the Suppliant Prime was in no way beyond her reach, beyond her influence. To take Neryn on the journey with her, she needed to use the tongue of a poet. She had written her thoughts on scraps of paper, rearranging them into phrases that would prick his ears. She imagined a map, with her chosen words becoming the roads leading to the destination. She had crafted a cadence, a rallying cry hidden between the phrases.

"I wonder if, within the Remnant, there are other women like me, even other men, who have within them a voice that continues, never stopping, never slowing, telling them that to love Erjunn is not to *breed* for him but simply to *be* as he is, people for whom intimacy brings great fear or shame or pain, but who dearly wish to please their god, who thus steel themselves with prayer and meditation, and who accept great fear and shame and pain in sacrifice to him, offering their bodies and their wills and their lives, when Erjunn has never, never requested such things? Have you considered, dear brother— my *dearest* brother—that such sacrifices bring our god sorrow instead? That he weeps over wives and husbands who deny themselves the comfort of each other's intimate embrace, the daughters who are auctioned off to males who see them as little more than vessels for the next generation, and the silent women whose husbands are, in secret, no better than Bram." Her voice remained clear, but her words grew urgent. "Men are given wives they rarely see, children they rarely see, when the Disciple claims every waking moment of theirs for himself? For his meetings, his missions, his missives. There are two worlds in Dirgil, Neryn. There is one in which women are denied mage training, denied study of the holy books and of history, denied the privilege of living as Erjunn's daughters, but instead live as their husbands' servants. And they walk about as ghosts, their bellies round with children and their brains smooth with disuse. And in the other, men celebrate the idea of spiritual castration, in which they play as soldiers waging an unseen war, where they fashion themselves after a man who could not be brought to mourn his dead wife or to comfort his only son?"

Neryn's head was between his knees, and Orlaeth was unable to determine if he was weeping or retching or both. She waited, patting his back as she imagined Rinah might do in this situation. He stood up, breathed deeply, wiped his mouth, and then looked down at her. Distress painted his face a weak shade of gray.

"You think so poorly of me? You think that *I* would have used you in such a way? Treated you as a handmaid? A *slave*? That I would not have placed your comfort and care above my own?"

"I know your heart, Neryn. But I also know that there are many men within the Remnant who do not possess hearts like yours, and it is for those men and their wives I mourn."

"How easy it is for you—you with a loveless soul and a lifeless womb—to speak of a wife's burden and a husband's neglect when *you* have fled your responsibilities, fled your family, and left *me* with the weight of seeing them morning and night, the truth at the edge of my tongue remaining always and eternally unspoken!" Neryn was flushed and tense, a man in the heat of battle within his own mind. "Your gift to me is an empty bed and an empty home and cursed me with a yearning that I can *never* satisfy!"

Orlaeth was unmoved by his accusations. "I am sorry that my request has become so unbearable a burden for you. It was not my intention to bring you suffering, but I stand by what I have said. Your women are wombs and nothing more, Neryn; they have no curiosity, intelligence, wit, wisdom, joy, or laughter. Neither they nor men are allowed to make mistakes, to learn and grow, to fail and try again. In Dirgil, there is a narrow path males and females walk, parallel to each other but never intersecting. It is a lonely existence. Before Rinah found me here, I had never *lived* a single day in my life."

She had memorized those painful words and wrapped them in pretty packages, and now they were open, exposed, raw. All her thoughts had been delivered, and she said no more. They were quiet for a long time, both silently considering the gravity of the conversation they had just shared. When Neryn spoke, his voice was small. "I wish that I had known all of this before you left." He sat down heavily next to her. "Even so, I should not hold you accountable for my own struggles, the silent sins that seek to strangle me in the night. It is not *your* face that haunts my dreams." He seemed to shrug off some invisible weight, then graced her with a small smile. "No. Your secret is not a burden. I do not regret my decision to honor your request. I apologize. I am speaking out of frustration. And perhaps... shame."

She sensed that another pause was necessary, then asked, "If you have shared with me all that you wish to, then I would like to go to the library and begin work on a new assignment." She noticed with some concern that

Neryn's beautiful face was haggard. Orlaeth could not recall seeing him so distraught, other than the day he discovered his mother, nearly dead, inside their home. She added, "Do you have more to share? I do not wish for you to retire to bed this evening with words unsaid or a heavy heart."

"Yet heavy it will be," he said. "Please forgive my thoughtlessness. I spoke in anger rather than in truth. I am ashamed to reveal that, even now, I have much to learn in order to be a suitable mate for anyone... or even a suitable friend. I will have a great deal of thoughts to ponder this evening as I meditate."

"Of course. You need not ask. You are forgiven."

*

Dargah, draped in a thin, billowing dressing gown, was returning to her room when she noticed Neryn pacing in the hall outside her door. Plaiting her wet hair into a fat braid, she raised an eyebrow. "Can I help you?"

"Oh!" He froze, stiff-backed and wide-eyed, like a soldier at attention. "Yes, hello, Dargah. Your brother informed me that you had gone to the bathhouse."

"Why did you ask my brother where I was, and why did he actually tell you I was taking a bath?' Neryn turned the appropriate shade of pink and began to apologize, but Dargah smiled wickedly, hands on hips, and asked, "Were you planning on joining me?"

To her surprise, he replied, "A bath sounds like exactly what I need before I leave for Dirgil. I assume there are separate facilities for males and females?"

She nodded. "And *why* are you here?"

"I wanted to speak with you before I left."

"And waiting outside my room didn't feel just the tiniest bit creepy to you?"

He cocked his head.

"I swear, you have the social skills of a five-year-old. What do you want?"

He wet his lips. "To thank you."

"This is a first for you, isn't it? What are you thanking me for? Lending you the coin for a room? The dagger?"

"For caring for Orlaeth."

She shrugged.

"No. Do not make light of this," he admonished. "Orlaeth is... very valuable. Not merely as a female. She is a valuable person, a valuable part of my life. My discussion with her today reinforced this truth. Her absence is keenly felt in Dirgil, but I am at peace knowing that she feels safe here, with you and Rinah."

"She's probably safer here than she was in Dirgil."

"As are you."

"It's not like I'll be sightseeing up your way anytime soon."

He drew himself up to his full height - a solid two inches taller than her. "May I write?"

"What?"

"You agreed to allow me to communicate with you. To express my... *feelings*, if I did not mistake you?" For the briefest second, he was not the arrogant son of an arrogant man. His half-smile was boyish. Hopeful. "As it would not be possible for me to visit as often as I might require to discuss such things, I will be writing letters. Is that acceptable?"

"And no one will question why the Disciple's son is suddenly writing to a friend in Lindenvale?"

A friend. The word came from her lips, not his own. His heart leapt. He struggled to maintain his composure. "I

541

will post my messages in the hamlet not far from Dirgil. I will be cautious." At her doubtful smirk, he raised his chin. "No one among my people has ever questioned my story about my father's horse. I am quite capable of subterfuge."

"Can't promise I'll write back. I'll probably be busy doing dirty, nasty orcish things."

His lips thinned into a grim line. "Good day, then." He held his head up high, once again the statuesque martyr, and strode down the hall toward the stairs.

If the entirety of the Remnant was as insufferable as Neryn, Dargah wouldn't have blamed Orlaeth if she razed the place to the ground instead of just running away.

Chapter Twenty-Seven:

Of Predators and Prey

The evenings had grown cooler since summer's glory faded from Lindenvale for the year. Autumn was a time of richness and harvest, warm scents and comforting flavors, and nights falling asleep by the fire. This was the season in which Rinah felt most alive, experimenting with new spices and flavors, watching Kaylor paint the trees in fiery shades, and savoring the garden blooms that would sleep for the chilling rains of winter. She had always suspected that she hadn't been born during the spring but was a child of autumn, born under the boar, the hawk, or the stag.

Wrapped in a lightweight woolen cloak, Rinah stepped out of the cottage to breathe in the fragrance of her garden. Sage, rosemary, basil, pine, and rose swirled on the breeze like a melody, each with its own distinct aroma but blending together like a soothing song. She moved farther from the house into the thicket beyond Alvyx's property. And she breathed in the night.

A low chuttering sound drew her attention toward the great maple tree to her left. With wings outstretched in greeting or threat—Rinah couldn't tell—perched a huge, golden-eyed owl.

A pleasant humming brewed in her blood, whispering a secret. "So, I finally get to meet you, Nell."

The owl extended her wings once more, then cocked her head. She hooted, soft and low.

"Oh, if you're here for Papa, I'm afraid he's already gone to bed," she admitted.

The owl narrowed her eyes and flexed her talons. The tufts of feathers on her head looked like horns—a bit intimidating. "I'm sorry. Shall I tell him you stopped by?"

Without warning, Nell dropped from the branch and swooped past her, so closely that she ruffled Rinah's curls. With a startled cry, she leaped out of the bird's path, only to watch her circle back to the maple branch with a wriggling mouse hanging from her claws. With an almost imperceptible crack, she snapped the mouse's spine. Rinah winced. Then, the owl dropped to the ground again, carefully placing the dead mouse in front of Rinah before returning to the tree.

"Oh. Um, thank you," Rinah managed. Nell stared at her with unblinking eyes, waiting for her to taste her dinner. Rinah snatched the limp rodent from the ground and quickly wrapped it in her apron. "I've already eaten. I think we should save this for Papa."

"Hoo-*ooo*," Nell agreed.

"How are your boys?"

Nell made a whuffling sound and shifted on the branch.

"Are they hunting on their own?"

The owl sniffed and squinted one glowing eye.

"Well, excuse me! I must have lost track of how old they are! It didn't help that I assumed you were all *people* for so long." She smiled at the speckled bird. "I should try to get some sleep. Thank you for the meal," she said. "I'm glad I finally got to meet you. Please feel free to stop by any time." She offered a wave in Nell's direction, then paused. "Oh. You've probably already noticed that a faerie stops by the garden most nights?"

Impossibly, the owl's eyes grew rounder. "*Whooo*?"

"Oh, hush. I know you've seen him! His name is Makoa. He has bright orange wings, and he probably looks delicious to an owl. Can you please not eat him? I rather like him. And so does Papa."

Nell let out a low grumble and ruffled her wings.

"I know it's asking a lot. Thank you. Good night, Nell."

It was only after she'd closed and locked the door behind her that Rinah realized she'd just had an entire conversation with a two-foot-tall bird of prey in her backyard.

It appears that rogue magic could do a great deal more than she'd anticipated.

*

Dargah had just returned to the inn after a shift at the forge when a high-pitched squeal of joy sliced through the buzz of customers and cooks. When she saw the source of the sound, she sauntered over to the smiling group in the corner—Charis, Xinila, Rinah, and Charis's younger cousins.

"It's official! In two months' time, Charis will be the new Mrs. Rallis," Rinah announced to Dargah.

"After the Adoration," Charis added, "we're going to Sterlingshire to visit one of Mama's old friends. She's the most incredible tailor. She can even make dresses just like the ones the rich ladies in Reefside wear! And she said I can pick out any fabric or style that I want for the wedding!"

"Something purple!" her cousins chorused.

"You'll certainly *need* a new dress," Xinila remarked under her breath.

Taking a break from cleaning dishes, Runo also plopped himself down with the group. "Congratulations!" he said. "And yes, Miss Charis, I would be most honored to perform at your wedding." When Xinila gave him a cold stare, he eased himself out of the chair and, backing into the kitchen, added, "If you like."

"Yes! I'd like that, and I know Gale would, too. Thank you!" While her cousins and Xinila tucked into their roasted pork, Charis whispered to Rinah, "Will you come with us? To Sterlingshire? It would mean a lot to me and Mama if you could be there—you're like a sister to me."

"I'd love to! I haven't been there yet this year."

As she and Rinah talked, Charis's cousins devoured Xinila alive with questions. Was she going to help pick out the dress? Was Xinny married? Why not? Did she have a secret beau? Did she fancy anyone? Was he handsome? Was he tall? Where had she met him? She'd seen him *here*? At this very inn? Was she going to propose to him? Yes, that sort of thing *was* done nowadays! Why was she so uptight about it? And *where* did she have her shoes made? The embroidery on them was fine, indeed! And it looked expensive! Was Xinila's family rich? Would Charis be rich, too, after she married Galen?

As Dargah watched, amused with Xinny's fraying patience, Rinah asked her, "Did you decide what you're doing for the Adoration?"

The half-orc groaned and let her shoulders droop. "I tried everything in my power to prevent it, but Umma and Appa arc coming here after all. They probably left Dehlkia yesterday. It's a haul for them. They say they've already forgotten what Runo looks like."

"What about you? You haven't seen them in… four years?"

"No, Rinah. Almost six now. And I'd have preferred to keep it that way. But," she said with a cheerier tone, "I was able to reserve rooms for them at the Lady Tilia, so they will be as far as possible from Runo and me. At least, in a town this small."

550

"They'll only be here a few days. It won't be so bad."

"If you're so sure about that, I'll be happy to send them your way for an afternoon."

*

They were ashamed of her. Dargah had known that for a long time. But now, their disapproval of her was spilling over into their concern for her brother. They didn't think she was taking proper care of Runo, never mind that he was *technically* an adult orc. Now, they were coming to see for themselves what a dreadful sister she'd been to him. And then they'd try to convince him to go back with them, just for a visit. And then they'd find more and more excuses and reasons to keep him there. And maybe he'd decide that Lindenvale—and, therefore, Dargah—wasn't good for him after all.

And that terrified her.

She'd always been a scrapper, the smallest of the four children in their family at the time, and had learned to be tough and stand her own ground with her brothers. She'd even been mistaken for a boy more than once while training with them. But when Runo was born, a protective streak was ignited within her, and it continued to burn brightly throughout her teenage years. Once, when her twin brother Hashem crushed one of Runo's toys out of spite, Dargah tackled him to the ground, breaking his nose. Their parents hadn't intervened, but their father later suggested to Hashem that he watch his back.

That protectiveness was the reason that, in spite of learning that Orlaeth had lied about her situation, Dargah was ready to defend her. She was so clearly helpless, so frail and brittle, like glass, that the same swell of compassion Dargah felt for her newborn baby brother rushed into her heart for Orlaeth. It didn't matter that Neryn and Tiarnán wanted to haul her off to that horrible place.

Dargah would have found a way to cut them both down if they were a genuine threat.

She sat up, a frown forming on her face. No, Neryn declined to take her back to Dirgil in the end. She wouldn't pin that cruelty on him.

As she lay back down on the bed, Dargah accepted that she was afraid. Afraid of being rendered *completely* useless. She was already an embarrassment in her parents' eyes, she knew that. Their only daughter had the misfortune of appearing far more human than orc, but she'd redeemed herself with early success in the Games. Her parents had been pleased, assuming—as everyone had—that, with time, her star could only shine brighter.

But she'd walked away from Gora-Vekiri. Walked away from her heritage, her family, her homeland.

Without a mate.

And it wasn't something her mother would *ever* forgive.

No matter what her parents assumed, over the past several months, Dargah had made it her job to keep Runo safe, to make sure that he'd never gone hungry, never gone without a warm place to sleep. Even now, he was probably snoring away in that mop closet, sleeping peacefully because he was content. She'd kept herself safe, too, by being selective about her friendships and even more selective about intimacy.

Dargah let out a derisive snort. *Selective* could only apply if there had been a vast number of males to choose from. Neryn had seemed to think that she spent all her nights seducing men from one end of Argodoth to the other. That she sought only physical pleasure. That her body was a snare. Well, perhaps *parts* of her body could be, she reconsidered with a prideful smirk. And she *did* love to flirt. She liked attention; she'd readily admit that.

But she hadn't taken anyone to bed in quite some time.

What Neryn—and probably most elves—failed to understand was that while orcs absolutely enjoyed wildly fulfilling sex lives, monogamy was just as important to them as it was to the Children of Erjunn. A pious, mature orc was unlikely to succumb to a one-night stand solely to scratch an itch.

No, to the people of Dehlkia, sex was sacred. Almost a way of communing with the goddess herself. It was a gift.

And the idiot elves of Dirgil considered it a punishment.

Neryn considered it a punishment.

Her lips twisted into a slow, wicked smile, though, and her memories brought her a flush of victory. She'd gotten inside his head, that day in Dirgil, when she'd quoted the erotic poetry of the ancients. She could practically see the sweat beading on his brow as he did everything he could not to listen to her voice. He'd done an admirable job of trying to hide it, but his discomfort had delighted her.

Which reminded her that she had an unopened letter from him. The first package he had sent included the coins she had lent him earlier in the year, as well as a missive nearly six pages long, and a carefully organized chart of prophets recognized by the majority of Erjunnian officials, those who were dubious, and those who had been outright rejected. In addition, he'd cited verses from a variety of so-called holy books, all of which discussed the end of the world and its rebirth, and none of which foretold the destruction of half-blooded peoples. Then, he 'respectfully requested' details from certain portions of Dehlkia's sacred poetry. None of the parts referencing sexual intercourse were necessary, he'd reminded her. Twice.

It had been dull enough a missive that Dargah was in no hurry to read the second. She unearthed it and broke the wax seal, noting that the sigil on this one was different than the last. And he didn't mention personal names or details. This male was going out of his way not to get caught.

For an elf whose religion demanded honesty, he was a damn sneaky guy.

My duties as a messenger have been suspended; I assume this to be temporary. It now appears that I and several of my colleagues are to focus only on diplomacy. It is expected that we will begin traveling abroad before the spring Adoration. Please let our mutual friend know that her loved ones remain well. And, should you consent, I would not object to reading more sacred poetry from your people. I find the use of metaphor and allusion unusual but appealing, and can perhaps use them as reference for new works of my own.

Dargah snorted a laugh. She was going to send the lyrics of "The Ballad of the Orcish Fishwife" and tell him it was a high holy hymn.

Interlude III:

Of Murder and Misplacement

Nineteen Years Ago

Elpida remained at the edge of the clearing, thankful that Charis was still asleep at her breast, and that the orphan was preoccupied with her breakfast. She watched as Hector, Alvyx Autumnsong, Cyril Rallis, and her own husband, Kephas, carefully searched the campsite for a hint as to what dreadful things might have happened there.

At last, Hector ambled over to her. "We've got ourselves a dead man in the tent," he told her soberly, then dropped his voice even lower. "Stabbed. Blood everywhere. I can't find no trace of the little girl's mama, but for a lady's chemise over yonder. Got a good amount of blood on it, and it's tore up, too. We're thinking that whoever killed the father probably had his way with the mother afterward. No sign of where she's gone. Coulda drowned or been carried off. A sad affair."

"Alternately," Cyril added, approaching them, "It's entirely possible that this child's mother *was* the culprit. Who is to say she didn't murder her companion, then arrange her belongings to look as though they were attacked?"

"Wouldn't be the first time a wife turned on her man," Hector replied grimly.

Elpida shook her head. "Absolutely not. No mother would do something like that with her child so close by."

Kephas took her hand. "We cannot be certain, love. Perhaps she was protecting the child from *him*?"

"At any rate, we'll continue to search this area. If someone is injured out here, we'll find them." Cyril smiled wistfully at the little girl, who was still gnawing on her hand pie. A caterpillar had caught her attention, and she was inching closer to it as it crept along beneath a shrub.

Hector waved Cyril back to the search. "In the meantime, Miss Elpida, you take our new friend and give her the best welcome you can, given the circumstances, yeah?"

*

Once Elpida returned home, she made sure that the little girl was cleaned up. Despite her dirty tunic and smudged face, the girl's hair, a crown of gorgeous, thick, rusty-brown ringlets, seemed well cared-for. Could the hands that tenderly brushed her hair each night be the same ones that ended her father's life? Elpida put the thought out of her mind. "I think we are going to be good friends," she announced as she unbuttoned her tunic to nurse her daughter. "My name is Elpida and remember, this is Charis," she added, positioning the baby on her breast. "What shall we call you? What is your name?"

"Rinah," the girl said absently, watching in wonder as Charis stretched her tiny limbs, yawned, and then buried her face in her mother's bosom.

"Well, Rinah, as soon as Miss Charis here has had her breakfast, we will find something lovely to do today." Her smile was bright, but Elpida knew that nothing she could provide to entertain Rinah would erase the horrors the girl had witnessed hours earlier.

"See Mama?" Rinah chirped.

Elpida blinked back tears. "I hope so, baby."

Chapter Twenty-Eight:

Of Adoration and Aggravation

Dargah would have worn her finest clothing to celebrate the Adoration of Dehlkia anyway, but the threat of her mother's critical eye ensured it.

Her typical daily attire varied; though her work at the forge demanded she wear simple, practical clothing, Dargah preferred to express herself with bold, feminine pieces. She paired vividly colored, breezy dresses with soft, suede vests or bodices and rarely went without her signature hammered-gold bracelets.

But today, she honored the goddess. The autumn festival was a time to celebrate the coupling of Dehlkia and Erjunn, the conception of spring, and the gift of Dehlkia's blessed and abundant harvest. Centuries ago in Dargah's homeland, the Adoration had been a convenient time to find a mate or discuss alliances or trade deals. So, when communities came together to celebrate, orcs wore whatever made them appear most attractive to a prospective love interest. Males often wore leather armor, a harkening back to when champions in battle were seen as ideal mates. Some females did, too, as women were just as likely to go to war as men. Other females wore the flowing, gauzy, and often revealing gowns said to have been worn by Dehlkia's attendants at her marriage ceremony to Erjunn. Either way, everyone looked their best. The custom never died, although now, married and engaged women veiled their faces as a sign of their status during the festival. Adult females looking for a mate lined their eyes with kohl and painted their lips ruby red, freely revealing their hungry smiles.

Though no longer in the heart of her homeland, Dargah donned the airy, diaphanous layers of her treasured pomegranate-colored gown, cinching it with a narrow gold belt. The autumn weather in Lindenvale was unpredictable, so she left her golden sandals in her trunk, opting for practical leather flats. Her bracelets clacked as she released her hair from its braid. Waves spiralled down her back, reaching her waist. She flicked a bit of kohl along her lashes, studied her catlike eyes in her hand mirror, then walked out of the room as though heading toward an executioner's block.

*

Runo, clad in lightweight leather armor slightly too large for his frame, chatted with Ioanie as Dargah descended the stairs. He nodded at her approach, murmuring, "You look very pretty. Now let's get this over with."

"*You* have nothing to be worried about," she insisted.

"Dargah, you look like a princess!" Rinah laughed delightedly as she hurried to hug her friend. She wore her finest dress, too, although Ayusan garb was far more practical for the cooler weather than Dargah's sheer, voluminous gown.

Orlaeth, bundled in layers, was also waiting to join the party. Though everyone had insisted she needn't join them, she promised she would at least attend the first event. She told them that observing a holy ceremony in honor of Dargah's goddess was important to her but that she would retire shortly after.

In spite of tending to a packed house and an overflowing tap room, Ioanie had managed to whip up her version of a cherished Dehlkian lentil soup, and she offered a bit to Runo and Dargah. When they approved, her face lit up with pleasure. She wished them a wonderful celebration, then she, her parents, and the newly-hired Estia set out to serve the soup to their hungry patrons.

The warm smile Dargah had given Ioanie froze on her lips when she saw her parents enter the room.

*

Both Umma and Appa were half-orcs, excessively proud to have been born with distinctly orcish features. Hardly a hint of his human ancestry was revealed on Appa's face, other than his muddy green eyes. In his youth, Appa had participated in the games, never reaching Champion but winning an event every year he competed. At forty-five and also an athlete in her younger days, Umma was still the height of orcish beauty. Her tusks were pearly white and sharp (and one was capped with gold; that was new), her hair lustrous as a raven's wing, her skin a dewy, mossy green, and her figure thick, muscular, and well-proportioned. Only her height—several inches shorter than her husband—hinted that she might be anything other than full-blooded.

Runo squeezed Dargah's hand in a show of solidarity. Both their palms were clammy with sweat. At last, Runo said, his voice ringing across the bustling room, "Greetings and Dehlkia's abundance to you, Umma and Appa!"

The two turned as one, exchanged a glance, then made their way through the throng of revelers to stand in front of their wayward children. Umma walked with a powerful grace the poverty of Gora-Vekiri had never been able to take from her. Taking in her mother's fashionable attire and shimmering silver rings, Dargah wondered how much of the jewelry had been purchased with money she herself had sent them. She and Runo welcomed their parents with a traditional, reverential bow, then awaited their response.

"Dehlkia's abundance to you, Darah-Gohar and Ruh Noor," Appa's richly accented baritone rumbled.

After a stiff embrace, Umma asked, "What is this mockery, daughter?" The eyes above her veil were cruel. With an elegant hand, she caressed Dargah's cheek. "Are you still advertising your wares? Who will pay for a broken bride?"

Dargah's posture was perfect. Her voice was clear. But she could not meet her mother's ebony-eyed stare. "I am unmarried. Though I seek no mate, I honor tradition today."

"If only you'd had such passion for tradition a decade ago, we wouldn't be in a cheap tavern, reeking of ale and spoiled pork, right now. We'd be celebrating the goddess back home, where we *all* belong." Umma inclined her head, then turned with an indulgent smile to her son. She opened her arms and pulled Runo into them, then held him out and looked at him. "You've gotten too thin, my child."

Appa murmured, "He's still young. He'll be fine." And he, too, embraced Runo.

"I eat all the time," protested Runo. "And I make our flatbread hand pies here every week. People love them!"

"I can attest to that," Rinah said with a nervous smile. She tried to reach out a comforting hand to Dargah but couldn't do so with any degree of subtlety. "Runo is a wonderful cook!"

"Of course he is," Appa said, a smile curving around his tusks. "I taught him everything he knows."

"Are these your friends, Ruh?" asked Umma.

Not Dargah's friends. *Runo's.*

Runo beamed with pride as he introduced Rinah and Orlaeth, then got even more excited when he saw Galen, Charis, and Xinila enter the inn. "Yes! All of them. These are our friends! And Miss Ioanie is, too, and Estia is new, and kind of shy, but she's nice. And Mr. and Mrs. Adelfi are really friendly, too. And Vigga—she's the lady who runs the forge Dargah works at—she's something else. Appa, you'd love her. She's half your size and with twice your brass. Maybe we'll see her later. And Mr. Autumnsong—where is he?" he wondered.

"Papa is out delivering his orders. He might be able to join us later." Rinah's pleasant demeanor became strained as she noted the tension between Dargah and her mother.

Runo, too, saw Rinah's smile start to droop. "Let's get out of this stuffy room and go find a place by the temple," he suggested, heading for the door. Everyone followed his lead, falling into line behind him like obedient ducklings.

Dargah was the last to leave.

*

Due to its proximity to the Dehlkian border, Lindenvale was home to a substantial number of orcs and orcish patchworks. Therefore, the Adoration of Dehlkia

571

was an even larger event than that of Ayusa, and it was no surprise that both of the Dehlkian temples in town were full to bursting with worshipers today. Chairs and benches had been arranged on the grounds, but people were also on the gentle sloping green next to the larger temple, making themselves comfortable on blankets and pillows they'd brought from home.

Runo, leading the pack, found a decent spot on the hill, warmed by the bright sunlight but not too far from the outdoor stage, on which a pantomimed version of *The Courtship of the Goddess* would be performed by the visiting troupe.

As always, the hours-long service opened with an invocation and a series of songs praising the goddess, the earth, and the harvest. Dargah had always loved the throbbing, urgent rhythms of Dehlkian worship, the rattling of tambourines, and the pounding of drums. Some folks without an appreciation for orcish culture dismissed the music and dance as too sexualized, too erotic. But to Dargah, it had always been a wild and joyful expression of life, the promise of new beginnings, and the celebration of rebirth. As a child, she'd jumped and pranced, celebrating the goddess with a fervency that her parents hadn't quite understood.

But today, as hundreds of people rose to dance before the goddess of earth with gratitude and excitement, Dargah quietly stole away to the Temple of Erjunn instead.

*

The wind god's shrine was empty.

Many elves observed Dehlkia's Adoration Day out of respect, as she was their god's consort. They usually did so in the privacy of their homes, however, to avoid the loud, sweaty, potentially lewd mobs of revelers in the streets. Not all elves were as uptight as Neryn, but as a people, they did tend to be on the reserved side.

The building was small, more of a pavilion, allowing the scented autumn breeze to flow freely over the altar and the supplicants that ordinarily prayed within. Unlike the temple of Dehlkia, wreathed with flowers and ripe fruits of all kinds, Erjunn's shrine was simple and unadorned but for a row of wind chimes above the entrance. Sheer curtains separated the altar from the worshippers. They did not appear to be in place to keep the altar hidden. More likely it was a visible representation of the Breath of Erjunn, said to give life to all elves.

Kaylor's children came trembling before his power. Ayusa's people came bearing beautiful art of their own making. Dehlkia's worshipers came with drumbeat and dance. The god of the winds and the air, the breezes and the songs that whistled through the trees—what did he require?

Perhaps her words alone would suffice. Erjunn—the Erjunn of the sacred books she'd read—gave her the impression he cared less about the presumed value of an offering than he did about the attitude with which it was offered. Maybe this was why his shrines were not gilded and filled with elaborate scrollwork, silver, and fine gifts. Instead, words of gratitude had long been laid down here, an unseen foundation of his followers' thankful hearts.

Dargah sat.

"It's your day, too, isn't it?" she began, her voice sounding thin in the wind. "You were the one she chose, her lover for eternity, but we celebrate Dehlkia today because it is she who nurtures life, grows spring within her womb. And it is she who brings us the richness of harvest before the year fades to gray. It's been a long time since that part of her power resonated with me."

There was no reply. She did not expect one, of course. The wind chimes jingled a gentle melody.

"I don't really understand Orlaeth," she continued. "She's so different from anyone else I've ever met? But is she different *because* she listens so hard for your voice, or is it that hearing your voice that has *made* her different? And I don't understand Neryn, either. I can't comprehend how anyone could read the books of the elves and conclude that you are some kind of celestial dictator who gets off on seeing his people suffer."

Unable to think of anything else to say to the god, Dargah closed her eyes for several minutes, reflecting on her life. She was grateful for the gifts of the earth—the ingredients for sweet potato hash, and for pumpkin cakes, for fig paste, and sweet, golden honey. She was grateful for the town that had been quick to welcome her during a time when she needed a home. She was grateful for the friends who encircled her, grateful that her brother had found this town as welcoming as she did. She was grateful that Bram was probably rotting back in Black Lake, though Dargah doubted someone else's suffering was supposed to be a reason to celebrate the goddess.

"It's calm here," she finally said to the air. " I love the Adoration of Dehlkia, but it's always so full of sounds and colors and flavors and movement that it's impossible to think."

That had been one of the reasons she left her hometown in the first place. Sure, it had been little more than a slum, but she'd never had a moment's quiet there. Between the five children in her own household and the countless children of neighboring families, every day was an endless jumble of nursery songs and stories, games, laughter, the rattling of homemade instruments, her mother's tirades, the other mothers' tirades, and the shrieks of squabbling siblings. As she had gotten older and spent more time in the arena, the sounds were just as raucous. The slapping of fists against leather dummies, the shuffle of bare feet on dusty ground, the merciless shouts of her trainer as he urged her to push herself harder. And there had been nothing more deafening than the roar of the crowd when Dargah of Kuvaat-Asi, the publicly disgraced daughter of Kadir Kuuvat and Sefa Asi, was crowned with the golden diadem of a Champion.

All of that was behind her now. Her comeback had been spectacular and short-lived, just as she'd planned it.

And then she'd walked away from everything. Her career and the further wealth it could amass, her fans, who had rooted for the underdog, her family, who was suddenly again on her side, and the vain hope of a second chance with the man who had broken her heart.

She had made a life for herself. Found steady, honest work. Resided comfortably on her own. Kept learning, kept growing. She was proud of herself most of the time. But not right now. Because, after all, today she was alone in the temple of the wind god, still running away from her family.

*

It wasn't Runo's fault, really; still, Dargah couldn't help but cringe when her brother announced to their parents over dinner that Charis and Galen, whom they'd met at the opening service, were engaged to be married. He was only making conversation, she knew, but he couldn't have chosen a more sensitive topic if he'd tried.

"Ruh, did you read Umma's last letter to your sister? The news about Hashem?" Appa asked over his honey-soaked date cake. "We are so delighted."

"Yes! I've always thought he and Janan would be good for each other if he could ever get his head out of his ass and see how great she is."

"They are going to have a full, traditional Dehlkian ceremony," Umma added, gleeful as a child. "Everything. The feasts before and after, and they're even talking about bringing in High Priestess Uretken to preside!"

Where they'd be getting the funding for the wedding, and to pay the Empress's own personal spiritual advisor, she didn't say, Dargah noted.

"You both will be joining us for the celebration in Khusuba, I am hoping," Umma said. "Daughter, you have not seen our new home! Let your brother's wedding be an opportunity to rejoice for him, then come see our house in Zumurrud!"

The capital city of Dehlkia was quite a step up from the slums. So. Dargah's monthly funding was embraced, but *she* was merely tolerated. "I will try my hardest," she said, her tone indicating that she had no intention of trying at all. "I've told you how hard Vigga works me. I hardly think she would be pleased with my being gone for over a month."

"Well, then perhaps do not come for the week of the Bridal Bonding. I can serve in your role there. Just come for the day of the wedding, then leave before the days of feasting. The dwarf cannot begrudge you that," Umma said dismissively.

While her mother's suggestion was logical, it still stung. The Bridal Bonding took place over several days, during which the females of both would-be mates sequestered themselves and celebrated, worshiped, offered advice, indulged in wine and candied fruits, and finalized the design of her bonding tattoo, which she and her new mate would receive during a private, intimate ceremony after the celebration. As Hashem's only sister, Dargah would have had a place of honor among the women. She would have been expected to lead certain rituals and even invoke the Dehlkian blessing of fertility for the couple. The days of feasting were essentially a three-day-long party during which both families provided food, drink, gifts, and necessary items for the new couple to build a household. In essence, her mother was telling her that she wasn't needed in Dehlkia for any of the intimate moments *or* the parties.

"Did Hashem decide to go for the traditional wedding, or was it Janan's idea?" Runo wanted to know. Likely, he wondered, as Dargah did, how Hashem would fund the kind of event that had become rare nowadays, even for the wealthy.

And here was where Umma's smile turned smug. "Didn't I mention it in my letter? It seems that Janan is now related by marriage to some *very* wealthy people, and they have offered to pay for the whole affair!"

Dargah raised an eyebrow. All the requirements of a traditional wedding in Dehlkia could easily equal a year's pay—or more—for the average laborer. The prohibitive cost was exactly why they were no longer commonplace.

"Damn, lucky her," moped Runo. "Whose family? Do I know them?"

"I would say that you do! Janan's cousin married *Kelia*'s youngest brother last year."

Dargah's appetite vanished. The cake on her plate may as well have been ox dung, for all she wanted it now.

"With Kelia having such a good head on her shoulders, you know, and with both her father and her *husband* doing so well with the arenas—did you hear, they built another? Three, now, and all of them filled to bursting with contenders!—it just made sense for them to handle all the details," she chuckled. "What a *blessing* for Janan and Hashem!"

With a poise and icy grace she could have lifted from Neryn's playbook, Dargah rose from her chair, smoothed her dress, and placed a few coins on the table. "This should cover my portion of the meal. With this, I have more than fulfilled any debts I have owed you. I will be returning to my room now. I will not see you again before you leave. Travel safely." Pointedly withholding the customary bow of respect, Dargah swept out of the dining hall and, without slowing her stride, started down the path toward Adelfi's.

*

The evening had grown chilly, even for autumn, but Dargah's blood was colder still. After all this time, she'd moved on from her debacle of a breakup, but apparently, her mother hadn't. And the worst part was that Kelia wasn't even a home-wrecker or cheap whore. Dargah had tried to hate her, to resent her. But she couldn't. Kelia was a clever, cheerful girl from a very wealthy family, whose father was itching to invest in athletic training and facility construction. It had always been lucrative, but the popularity of the Games had steadily risen across Argodoth for the past few decades. It only made sense for him to partner with a well-known, successful trainer. And wouldn't it be just brilliant if that trainer could be roped into the family as well? Genius!

The only problem was that the trainer he picked was Parviz of Olasi-Memnun.

And Parviz's heart belonged to Dargah.

Or so she'd thought.

She'd been humiliated enough when she'd heard the very public announcement about his upcoming wedding—before he'd even officially ended things with Dargah—but even at home she found no relief. While Appa was somewhat disgruntled about the thoughtless way in which Parviz had behaved, Umma was incensed at Dargah.

"You've been given *everything*!" she hissed across the dinner table. "We spent every single coin—money we don't have to spare—to get you armor, get you training, get you every gods-damned thing you needed to succeed in the arena. Gods, you even caught the eye of a trainer! You had him by the *balls*, daughter, and you couldn't even bag him then! If you hadn't been so gods-damned picky about a mate, you'd have been married with half a dozen children by now, happy and out of this house. So now, we're supposed to find you a new trainer mid-season? With what money, child?"

Dargah had glanced at her three adult brothers, none of whom looked any happier than she felt, and said nothing.

That night, little Runo had snuck into Dargah's room, curled up on her bed, and hugged her. In innocent whispers, he reassured her it was all right if she lived there forever because he would, too, and they'd never ever have to be apart.

*

"They left early."

Runo's face, though weary, was a happy sight for Dargah the next morning, as it meant that he'd survived the rest of dinner with their parents. "What do you mean?"

"Umma and Appa left for home just after dawn."

"Why? They weren't planning on leaving until the closing rites."

"I told them to go."

"Come here and explain." Dargah patted the bed, and Runo, still dressed in his finery from the night before, shuffled over and flopped down next to her. He buried his face in her pillow for several seconds before speaking.

"I told them to go," he repeated. "After what Umma said to you. She could have answered my question without mentioning Parviz's mate. But she did, and I know she did it to hurt you. And I also know that's nothing new. You're gonna kill me for it, but I've read some of the other letters she sent you. The ones you thought were hidden inside that cookbook?"

"You little bogsucker," Dargah said admiringly.

"Like, every letter is how much better the family's doing without you. She doesn't come out and *say it*, but 'oh, Hashem was so happy to move into your old room,' and now it's 'the new house is so nice and quiet these days,' and that crap—it's obvious. I think she treats you like that because she's jealous," Runo announced. "If we're being honest, I think she wanted you to marry Parviz so *she* could drool over him."

Dargah gave a derisive snort.

"She acted like *you* ended things and that you did it to spite her! I never understood that."

"Maybe it's a good thing I won't be having children. They'd have the worst grandmother ever."

Runo frowned, pointing to himself. "But the greatest *uncle* ever."

"Even before you were born, it was like this. It's not just that I'm a disappointment. It's like she's angry I exist. Like, angrier than Neryn is that I exist."

587

"I don't think he's angry that you exist anymore." Runo's face was back in the pillow, and his voice was muffled. "Maybe vaguely irritated. But not *angry*."

"Ugh. Write to Umma and tell her I died. Then at least she'll get all kinds of attention for having a dead daughter. Maybe she'd like that."

"That's a very Orlaeth thing to do."

"For a very un-Orlaeth reason."

"I told them they could stay in Lindenvale for the rest of the festival, but I wouldn't be joining them. They came to say goodbye this morning." He shrugged. "I'm not going home either. Ever."

"They aren't mad at *you*. Go, enjoy the wedding. Maybe you'll get the chance to play or sing, and then you'll become famous or something. And there will be *so many* eligible females there!"

"No."

"Are you signing on as a permanent part of my rebellious little posse? For keeps? Even though you sleep in a mop closet, and it's a really *small* posse?"

"Wouldn't have it any other way."

The room was quiet for a long time.

"Hey, Dargah?"

"Hm?"

"Good deeds can outweigh bad ones, right?"

"I guess, sometimes, sure."

"And standing up for you was a good deed?"

She grabbed a hunk of his hair and pulled his head up off the pillow. "What bad deed are you trying to outweigh, Ruh Noor of Kuvaat-Asi?"

"I might have kissed your best friend."

Dargah was deadly silent for far too long.

"In your mind, you've already dismembered me and hidden all the parts, haven't you?" Runo asked.

"Twice."

"Lemme explain, all right?" When she didn't immediately protest, he said, "I left dinner not long after you did. And when I was coming home, I ran into Rinah. She could tell I was really emotional because I hate the way Umma talks to you, and so she gave me a hug, and I might have held on like a little teensy bit too long and then kind of gave her like a friendly sort of squeeze, and it might have been kind of more than friendly because, I mean, I *am* lonely, and I've *kind* of had a bit of a thing for her like since the first day I met her even though she's an Older Woman, and I never said anything, but she looked really pretty in her dress, and I just really appreciated her caring about me, and I told her she was beautiful, and then I got really, really nervous, kind of smooshed my mouth into hers, and then ran away."

"…Was that your first kiss?"

Runo appeared mildly offended. "Oh, my gods, *no*. And I am usually much smoother than that but I got nervous, and my tummy started to hurt, so I just—" He mimed vomiting all over the floor.

"You'd better thank the goddess that I am too emotionally drained to do anything but give you the stink eye right now, boy."

Chapter Twenty-Nine:

Of Lilacs and Lavender

"*How* long will you be gone?"

Rinah folded a chemise and placed it into her satchel. She'd nearly finished packing and could hardly contain her excitement at the prospect of a trip to Sterlingshire with friends. She'd organized all her belongings, promised Alvyx that she would continue her druidic studies while she was away, and baked a fresh batch of muffins for the journey ahead. Charis, Xinny, and Elpida would arrive in the morning to pick her up.

"It's a solid two days to Sterlingshire, and that's with good weather. We'll be staying a few days for Charis to have her dress made, then coming home. A week, at most?"

Makoa reacted as though she told him she was permanently relocating to the frosty mountains of Kaylor to frolic among feral dwarves.

"You're welcome to visit Papa while I'm gone. He'll need supervision, I'm sure," she said with a wink. "And, you can stop by the inn to see Dargah and Runo."

"But Runo doesn't know anything about earthworms!"

Rinah laughed so hard she almost choked. "Why does that matter?"

"He can't teach me about them. You can."

"I already taught you everything I know about earthworms."

"Forget the earthworms, then. Anything. Teach me anything. Because you get so happy when you talk about something that interests you. And then you kind of get a little glow, sort of a blush, but I think it's just excitement, and that makes me get excited too, and I want you to talk about earthworms—or whatever it is—for hours." His voice softened a bit. "You get like that whenever you're doing something you love: baking muffins, or gardening, or when you're reading to your papa—and to me. It's like you're happy just *existing*. I like that. A lot."

"The glow is probably just rogue magic getting fired up," she said dismissively. "I've seen Papa like that sometimes, too." Rinah moved her bag from the sofa to the floor, making room for Makoa to join her. "Is that why you're coming over more often? Because life as a faerie is really that boring? Or is it because you love muffins so much?"

594

He sat. "You'd think faeries are social, but we're about as fun as that elf from the weird village. It was Neryn, right?"

Rinah smothered a giggle.

"It's *really* boring being a faerie. We're considered a colony because we live near each other, but we're not close like a family or anything. Not even like neighbors. We don't have festivals like you, worship at temples, have hobbies, or go to shops. There's not much to do except patrol, sleep, and have sex."

Rinah coughed to hide her surprise. For obvious reasons, casual sex had never been part of her childhood faerie daydreams. "So, you... faeries can... oh. Well, I mean, of course you can. You're earthborn, after all. You obviously came from...uh."

"It's usually for different reasons than humans," Makoa hurried to explain. "Elemental mages get power from the gods, and their strength is based on their training.

Rogue mages, the way your papa explained it, get their power from scavenging."

"I suppose, for lack of a better word," Rinah said with a raised eyebrow.

"*Lorica* is a different kind of magic altogether, and, well, faeries get it from each other. When our supplies are low, we can, uh, restore each other. With...sex. It isn't exactly the same as what you do. I mean, not *you*, specifically, I just meant... it's just... it's over fast. It's not *romantic*." When she looked away, flustered, Makoa patted down his body briefly as if reminding himself he'd shifted. "So, I guess things would work a *little* differently in this body, but not much. My wings wouldn't get in the way. That would be nice for a change. And from what I've heard, the Created races like to take their time and create an atmosphere... with poetry and music, and good food and wine... and they start out with something called foreplay?"

"*Who* have you been talking to?" Rinah blurted, torn between a giggle and a groan. "Runo?"

"And Dargah," he confessed.

"Oh, gods, Makoa. Orcs and humans are not the same!"

"So you're *not* interested in this 'foreplay'?"

"Go finish your patrol," she commanded, leaping up from the sofa. She pushed a pumpkin muffin into his hands and shooed him out the door. He stuffed the whole thing into his mouth, gave her a cheeky grin, then disappeared to protect the forests of Ayusa.

*

The road to Sterlingshire was paved with Xinila's complaints.

Their little party had barely piled up in the wagon, pulled by dumpy, faithful Apple Blossom, to leave Lindenvale when she began to comment about her discomfort. "I think I snagged my dress on a splinter..."

Rinah was glad that she'd volunteered to sit up front with Elpida. At least it gave her an excuse to pretend not to hear every one of Xinny's lamentations. Still, the journey ahead was going to feel much longer than it really was. She should have brought a book.

"Is that the horse I smell, or did someone forget to bathe?"

Rinah should have brought *several* books.

*

Late into their first day of travel, as the sunlight was fading, they found rooms in the town of Warrick's Wood. It was there that Rinah's good fortune finally ran out, and she drew the short straw, earning Xinny as a bedmate. All the ladies shuffled into their room, with Charis's excited chattering finally dissolving into a gentle snore as she snuggled up next to her mother.

Xinila lay with her back to Rinah. After a moment, she asked quietly, "I guess things didn't work out with Bram?"

Rinah's breath caught. Four months had passed since Vigga's nephew had suddenly "disappeared" from Lindenvale, and no one had seemed to miss him. "No," mumbled Rinah. "He wasn't the kind of person he led me to believe he was."

"Hm. What about this new boy of yours? The redhead? He's a pretty one. I've seen him with you at the inn a few times but never around town. Are you keeping him to yourself, Rinah?"

Rinah's cheeks warmed, and she blurted out the backstory they'd chosen for him. "Oh. Makoa, uh, he's an astrologer's apprentice, so he's mostly only up and about at nighttime."

"I wonder if he'd be able to draw up a birth chart for me," Xinny mused.

"Oh, he's nowhere near ready to do anything like that," Rinah assured her, certain that anything Makoa drew at this point would be on par with a toddler's scribbles.

"...then I wonder if perhaps I can plan a trip to Reefside. To see the Oracle."

Rinah imagined Xinila threatening the trio of prophetesses if they told her something she didn't like. "I've always wanted to go there, too. To see the Archives, though."

"Who would want to waste time on history when you have the chance to see the future?"

Oh, Xinny. "You think the goddess really speaks through them? I've always thought the Oracle was more ceremonial than anything else. It's been years since they accurately predicted a natural disaster or the outcome of a battle..."

"What do I care about natural disasters? I just want to know if I'm going to be stuck in Lindenvale forever."

Ah. There it was. "What's wrong with Lindenvale?"

Xinila sniffed. "There's nothing there. Little boys, and old men, and smelly fishermen, and ignorant farmers, and traveling merchants peddling junk."

"Oh. I think I see…" Rinah felt her shift in the bed, temper brewing.

"Every time someone new shows up in town, he gets snapped up in a heartbeat. Bram made a beeline for you. I didn't even have a chance! And that big, burly trader who comes through every so often, the one with all the rings on his fingers? Who does he make eyes at? Dargah!" Her voice, already a hiss, dropped even lower. "Even Charis. Charis has a pet goose and no sense at all in her head, and she still gets *my brother* for a husband!"

Rinah stewed for a moment, swallowing the curse on her lips. Then, as though speaking to a young child, she said, "Xinila Rallis. Bram fathered two children to two different mothers, neither of whom he married, and then he tried to *rape* me."

"*Well*," was all she said.

Her rogue magic was squawking inside her like a ruffled bird, only adding to the frustration in Rinah's words. "I know for a fact that Baros is *not* courting Dargah, and even if he was, I would not begrudge her that because she's long overdue for a little romance in her life. And Charis is a gentle, sweet girl who will be your sister-in-law, so maybe you should learn to speak kindly of her, or at the very least, hold your tongue for once."

As though she hadn't heard anything Rinah just said, Xinny hissed, "And now you've snagged this redhead! If I don't get out of that stupid little village, I swear, I'll just *die!*"

Maybe it was hearing Neryn, an avowed pacifist, slam Bram into a tree. Maybe it was hours of watching Dargah rain blows onto steel and iron, forming a weapon out of a shapeless mass. Maybe it was the whisper of Orlaeth's strange and courageous faith. Whatever it was,

Rinah felt a surge of bravery, and she was tired of playing nice. She pushed past her bedmate, made herself comfortable on the floor, and answered, "It's not the village, Xin. It's you. It's always been you. You don't deserve someone like Makoa, and do you want to know why?" *Oh, dear.* She'd blame the magic later when she looked back on this, she decided, but for now, she plunged ahead. "Do you know what things matter to him? All the things you consider useless. He likes learning about gardening with me and Oraleth. He thinks it's wonderful that Runo cooks and uses his family recipes. He loves listening to old children's stories, and he thinks my papa is a good person and not a madman, and *he likes me*, Xinila."

The only response was the shifting of the mattress as Xinny slid closer to the wall.

*

It was probably Rinah's fault that Charis's dress-fitting was a rather chilly affair. Xinila had frozen over entirely, refusing to speak to either girl and only allowing for brief exchanges with Elpida.

Charis didn't seem to mind in the least, however, and chirped merrily to the tailor, who tucked and measured and cuffed and poked, all in the name of beauty. The mother and daughter had narrowed down their fabric choices but still flip-flopped between a rich, velvety plum and a light, dreamy lilac.

"Use both!" Rinah suggested. "The darker color is perfect for autumn, so the bodice and overskirt can be plum, but if the underdress is lilac, she can wear it in the spring, too."

"With green lacing! And green ribbons in my hair and green shoes!" sighed Charis, imagining herself as a beautiful, blooming flower of a bride.

"I'll see what we can do," said Elpida with a smile.

The tailor jotted some numbers down, then said, "Two days. I cleared the schedule for my girls and me to work on nothing but Miss Charis's dress. Now go and spend money in my town." She hugged Elpida and Charis, then ushered all four ladies outside.

Charis drifted toward the fragrant cinnamon and vanilla aroma of a baker's cart. Xinila's eye was caught by a cobbler's display that featured shoes with an impractically high heel. Elpida pulled Rinah aside and whispered, "I heard what you said to Xinny last night." Rinah opened her mouth, unsure if she should apologize, but with a motherly smile, Elipda continued. "Thank you for standing up for Charis. She *can* seem a little simple-minded sometimes, but I think *that*—the fact that she doesn't put on airs or pretend to be someone else—is exactly why Galen adores her." Allowing herself a sly smile, Rinah nodded and decided to reward her bravery with a little treat. She hurried back to the cart they'd passed earlier and smiled at its proprietress.

"Hey, Lindenvale!" the young woman cried in recognition. Nikola giggled and gave Rinah a hug. "What are you doing in my neck of the woods?"

The pleasure of meeting Nikola at the summer Adoration had been nearly erased by Bram's assault, but Rinah hoped to kindle a new friendship. "One of my friends is having a new dress made for her wedding, and—"

"Ooh, I bet she came out to see Meldri Kalogeros! Do you know, she's the only person the temple priestesses trust to make their gowns? There are half a dozen tailors and clothiers in this town, but she's had an exclusive agreement with them for *decades*."

Like their goddess, the temple servants of Ayusa were reputed to be vain and fussy. They'd been known to dramatically halt worship services if they perceived sacred objects to be out of place or if supplicants were kneeling too close to the altar. "Then she must be remarkable."

"Yes, and she's a sweetheart, too. My Zoie is only six, but she's always dressed in the most popular styles from Reefside. Mel says she's using my girl as her dress form, but it's just an excuse to put another pretty dress on that child. Zoie'd better get rich or marry a rich man because gods know that I will not be able to afford all the clothing she's going to want when she gets older."

"Zoie sounds a lot like Charis was as a child," laughed Rinah. Her friend had always loved to dress up, once going so far as to pull her mother's curtains from the windows, wrap herself in them, lie immobile on the floor, and insist she was a mermaid. The only way Elpida had been able to salvage the drapes was to remind Charis that mermaids didn't eat roast beef, and that's what they were having for dinner, and it would be a shame if she went hungry.

"Did you come to shop, too, maybe?" Nikola asked, her eyes sparkling.

"I did!"

"For yourself? For a boy? No! For a *man*!"

Rinah's face was radiant. "Yes. For a young man who means a lot to me."

"Brother, lover, father, or friend?"

"Um, friend?"

"Friend for *now*," corrected Nikola. "Tell me about him." The craftswoman opened a small chest and rummaged through it.

"He's brave and funny. And he's very sweet. And humble. He is honest, and he gets along with my friends. And they like him, too."

"He sounds like husband material to me, darling." Nikola held out her hand. In it was coiled a bracelet that glittered like a fallen star. "Sunstone for joy and moonstone for new beginnings." With a wink, she added, "And *fertility*."

Rinah jerked her hand back and made a face, but Nikola just laughed. "It's just tradition. I promise, I can't afford to use any *genuinely* enchanted gemstones in my work." Then she slipped the bracelet around Rinah's wrist. "Give it to him with love from Sterlingshire. He sounds wonderful."

Rinah thanked her, paid, and hurried to meet up with the rest of her party. They were all hungry, and everything smelled delicious.

*

"Go where the magic calls you."

With a belly full of potato soup and her papa's reminder thrumming in her head, Rinah shrugged and closed her eyes. Finding rogue magic was so much easier in the peaceful calm of the woods. Here, even as far from the heart of the bustling market—and Xinila's reproachful glare—as she could get, she was still distracted by the rattling of carts, the shouts of vendors and merchants, the buzz of nearby conversation. She could smell the faint aroma of bacon grease, which she'd dripped carelessly onto her skirt earlier, and the wild violet perfume of a passerby. She could feel the brisk breeze, carrying traces of elderberry and pine.

Rinah breathed in lungfuls of chilly air and released them slowly. She imagined she could blow away her worries with each puff of air, and soon, her mind began to clear. The jangle of nearby shop bells faded. The conversations turned from words into sounds, and then from sounds into vibrations. The sharp, green scent of pine faded.

And there it was.

Rogue magic was dancing all around her. Some of it taunted her. Some of it beckoned her. And some of it loved her. *Courted* her. Wanted to belong to her. She opened her eyes and pointed. "It's there."

She was staring at an outdoor privy.

Ah. Even magic can play jokes, it seemed. She was directly facing a row of five discreetly painted doors, each of which led to a small, private hutch containing an enchanted, self-cleaning chamber pot. Rinah was certain that her bodily needs weren't interfering with her sense of wonder. "Here we go, then," she said under her breath. She crossed the street, disrupting a boys' ball game, and traced the path of magic, which wound around behind the necessary rooms.

There was nothing but a patch of trampled grass and a discarded kebab, likely bought from a street vendor. Insects were already making short work of the meat, and only a shriveled hunk of pepper and a quarter of a red onion remained. Nothing else on the ground.

Maybe she *did* just have to pee.

No, there it was again, calling out to her like a long-lost friend. She looked around, then up into the shady trees above, convinced she'd missed something. "Where are you?" she whispered. She felt a tug from the trunk of the oak and gingerly placed her hands on it, waiting for it to tell her its story.

When it did, she gasped.

Rogue magic had never regaled her with elvish erotica. Not until now.

"Am I even I *allowed* to take that kind of magic? Seems sort of... personal," she wondered aloud, withdrawing her hands. Unseen, it rippled with something like a shrug. Magic is magic, it seemed to laugh in her ear.

And at least *this* magic had seen a good time. Maybe it could give her some pointers?

She glared at the tree. "That isn't necessary, thank you. But if you can behave yourself, you're welcome to climb aboard."

When it did, she felt its warm fluttering under her skin and then a happy spark, offered in gratitude.

But she *did* also have to pee, she realized, and she slipped into one of the rooms.

Chapter Thirty:

Of Homecomings and Hook-Ups

"I really missed you," Makoa said for the third time that evening.

Rinah stretched, her limbs still stiff from being wedged in that wagon for so many hours. In spite of his delight upon her safe return, Papa managed to steal away for a bit, pretending he didn't realize he was leaving Rinah and Makoa alone. "I missed you, too," she replied. "But it was really nice to spend time with Charis. Her mother was the one who found me after my father died."

When Makoa's eyes bugged, she laughed and looked down at her tawny-hued skin. "I thought it was pretty obvious that Alvyx isn't my real father. I mean...he's almost as pale as Orlaeth!"

"I just assumed you looked like your mother."

"Maybe I do. I wouldn't know."

Makoa drew in a sharp breath. "Oh, no. She isn't alive?"

Rinah shook her head. "I don't remember a lot about her or my father. I was really young when Papa took me in. What about your parents? Do you look like either of them?"

He shrugged. "Earthborns aren't raised by our parents' colony. I guess maybe the idea that some faeries would have a family unit, like the Created races, while others didn't... maybe it wasn't a popular idea. So we grow up in a colony different from our parents'. No one has any special ties to each other that way. I mean, even our King and Queen aren't in a relationship the way you'd think of one. They're partners, consorts, but it's for the sake of managing the colonies, keeping us united, you know?"

No. She did not know. Rinah blinked. "And you have never had any desire *at all* to find out who your parents are?"

"No."

Her eyes went wide. "How? Why?"

"My situation is different from yours," Makoa insisted, worried by her expression. "Humans are *supposed* to have a mother and a father, and siblings, and a job, and hobbies, and a spouse, and children. I'm not. Faeries, I mean. We're just made to work."

Put that way, Makoa's life seemed bleak. Faeries - creatures said to have been born out of the Unseen God's final breath - seemed to have little more value than the bees that visited her garden. But even the bees had sisterhood when they returned to their hive, working together to rear another generation! Did Makoa truly have nothing apart from what he had found in Lindenvale?

Perhaps it was the unexpected mention of her dead mother, or perhaps she was just overtired from her journey, but Rinah's eyes welled with tears. "That's so cruel."

Makoa shook his head, but his tone was gentle. "And *this* is another reason why we never shift. Trying to explain this to a Created one is just... it's just not something that makes sense to you."

"No, it doesn't," she agreed, trying to imagine her life without Alvyx's compassion. Without Runo's easy companionship. Without Charis's joyful laughter.

It wouldn't be a life at all.

"But that's why I missed *you* so much," Makoa said, brightening. "Your papa is a good person, but he falls asleep mid-conversation, and the books he reads are kind of dull."

Rinah allowed the change of subject. "What else did you do while I was away?"

"Stargazed. Got chased by an owl. Twice." He reached over and twisted one of her curls around his fingers, then released it like a spring. "Worked. Scouted. Slept in a new tree yesterday."

"That sounds lonely."

"It is. That's why I'm glad you're my friend. My best friend. I'll fight Dargah for the title." Makoa had taken Alvyx's seat in front of the fire. He put his feet up and closed his eyes, enjoying the warmth of the hearth.

Rinah watched him for a moment, taking in his relaxed, peaceful attitude. "Oh, will you?"

Without opening his eyes, he replied, "Come sit with me." He patted his thighs.

Rinah wasn't often self-conscious about her body, but Makoa was on the lean side, and she... wasn't. She looked down at her generous hips and insisted, "There's not enough room."

He took her hand and pulled her into his lap, then embraced her. "Sure, there is."

Rinah couldn't tell if it was his heart pounding or her own. "Makoa, best friends don't... snuggle."

"Why not?"

She couldn't think of a reasonable answer. "They just don't?"

"They should. From what I've learned, best friends like spending time with each other. They eat together, and they talk together. And they look at the stars together. Why shouldn't they sleep together?" Rinah tensed, but Makoa carried on easily. He didn't mean sex. He meant *actually sleeping*. Right? "This is what I want. I want the rain outside, and the fire inside, and muffins, and you—talking to you. If it could be like this all the time..." He quieted for a moment. "I like how your body feels. You're warm and soft, and you always smell like good things. If you don't like snuggling, we don't have to. But we shouldn't not snuggle just because best friends aren't supposed to snuggle."

"I do like snuggling," she said faintly. She didn't know where to put her hands. Around his neck? On his chest? She settled for folding them demurely in her lap. Then, she wondered, "Shouldn't your best friend be maybe a small woodland creature?" She looked at him hard. "Oh! Can you ride squirrels or rabbits the way humans ride horses?"

"Squirrels are stubborn as hell, and rabbits are too skittish. Skunks are friendly enough, but, well, the problem there is pretty obvious. Usually, a fox is your best bet, but not a mother with kits. A juvenile male."

Picturing a tiny Makoa attempting to saddle a frisking polecat, Rinah stared. "Seriously?"

He laughed. "No! Any one of those things might eat me, except maybe the rabbit. I steer clear of anything with teeth, for the most part. And even if I could understand animals, I don't have a lot of free time for deep, meaningful conversations." He looked at her with affection, the corners of his eyes crinkling as he smiled. "So, yeah. You're my best friend. If that's all right."

"So faeries don't even..." Rinah hesitated. "You don't have families like we do, but you don't even have a, um, a sweetheart?"

"You mean a regular lover? A partner?"

"I guess?"

"No reason to."

Oh. All right. Wait. Was that a good thing or a bad thing? "I thought you said before that faeries have nothing to do except sleep and have sex..." Rinah shouldn't be asking him anything like this. Definitely not when she was in his lap. She should let the conversation die. She should just enjoy the feeling of his heartbeat against her cheek and the sage-and-mint scent of him. Be happy that this mysterious creature chose to befriend her. Chose to visit her nearly every night. Chose to invite her into his arms, even now...

"Yeah, but it's not about connection for us. It's more about survival. For you, I mean, for the Created races it's for children, or for love."

"Or lust." Her face was hot, she knew, so she looked down at her hands. She hadn't realized until then how comfortable she'd become with having Makoa in her life. With having him as *hers*, somehow. How was she supposed to tell this man, this magical, mythological creature, that the idea of him wrapping a female faerie up in his arms—for whatever reason—was enough to make her sick? Tell him that she knew she'd never been given the slightest hint that there could ever be anything beyond friendship between them, anything beyond nightly chats over tea and scones, but that she felt so safe and relaxed with him? That every time she saw the sun rise, all she could think about was his brilliant, flame-colored hair and those snapping amber eyes?

"But what if you *did* fall in love?" Rinah's words were barely a whisper.

Makoa rested his chin on the top of her head, and she heard his response rumble in his throat. "Were you in love with Bram?"

She did not appreciate the mirror being turned on her. "No."

"Have you ever fallen in love? What's it like?"

I imagine it's like this, right now, breathing in your scent and feeling it wrap around me like a blanket. Your skin touching mine and feeling like home. Never wanting this moment to end because when it does, I'll feel like I'm waking up from a dream, and all I will want to do will be to fall asleep again so I can have you like this, all to myself, just for a little longer.

The intensity of her reaction terrified her. She squeezed her eyes shut to keep all the fear inside, then let out a deep breath. She carefully untangled herself from his limbs and stumbled to her feet. "Sorry," she murmured. "I didn't get much sleep while I was away. I'm... I'm really tired. I think it's just hitting me now."

"I wouldn't mind," he said gently, reaching out to her, "if you fell asleep here."

Unsure of herself, Rinah was grateful to have Alvyx as an excuse this evening. "Oh, absolutely, Papa would *love* walking in the door and seeing you in his chair and me sleeping in your lap," she snorted, still unable to look at him.

"I'll see you tomorrow, then?" he asked, rising from the chair.

"Maybe."

Her response hung in the air, unanswered, for just a second too long.

"All right. Next week then. Sleep well, Rinah."

She couldn't bring herself to watch the wings waving goodbye to her that night.

*

Erjunn had not spoken to Orlaeth since he'd given her the vision of Rinah's death.

At first, Orlaeth assumed that he remained silent because of how thoroughly the experience had exhausted her. Perhaps, in his mercy, he was allowing her fragile mortal body the time it needed to recover. Then, she wondered if it was because she'd failed to react appropriately upon receiving the vision. Should she have hurried to prevent it herself? Sought further clarification from her god? And, ultimately, why was it that the terrible ending she saw for Rinah did not come to pass?

Orlaeth's time at the library, previously spent only on dutiful copywork for Mr. Naoum, was now also spent on study. There were few elvish texts there, and fewer still that focused on magic, but Orlaeth would solve that problem.

Providing her employer with a tidy list of every piece in Lindenvale's literary collection, including its title, author, topic, and approximate date of completion (if known), the elf presented a thoroughly convincing argument in favor of a resource exchange between themselves and other small, nearby libraries. "If an individual can be trusted to borrow and return a book," she had pressed, "then let us treat a sister library with the same good faith. What do you think?"

Within weeks, Mr. Naoum had arranged a lending circle among the small collections at Sterlingshire, Warrick's Wood, and Black Lake, and Orlaeth pored over every elfish chronology, religious text, and scroll she could get her hands on. She needed to know: what was expected of a prophetess of the wind god?

*

"Come in. You're soaked. How long were you standing outside?"

A week after her intimate fireside chat with Makoa, Rinah had tucked her confusing feelings safely inside her heart. She was ready to forget the way she'd felt, but it wasn't easy seeing him now, like this, his soaked clothing sticking to the hard lines of his body, to pretend that she hadn't pressed her cheek up against that chest. "I couldn't remember where we decided to hide my clothes," he admitted.

"Under the bench," Rinah answered, ushering him inside. They'd agreed to pack them up in beeswax-coated paper to keep them safe and dry, but they hadn't been able to decide on the best place to hide them at first.

"I realized that after about five minutes of standing naked in the rain like an idiot."

"Let's get you warmed up," Rinah laughed, leading him by the hand toward the hearth. "It's just going to be us for now. Papa will be around a little later. Orlaeth isn't feeling well, and he took her some soup. Runo has to work, and Dargah's too tired." As he shucked off his boots, she pawed through the wardrobe until she found her papa's old winter cloak. It was worn and well-patched, but it was lined with fur and very soft. Even when Rinah had arranged to have a new one made, he couldn't bear to part with it. She turned to offer it to Makoa, not realizing he'd already removed his wet tunic.

He stood facing the fire, the flames glinting off his torso. Though trim, he was all muscle, with broad shoulders and a narrow waist. Not for the first time, Rinah drank in the sight of the magical wards branded onto his skin—ineffective in his human form but still stunning. Sinewy, vinelike runes snaked up his arms and legs and stood out in sharp contrast to his fair skin. He turned to her with a bright smile.

She didn't have the words to properly convey the feelings flooding her body at that moment and would have sworn to anyone who asked that the heat on her cheeks was from the fire. "Here," she said faintly, offering him the robe. "Ready for dinner?"

"Maybe I can help you make something! I think it's time I repaid your hospitality," he joked.

"No need." From the pantry, Rinah pulled leftover pastries, dried beef, a jar of peach preserves, a large hunk of hard yellow cheese, half a loaf of brown bread, and an entire bag of apples. "Take your pick."

He ignored everything except the pastries, eating three of the scones. Rinah cut a wedge of cheese for herself and drifted over to sit in Alvyx's chair. The fire crackled lightly. An owl hooted nearby. It wasn't the one that chased him, Rinah told him before he could ask. She'd need to have another chat with Nell.

They enjoyed the warmth in calm, companionable silence for a while. Then Makoa said, "This is my favorite place of all the places I've ever been."

"In front of the fire?"

"No. With you."

Rinah forced a laugh. "Your colony must be duller than I thought, then." She bit the inside of her lip, then added quietly. "You can't say things like that, Makoa."

"Why can't I?

"It makes it harder to say goodbye every time you leave." She dared a glance in his direction. "I've gotten used to having you around."

He leaned his elbows on the chair above her head, a satisfied smile spreading across his face. He said nothing.

Interlude IV:

Of Rumors and Risks

Two Months Ago

Queen Talu didn't mind travel; in fact, she enjoyed the variety of landscapes the territories of Erjunn and Ayusa had to offer. No, it was the seeming endlessness of the journeys themselves that grated on her.

For the past thirty years, she had left the comfort of her home for just two reasons—to welcome life and to oversee death. She delighted in the former, of course, though it was an infrequent joy. The need for younglings was so rare among the Guardians that, in the fifteen hundred years of her reign, she had personally witnessed the birth of fewer than fifty infants. Some of the more arrogant members of her race insisted, under their breath, of course, that earthborn faeries were inferior to their sky-blessed kin, but Talu had never entertained such a foolish notion.

Still, she had to wonder if there *was* something different about the earthborns. Something that made them more prone to wander away from their true calling, something intrinsic that came from being crafted within a womb, a curiosity that was never passed from The Unseen God into the Guardians formed from his own broken form. Her own body had never nourished an infant. Unlike human queens, she had no need for progeny of her own, nor did she need to concern herself with any of their oddities or habits.

Talu, for one, had never wondered what humans liked to snack on, or what their courtship rituals were like, why they seemed so concerned with the cut of their clothing, or why they bothered with clothing at all. And she could hardly imagine drakes or nixies concerning themselves with such things, either.

The leader of her Queensguard inelegantly interrupted her thoughts. "My lady, this colony's wards are adequate. I am confident in the safety that they will provide this evening, but the decision to stay is ultimately yours. What say you?"

"I say that I am tired, Kapena," Talu sighed. "Let us rest within the boundaries of Riverwatch Colony tonight."

With a firm nod, the captain unfurled his peppery-brown wings - unremarkable to look at, but stronger and larger than those of most faeries - and took off to notify the clan's leaders that they should prepare a meal, for they would be graced by the presence of their queen this night.

Chapter Thirty-One:

Of Reflection and Repentance

"Brother?"

Tiarnán's face came into focus, and Neryn realized that he'd again spent half of the service lost in thought. He leaped to his feet, clapping Tiarnán on the shoulder and taking the lyre from his hands.

As always, his pitch was flawless, the lyrics clear, and his head high. But as it had been for some time now, his voice lacked its lilting joy. No confidence in the men around him. No humility for Erjunn's kindness. No reverence for his station as a leader.

Nothing but the confusion a woman's question had created.

"Why do you hate me?"

The service ended as soon as Neryn struck the final chord, with the men free to socialize and pray with each other as they proceeded to enjoy a simple, communal breakfast. This morning, Neryn sat with his peers, but he barely glanced at the kettles of boiled oats and the baskets of dried fruit. A different kind of hunger gnawed away at him, and he made a plan to satisfy it as efficiently as possible.

*

Kaedryn Sunstorm, Disciple of Erjunn, was a leader to all, a mentor to many, and a patriarch to the Counselors, his cadre of twelve trusted advisors, which included Neryn. It was the sole reason he was able to secure private meetings with his own father, and even then, their conversations were frequently didactic, with Neryn jotting down notes to review afterward. Today, however, he had determined that *he* was going to steer the discussion.

Neryn arrived earlier than his scheduled appointment, bearing a hot mug of the Disciple's favorite herbal brew. In his other hand, he held his well-worn copy of Erjunn's holy book.

"Welcome." Kaedryn greeted him with a grateful smile as he took the tea. "Sit and pray with me for a while." He took his customary seat behind a large wooden desk and offered Neryn the low-backed chair opposite him.

With resolve in his tone, Neryn placed the book in front of him and began, "As always, I am honored to sit in your presence, Revered One. Yet first, and with all respect that is due your office and your person, I crave your indulgence." When the Disciple patiently raised an eyebrow over interlaced fingers, he continued. "You have never failed to share with me timeless wisdom and truths from Erjunn's own heart. And so I hold the hope that today, I may receive clarification on a variety of verses found within—"

The Disciple shook his head, chortled, then composed himself. He placed one slender hand on top of *The Path of the Wind*. "Neryn. You are an adult, and you need robust, hearty meals to nourish you. This is but milk, suckled at the breast of a new mother. Sweet it may be, but it is not long before the infant requires more than his mother alone can provide. He has felt her warmth and love, but he cannot remain coddled on her lap all of his days. He must cut his teeth on the fundamental truths and wholesome directives given in *The Wind Walker*. You know this, and you have always known this." The Disciple sipped his tea, leaned forward in his chair, and regarded Neryn for a long moment. He asked, "So how can it be that my Suppliant Prime of eight years, my advisor of six, and my son of thirty-two, has unanswerable questions about a child's primer?"

My son.

Kaedryn had not referred to him as anything other than a colleague for nearly seventeen years. Neryn felt a pang of sorrow; he'd hoped that, when he at last heard those words from his father's lips, they would be as rich as honey and twice as sweet. Instead, they sounded to him as hollow as an empty barrel. He did not, however, falter. "In all things, I have learned, a firm foundation is the key to success. So too is it with our faith. This book, simple though it is, creates for our people the groundwork we need to build ourselves and each other up into a people in whom

Erjunn can delight. And so, it is with that in mind that I humbly ask you to walk me, as a child, if you must, through the final passages in discourse three."

"So be it," the Disciple said.

Neryn didn't need to open the book to quote the passages, but for the Disciple's benefit, he did so and drew a finger, long and graceful, nearly identical to his father's, down the page. "'And with solemnity, Erjunn brought forth his children, presenting them as his beloved treasure, to his consort Dehlkia. The goddess was delighted with the creation of elves, as was Erjunn with her creation, the orcs. As elves reflected his gentle and thoughtful nature, so too, the orcs shared Dehlkia's passionate and robust character. How could Erjunn not adore that which so clearly bore witness to his esteemed queen? And, together, the god of air and the goddess of earth went to meet the creation of Kaylor, finding the dwarves equally agreeable. In those days, the gods walked among their people, instructing them in the ways of magic and teaching them how to care for themselves and each other.'" Neryn closed the book with gentle reverence.

"And what is it in these verses that you would like me to clarify?"

"I cannot find a passage in this book in which Erjunn changes his opinion about the creations of the gods."

"What do you mean?"

"Here, the holy text tells us that our god delighted in Dehlkia's children. At what point did that change?"

The Disciple shook his head sadly. "Oh, to be certain, in the earliest days, the orcs *were* appreciated by Erjunn. I have no doubt that he loved them as dearly as his own children. But, as time passed, they retained fewer and fewer of the qualities that our god loved in Dehlkia. The goddess of earth brings forth all things green and growing, but among the roses, there are thorns, and among the healing herbs hide poisonous blooms. It was not long until orcs fully embraced the feral nature of their double-faced goddess, and so they have become as wild animals. They are unpredictable and led not by reason but by desire alone. But elves—at least, these elves here, your brethren—choose to remain close to the heart of Erjunn, valuing his commands as others may value gold or gemstones. Because we seek to reflect his purity and integrity, how can we take into our spiritual embrace something that has become so foreign to our god?"

Tears of frustration pricked at Neryn's eyes, but he refused to let them fall. "What if Erjunn," he asked, "loves them still? The wild orcs, and the fickle humans, and the stubborn dwarves too? Has he not enough room to hold all of us in his heart?"

Kaedryn gave him a wistful smile. "You mistake pity for love." He stood. "Yet I appreciate your candor,

Neryn. And I am grateful for the opportunity to direct you towards the truth. Remember always that the book in your hands is nothing more than an *introduction* to Erjunn and an invitation to worship him. Only *The Wind Walker* contains the instructions to live a life pleasing to him."

Neryn nodded and stood, understanding that their brief meeting had come to a close.

His father smiled warmly. "I am eager to hear the newest song of invocation you have been working on. Will it be ready to present at next month's wedding ceremony?"

"It will be."

"Let us close our time together in prayer."

"It would be a blessing."

Kaedryn's voice took on the soothing cadence it did when he taught the women and children. "Great Erjunn, we humbly receive your teaching and thank you for your refreshing wisdom. Guide us, O god of air, as we go about our daily tasks, reminding us that every decision we make is an opportunity to honor you and that we should never take such things lightly. May it be so."

"May it be so," Neryn echoed. He offered a respectful bow, then escaped the room, his hope in tatters.

*

The evening vigil concluded at moonrise; it always did. As had become his post-service custom since he'd last returned from Lindenvale, Neryn ignored the rest of the men and escaped to the silent solitude of his own small cabin. He sat on his bed, staring moodily at absolutely nothing.

His cabin faced east, like all of the dwellings in Dirgil. Because Erjunn is the land farthest east in Argodoth, tradition claimed it as the god's preferred direction, though Neryn never understood why a deity needed to have a favorite orientation. His modest home had been next to those of two of his father's other trusted counselors. Three dwelt in the southernmost portion of the village, three to the west, and three to the north. Neryn, Tiarnán, and Ylthet Evermorn lived in the homes on the easternmost boundary of Dirgil. Tiarnán lived with his wife of fourteen months, Imogen, and Ylthet's wife was expecting their second child.

Only Neryn lived alone.

Although he would have enjoyed welcoming Orlaeth into his humble house, at the moment, he appreciated the privacy. His thoughts were too troubled for him to continue to maintain his composure, and he was finally able to sift through them, unbothered.

He revered his god and wanted to approach him with a pure heart. He'd lived according to the rules. He sang, he smiled, he served, he studied.

Then, his bride had disappeared, and he'd traveled to Lindenvale...

And met Dargah.

She was candid and confident and *irritating*, and unlike any woman Neryn had ever encountered. Worse, she was a half-blood and a wildling. She had nothing to do with Erjunn, save for a tenuous connection to his consort's ancestral homeland. Neryn was supposed to despise her. And he did, that first time he saw her.

But by the time she asked him why, he realized that he'd already changed his mind.

Therein dwelt the problem.

For the first time in his life, today, he'd brought himself to voice questions about his own faith, and his trusted leader dismissed it as childish bewilderment. Oh, how humbling it was to be righted by the Disciple.

Still…

His face warmed uncomfortably. The memory chafed, but his father was right about Dehlkia's children.

His preoccupation with Dargah was fascination more than it was anything else. Fascination that she was a distorted reflection of his own god's beautiful but primitive lover, and fascination that there were creatures in the world so unlike himself.

The fact that he didn't hate her he would keep to himself. None of his brethren needed to know that not all half-bloods were as repulsive as they'd feared. Nor did he want to brand himself a libertine for admitting he'd let one enter the sacred lodge and stay overnight.

Or that he had dreams about her, and each morning after he did, he allowed those forbidden images cling to him like her perfume, dark and heavy and so very captivating.

Interlude V:

Of Daughters and Destinies

Nineteen Years Ago

Alvyx Autumnsong hadn't realized how striking the similarities would be between the daughter and the mother, but he kept his surprise to himself.

Rinah leaned over the baby's cradle, giggling as she tickled Charis's little pink toes. Though too young to respond with a genuine laugh herself, Charis cooed, gurgled, and swiped clumsily at Rinah's fingers. Seated on the sofa, Elpida stretched and smiled over at Alvyx. "She would be a fine big sister, at any rate," she said. "If she was only old enough to help wash the soiled linens and prepare dinner, I'd fight you for her."

He reached over and placed his hand atop hers. "You understand, Elpida, don't you? You and Kephas both? This has nothing to do with you as parents. There isn't a doubt in my mind that Rinah would be happy here, and healthy, and live a wonderful life with the three of you," Alvyx said gently. "But the choice isn't mine to make."

Elpida squeezed his hand. "Of course. But *you* need to understand, you won't be doing this alone. Not for a minute. Kephas and I, and Basilia and Cyril, and the Adelfis… we are all here for you. And Rinah."

"She is a sweet girl. How hard can it be?"

Charis chose that moment to vomit all over herself. Rinah shrieked and started to cry. Charis cried louder.

"Oh, sure, it's easy as pie," Elpida laughed as she got up to tend to her daughter.

Alvyx knelt down and touched Rinah's shoulder, gently hushing her. "It seems that the gods have bound your fate to mine, little one. Can't say it's unexpected, though I would have liked a bit more time to prepare. Let's go to the cottage, Miss Rinah, and bake some muffins. I wonder—do you like blueberry best, or strawberry?"

The girl placed her tiny hand in Alvyx's large one, looked up into his face with a gap-toothed grin of pure delight, and announced, "Stew-berries!"

He nodded solemnly. "Yes, that's my favorite, too."

Chapter Thirty-Two:

Of Mistakes and Making-Up

"The elves have entirely different names for these constellations," complained Makoa. "And the faeries don't name them at all. Well, we do, but we don't have all these nonsense stories to go with them. I don't want to be a pretend astrologer anymore."

Several weeks after he and Rinah concocted their half-baked plan to pass Makoa off as a stargazer-in-training, he'd become a regular at Adelfi's, but only after sunset and only for a few hours at a time. Tonight, he and Rinah were standing at a large table at the inn. He smoothed the star chart across the table's knotty surface and groaned, trying to compare the dots on the chart to the pictures in the book Rinah had given him. "What is this? 'The Moored Fishing Boat'? Anyone can tell it's an eagle's nest. Who came up with this?"

"Quiet," hissed Rinah. "You're supposed to be a normal human. Don't make this weird."

"We are so far past that point already," Makoa mumbled. But then he caught her eye, and they both smiled.

"You've gotten much better at reading," Rinah praised him.

He laughed, "You wouldn't think Mr. Ikraam has the patience, but he's been a great teacher."

"Anything to drink for the apprentice?" Ioanie called out from the bar. She hadn't questioned Rinah's halting tale about Makoa being a visiting Autumnsong family friend who had taken up astrology as a hobby, and could he please have a room for the night? Coin was coin, and had Ioanie been told that Makoa was secretly a nine-headed hydra beast in hiding, she'd probably still rent him a room as long as he could pay.

"Yes, please," Makoa replied as Rinah furiously shook her head at him. He'd only had water or tea up until now.

"Cider, ale, or wine, love?"

"Nothing, thanks," Rinah called back at the same time Makoa asked for "whatever."

"I can't imagine faeries can hold their drink," she sniped.

"No, but this body might," he responded with a wink. "Guess you'll find out tonight."

"Guess *you'll* find out tomorrow what a hangover feels like. The ale here is piss and vinegar," she warned. "Only the wine is worth the headache later. Ioanie and her father make it the same way Papa does." The youngest Adelfi delivered the drink with a smile, then disappeared off to flirt with her patrons.

Rinah watched as Makoa swilled some of the ale. "TOld you it's awful." He was clearly refraining from expressing emotion, so she rolled her eyes and returned to the star chart. She scratched a few notes in her journal with a stick of charcoal, then rested her chin in her hand.

"We've kept your secret here," she said quietly, "but I never asked if you've been able to keep your secret *there*. None of your people know about your visits?"

"I make my rounds every night and report in every morning; that's all that matters. No one asks any questions. As long as I can keep my visits here short, there's no reason for anyone to be suspicious. But it's my night of rest anyway, so I can do whatever I want. Which is drinking this horrible stuff, apparently."

"Good to know. Now, get to work." She pointed to a passage she'd bookmarked for him.

"Yes, milady." At that, he finished the dregs. Finally, he made a face. "Ugh. I guess after you've had a few, the taste doesn't really matter anyway, does it?"

"You don't need to find out." Several minutes passed by, and Rinah found herself watching his facial expressions as he pored over the book. He wrinkled his nose a lot and squinted when he didn't understand what he was looking at. His fingers twitched sometimes, like he couldn't sit completely still. Then he said in a low voice, without taking his eyes from the page, "See something you like?"

Startled, Rinah sputtered, "Oh, let's read the next chapter, why don't we?" as she turned the page for him "This star formation is called The Mourning Queen. Not much of a story behind it. Many years ago, there was a human queen named Elinora. Her husband was killed on the battlefield. And when Elinora got word, she was sitting on her throne. The legend says she never stood again and pined away until she died, still sitting on the throne. The end." She pointed. "All right, now let's see if you remember the Boot of Ozias."

"No. Now it's my turn," he corrected her, closing the book and signaling to Ioanie for another ale. He leaned in and adopted the tone of a seasoned storyteller. He must have picked up the manner from Runo. "You hear things at night, sometimes, and once, I came across a band of travelers. Among them was a bard. And he told what he said was a very old tale. The tale of Serennog the Reaper. Serennog was once a king. A wise and noble king. His advice was heeded without question, as he was as virtuous as he was brilliant. He was adored by all, but he longed for a queen who would rule beside him. Then, one day, a beautiful maiden appeared at court. Serennog had never seen eyes so... what color would you call your eyes?" He nodded his thanks to Ioanie as she handed him the ale.

"I guess they're brown," Rinah replied, vaguely amused.

"No, no, no. Brown is the color of dead grass. Your eyes are the color of that spice you put in the scones. Those dried-up sticks you crumble up?"

"Cinnamon?"

"Cinnamon! Your eyes are *cinnamon*! Serennog had never seen eyes so remarkably cinnamon in his life. And from that moment, his loyalty shifted from his people..." He paused for dramatic effect. "To this mysterious, cinnamon-eyed woman. That very night, he sought her out, pledged his undying devotion, and swore he would be forever true."

Rinah raised an eyebrow. "And they lived happily ever after," she murmured.

"Nope. I'm not done yet." He downed the ale.

"Too bad. It's time for bed," Rinah sighed. The dining hall was beginning to clear as patrons retired to their rooms. "Humans sleep at night, and you've got to keep up appearances." She rolled up the star chart and slid it back into its cylinder, piled the books into his arms, then jingled his room key. "Come along, then." She waved good night to Ioanie.

Once in the room, Makoa gagged, "That ale was disgusting. I don't think I'll ever get the taste of it out of my mouth!" He dropped the books, kicked off his boots, and shrugged out of his vest.

"Serves you right. What were you trying to prove, having two mugs of it?"

"That I'm a human." He threw himself onto the bed.

"There are far more pleasant ways to act like a human," chuckled Rinah. "I'm going back downstairs to get you something to eat. It'll help. I'm sure Ioanie has leftovers."

*

When Rinah returned and offered him a bowl, Makoa ignored it, focusing instead on her face. "Do you want to stay with me? Just for a little while."

His words stabbed her. Rinah closed her eyes. *Yes!* More than anything else, she wanted to. For *weeks* now, she had wanted to. And lock the door behind her, push herself up against that strong chest, trace the tattoos on his arms with worshipful fingers, and kiss him. Again and again, until his lips no longer tasted like that piss-poor ale but like *her*. And then she'd pull him down on top of her and run her hands through that gorgeous, silky hair. After that, well… she might let him take the lead.

"You're not afraid to be alone with me, are you?"

Yes. I'm afraid of ruining this precious friendship.

"I've spent *hours* alone with you since we met," she scoffed. "No, I'm not afraid."

"In your own home. Your garden. Your safe place." His body was relaxed, but his words were a challenge. "Not here, where no one's watching us."

"Please just eat something," she begged. "It's cold leek soup. It tastes better than it smells, I promise."

He looked at the bowl briefly. "I don't want to eat soup," he mumbled.

Rinah let out a frustrated sigh. "For Ayusa's sake, Makoa, I'm trying to help you. What do you want to eat?" Her eyes darted to his fingers deftly unbuttoning his shirt.

Makoa's hair was rumpled, his eyes half-lidded. He smiled, sleek as a cat, as he raked his gaze up her frame and rumbled, "How about a taste of *you*, Rinah Autumnsong?"

She tried to ignore the spark of desire that sizzled through her body, but her efforts were in vain. So she leaned in toward him, just a bit, and forced herself to tease, "Aw, is that the best you can do?"

Makoa shrugged off his shirt as he stood. It fluttered to the floor. He took a step toward her, his arms above his head in a languid stretch. He stood so close to her that her nose nearly touched his firm, naked chest.

"You want me to try harder? Then let me finish the story of Serennog the Reaper." He drew a single finger down her cheek. "The night he pledged his devotion to the mysterious woman, she took him to her bed. They made passionate love the whole night through. Serennog had never known such pleasure." His voice went soft, snaking between her curls and into her ear. Rinah shivered. "But this beauty was no ordinary maid. She was a succubus, a spirit born of jealousy and spite, and every time their bodies came together with the force of their desire, she devoured a little more of his soul. Once she was satisfied, she left Serennog a shell of what he was, and she stole his throne. It's said that she lives on and, with an ever-changing face, continues to seduce handsome, powerful men all over Argodoth. Serennog, like an empty husk, continues to follow her to this day, dragging behind him the souls of all the men the succubus has consumed.

He has become their keeper, a hollow reminder of the danger of playing the foolish game of love."

Makoa's voice was a melody, and Rinah was drowning in it. He put a finger under her chin and tipped her face up toward his.

"Is love too foolish a game to play?" Rinah whispered. "Do you think?"

"Do you?" he murmured. "Oh, I don't need the ale, Rinah. I could get drunk just looking at you. Could lose myself in your eyes. In imagining what your body feels like on top of mine. Or beneath." She shuddered, another bolt of pleasure crackling through her. The sigh that escaped her lips bordered on a moan, and she bit her lip to quiet herself. "Since I don't sleep at night anyway, I'm sure there are some things we could think of to do to pass the time, you and me. And if you, too, prove to be a succubus, then I would give my soul up for a single kiss from those impossibly perfect lips." He placed his hands on her waist, and when he pressed his hips into hers, it was *very* clear why he wouldn't be falling asleep anytime soon.

She suppressed a gasp. Her skin felt like it was on fire. Her breath was ragged. Her eyes were fever-bright. For a moment, she felt faint and couldn't speak at all, couldn't move. After an endless moment, as she was just forming his name on her lips, he let out a laugh like a cackling bird and threw himself back on the bed. "Was that attempt more to your liking, milady?"

The heat in Rinah's body turned from lust to fury in a heartbeat. She picked up the bowl of soup and poured every drop of it into his lap. He was still yelping his apologies when she slammed the door shut and thundered down the hall.

*

She'd made it halfway home when, out of breath, Rinah slumped down on a bench overlooking the river. Her skin was ablaze with anger and the bloom of embarrassment, so warm that she nearly stripped off her cloak. She pulled her knees up to her chest and covered her face. What a fool she'd been. Again.

Against her will, she savored the memory of his lips so close to her ear, his arms holding her. She had been a willing captive of his voice, lulled into letting down her guard. And her body had thrilled to every single word dripping like honey from his mouth. She had been ready to melt into his arms. To give him everything. To finally give voice to the feelings that had been strangling her these past few weeks.

And then he shrugged it off and *laughed* at her.

Shame burned through her veins, and even in the dark, she knew her face was glowing red. *Best friend*, huh?

For gods' sakes! She was so naive, getting swept up in that stupid story about the succubus. Succubi weren't even real! And now her thoughts tumbled together, growing ever larger like a storm of buzzing locusts. Bram had charmed her only to try and sleep with her, to use her as a shield against the mothers of his children. All of his kindness had been a façade. Makoa was proving himself to be the same sort of man, albeit one with smoother pick-up lines.

When Bram revealed himself to be a snake, Rinah wasn't disappointed, only angry, and her pride was hurt. But now, her emotions were so much sharper. And her distress ran deep. Bram had cared to learn very little about Rinah during their time together, but Makoa—she'd grown comfortable enough to share all of herself with him. He seemed to love learning about her. Not just humans. About *her*. Was it all for this? A chance to take her for a tumble? To see what a wingless woman was like in bed? For some kind of crude bragging rights among his fellow faeries?

No. He hadn't wanted her. He had just wanted to toy with her, like a sly cat with a frantic mouse. To see how far he could get. To bait her. Test her. And she'd failed. Was she truly so gullible? Willing herself to forget his striking amber eyes, she hugged herself tightly.

And then, of course, there he stood, still shirtless, shivering, and dripping soup everywhere, his face as pale as the moon, his expression contrite, and his hand extended toward her.

"Hey. It's cold. Come back inside?"

*

Rinah allowed herself to be led back to the inn only because her burst of fury had faded, and the evening was indeed chilly. Still, she refused to go inside Makoa's room, forcing him to stand in the hall, still smelling of leeks, to speak with her.

"I can tell I upset you. I'm sorry. What did I do?"

666

"You can blame the ale. That's what 'real' humans do."

"Rinah. You know I'm not drunk."

"No, I *don't* know that. And so what if you're not? What is all this, then? A joke? Am *I* a joke?" Rinah felt tears stinging her eyes. "By the gods, Makoa, how cruel can you be? What have I done for you to make fun of me like this?" She started back down the hall, determined that he would not see her cry.

He stopped her with his gentle tone, and she turned, helpless. "I wasn't making fun of you, Rinah." His beautiful face was open and earnest. "Why would I do that?"

With her jaw set, she replied, "Obviously, I'm an easy target."

"Target? What are you talking about?"

She struggled to keep her voice down. "I'm talking about how stupid I am! How naive! I'm talking about Bram and how he had me convinced he was a good man! And how that kind of thinking put me in a terrible situation—but then you showed up and... but now, you're just... you're doing the same thing he did! And it hurts, Makoa, because I wanted you to be different. I *needed* you to be different!"

"Gods," he said, hushed. "You thought I was trying to take advantage of you?"

"Yes! What else was I supposed to think?"

At once, he was kneeling in front of her, his hands wrapped around hers. "Never, Rinah. Never." He pressed kisses on both her palms, one after the other.

She didn't pull away but whispered, "It felt like you were making fun of me."

Humbled, he walked her back down the hall. "I thought that you... you looked like maybe you wanted *me* to… uh…" He let out a nervous chuckle. "You know… seduce you? I'm not entirely sure how that works with humans, so, I took a chance… Figured I was doing pretty well, but then you weren't responding the way I, uh, assumed a human woman would, so I figured I read the situation wrong. I laughed it off because *I* was embarrassed."

"Oh."

He stopped and looked down at her, his grin subdued and a little dreamy. *"Rinah.* You looked so perfect standing right here, with the lantern light dancing in your curls, and with your lips looking like ripe cherries, and your eyes fluttering closed when I touched your skin… I thought you were waiting for me to make a move."

This wasn't happening. Was it? Right now? Confessing his attraction to her while he was wearing an entire bowl of cold, creamed leeks? Her cheeks were blazing.

He slumped. "But then I thought... maybe since your hands *weren't* already down my pants, maybe I got the wrong idea about... what you wanted. Want. What you want. What *do* you want?"

She swallowed hard but didn't speak.

"Look. I can't lose your friendship because I messed up like this. I wasn't trying to *hurt* you. I was—I *am* trying to protect myself. Because this is bad, Rinah. This is so, so bad."

"What are you talking about?"

"I'm trying to say—"

She put her hands up, reluctant to interrupt him in this potentially pivotal moment in their relationship. But there was no helping it. "Hold on a minute. I'm really sorry, but I'm not going to be able to take you seriously unless you put on some clean clothes. You've got garlic and leeks dripping down your legs, and it's starting to make me feel kind of nauseated."

He laughed a bit. "I don't have anything else to wear. And it's not a good idea for me to be naked with you right now. Unless…?"

His grin sent a wave of goosebumps marching up her arms. But no, this wasn't the right time. Biting her lip, she turned away. "Let me see what I can do."

*

"These are the only clean pair I have," warned Runo, "so he can't get them messed up!"

"Thank you."

"Why are you here so late anyway? Are you two gonna do it?"

Rinah didn't even bother to act embarrassed. "Maybe? But he currently smells like onions, so… it's sort

671

of killing the mood." *Also, I am very good at killing the mood, apparently.*

"You really, *really* like him, don't you?"

She sighed and looked at him. "I'm really sorry to disappoint you, Runo. I don't think there can be anything between you and me. Nothing romantic. I thought you kind of figured that when—"

He let out a sigh of relief so loud that it was borderline insulting. "Oh, thank the *gods*, Rinah, because kissing you was like what kissing Dargah would probably be like, and *ew*."

"I'm going to try not to take that personally."

"I was kind of hoping neither of us would ever have to think about it again, especially because I am way better at kissing than that and I don't need you telling girls I suck at it."

"Wasn't on my agenda," she assured him with a smile.

"I'm sure Carrots will have the time of his life, though. Go with my blessing."

"I thought you didn't like him."

"Not at first. It looked like he was just here to take advantage of you like Bram did." His face hardened. "I wasn't gonna let that happen again!"

Rinah's heart swelled with affection at his words. "But you don't feel that way anymore?"

"Nah. I mean... look. He always makes sure Orlaeth is served first at dinner so that the serving spoon doesn't even *touch* any meat before it gets to her. He helps clean up after we eat, even though no one asks him to. He helps cook half the time. I mean, he's kind of not great at it, but he's trying, right? And a coupla times, I saw him feed that weird-looking stray cat that sometimes hangs around the cottage. Bram would have kicked it. Or lit it on fire or something. Like, I think Makoa's a genuinely good person. Faerie. Whatever. And I think Dargah does, too."

"How can you tell?"

"He's still alive, isn't he? See, that's a good sign. Go for it." He gave her a little punch on the shoulder.

"That means a lot. Thank you. Oh. I need to borrow a mop, too, please."

"What *are* your plans for the night?"

She shook her head and smiled. "Good night, Runo."

"Good luck, Rinah."

*

With Makoa's pants soaking in the bedside basin and Rinah having scrubbed the remaining soup from the floor, the rising tension between the couple had been utterly shattered. They had decided to return to the late-night quiet of the dining hall, and now they sat on the couch, alone in front of the crackling hearth.

"Can we agree that, in the future, if you feel the need to throw food at me, you at least pick something that smells good?" Makoa asked sheepishly.

"Can we agree that, in the future, you're not going to say things that make me want to throw food at you at all?" Rinah replied with a pert tilt of her head.

"That's fair." He gently drew his fingers through the soft curls on the nape of her neck, and she shuddered with pleasure. "This is nice. I could fall asleep right here."

She rested her head against his shoulder, her face glowing in the warmth of the fire."You never told me exactly where you sleep, anyway. You mentioned trees. Do you have a regular tree? What do you do during the rainy season?"

"Depends on the colony. The border of Erjunn and Ayusa is a good place for us since it almost never gets cold enough to snow here. But the colonies up north actually make shelters out of ice. I hear it's pretty incredible. I have a tree I like, I guess it's not far from your cottage, actually."

"Oh."

Silence again.

"Fire makes me think of you," Rinah blurted.

A soft smile crossed his face. "Why is that?"

"Well, maybe because of your hair," Rinah hedged. "But… mostly because a fire is warm and comforting and makes you feel safe. But," she hurried on before losing her nerve, "fires can be unpredictable, too. And I think that you have some of that in you, maybe."

"Well, you remind me of a bee," he said. "You're small, but you're dedicated. Focused. And because honey is sweet."

"But honeybees can sting," she whispered.

"Only once, and then they die," he whispered back. Then he pulled away from her. "On second thought, maybe you're more of a wasp. I imagine that if you were really in a snit, you could do a lot more damage than a single sting."

She made a sour face at him and playfully pushed him even farther away. "See if *you* get any honey."

"Are you saying there's still a chance I could?" Looking up at him, she saw the fire reflected in his eyes, and her breath caught in her throat. "I know I really messed up tonight. But you still feel safe with me?"

"Yeah," she said, her voice smaller than she would have liked. "I think we both jumped to conclusions tonight. I assumed you were trying to insult me, and you assumed I *didn't* want to put my hands down your pants." He grinned slyly. "You're not like… like *him*. I don't feel like you're trying to put me down or twist my words. Or that you're trying to keep me away from the people I care about."

"What *do* you feel?"

"With you? Happy. Really happy."

"Can I tell you something? Your garden was the first place I felt something like happiness. It's so welcoming, and even at night, it's easy to see that every living thing in that place is loved, and cared for, and cherished. It made me feel that way, too. I'd been going there a while before your swim in the stream." He brought her hand to his mouth and kissed it softly. "The first time I saw you was a mistake. I had no right to see your body in the moonlight. It was a violation, I know that. That's why I left. But on the night when that *animal* was touching you, when he was clawing at you… You didn't deserve that.

678

Your body is too precious for that. Your body should be *worshiped*, Rinah."

She stopped breathing.

"I just wanted to keep looking at you. At first, I didn't need anything else. But then you turned out to be clever. And compassionate. And sweet. And generous. And so much more than beautiful. I'm feeling things I haven't felt before. Things maybe I'm not even supposed to feel." Abruptly, he swiveled to face her. "I need to know I'm not imagining this, Rinah."

The gravity of his words and the flicker in his eyes stoked something inside her, something primal and urgent and powerful. "Tell me what you're thinking, and I'll tell you if you're imagining it."

"I'm thinking that the woman sitting with me is the most captivating being I've ever seen, faerie ladies be damned. Every last one of them." Carefully, he brushed his fingers against her cheek. She melted into his touch. "I'm thinking that the best times I've ever had in my life are when I'm with her and her friends."

"Our friends. They're *our* friends, Makoa."

"I'm thinking that this, right here, could be the perfect moment. The moment when I tell her that she makes me feel like I mean something. Like I matter in a way I've never mattered to my colony."

She couldn't think of anything to say. Not a witty comment, not a flirtatious reply. Nothing. She could only hear the stumbling thuds of her heartbeat, only see the sunset eyes staring into hers. He put a trembling hand on either side of her face.

"I feel like I'm *alive*, Rinah. Like I'm home."

She finally found her voice. "Kiss me."

Makoa pulled her back into his arms and kissed her, long and gentle and sweet, exactly how she wanted to be kissed. She breathed in his warmth, delighted in the feel of his arms surrounding her, and finally dragged her fingers through that brilliant, shaggy, orange mane.

Chapter Thirty-Three:

Of Sweetness and Spice

In the silent moments just before dawn, Rinah opened her eyes. The fire was dying, the sun was rising, and a beautiful man was sleeping in her lap. She nearly purred with contentment.

She hadn't been dreaming.

She and Makoa had fallen asleep, curled in each other's arms. Sometime in the night, instead of waking them, someone had draped a blanket over them and carefully placed a pillow beneath Rinah's head.

They had not shared more than a few tender kisses the evening before, but Rinah let out a deep, happy sigh. She'd never woken up with a man in her arms; it was a delicious new experience.

Even in the entirely public and not even a teensy bit private tap room of the local inn.

In spite of her pleasure, Rinah knew that Makoa needed to return to the colony. She stroked his cheek and whispered, "Hey, handsome."

He opened his eyes, a sunrise in his face. "Honeybee." Then he made himself comfortable again, squeezing her tighter and letting out a happy little grunt.

"Please! Allow me to be the first to tell you two to get a room! And also, I need my pants back."

Runo's gleeful announcement startled Makoa so thoroughly that he fell off the sofa, taking the blanket with him. Rinah turned to see the teenaged half-orc standing in the middle of the empty dining hall, eating a leftover pork chop and wearing only his linen underpants. "I'm freezing!"

"For gods' sakes, stop being dramatic." Dargah strode through the room, eyed her friend with something like pride on her face, then asked, "Are those pants a bit *tight* on you, Makoa?"

He looked down. "Oh, hey, that's new!"

"*Dargah!*" Rinah hissed. "You're embarrassing him!"

"Oh, I think I'm embarrassing *you*, little lady. That boy's perfectly fine with it."

"I don't know what's going on over there, but my guests didn't pay extra for a show, so knock it off," called Ioanie from the counter. "Runo, that means you, too. These eggs aren't going to scramble themselves."

"He's *wearing* my *pants!*"

"I don't care what you do on your own time, but in five minutes, you're on the clock, and you'd damn well better be dressed." She disappeared into the kitchen, mumbling to herself.

"I'm going!" Makoa groaned. He climbed up to give Rinah a much longer good morning kiss than she'd expected, then shifted and disappeared in a wink.

"There. Pants," Dargah told Runo, gesturing grandly.

"Eggs!" thundered Ioanie from the kitchen.

"I bet you don't talk to your man like that!" Runo accused.

"Ikraam likes it!" Ionie shot back.

While Runo grumbled, Dargah perched next to Rinah, crossed one leg over the other, and smirked.

"Shut up," Rinah muttered.

"I didn't say a thing!"

"Your face talks, even when your mouth doesn't."

"How long?"

"I don't know. We didn't get that far." Rinah let out a disappointed groan.

Dargah snorted with laughter. "How long have you been wanting to *kiss* him?"

"*Oh.*" Of course. Gods, this whole morning was turning out to be rather awkward. "Probably since the beginning of autumn," she admitted bashfully. Then her eyes narrowed. "Hmm… around the time Papa stopped leaving me alone with him."

"They know, Rinah. Parents know."

Ioanie's guests slowly began to shuffle into the room, eager for a hot breakfast and a chat with the friendly faces behind the counter.

"Be careful."

Rinah was indignant. "He's not like Bram."

"You didn't think *Bram* was like Bram, either."

"I promise. I'll be careful."

*

Rinah was not, in fact, careful.

The next time she saw Makoa, she yanked him into the cottage and wrapped her arms around his neck, pressing her body hard into his.

"Is this gonna be a regular thing now?" he asked with a crooked smile.

"Do you want it to be?" She loved how her voice sounded with him—soft but confident. She'd never talked this way to anyone before.

He answered with a hungry kiss, daring to dart his tongue between her lips.

Emboldened, Rinah stood on her tiptoes to pull him into a deeper kiss. She muffled a gasp as his hands slipped around her waist to give her a gentle squeeze. Then she dissolved into giggles. "I'm ticklish," she confessed, doubling over.

"I'm going to remember this for later," he threatened, squeezing her again. After she stopped laughing, he added, "Hey, I can't stay long tonight."

"Why not?"

"Once a season, everyone in the colony gathers together, kind of like a reunion. It's sort of an opportunity to check in and make sure everything is going smoothly." His cheerful expression dimmed. "Sometimes, we get shuffled around, and our assignments change."

Rinah tamped down the panic that flared in response to his words. "Are you telling me that you might not be able to visit as often? Or at all?"

"It's a possibility. I just wanted you to know if you don't see me tomorrow night, that's probably why. I'll show up as soon as I can."

Rinah moved toward the table. "Thank you. I would worry." She sliced into a fat loaf of brown bread. "Do you have time to eat?"

"I just came to talk."

Her hands went clammy, and her stomach jumped, the same way they did years ago when Papa caught her sneaking spoonfuls of honey straight from the jar. "Those words always make me nervous."

He leaned over to kiss her forehead, then looked at her, his eyes searching hers. "I need to know. What do you want, Rinah?"

If it had been anyone else standing before her, she would have blushed and hidden her face, flustered and charmingly confused, unsure about how to respond. But it was Makoa, and she met his gaze with boldness and certainty. "Just you."

"I can't stop thinking about you, either." When she smiled, he looked away, suddenly bashful. "But, uh, it's not a good thing. Not at all. For me, at least."

She took a deep breath. "Makoa, in the world of humans, this is called 'giving mixed signals,' and it's confusing me."

"I'm sorry. It's kind of hard to explain."

A lump formed in her throat, and she placed her hands on the table to support her weight. She addressed her reply to the bread instead of Makoa's face. "I promise it's not. If you think this—'us'—is a mistake, then please just come out and say it. It will be easier for me to accept—"

He grabbed her by the shoulders. "Rinah, *no*. I don't feel that way at all. That's the problem. I'm afraid you're going to get hurt, and I don't want that to happen."

Her insides were shaking. "Hurt how?"

He placed a finger over her lips and tilted his head, listening to something in the distance. "Damn. She's calling us in. I can't stay any longer." He looked back at her, eyes shining, full of fear and... something else. He pressed a kiss to her cheek. "I messed up. There's so much more I wanted to say."

"She? Who's *she*? What's going on?" Rinah asked, only to realize she was alone again, Makoa's clothing in a heap at her feet.

*

Good for her.

Dargah grinned to herself as she worked, pleased about her friend's budding relationship with Makoa. Of course, they'd all been wary of him at first, but it had become clear early on that the kid was genuine. She remembered the time she stopped over after work to deliver a padlock to Alvyx. She'd heard shouting from within the cottage and burst through the door, ready to fend off an intruder or interrupt an attack. Instead, she'd walked in on Rinah, Makoa, and Alvyx, covered in flour, a cloud of it still hanging in the air. Apparently, Makoa had accidentally tipped over the sack, resulting in the mess. The shout had been Rinah's too-late warning to be careful, but now they were all laughing. Dargah had offered to help clean up, then chatted with them while they finished preparing the dough for a savory pot pie. She'd stayed long enough to force their hand in inviting her to eat, and that pie had been delicious.

And the time he learned that Orlaeth had declined her standing dinner invitation as she was recovering from a mild cold, he'd asked for help packing up a meal for her, then delivered it himself before heading off into the forest.

He wasn't without his faults, of course. His still-rudimentary understanding of human behavior and interaction prompted some strange conversations at the dinner table, including a debate on the virtues of eliminating one's waste in the forest versus the cost of purchasing an enchanted chamber pot for one's home. No one felt much like eating the chocolate custard offered for dessert that evening.

But his playful, inquisitive nature meshed so well with Rinah's nurturing, indulgent one. Dargah enjoyed seeing them interact, seeing Rinah's face light up with affection—not hero worship. The only thorn in this rosebush, of course, was whether the girl would be willing to take on a part-time lover. Knowing that Makoa's life would always be split between his obligations as a faerie scout and his role as a "human friend of the family" might prove impossible for Rinah to manage. Dargah knew that she would have a hard time letting go of a lover so often, knowing that the other life he lived was so violently opposed to their relationship.

But maybe Rinah was a stronger woman than her.

Interlude VI:

Of Crime and Consequences

One Week Ago

More times than she could count, her closest advisors had strongly urged Queen Talu to permit them to use their human-like forms when traveling. The journey would be much shorter, and much easier, they insisted this time around. Kapena was the lone holdout, answering them on Talu's behalf, "You would have your queen unguarded? Vulnerable to any manner of attack or illness?"

"It's best for you this way, too," Talu added mildly to her courtiers. "I can't bear the thought of losing any of you to a stray arrow or wayward dagger. In Erjunn, perhaps things might be different, but Ayusa'a humans are violent. Unpredictable. And the last thing any of us needs is the loss of another one of our kind."

Besides, Talo told herself, perhaps Kapena, with his tan skin and rusty-brown hair, might pass for a human, but her own cascade of waves was the color of a ripe pear, and her purplish complexion wouldn't fool a genuine human for a second.

No matter. She had no need to walk among them. She and her attendants stretched their wings, and took to the skies towards Duskweaver Colony.

Chapter Thirty-Four:

Of Pain and Promise

If she hadn't decided that her chrysanthemums needed a bit more attention, Rinah wouldn't have seen the body in her garden, nor would she have heard the soft whimper coming from it.

When she realized that the body was Makoa's, she cried out his name and ran to him. Blood seeped from two deep wounds in his back, and his entire body was purple with bruises. He was barely breathing. "Dargah! Help!" she screamed back toward the cottage. She then brushed Makoa's matted hair out of his face, whispering, "Please be all right. Please live. Please be all right!" She groped for a pulse. Faint. Was she imagining it?

Dargah, who'd been enjoying a peaceful breakfast inside, wasted no time coming to her aid. On her knees next to Rinah, she swore under her breath. "Oh, my gods."

"Papa's at the temple of Kaylor," Rinah whispered. "I need him. I need him right now!" At the farthest edge of town, Papa was restocking the dwarves' stores of incense. He couldn't return quickly enough, even if he took the form of the owl. Dargah took off in a dead sprint.

Rinah was vaguely aware that shock kept her tears and horror at bay for the moment. She also knew she was supposed to separate the part of herself that cared for Makoa from the part that saw him as a dying patient and that she wasn't going to be able to do it. She tore off her apron, wadding it and pressing it into the gaping holes on his back.

Oh, gods.

His wings. His wings had been cut off, cut right out of him.

Her apron was soaked through in seconds, and she slid one blood-slicked hand toward his throat. His pulse was barely a flicker.

He was dying.

Right here in her garden.

Right where she'd met him.

NO.

Rinah's frame lurched as though she'd just been doused with a basin of icy water. She shook violently and struggled to catch her breath.

In her mind's eye, she saw her own will, her own strength, cease to be. Her own power, her sense of self, shriveled into nothing. Swirling in colors Rinah had never before imagined, the rogue magics of the joyful little boy, the good-natured ancient orcs, and the clandestine lovers came together underneath her skin, bubbling and simmering like an overflowing kettle.

WHAT IS IT THAT YOU WANT, KEEPER?

Papa told me that you always know—you always know what to do.

But I'm afraid.

And I can't do this without Papa.

I can't do this at all.

Oh, gods, Makoa.

I can't lose him.

I can't save him.

WHAT IS IT THAT YOU WANT, KEEPER?

Rinah glimpsed an image of herself, shaking violently as she tried in vain to staunch the blood, saw the blackish pool spreading in the grass around them, saw the flecks of scarlet spray on her asters, saw her hope and her future writhing in the dirt of her garden, fading like the colors of dusk into a moonless night, saw herself screaming and weeping—slow and silent—over the body of the man who'd stood there, right there, and—

GO BACK TO THAT NIGHT.

As freely as Makoa's blood flowed, she allowed the memories to come. The glint of the blade as Bram slipped it from his boot. The violent rip of her skirt tearing. The numbness in her fingertips as she crushed the tansy into the cup. The staccato beat of her heart, madly fluttering like a caged bird. The sound of Makoa's voice interrupting. The shape of his silhouette. The flood of gratitude so overwhelming she wept. The raw trust she'd placed in this moonlit, naked stranger. The scorching shame that—

STOP.

GO BACK.

The trust.

WHAT IS IT THAT YOU WANT, KEEPER?

You know what I want.

I trust you.

The impossible colors burst into flaming whorls in her blood, pawing and straining like hounds scenting a hare.

I trust you, and I release you.

The magic tugged on her, pulled at her, drew from her all of her natural strength as it leaped headlong from her body into Makoa's. Gossamer threads of magic—tethers with their anchors in Rinah's soul—plunged into throbbing darkness that smelled of blood and wet marrow. She stood at the precipice, watching them dive deeper until they were barely points of light being swallowed up by endless night. And if they fell any further, she knew, she knew, she knew, that she would fall with them, and there would be nothing left of her, no body, no thought, no soul, no life. The darkness grew louder—can darkness make a sound?—and something velvety soft and impossible to understand crawled up from the pit, eyeless and soulless, broken of heart and of body, and reared itself before her like a thrashing animal, and then the form was no longer like clay, dark and unreadable. It was Makoa, white-skinned and wide-eyed, gasping for air. Then he was gone, replaced by faceless clay, and again he returned, clawing at his throat for air. Rinah reached out and held him, held him so fiercely that she would rather break him than lose him again. Then everything was quiet, and nothing was real, and darkness was everywhere.

*

Dargah kept an eye on the furiously flapping owl just ahead of her, hoping that they could reach Makoa in time, hoping that no one in the streets noticed a huge, nocturnal bird of prey screaming through the morning sky, hoping that this wasn't happening. Not really. Not to Makoa. Not to Rinah.

But it was.

Dargah cried out when she saw the two motionless forms at the foot of the splintered oak tree in the garden. Feathers unfurled from Alvyx like a cape, and in his true form again, he draped himself over the bodies.

Dargah fell to her knees and prayed.

*

A delicate hand, cold but comforting, caressed Rinah's brow. Her eyes fluttered open to see the blur of a milk-white face above her, silver-eyed and smiling.

"Mr. Autumnsong, she is awake!" Orlaeth declared. She rose and withdrew to a corner of the room, releasing a quiet but joyful prayer of gratitude to her god. The elf's face was replaced by her papa's, and his expression was grim. Rinah closed her eyes again, trying to recall what could have made him so solemn. She was dizzy, and her muscles throbbed with an angry ache. She felt herself slipping back into a place of hazy, fuzzy comfort, then heard her own voice, cracked and pleading, whispering Makoa's name.

A sigh came from Papa, a sigh so heavy that it dragged Rinah's heart into her stomach. Tears dribbled from her eyes, and she breathed a single sob before she felt strong arms embrace her. Dargah's body was powerful and solid, her scent, musky rose mixed with the sharp tang of sweat, still sticky on her skin. Dargah's voice was hushing and soothing her like a baby.

Then Papa spoke, his words measured and slow. "You almost killed yourself. You released enough rogue magic—raw rogue magic, untested—to reduce this cottage to dust."

"*Makoa.*"

"He lives."

She was dizzy again, light-headed with relief. Everything was spinning, and the tears were now a cascade of joy streaking down her face. She was shaking again, still in Dargah's embrace, and then she realized she was laughing, laughing and sobbing, and nothing mattered beyond the words her papa had just spoken.

"Rinah," he said, his grim tone silencing her. "He lives, but at a great cost."

She looked up, past Dargah's ebony waves and into Papa's watery blue eyes. "Zealots?" she rasped. They rarely appeared so soon after Dehlkia's adoration. But what if they were passing through Lindenvale and learned what she'd done? Panic clutched at her throat, and she gasped to breathe.

"No, thank the gods. We'd both of us be in shackles right now, and Makoa dead if Zealots caught wind of your recklessness." He paused, watching horror and regret wash over his daughter's face. "The magic took on the form of fire and cauterized Makoa's wounds. It stopped the bleeding, but it also separated him from his own magic forever."

*

Orlaeth knew she was seen as frail, but neither blood nor wounds bothered her. It was she who cleaned Makoa's skin, her touch as tender as a mother's as he lay on his stomach, motionless, in Alvyx's bed. It was she who carried the blood-soaked towels and sheets outside, scrubbing them clean in the stream and pinning them on the line to dry in the pale, fleeting warmth of the autumn sun. It was she who poked through Rinah's herbs and oils and prepared a poultice for the cuts on his arms and legs. And it was she who sent Dargah to the inn to bring back Runo, and food, and drink, then to the temple of Erjunn to ask her fellow elves to pray on behalf of Rinah and Makoa.

Alvyx moved around the cottage, briefly squeezing the hand of his sleeping daughter, then peeking in as Orlaeth cared for Makoa. With a breezy authority she'd never before displayed, she gave him task after task, sending him searching outside for chamomile, then to the inn for more vinegar, then to the clothier for rolls of gauze. After he'd spent a day and a half in continual service to the elf, he finally stepped into his bedroom and glared at her.

"You have been sending me all over town to keep me from becoming consumed with worry," he accused.

She nodded serenely. "It is a technique that my mother often employed when my curiosity threatened to overwhelm her. Rinah is well enough, I believe, to move about, should she want to. But first, please make sure she eats something. There is vegetable broth on the hearth and some bread that Runo dropped off earlier."

"Orlaeth," uttered Alvyx, "I can't thank you enough."

She said nothing to him but returned to the quiet string of prayers she'd been speaking over Makoa for the past several hours.

*

As soon as Rinah was able to sit upright without dizziness, she staggered her way to Makoa's bedside. Orlaeth began to ask her if she was sufficiently recovered, but the determination on Rinah's face silenced her. The elf placed her arms around her in a hesitant embrace, then, leaving behind a basin of cool water and a clean washcloth, closed the door behind her.

Rinah stood still for several seconds, taking in the destruction her foolishness had wrought. A charred, gnarled black scab sat on either side of Makoa's spine, just below his shoulder blades. A morbid rainbow of bruises colored his skin, and his cheeks were sallow, his eyes sunken. His hair, pushed back from his face, was slick with sweat. A blanket had been draped over the lower half of his body, and his breathing was slow and shallow.

She curled up on the floor beside the bed, her body screaming in protest, and hugged her knees. She said nothing for a long time, and when she finally spoke, her voice was rough and weak. "I'm sorry. I'm so, so sorry. I never meant to…" She thought her tears had dried up, but fresh ones sprang to her eyes. "Papa told me that if I'd just waited a little longer, then he—he probably could have saved you without… what I mean is, he has a better control of his magic than I do. So much better. And he could have stopped the bleeding another way, or we could have worked together, and then your body could have healed itself. And your wings could have regrown. It would have taken a long, long time, he said, but they would have grown back. And I took that from you. I trusted the magic, like I was supposed to, and it… it ruined you. I might have the rest of you alive, but I killed that part of you, and I will never forgive myself for that. I never wanted to hurt you. I just saw you there and, Makoa"—she paused to catch her breath and scrub her tears away—"your heart was barely beating. I didn't think I had any time left. And I knew I couldn't lose you. I'm sorry."

She dissolved into silent sobs, her arms covering her face, and sat with him until the sun hung low in the sky. She recited stories to him, the ones from the book Elpida had given her, stories she'd memorized years ago. She sang him an Ayusan lullaby but stopped after the first verse because her voice kept cracking. She told him the news

711

she'd been meaning to tell him—that Charis looked like a princess in her new purple dress and that Dargah and Runo had made a clean break with their family back in Dehlkia (it was a good thing, she added, because Dargah's mother was a horrible person), and that the odd little stray had returned to her cottage, and she was convinced the animal was looking for him because it hid when anyone else tried to offer it food. She suggested possible names for the cat, settling on Bunny because it loped about more like a rabbit than a feline.

"It's a fox."

Rinah's heart threw itself against her ribcage.

Makoa slowly reached a finger toward her face and touched the tip of her nose. His voice was little more than a croak, but he went on. "It's a baby gray fox, honeybee. And it limps because one of its legs is twisted."

She looked up at him and watched his split lips curve into a smile. Relief flooded her, and she kissed his bruised fingers. "How long have you been awake?"

"Long enough to know that you've still got a little crush on me." He twitched an eye. "Never mind, I can't wink. It hurts."

Her smile was wistful. "You heard about your wings, then."

"You saved my life."

"I stole your magic."

"You stole my heart, Rinah Autumnsong."

She kissed his hand again, then held it to her cheek. "What happened to you?"

"You," he said, booping her on the nose again, "are a smart woman, and I bet you can figure it out."

Her face fell. "Did your colony do this? Is this what you were trying to tell me that night before you left? Who's the 'she' you were talking about?"

"The Queen." Makoa's voice was as weak and hoarse as hers, but he continued. "Ultimately, she's supposed to keep all of us in line. There's a strict look-but-don't-touch policy among the Guardian races, honey. Drilled into all the earthborn Guardians from day one. We're here to protect. Not to make friends. We can't do our jobs unless we stay hidden. So there's a high price to pay if we break the rules. I guess word got back to her that I'd been a bad boy."

"...So you were *aware* that this... mutilation, this *amputation*—"

"Penalty for disobedience," he corrected her mildly.

"*Makoa*! This is not the same as a child being sent to bed without dessert! This is terrible!"

He grinned at her, his eyes half-lidded. "You're worth it, though."

His words flooded her chest with warmth, but she drew her brows together. "If I had known that there was any chance of this happening to you—"

"You would have pushed me away to save me."

"Absolutely, I would have!"

"Which is why I didn't tell you. I get to make my own choices. I chose this. I chose you. I chose *us*. I don't even know what we are or what we could be, but this is still what I want."

She didn't dwell on his implication, her emotions already too jumbled for her to untangle now. "If you knew all this would happen, why did you go to the Queen? Why not run, or hide, or stay in this form?"

Makoa blew a puff of air between his lips. "Because that's what a coward would do, and I'm not a coward.

715

Besides, I couldn't run forever. I'd always be looking over my shoulder. I'd never feel peace. I'd rather be dead than live like that."

She hated to admit it, but Rinah knew the feeling. When rogue magic was swirling inside her, she was one mistake away from any number of disasters. "But they think you *are* dead?"

"They don't care one way or the other. I've been exiled. If I live, I live without a colony and without my wards. Without a role or a purpose, wings or no wings. And if I die, I die. That's how it works. Good thing you've taught me so much about being a human. I'm ahead of the curve. And I think I'll be all right. I know I don't understand everything about your world. I probably never will. But I know what's important." Weakly, he reached out a hand to stroke her curls. "I know what matters."

"I never would have asked this of you, Makoa. I never, never would have put you in the place of having to choose between your magic or me."

"I know. And that's why I love you."

Tenderness wrapped around her heart and squeezed. She closed her eyes. "Makoa. Please don't." Her voice was weaker than she'd intended. "You told me faeries had no use for love or companionship."

"Oh, but milady... I'm not a fairie anymore."

Pulling herself to her knees, she pressed a kiss to his bruised face. "I was afraid to hope," she confessed, unable to explain further.

He attempted to wrap an arm around her, but winced in pain. "This isn't a very romantic moment, is it?"

"Love isn't always romantic, Makoa," Rinah said solemnly. "It can get messy. Sometimes, it hurts. Is that really what you want?" She hesitated before asking the question that had been hidden in her heart for weeks. "Am *I* really what you want?"

"More than anything."

Chapter Thirty-Five:

Of Recovery and Renegades

Rinah was pleasantly surprised to see Makoa sitting up in bed, attempting to pull on Alvyx's old tunic and looking far better than he had all week.

"Careful," she said, placing his food on the bedside table. She helped him ease the soft linen over his head, then checked his bandages before she allowed him to finish getting dressed. "If Papa knows you're up and about, you're going to have to start joining us for meals again. Are you sure you want to do that? He's been talking a lot more about predatory birds lately. Over dinner."

Makoa laughed tiredly. "It's fine."

"Are you feeling better, though? A little?"

"It still hurts like hell, but I've got to start moving around, or I'll go crazy." He took a bite of the apple she'd brought him. "I'm not complaining about having a gorgeous lady waiting on me hand and foot, though. Can your papa prescribe a few more days of that?"

She leaned in to kiss his cheek, then his neck. In the purr she saved only for him, she asked, "How long until you're comfortable on your back, do you think?"

His inviting grin made her insides flutter. "Rinah Autumnsong, whatever are you suggesting?"

"You're a smart boy. You can figure it out." She disappeared before either of them could do anything to sabotage his recovery.

*

"I would like to formally offer my apologies to you all."

Orlaeth stood as still and stiff as a schoolchild reciting a poem she still hadn't fully memorized. Makoa and Rinah sat on the sofa, their fingers intertwined. Runo lounged in the armchair, his legs swung over one side. Alvyx stirred the pot of stew in the hearth. Dargah and Neryn—yes, Neryn, for Orlaeth had asked Dargah to write and invite him when he would not be missed in Dirgil—sat on opposite sides of the table, treating each other with cautious civility.

"You don't do anything wrong ever, except for that time you died," Runo pointed out. "What're you sorry for?"

"I have come to believe that, perhaps, my actions leading up to the thwarted attack on Rinah... perhaps they were ill-advised."

"What do you mean? You had a vision, freaked out, got Neryn here, and Bram got thrown into a tree. Worked out pretty well, I'd say," he answered.

She glanced at Rinah, nervous that her words would stir unpleasant memories. But she just leaned in a bit closer to Makoa, her eyes clear and focused on the elf. "I mean to say that... perhaps the reaction I had to the vision was unnecessary."

"You said you saw her dead." Dargah refilled Neryn's mug with mint tea and slid it back to him. "I think that would make any of us worry."

"I believe now that what I saw was not an unchangeable vision of the future but more like a warning. A symbolic expression, open to interpretation. It is difficult to put into words, but I believe what I saw was the potential death of a *part* of Rinah had Bram been able to succeed in his goal."

"That kind of makes sense. My honor? Innocence?" Rinah guessed.

"Your joy."

The room fell silent at that.

"Your physical recovery, I feel, would have been swift. But the brightness that surrounds you, the gentle and persistent spirit of kindness that blooms within you, that which makes you who you are, Rinah, what makes us all love you..." Orlaeth fumbled here, realizing that she was speaking on behalf of those whose feelings remained unknown. She glanced at Neryn. "That is to say, Rinah, what makes us all admire you—"

"There is no need to amend your statement," Neryn said pleasantly. "I have come to hold affection in my heart for those who have welcomed you here, Orlaeth. And indeed, it is Rinah's compassionate nature that sets her apart from the majority of people in my life, also."

"Did you have a vision of Neryn being nice?" Runo asked Orlaeth. "'Cause none of us saw that coming."

"Shut up, Runo," his sister said.

"Ultimately, what you're trying to say is that you're still trying to understand your visions, or dreams, or whatever these things are, is that right?" Makoa wanted to know.

Orlaeth nodded. "They are a gift from Erjunn, I know this. In the past, the visions have been very brief, mere flashes, really, but far clearer." Her attention darted to Dargah, then away again. "It seems that the longer they last, the more work I have to do in deciphering them. But this is work I do in service to my god, and therefore, I do it with pleasure. I hope that, should our mutual friendship continue, I will have an increased understanding and will not cause any of you undue worry or fear."

"Well, regardless of what you thought the vision meant," Makoa said, pulling Rinah a bit closer, "you acted to protect Rinah. And I can't fault you for that."

"Nor I," Alvyx said. "I have always held seers in high regard, Orlaeth, and I encourage you to continue to nurture this gift, however you are able. I am no son of Erjunn, but I feel confident in saying that I believe his trust in you as his mouthpiece is well-placed."

The words of praise filled Orlaeth's heart with such gratitude that she found it hard to speak, nodding her thanks instead.

"I wholeheartedly agree. My only regret is that your gift cannot be put to use under the Disciple's leadership." Neryn's voice grew soft and thoughtful. "I realize now that it could only have been a benefit to us, and especially to our women."

Orlaeth looked into Makoa's cunning amber eyes and noted the tenderness with which Rinah rested her head on his shoulder. She saw the depth of emotion that swam in Runo's gaze and felt the fatherly acceptance with which Alvyx had come to offer everyone in the room. She observed Dargah's dark-eyed intelligence and the peace on Neryn's face as he relaxed, no longer out of place among these, her adopted family of eccentrics. "Our god has led me to many strange and wonderful people and things," she said with a rare smile. "And it is here, among the strangest and most wonderful, that I have found my home."

Postlude:

Of Dust and Dreamers

Nine Days Later

Dargah looked down at the dried rose in her hand, its petals the color of a skinned knee. It was the last link, the final, tenuous strand that kept her bound to the life she'd once had. The day she claimed her second title for unarmed combat, she received the traditional bouquet of desert roses—a symbol of resilience and inner strength. In the flurry of excitement after her win, the flowers had gotten jostled. One of the blooms fluttered to the ground. Parviz had plucked it and secured it behind Dargah's ear before embracing her and telling her how proud she'd made him. She had been so touched by the gesture that, while she allowed the rest of the bouquet to wither, she dried and preserved that single rose. It had been kept safe in a small wooden box she'd brought from Gora-Vekiri, and most of the time, she stored it safely out of sight and out of mind underneath her bed.

She really didn't know why she had it anymore.

It was Runo's initiative in sending their parents packing that inspired her to sit down, after these six seemingly endless years, and revisit this memory.

She hadn't known that bright and glorious day, that, just four months later, nothing would be the same. She had nearly destroyed the rose in a fit of anger but decided to keep it to remind her to be strong. Resilient. Unbreakable.

She had finally reached the place in her life where she no longer needed the reminder. She now had the strength to let go of the family that tied her to her homeland. She had the resilience to embrace the family she'd found in this colorful little town. And her heart was unbreakable now, beating only for the friends who'd chosen her, who loved her freely and faithfully.

She took in the curled petals, the twisted, crisp leaves, smiled, and closed her hand, crushing the flower entirely. When she held her open palm up to the sky, the wind took the rose-colored dust, and her broken dreams were finally laid to rest.

Pronunciation Guide

Adelfi*: ah-DEL-fee*

Aine: *EE-nuh*

Akeldama*: ah-KELL-da-ma*

Alvyx: *AL-vix*

Asi*: OSS-ee*

Ayusa*: EYE-oo-sah*

Betris*: BET-riss*

Bram*: BRAHM*

Charis: *KARE-iss*

Cyril: *SEER-ill*

Dargah: *DAHR-guh*

Dehlkia*: dell-KEY-ah*

Dirgil*: DUR-jhul*

Elpida: *ELL-pih-duh*

Eorna*: YOR-na*

Erol*: AIR-oll*

Erjunn*: ER-yunn*

Estia: *es-TEE-ah*

Farzaan: *far-DJAHN*

Felan: *FEE-lun*

Fritjof: *FREE-tyoff*

Fyoled: *fah-LEED*

Galen: *GAY-lin*

Glanhau: *GLAH-gnaw*

Granaat: *gruh-NOT*

Gora-Vekiri: *GOR-ah veh-KEE-ree*

Hallor: *HAL-orr*

Hashem: *hah-SHEM*

Ida: *EYE-da*

Ikraam: *IKH-rum*

Imogen: *IM-uh-jhun*

Inbar: *INN-barr*

Ioanie: *EE-uh-nee*

Janan: *dja-NOHN*

Kadir: *kuh-DEER*

Kaedryn: *KAY-dren*

Kapena: *kah-PAY-nah*

Kaylor: *KAY-lore*

Kelia: *kah-LEE-ah*

Kephas: *KEE-fus*

Kasdeya: *KASS-dee-ah*

Kuvaat: *KOO-vaht*

Kyrell: *KY-rel*

Makoa: *muh-COW-uh*

Meldri: *MELL-dree*

Maolyr: *MULL-er*

Neryn: *NAIR-in*

Nikola: *NEE-co-la*

Rinah: *REE-nuh*

Orlaeth: *OR-luh*

Parviz: *PAHR-viss*

Peruuz: *pah-ROOZ*

Quadira: kuh-DEE-rah

Rallis*: ROLL-iss*

Raserri: *rha-SAIR-ee*

Runo: *ROO-no*

Sammot: *SAM-mitt*

Sefa*: SEE-fuh*

Serennog*: SHEER-nok*

Solon*: SO-lawn*

Soter*: SO-tuhr*

Talu: *TAY-loo*

Tiarnán: *TEER-nun*

Titus*: TIE-tus*

Tzaki: *ZOCK-ee*

Vigga: *VIG-guh*

Xinila: *zih-NIL-uh*

Yalniz*: ALL-neez*

Ylthet*: al-THEET*

Ysella*: ah-SEE-lah*

Zoie*: ZOE-ee*

Zumurrud*: Za-MOR-rud*

Bonus Content

I'm an elder millennial. My generation is *the* mixtape generation.

We know the deep magic needed to create the perfect Road Trip Playlist. I applied that magic to creating a soundtrack for this novel. Headphones on, kids, and turn those Walkmans up.

(P. S. - There are potential spoilers on the next page.)

Page 34 - *Best Day of My Life* - American Authors

Page 37 - *Exile* - Enya

Page 45 - *Little Talks* - Of Monsters and Men

Pages 48-49 - *shouldn't i give up* - Mehro

Page 52 - *Moondance* - Van Morrison

Page 53 - *How My Heart Behaves* - Feist

Page 55 - *Safe and Sound* - Capital Cities

Page 64 - *Shake It Out* - Florence + The Machine

Page 80 - *The Places You Have Come to Fear the Most* - Dashboard Confessional

Page 121 - *Policy of Truth* - Depeche Mode

Page 137 - *Little Lion Man* - Mumford & Sons (explicit)

Page 228 - *Stay (Wasting Time)* - Dave Matthews Band

Page 236 - *Enchanted* - Taylor Swift

Page 237 - *Wrapped Up in Books* - Belle and Sebastian

Page 258 - *Borderline* - Tame Impala

Page 275 - *How to Save a Life* - The Fray

Page 300 - *Sweetness* - Jimmy Eat World

Page 301 - *The Middle* - Jimmy Eat World

Page 331 - *Ophelia* - The Lumineers

Page 337 - *Out of the Woods* - Taylor Swift

Page 368 - *Budapest* - George Ezra

Acknowledgements

This book could never have been written without the help and inspiration of a number of special people—and most of them have ended up as minor characters in the story!

Thank you to Em, without whom I probably never would have opened *A Court of Thorns and Roses*, which led to my re-awakening as a reader and writer. Em is also my cover artist, and since she's been a part of this project since very early on, I knew she'd be able to do Rinah justice! (Emily is also the inspiration for a character that will be introduced later in the series.)

Thank you to Jean, who was my number one cheerleader from the start, despite having not yet (at the time) met me in person. Jeannie was the inspiration for Ioanie Adelfi in this book—genuine, no-nonsense, kind-hearted, and perpetually putting up with stuff you *cannot* even make up.

Thank you to my husband, my tireless research assistant, who has endured an embarrassing number of personal questions and been willing, at any given moment, to help me determine if a romantic scene is plausible. Wink, wink.

Thank you to my absolutely wonderful editor Nevvie, who will hopefully come on this seat-of-my-pants journey with me 'til the end!

And thank you to Courtney, whose hastily scribbled letter, written in black

738

Sharpie almost 20 years ago, sits on my desk

to this day:

Do the world a favor and become a

professional writer.